EMPIRE BUILDERS

Will Cardigan: a former riverboat gambler, he came West to claim a spread of unfenced prairie.

Jennifer Waverley: a Denver socialite, she could drink any miner under the table in a Telluride saloon.

Redge Cardigan: the healer, he showed one gunslinger why putting a Cardigan in the grave was just like digging your own.

Mark Cardigan: a man of vast drive and vision, he built a giant construction business, but could never marry the woman who made it all possible.

Dolores Montez: the fiery Mexican beauty and financial wizard behind the Cardigan empire, her scandalous love for Mark had to be accepted— even by Mark's wife.

Their story spans seven decades, from horse to helicopter, gunplay to graft, in the building of a great family empire on the vast Colorado plains— GRASSLANDS!

CLYDE M. BRUNDY

GRASSLANDS

AVON
PUBLISHERS OF BARD, CAMELOT AND DISCUS BOOKS

GRASSLANDS is an original publication of Avon Books. This work has never before appeared in book form.

AVON BOOKS
A division of
The Hearst Corporation
959 Eighth Avenue
New York, New York 10019

First Avon Printing, June, 1980

AVON TRADEMARK REG. U.S. PAT. OFF. AND IN
OTHER COUNTRIES, MARCA REGISTRADA,
HECHO EN U.S.A.

Printed in the U.S.A.

To Viola, Roy, Dorothy and Marie,
for upon them too is
the *mark of the grasslands*.

Preface

It is still the quiet land. In summer its distances lie sprawled under dappling sunlight and shadows. In winter a snow-bound solitude marks hills that gently undulate toward an ever-receding horizon.

Where once unbroken grasslands spread silence and lone-liness, there are now fenced pastures, contoured wheat-lands, oil wells, and missile bases.

The great valley of Crow Creek stretches from Wyoming mountains across the high plains to the South Platte River. Modern irrigation wells, with electrically powered pumps, have lowered the valley's water table. Drought is rapidly killing myriad stately cottonwood trees, thickly clustered willows, and the thickets of wild roses that once edged the stream's course. There is no running water now, only a twisting ribbon of sand scrawling across desolate reaches.

About midway down the creek's course is a long-deserted two-story frame house. Once it was painted white; now it is weathered and windblown and shabby. There are rem-nants of sizable cattle sheds and of extensive corrals. Only these neglected and decaying landmarks tell that this was once the site of the immense and powerful Diamond-7 Ranch.

Some twenty miles upstream is a four-mile-square pas-ture. Locks on the gates of its fences deny access along what was once a graded country road. This carefully chosen and secluded spot is entered only by the few who can prove their right to keys matching the gate locks.

But neither gates nor an abandoned roadway can deny a helicopter's way above the sun-splashed land to the six old, old graves—*and to the new one dug only yesterday.*

PART I

THE HERITAGE

Chapter 1

In the warm sunlight of midmorning they came to the crest of a gently sloping hill. The infinite grasslands of Colorado and the quietness of that April day in 1897 lay about them. Redge Cardigan gazed about, overwhelmed by the sureness so suddenly upon him, the certainty that this was the place. He had never been here before, had never viewed this plains solitude. Yet his mind knew, as did his heart. The long journey was over—he had come home.

A small valley lay before them, with a creek along which tall cottonwoods and screening willows assured the presence of water. A mile farther west the prairie began a slow climb toward distant foothills. The vista beyond was of snow-speckled peaks thrusting above the dark tinge of forests. A great sawtoothed barrier lifted from the distant wilderness to the south, loomed boldly, then receded beyond the horizon to the north.

Redge Cardigan halted his bay mare, swung down from the saddle his father had given him a month before on his birthday, and stood in silent wonder. Perplexity still clutched him as their freight wagon drew alongside and halted. His father climbed down and strode to the boy's side. The man too was wordless for a time as his gaze probed the immensity ahead, the lonely grandeur leading from grassy creekbanks to the far-off rim of the world.

Presently Will Cardigan placed a firm hand on his son's shoulder. "Redge, look at the big, clean emptiness of it. Out there is new land and a new life for us. Sort of makes the seven hundred miles we've jolted along worthwhile. In two days we'll reach the mountains."

The boy had to say it then, to voice this new and urgent certainty. "We won't be traveling tomorrow, Pa. Not even an hour from now. Can't you feel it . . . know it? This

3

valley. The creek and these meadows. They've been waiting for us."

Redge paused and pointed to a spot where cottonwoods studded a couple of acres lifting to form a knoll. "There's room for a cabin, a barn, and corrals." He surveyed the undulating grass country as he added, "And graze for a thousand cow critters."

Will Cardigan looked thoughtfully about, then replied, "I'd hoped to get up into the forest country, Redge. Along a river. But could be you're right, son. Winters up there would be longer and snow deeper."

Redge was quiet for a time. His words, when they came, were quiet and laden with the odd and unexplainable sureness with which he recognized this place as home, a spot to which they had been inexorably drawn.

"It's sort of scary, Pa—this knowing we've reached our land and our time and place to build."

His father's arm swung the boy about; eyes held firm to Redge's face. "It's your future we're after, son. So you call the turn. Let's get down to the creek and unhitch."

In this way, simply and irrevocably, their decision was made. They sought out a cottonwood-skirted spot on the knoll. By evening they had fashioned a corral of posts and poles; it would suffice to hold their horses that night. A tent, fronted by a pole-roofed area for cooking, would serve as their home until pine logs could be hauled from the mountains.

As dusk deepened, they sat facing each other across a small campfire. Will Cardigan, somewhat over fifty years of age, showed gray strands in hair that was dark, almost black. He was a man of quiet words and quick movement. A hint of military bearing lingered about him—something he had carried since the years of Shiloh, Bull Run, and Antietam.

Redge's straw-colored hair shone in the dancing light and fell across his sun-roughened but fair-complexioned forehead. His steady eyes, dark and wide-set, were a heritage from his father, but he would never attain Will Cardigan's lean height. Already his shoulders were broad and powerful, contrasting sharply with the flatness of his waist. His mouth favored that of his mother and was often molded in an attitude of stubborn determination. Already

4

young Redge sensed his future—he would not easily relinquish it.

They were both tired from the day's labors yet eager for another sunrise. They spread blankets. Redge preferred for his to be outside, where stars began to appear, hanging low in the sky.

Moments after they had turned in, the rhythm of hoofbeats drew them erect. Will Cardigan lifted a rifle in readiness. The hoof sounds told of a lone rider coming near at an unhurried gait. He came into view, a small leather-faced stranger astride a tired piebald gelding.

He halted fifty feet from them and lifted a hand in greeting. The movement was casual, but it indicated restrained surprise. "I saw your campfire and then caught a whiff from your coffee pot. Thought mebbe . . ."

Will Cardigan appraised the stranger and his manner of speaking, then laid the rifle aside. "Light down while I pour a cup for you." He poked the fire's embers, then added, "I'm Cardigan from Iowa, and this is my son, Redge." The words carried neither insistence nor invitation for the stranger to reveal his own identity. In this time and place, men were left to their own choice in such matters.

The stranger accepted a steaming tin cup as he scrutinized Cardigan's face. "Glad to meet both of you. It's a lonely land." He sipped the coffee, then added, "People call me Hank—Hank Kutcher. I ride for the Diamond-7 Ranch."

Cardigan offered his hand in greeting, then studied Kutcher's tired horse. "You've ridden a far piece, I'd surmise. We haven't spotted a ranch or settlement for three days."

"Headquarters are off to the south. Mebbe fifteen miles, crow-flight reckoning."

"We can scare up some grub if you're hungry and have the time," Redge volunteered.

"Thanks." Kutcher grinned. "I'm the fellow who can stow it away."

They squatted close to the rekindled blaze. Will Cardigan noted the intense but seemingly disinterested thoroughness with which Kutcher took note of their corral and the lean-to afront the tent. "We plan to settle here . . . start a small outfit." The words were quiet and probing.

"You've come to a likely spot," Kutcher answered. "But iffen I was you I'd get in touch with old Andy Purcell."

5

"Purcell?" Cardigan repeated.

Kutcher lustily wiped a biscuit across his plate, bit into it, then said, "He's the one to see. Purcell owns the Diamond-7 Ranch. You're squatted on his graze."

Redge flipped a pebble toward the stream, then asked, "Does Purcell lay claim to the entire creek? Full length?"

"Good Lord . . . no," Kutcher said. "This winding waterway is Crow Creek, more than a hundred miles long. It rises in them mountains west of Cheyenne, flows eastward, and makes a big bend to the south out here on the plains. Then it heads for the South Platte River."

"But up here," Redge persisted, "maybe twenty miles from his headquarters, Purcell claims all the water—and all the grass—is his?"

"Lad, the situation ain't of my making. Now me, I'd like a neighbor or two. It's a mighty lonesome land. Just tarnation steady wind, gully-washing summer rains, and months of blizzards stacking snow over the short grass."

Will Cardigan had listened attentively. He refilled the visitor's coffee cup, then said in a noncommittal tone, "Seems a man would have to have been here a long spell to get domination or government deed to nigh onto a hundred thousand acres."

Kutcher lighted his pipe, then spoke, seeming to choose words with care. "Andy Purcell ain't no ordinary man. He came here right on the heels of the Union Pacific's rail-laying up north. He claimed land—and somehow made his claim stick. Maybe he's got paper deeds to his holdings. Maybe not. The deed to a lot of grazing land west of the Missouri River is carried in a leather holster . . . and if need be, signed with lead."

Will Cardigan watched his son clench his fists in anger. He spoke quickly to forestall Redge's brewing retort. "We'd be happy to have you bunk here tonight, Mr. Kutcher."

"I'd sure like to," the stranger said, grinning. "But I'm expected in at headquarters tonight." He mounted, wheeled his horse, then looked back. "When you ride down to the Diamond-7, be sure it's Andy Purcell, the big boss, you talk to. Stacy Murdock, the foreman, may try to shoo you off." Kutcher waved a parting gesture, then rode into darkness.

As the hoofbeats of their visitor's horse died in the distance, Redge turned with a troubled and stubborn face to his father. "We're not going to slink away?" he demanded. "Pull stakes just after getting here?"

Will Cardigan's eyes roamed the night, then lifted to the brilliant sweep of the Milky Way. He was quiet for some time as memory sought out events long past. "No, Redge," he said at last. "We're here to make a stand. A man can roam and search just so far. But we will visit Andy Purcell before the weekend. Let him know we didn't come here seeking trouble. The man should at least hear us out."

As Cardigan's words ended, his mind was tolling a half-wistful, half-desperate thought: Perhaps it is he. Just perhaps it is Purcell of Shiloh, of Grant's determined, bloody stand.

The country through which father and son rode southward, two days later, seemed an eternity of grassland flung to the world's rim. Often their course followed the meandering of Crow Creek, through fringing willows and wildrose thickets; often they crossed parklike areas dotted by tall cottonwood trees.

From safely distant ridges, antelope watched them ride by. There were signs that buffalo had grazed here recently, but none were seen. But as they skirted the creek's broad valley, cattle became more and more numerous, feeding in groups or in solitary seclusion.

Headquarters of Purcell's Diamond-7 Ranch were visible when the sun was hotly near noon. The place was dominated by a square two-story frame house, painted white, located in a sheltering grove of cottonwoods. Behind it was a long weatherbeaten shed, built in ell shape for wind protection, and open to the south and east. Beyond this, the corrals spread out, reaching so far they brought an amazed whistle to young Redge's lips.

Will Cardigan motioned for his son to follow, then rode directly toward the ranch house. They were within a hundred yards of it when a man afoot, trailed by two large dogs, strode out from the corrals and stood blocking their progress. His manner was neither friendly nor hostile, but a Colt .45 revolver hung in readiness in his hip holster.

"Something I can do for you?" he asked.

Cardigan reined his horse to a stop; a glance satisfied him Redge had also halted. "We're looking for a Mr. Pur-

7

cell . . . Andy Purcell," he explained quietly. "Your man Hank Kutcher suggested we drop by to see him."

"You're sure Kutcher sent you here?" There was disbelief in the stranger's voice.

"What reason would I have to lie about it?" Will Cardigan answered.

"No need to rear onto your hind legs, stranger. It's just that likely Stacy Murdock is the man you want to see. He's foreman. Does the hiring. Besides, Purcell isn't due in till toward sundown."

"Then we'll wait," Cardigan responded firmly. "Mind if we rest in the shade . . . water our horses?"

The stranger glanced toward the dogs, which were now sniffing Redge's boot. The boy had leaned far over in the saddle to scratch their ears.

"Hell," the man muttered. "Purcell would have my hide iffen you missed a noon meal. See that first shed behind the main house? It's the cook shack. Get over there after you water your hosses." A twisting grin of approval marked the stranger's face as he watched Redge dismount and walk toward the creek, followed by two tail-wagging hounds.

Will Cardigan joined the procession. He felt slightly hopeful. At least neither the hired hand nor the dogs at the Diamond-7 were seeking trouble.

During their afternoon of waiting, Redge's thoughts turned often to their own camp far up the river. Would it be molested during their absence? They had prepared for the eventuality of being gone from camp until evening. Now it seemed certain they would be away most of the night. Instead of waiting idly here, they could be getting a head start on all those urgent things that needed doing for the winter ahead.

His gaze swept ruefully over the seemingly endless reach of pole corrals. When would the Cardigans, father and son, need even two corrals? Time dragged on toward evening.

The man leading the Diamond-7 crew, riding into the home yard in deepening twilight, was tall, with a deeply furrowed face. Both his hair and his eyes were gray. He stopped at the stables, gave his horse to the care of others, then walked with tired but firm tread toward the Cardigans. He thrust out a work-hardened hand. "I'm Andy Purcell.

8

They tell me you've been waiting here since noon. Sorry for your long wait."

Will Cardigan studied the rancher's face and words, then answered, "You had no idea we were coming, sir. I'm Will Cardigan. This is my son, Redge."

A younger man, of powerful build and with an expressionless face, strode up close to Purcell, then ran calculating eyes over the Cardigans. "It's the pair Hank Kutcher warned us would be paying a social——"

The deliberately caustic words were silenced by Purcell's hand. "Murdock, you know anyone is welcome here for two things—a meal, and a chance to say what's on his mind."

Will Cardigan studiously ignored Stacy Murdock and spoke directly to the ranch owner. "My son and I are by ourselves. We came from Iowa. The boy lost his mother last year; we decided to trek west, to look for new surroundings and a place to shed some painful memories." Cardigan was aware of Purcell's interested silence, and of the sullen impatience sweeping Murdock. He continued with carefully chosen words. "We found a likely spot for a small cattle outfit some twenty miles up the creek from here. Then Hank Kutcher happened by and told us we're within your limits of claim. So . . . today we rode down to meet you. To let you know we're there, Mr. Purcell." He was neither asserting his right to stay nor was he offering to move on.

"Just two of them now," Murdock broke in coldly. "Boss, if they stay it'll signal a dozen or so more squatters to move in on us."

Redge felt the tightening of his face, the bitter dislike of Murdock that was building within him. He knew that he should keep silent, but he could not. "Pa," he said, "maybe it just ain't worthwhile, seizing some prairie that it seems is the sole property of an overfed ranch ramrod."

Murdock would have stepped forward to strike at Redge, but he was caught short by a sudden explosive laugh from Andy Purcell, and by Will Cardigan's stern order to his son: "Shut up, Redge."

The elder Cardigan turned back to the rancher. "We sort of had hopes of putting down some roots there along the creek." He continued, probing a bit, "I've had a hanker-

9

ing for homebound roots ever since the Rebellion—since the days and nights of that carnage known as Shiloh."

The words lessened perplexity that had been growing on Purcell's face. "Cardigan . . . Will Cardigan . . . the name has a familiar ring. Weren't you with an infantry company? One that was pretty well shot to pieces?"

Cardigan nodded. "Yes, I was, sir. How well I remember your being there too."

For a brief time the rancher seemed lost in reverie. Then he nodded and said, "It has been a long, long time. Yet so much remains strangely vivid. Why not stay all night . . . you and your son? We'll recall those war times."

"It would be enjoyable, sir. Perhaps at a later time we can. Just now all of our possessions are unprotected up there along the creek." He turned to Redge. "We'll be riding back now."

Redge had listened intently. He knew that immediately the gamble he had conceived must be brought into play. His hands were clenched and sweaty at his sides as he spoke to Purcell. "Sir, you need us up there on the creek."

Stacy Murdock had lost interest. Now he turned quickly back, laughing in scorn. Something about this stubborn boy fanned rancor within Murdock. He was also annoyed by Purcell's civil attitude toward the two interlopers.

"Sure we need nesters—squatters," he grated. "Just like we need cactus . . . rattlesnakes . . . blizzards."

Purcell hushed him in a voice laden with military brevity and curtness. "Stacy, get this straight. These people are here at Hank Kutcher's request. We will hear them out."

Reason cautioned Redge to speak slowly, so that each word might meet the test of sincerity and logic.

"Mr. Purcell, you *do* need us—my father and me. Our livestock, a half dozen horses and two milk cows, won't put any dent in your grass. We don't have money to buy a big herd. But we understand livestock. Especially ailing critters and those needing a lot of care. I looked over your penned cattle this afternoon, and a few horses. Some are in pitiful shape." Will listened to his son with great pride.

Redge continued. "We can take that kind of stock off your hands and care for it. Likely pull most of the critters through. Cows. Calves. Saddle horses. The sick stuff you have here is just going to die; you'll have to drag worthless carcasses off for the coyotes."

Andy Purcell pulled at his chin in thoughtful silence. After a time, he asked, "And just what would I have to pay you, lad?"

Redge bit his lip in shrewd concentration; his gaze remained unwavering on the rancher's face. "You'd owe me one out of every three we pull through . . . and half of the natural increase of the other two-thirds."

Murdock scowled. His boot lashed out in a vicious kick at a clump of sagebrush. "I say nothing doing. Andrew, it's just a scheme to squat on our range. We'll give them until tomorrow morning to pull stakes and head out."

Purcell wheeled about and stared bleakly at his enraged foreman. When he spoke, he seemed much younger than his years. "Just suppose you keep still a spell, Stacy. I don't recall you doing much to save ailing stock. And I sure as hell don't recall deeding the Diamond-7 to you—or relinquishing my say-so." His probing gaze moved back to the Cardigans. "Young fellow, you'd be taking on a tough task, both winter and summer."

"Redge is a rather tough boy," Will Cardigan said.

A semblance of doubt still covered the rancher's answer. "Redge, we won't be able to spend time helping you. Maybe we could spare a few medicines now and then. That's all."

"We'll go it alone," the boy answered evenly. "Expecting no help . . . and"—his gaze rested with dislike upon Stacy Murdock—"no interference once critters have been put in our care."

Purcell rubbed his forehead in silent thought. "Strange," he murmured, "how time turns full cycle. A young soldier —so long ago—at Shiloh, named Cardigan. Now one with a son ready to take on the accursed droughts and blizzards of these plains." A full minute slipped by before he thrust a hand at Redge. "Youngster, you've got a deal—for six months' trial. I'll have Hank Kutcher start hazing the nuisance stock—sick, hurt, and misfit—up your way this week. Let's have supper and iron out some details."

11

Chapter 2

Every man is inherently a wanderer, yearning for the sights and sounds beyond the horizon encircling the routine of his days. Yet, equally powerful is his need for a homeplace; there must be a certain spot to cherish, to defend, and from which to draw security and strength.

The urge and need for his own acres came early to Redge Cardigan. Though scarcely in his teens, he already sensed the futility of roaming, the elusiveness of seeking some distant splendor at a rainbow's end.

It is likely that the cause of his early search for a homeplace, for land to have and hold, dated far beyond his memory, or his birth. Perhaps its small and unrecognizable beginning with his father, Will Cardigan, went back to a summer evening in 1865—and to two blue-clad figures lounging tiredly in a lush Tennessee meadow.

Both men were young—if any man was young after those years of drill and disease, of infantry charges, and the carnage of Rebellion, of Civil War.

Emmett Willoughby, wearing his corporal chevrons, rose lazily to his feet, sizing up the contour and distance of a fence post yards away. Then with the speed, agility, and deadly accuracy of long practice, he brought his rifle into line and fired. Quickly he placed three bullets within a darkened knot.

He was reloading as Will Cardigan pulled off his boots and dropped reddened and swollen feet into a muddied pool. "I'll wager there aren't twenty men in this Union Army that can shoot as well," Cardigan said with admiration.

"And likely not that many places in the United States where one can make a living with firearms," Willoughby drawled. "Will, the war is about over. It'll be up to us to buck a new deal."

12

"Appears so," Cardigan agreed. "I was sort of handy with cattle before joining the army. I hope I haven't lost the touch during these four years of mud and blood."

Willoughby eyed his young companion thoughtfully and asked, "Do you plan to skedaddle back to your pa's place and farm?"

Cardigan shook his head. "No, I'll just go home for a visit. My two younger brothers do the farming now." He waited a while, then added, "I'd like to get farther west than Ohio, maybe see that railroad they're talking of building to California. Maybe I'll learn a trade to get me by."

"You already have it," Willoughby answered.

"Then you'd best inform me about it, Emmett. Being a newly discharged foot soldier ain't my idea of advancing to fame and fortune."

"Those hands of yours, Will," Willoughby explained with great care. "The way they can handle a deck of cards. Where did you get the hang of it—the perfection?"

Cardigan shrugged indifferently. "What else have I had to keep me occupied during month after month of nothing-to-do evenings but deal a greasy deck onto a blanket? Other bored men gather round. I win a few games. Lose a few."

"Maybe it was that way at first, Will. I've not seen you losing any games to speak of lately. Not where there's a gold piece or paper money on the blanket."

Cardigan shrugged. "Not likely I'd find work as a card dealer in my part of Ohio. Gambling is held to be the cardinal sin—by housewives, most town bankers, and the circuit-riding preachers."

A minute passed before Emmett Willoughby turned sharply and studied his friend's face. "Will," he said studiedly, "how about teaming up with me? Happens I don't have kinfolks left, or even a gal itching to hitch up with me. There'll be money—plenty of it—if one knows where to look." Willoughby paused, grinned wryly, then went on, "It'd be a shame to spoil those accursedly fast hands of yours, or waste them on a plow handle or brick hod. Those mitts of yours could be our insurance of good living from the day we're discharged." As the words ended, Willoughby raised his rifle and slammed another bullet dead center of the post. "Will," he asked, "how are we going to look in stovepipe hats and swallow-tailed coats?"

Cardigan eyed his bare feet as he propped them onto a

13

grass clump to dry. "What has either of us got to lose? We'll try it your way, Emmett, and find out—after we're mustered out and I have a month up home with the folks."

Within two years they were known wherever passenger boats ran on the Ohio, the Mississippi, or the Missouri. A likable and skilled gambler named Will Cardigan; his quiet and ever watchful companion, Emmett Willoughby, whose speed and accuracy with either a rifle or pistols was becoming legend. This display of firearms accuracy was part of their act; it usually assured a good crowd when the riverboat touched shore. It was also designed to instill a large degree of prudence among those inclined to slip marked decks and other such paraphernalia into Cardigan's games.

Other gamblers and opportunists were exploiting the riverboat business. Among them were some to whom expediency meant having something arranged to meet any contingency or turn of luck. Extra cards, carefully concealed; cohorts spotted in the crowd; the reassurance of a pistol handily placed for instant use.

Will Cardigan was shrewd enough to trust to honest skill. The laws of averages and probabilities, combined with intelligent play, would assure steady profit. For many others, it would have been sheer stupidity to wait and work for mathematical percentages. A fast game and a fast getaway. And why not, when lambs and suckers were just waiting to be shorn of their bankrolls.

One artist of the fast trim and fadeout was Hollis Devlin. His plan of action had been stripped of frills through months of experience. He was dedicated to relieving the rich of cash, jewels, and other negotiable items.

Devlin measured a lithe and erect six feet. His dark somberness seemed to speak of Latin blood and of subtle mystery. Some thought him to be Corsican; others were sure that his ancestry was southern Slavic.

There was no denial that Hollis Devlin was a handsome man. By careful styling of his black, wavy hair, and by choice of clothing, he carefully accentuated an illusion of being dashing and debonair. Women, upon first meeting Devlin, noted his deep and carefully modulated voice. He was well aware of this, and used voice, impressive features and grooming as advantageous facets in his daily search for introductions to men of position, power, money.

A different sort of Hollis Devlin masterminded the secluded gatherings of those who aided in his gambling ventures. At such times his innermost drives and calculating ways came to the surface. Then he was the gambler ridden by determination to win by any and all means. Then—and only then—was revealed the Hollis Devlin of greed, of cunning, and of ruthless cruelty.

It was inevitable that Will Cardigan and Devlin should come face to face. It happened one spring evening near Cape Girardeau. The boat progressed with a gentle murmur through placid water. Lamplight sheen spread above the thickly carpeted floor and three gaming tables. Two of the tables were quickly deserted, as twenty or more men crowded for closer view of the showdown between two extraordinary gamblers.

Will Cardigan was aware that this seemingly casual meeting had been deftly arranged by Devlin, probably with the desire to rid the boat and the river of one Will Cardigan, who played a more modest game, but who was no doubt cutting deeply into Devlin's projected profits.

And now, near ten o'clock of a pleasantly cool evening, nearly ten thousand dollars in coin and currency lay on the velvet green table. Most of it had been dropped by men who had lost and were already out of the game.

There was something about Will Cardigan and his manner of playing cards that caused an unfamiliar tenseness—an uneasiness—to creep over Devlin. He played this younger gambler with infinite caution, probing and testing Cardigan's moves and methods.

Within half an hour, Devlin realized that this night's work would call for either luck or expediency if he was to garner the stakes upon the table. And to Devlin, luck was something to be trusted only after taking diverse steps to assure winning.

With outward joviality that enabled him to take time for study of the entire room, Devlin prepared for the move he knew must be swift and decisive. Four men remained in the draw poker game, but Devlin was pretty sure two of them would throw in their hands if the fall of cards caused the betting to spiral upward. It was Devlin's turn to deal. There was a touch of arrogance in his sureness that his speed in dealing, which had trapped many gamblers, would confuse Cardigan. His fingering was smooth and without

15

tremor. He laid five cards before each player. There would be no draw; betting would be on the strength of the cards as dealt.

Devlin picked up the cards he had dealt himself. His eyes and his face were emotionless as he quickly read his hand, then gazed beyond the spectators ringing the table. With a quick, firm shove he placed the deck almost in the center of the table. For a moment Devlin turned his eyes toward the first eligible bettor, a young fellow in evening clothes who obviously had been drinking freely.

"What say, Henry?" Devlin asked with a flashing smile. "It's only money, you know."

The younger man's response was to pitch his hand face down to the table. "Hell's fire. I wouldn't bet a skunk skin on them."

Abruptly, attention turned to Will Cardigan. With slow deliberation, he picked up his five cards one by one, seeming intent on what each would reveal. Half a minute ticked by. "And you, Mr. Cardigan," Devlin said at last. "Is it your desire to wager?"

"I would like to. I would truly like to," Will Cardigan answered, in a sociable tone. "I would bet, provided . . ."

It was impossible for Devlin to mask the agitation within him. "Provided what, Mr. Cardigan?" he asked.

The expectant silence of the smoke-hazed room was shattered by Will Cardigan's voice—a voice of steel that matched his eyes. "Provided you give me the last card that should have been dealt to me—the ten of diamonds that you palmed to the bottom of the deck."

"You're a damned liar," Devlin snarled. His hand moved to retrieve and hold the deck. But too late. Already Will Cardigan had flipped it. The bottom card, the ten of diamonds, lay revealed. Close beside it was Cardigan's hand, needing only the disputed diamond ten to complete a full house.

In the next instant those onlookers not too dazed by fast movement and loud noise saw several things.

From the crowd about the table, a man with powerful shoulders and blond unkempt hair thrust suddenly toward Cardigan. His hand clenched a heavy pistol, swinging it in an arc that would bring it crashing against Cardigan's temple. Trained to self-defense, Cardigan would have

16

dodged quickly aside as he came to his feet. The attempt was forestalled by Devlin's grasp of his arm.

The pistol blow landed, but only as a jolting glance above Will Cardigan's ear. Across the room there had been the uplift of a revolver, a flash, a deafening roar—as Emmett Willoughby squeezed the trigger. The stranger who would have pistol-whipped Cardigan jerked in a strange, uncontrolled way, then crumpled to the heavy carpet.

Abruptly Hollis Devlin used his free arm to send a smashing blow to Cardigan's chin. As Cardigan staggered in an attempt to remain standing, Devlin was clawing for a knife that his open coat now revealed at his waistband. The savage attempt was Hollis Devlin's undoing. With quick but methodical sureness Emmett Willoughby used one more shot. The lead missile of that shot caught Devlin in the elbow, then plowed down toward his fingers as they clutched the blade. Hollis Devlin would never deal a hand of cards again.

The room buzzed with the excited hum of voices, and the strangely subdued aftermath of violence. Two men knelt beside Devlin's brawny henchman as he lay quiet, his blood spreading onto the rug. "He was dead when he hit the floor," one of them said.

Despite the bloody arm that dangled uselessly at his side, Devlin glared at Will Cardigan, who was busy exploring his sore chin with careful fingers.

"You bastard," Devlin gritted. "I vow I'll kill you, if it takes me the rest of my life." He looked toward Willoughby, who was standing nearby. "He won't always be by your side."

"I'll be expecting you," Cardigan answered. "With another crooked deal of some sort." He eyed the gaming table with distaste, noting the money still upon it. He turned to the men about him. "I saw two Catholic sisters—nuns—in the dining room. Give this to them. I don't touch blood money."

There were those who might have argued with him, but their indecision ended as Emmett Willoughby crossed the room, took his partner's arm and moved him toward the door. "You heard what Will said," he called over his shoulder. "See that it's done that way."

They passed from the room, redolent with the acrid scent

17

of gunsmoke, and walked into the clear, warm quiet of an upper deck. "I've an idea, Will," Emmett Willoughby said, "that we'd best get off this floating tub at the next stop."

Cardigan nodded. "We're due to dock in about an hour." After a time he added, simply, "Thanks, Emmett, for being there."

"Too many crooked deals on these steamboat runs," Willoughby affirmed. He strode to the rail, peered across the dark, lapping water, and spoke again. "Will, how about us leaving the river, and the gambling game? At least for a time. Try something a mite cleaner and fresher. Like maybe getting us a lead mine."

"What do we know about mining, Emmett? Besides, we'd have to locate a lead vein; there aren't any in the part of Ohio where I hail from."

"I don't know ores and assays either," Willoughby revealed, "but I've a friend who's plenty knowledgeable about such things. He's pretty well up in years now. He learned mining way back about 1820. Worked for Major Andrew Henry at the lead mines in Washington County, Missouri. We've corresponded a bit."

"Major Henry," Cardigan said with surprise and interest. "Wasn't he the chap that organized the Ashley-Henry fur-trapping expeditions?"

"Sure enough," Willoughby answered. "Major Henry took a passel of youngsters upriver to the Rocky Mountains. They pioneered the trade and got famous. The major put a lot of his earnings into business . . . including the lead mines. My friend's been urging me to try it. Says we can't lose."

Cardigan flipped a glowing cigar butt toward the darkened waters below, then grinned. "I'll be glad to be off this boat and set my feet on solid ground. Emmett, a lot of the thrill of a card game died for me during that fracas tonight." He was quiet for a while, then he added, "But we did right well for the months we've roamed the rivers. You foresaw that we would. Sure I'll join you for a fling at trying to become mining moguls. I've got ten thousand dollars from these years of card playing to back us."

"And I can match it," Willoughby said.

They stood then with a silence between them, the silence of friends who understand each other and have mutual trust.

18

But they were alert, knowing there were men on this river-boat who would like nothing better than to destroy them, to avenge the crippling of Hollis Devlin.

After a while lights appeared off the forward bow. The vessel gently changed direction and headed for shore.

Chapter 3

The details of those lead-mining years were fresh in Will Cardigan's memory as he and his son, Redge, rode homeward the following day from the Diamond-7 Ranch and their meeting with Andrew Purcell. The unexpected turn of events, Purcell's acceptance of the boy's offer to care for ailing stock, had stirred excitement within Redge. "You just watch and wait, Dad; within five years we'll have good foundation stock for a cattle herd of our own."

"Not if Stacy Murdock has his way, son." Will Cardigan was cautious of men who showed hostility against him—he had been so ever since his days on the river.

"Don't worry," Redge responded. "I'm not looking for trouble with that fat-gut Murdock as long as he leaves us alone." The boy dismissed the thought of trouble from that quarter. Already his mind was busy with plans for expanding the corrals and building livestock shelters on those tree-dotted acres they had chosen as a homeplace.

Will Cardigan's thoughts returned once more to past places and events. He and Andy Purcell had sat up far into the night recalling the excitement, the tumult, and the carnage, known as the Battle of Shiloh. The rancher had commanded a company of Ohio infantrymen. The toll of lives had been appalling—it had also practically wiped out the unit in which Cardigan had served. It was here, however, that he had first encountered the man who was to become his best friend and partner. Midway through the battle, Will Cardigan had received a bullet through the calf of his left leg. Not really a serious wound, but it bled profusely and he was unable to check the flow of blood. Gradually, he weakened, calling out the while for help that either did not hear or was unable to come to his aid. Unconsciousness covered him like a black, billowing cloud.

When he came to, weak and uncertain, he saw Emmett Willoughby. They were lying side by side in a shallow ditch, and this stranger had somehow stemmed the blood loss that would soon have claimed Cardigan's life. He struggled to sit up, but a swift shove, accompanied by prime cuss words, got him speedily to the ditch's bottom.

"Now, dammit, keep down and still. Some of those Georgia fellows out there could put a bullet between your eyes from a hundred yards or so."

They got out of the ditch and the battle alive. When Cardigan rejoined his unit after a brief stay in the field hospital, the tall, taciturn Willoughby sought him out. Emmett Willoughby was a quiet man who spent much time away from companions, and who seemed to dislike the routine and small talk of army life. Even Will Cardigan thought of Willoughby as a brooder who often sat silently at a campfire letting his thoughts drift upward with the smoke. He spoke very little of his past, but Cardigan pieced together indications that his companion's youth had been marked by some great personal tragedy that had left him with an abiding bitterness.

Somehow a trusting and unquestioning friendship grew between Emmett Willoughby and Will Cardigan. It led to their partnership on the gambling riverboats; it continued and strengthened when they chose to combine bankrolls in order to pursue a new and perhaps more respectable enterprise—that of opening a lead mine in the vicinity of St. Louis.

And now, thirty-odd years later, Will Cardigan still thought of his friend as though he had never left his side. Homeward bound, up Crow Creek from the Diamond-7 Ranch, Will Cardigan felt an urge to share more of his memories with his son. Presently he said, "Redge, did I ever tell you how I got started in lead mining—how I went into a new venture, just as you're nibbling at the ranching business now?"

Redge was at that moment struggling to devise ways to build a calf hospital of cottonwood logs. Yet he forced the plans from his thoughts, for it was not often that Will Cardigan spoke of the past, his years of soldiering, of gambling, of mining, of loving and losing the vivacious farm girl, Hazel, who had become Redge's mother.

Redge reined his horse alongside his father's mount and

said, "It seems you told me, a long time ago, that a mountain man, one of those fur-brigade trappers, put you and Emmett Willoughby in a likely situation at just the right time. Maybe I've forgotten the details, Dad."

"More likely I never told you much, son. Emmett and me got hold of one sweet little lead mine, all right. And know what? It came about because of that trapper—his name was Gervais—and a turkey shoot we hadn't even planned to take a part in."

Redge nodded knowingly. "If there's shooting involved in this, sounds like your sidekick Emmett Willoughby would have had a part of the act."

"You're reading my memory, Redge. Seems Emmett knew that Gervais character before the war. He was a Frenchman, and had worked at Major Henry's lead digging way back when James Monroe was President. He'd lost part of a foot to a grizzly bear, but had become an expert with a rifle. He'd also acquired a monumental thirst for hard liquor. But he knew lead veins and lead mining upside down; he was getting well-to-do as mining adviser. That's what enabled Emmett to find him about a month after we arrived in St. Louis. We spotted a newspaper item that Gervais was in Poplar Bluff as a consultant.

"We headed down that way. Got ourselves mixed up in the damnedest, biggest celebration of the year. Part of it was a turkey shoot that had a keg of whiskey as first prize. Willoughby wasn't one to show off his skill with firearms, but I argued we might as well have the keg. Emmett protested, and said there'd be a mob of rifle-crazy Missourians trying for that liquid first prize. So I agreed. I told him there wasn't much use of his taking part anyhow. From what I'd heard, I told him, Frenchy Gervais could shoot rings around Emmett."

"Then what happened?" Redge demanded.

"Old Emmett didn't even answer me. Just grabbed his prize rifle and took off from our hotel room. The coldness about his eyes was just what I wanted to prod up. Emmett didn't seem to want me along, so I just sat in the hotel lobby and waited. About dark, the door opened and in walked Willoughby. Behind him was a heavy-set middle-aged chap wearing one of those *coureur de bois* outfits, and with a five-gallon keg of booze on his shoulder."

"So the Frenchman, Gervais, did outshoot Mr. Willoughby." There was a tinge of disappointment in Redge's surmise.

"The hell he did, son. People around Poplar Bluff may still be talking about that match-up between Will and the Frenchman. Gervais had spent a dozen years in the mountains looking for beaver pelts. Out there, his own scalp depended on marksmanship. He showed it that afternoon at the turkey shoot, putting bullets nigh into center of a distant target. But Willoughby had come out of the war a super-shot, and had kept his skill honed." Will Cardigan paused, shaking his head in amazement. Then he said briskly, "I wasn't there to see the match. Didn't hear all the details. I just know that Emmett not only won the cask of whiskey, but in a shootout he won a bet that caused the Frenchman to lug it to our hotel."

"I suppose both you and Mr. Willoughby celebrated by tapping the keg." Redge laughed.

"Nope. Emmett did what I thought at the time was a stupid thing. He gave that liquor, all five gallons of a prime Kentucky brand, to Frenchy Gervais."

"It does sound like a crazy idea. Didn't either one of you have a single drink?"

"Not even a whiff from the bung. But we did get set up in the lead-mining business."

By now Redge's thoughts of the calf pen had succumbed to his curiosity. "How come that happened, Dad?"

"You won't believe how. That Frenchman, that hard-headed mining consultant, got sentimental—a sort of crying jag. Said that nobody had ever given Frenchy Gervais such a gift. He vowed that until the heavens cracked open, Emmett Willoughby would be his best friend, and in future years had only to ask any favor of his bosom friend Gervais."

"Neither of you took that seriously, did you?"

"I did, Redge, in a way. Presently the weeping Frenchman had to journey outside to the privy. He was gone long enough for me to suggest to Emmett that he try calling Gervais's pledges of future aid. Just try and get solid information about a lead vein, a good commercially feasible one, on land our financing would allow us to get hold of and develop."

Redge uttered a *whoa* that brought both of their saddle mounts to an abrupt halt. He stared in mingled doubt and amazement at his father. "You . . . you mean that's how you got hold of the lead mine north of Poplar Bluff, where I grew up? You mean you and Emmett Willoughby euchred a grateful old man into—"

"You can amend that description to include *'shrewd'* with the *'grateful.'* Sure we got a mining lode that became valuable. But don't feel sorry for Frenchy Gervais. He engineered the deal—put a couple of thousand dollars into his pocket."

When they urged their horses forward, that comforting quiet of understanding and unity was about them. They would be home to their creekside camp in about half an hour. There would be their livestock to care for, the work of getting a substantial cabin started, and the dreams and plans of a future to sustain them as the days marched on one by one, and the memories of those Missouri years receded.

24

Chapter 4

The next day Redge wakened to the incessant beating of rain upon the tent where he and his father had spread their bedrolls. A look outside confirmed his thought that this would likely be an all-day downpour. Dark clouds, laden with moisture carried up from the Gulf of Mexico, hung low above the valley of Crow Creek, creating a veil that obscured the sloping hills and the distant mountains. It would be a dreary day, but from this spring rainfall would be born tall, waving grass, myriad prairie flowers, and the freshly washed cleanliness of acres waiting to be ridden and explored.

The rainfall lasted two days, halting work on the lean-to shelter that served as their stable. Redge spent considerable time sketching out the pens he would need in order to care for even a few head of sick or crippled livestock. His immediate problem would be finding a suitable supply of corral poles. Only cottonwoods and willows grew along the creek; for good poles of lodgepole pine, such as he had seen at Andy Purcell's ranch, he would have to go with a team and wagon to the mountains off to the west. An even more ambitious and exciting possibility came to mind, and he asked his father, "Dad, do you suppose that up there in the mountains, beyond the scrub timber of the foothills, we might find some house logs? They'd sure beat cotton-wood poles or sod for fixing us a house."

"No doubt there are, Redge. But they'll be hard to get to—likely no cleared way or smooth going up there."

"I'd like to find out. Take our team and the running gear of a wagon. Strip off the box and just use rope to tie a load of logs to the bolsters. I could haul quite a few poles—and longer ones—that way."

"You're looking at a three- or four-day trip, son, count-ing time for cutting and trimming a load." Redge nodded, then peered into the gray falling rain off westward. He missed not being able to see the mountains with their dark, timbered slopes and snowy crests. He had no desire to settle or live among the foothills, the higher ranges, or the great river valleys he knew must separate them. Yet he wanted them always visible on the western horizon. Solid. Soaring. Eternal. Marking the outer limits of his world as they stood their vigil through every changing season. But this was the place he wished to live.

They discussed the idea of both of them being gone from their camp for so long a trip. Their livestock would have to be cared for, and although it wasn't likely that marauders would destroy their camp, it was common sense to protect their belongings.

The problem was solved in an unexpected way. At mid-morning on the next warm and pleasant day, a horseman hove into sight down Crow Creek and rode steadily toward the corrals. Will Cardigan watched the stranger, then grinned at Redge. "Seems we're about to receive a visit from our friend Hank Kutcher."

Now Redge could recognize the piebald gelding, the same horse Kutcher had been riding on the night of his first visit. His middle-aged figure seemed slighter than ever but moved with the grace of a man whose life had been that of the open range and a saddle. Will Cardigan lifted an arm in friendly greeting while Redge yelled aloud, "Hi, Mr. Kutcher. We've still got something in the coffee pot."

As the visitor reined his horse to a halt near them, his wind-carved face reflected the warmth of their welcome. "Howdy, neighbors. I see you're getting settled in."

Kutcher alighted, then dropped the reins of his gelding to the ground. The old rider's casual walk away from his horse caused Redge to ask with concern, "Shouldn't you hitch those reins to a post? Won't he wander off toward home?"

Kutcher beat dust from his pants with his old black hat. "Don't worry, lad. As long as those reins touch the ground, that bronc won't budge a foot. He's bridle-trained."

It was half an hour later, after they had shown Kutcher the corrals and their lean-to stable, that Will Cardigan complained of the shortage of suitable timber. "We just can't get much built with cottonwood and willow sticks;

I'd give a pretty penny for some of the straight hardwood timber we had in Missouri."

"It's a grass country," Kutcher agreed. "You may have to live in a dugout or shape up a soddy."

Cardigan glanced toward the foothills standing out clear and sharp in the distance. "The boy thinks we might be able to haul a few wagonloads of good poles and house logs from the mountains."

"It has been done. The ranch freighted in a lot that way."

"Trouble is," Redge chimed in, "we can't both be away for such trips. My dad says it's too dangerous for one man to try it by himself."

"And he's right, lad. This is a big, lonely country where the unexpected can happen. Where a man in trouble is likely on his own." Kutcher paused and again beat trail dust from his trousers. "Tell you what, lad. Maybe old Hank can lend a hand. I've got some time off from the Diamond-7. I was planning to mosey into Cheyenne. Get liquored. Get a woman. Go broke and ride home wonderin' why the hell a sane man would do that. You'd be doing old Hank a favor by letting me climb up into tall-timber country to fetch down poles."

It was decided around the noon-meal fire that Redge and his father would take turns staying to watch camp. Seeing the eagerness in his son's face, Will Cardigan suggested that Redge should accompany Kutcher on the first trip.

They left for the mountains at dawn the following morning. The wagon had been stripped to bare running gear. Onto this was tied a box of food, camping necessities, axes and a crosscut saw, a rifle, and a bedroll. Kutcher insisted that they take along fifty feet of stout cord, like plumb-line cord.

"What use would we have of that?" Redge demurred.

"Plenty of use. Just wait and see."

The weather held warm and sunny. Shortly after noon they came to a southward-stretching line of railroad track, bordered by the poles of a telegraph line.

"It's the Denver Pacific coming down from Cheyenne," Kutcher explained. "The colony started by that Horace Greeley fellow is mebbe twenty-five miles south—spot where the Cache la Poudre and Platte rivers come nigh to meeting."

Redge showed little interest in the new farming settlement. Instead, he was eagerly studying the foothills that loomed ever closer as he guided the team westward toward them. He sat alone on the wagon gears, since Hank Kutcher had chosen to ride alongside on his bald-faced gelding.

"Where does that Poodle River drop out of the mountains?" Redge asked.

"The *what* river?" Kutcher chuckled.

"The one you said runs down to the Platte."

"You mean the Poudre ... the Cache la Poudre. That's French for 'hide the powder.' We'll come to it at Laporte —and that means 'the Portal'—gateway to the Rocky Mountains."

But Redge was disappointed when they arrived at the hamlet of Laporte the following morning. He had hoped they would follow the clear, fast-flowing river into the canyon, and then upstream where timbered slopes ascended higher, tier by tier. Instead, Hank Kutcher pointed to a road that took off to the northeast through rolling hills and grassy valleys.

"Couldn't we get poles up there a short way?" Redge insisted, jerking a thumb toward the upriver course.

"It'd be danged hard, lad. The canyon walls are too steep. This other road probably was an old Indian trail up to the Laramie Plains in Wyoming. It was chosen for the Overland stage route. Up near the Wyoming border, there's a place called Virginia Dale, a stage station." The usually quiet Kutcher ended his explanation by deftly fingering tobacco into a brown paper for a cigarette.

"We're up here to cut poles," Redge reminded both Kutcher and himself. "These hills don't seem to have much timber."

"You'll change your tune, lad, once we're a dozen or so miles farther up the line. The north slopes of about every mountain carry prime lodgepole pine, straight, true poles up to a foot or more in diameter. We won't have to climb far off the road, either."

They camped that night in a small glade traversed by a cold, brush-bordered creek. Off to the south was a timbered slope. A short, preliminary jaunt into it caused Redge Cardigan to whistle in excited surprise. "Mr. Kutcher, we'll have a fine load of corral poles ready by sundown tomorrow." He paused, letting his eyes scan the area. He was suddenly very still. A short way across the meadowed

28

glade, standing quietly, curious but watchful, was a buck deer. It would be an easy rifle shot, and Redge's hand moved along the wagon wheel where he had propped the rifle.

"Hold it, Redge," the older man said softly. "It'd be a wicked waste; this time of year the meat won't keep."

Presently the deer bounded off into the shadows. When Redge turned, he noticed Kutcher measuring off a couple of rods of the heavy twine he had insisted they bring.

"So now what?" Redge asked.

"We're gonna have fresh meat for our supper. Trout. Suppose you slap your hat over a few of those grass-hoppers out on the meadow while I get us rigged." The old cowhand was already digging black hooks from a tobacco tin.

Redge never forgot the next half hour. It truly taught him that the land was his, offering rich bounties just there for the taking. As darkness gathered, they tramped a short way upstream and found a deep hole at a bend of the creek. Kutcher had cut willow saplings and trimmed them for poles. Now he slid a grasshopper onto a hook and cast it lightly toward the hole's center. Instantly a sizable shadow sliced through the water and struck the bait. Kutch-er's line jerked tight with the weight and fury of the mountain fish. There was no reel with which to play and tire the trout, so Kutcher seized his pole with both hands and jerked it over his head. The fish came out of the water, arced through the air, and lay squirming in the grass.

"Get your pole and get busy, son. This hole's running over with beauties. Likely some up to five pounds. Mostly native trout—cutthroats."

Minutes later they had landed enough trout for both supper and breakfast. After a splendid meal, when they had made final preparations for the night, they threw lengths of pitch-laden pine onto their fire and watched flames lick upward. A light breeze was whispering through the timber; the creek murmured protest of the boulders striving to impede its way. Both Redge and Kutcher sprawled on bed-rolls, knowing that soon they must seek rest for the long day of timber cutting ahead.

Redge watched Kutcher stare silently into the blaze, and his curiosity about this ranchhand got the better of him. Finally he asked, "Mr. Kutcher, have you worked at the Diamond-7 a long time?"

The older man stirred embers with a smoking stick. "Son, don't you think it's about time you knocked off that 'Mr. Kutcher' stuff? Just call me Hank. Well, I've been at the ranch for years, since '82. A bunch of us brought a trail herd up from south of San Antone, Texas, and delivered them on the Yellowstone River in Montana."

"And you never went back to Texas?"

"I started to, late that fall. Out along Crow Creek, mebbe a dozen miles downstream from your camp, I got a busted leg. I was alone and in damned bad shape. It happened Andy Purcell was riding home to his Diamond-7 from Cheyenne. He got me to the ranch and splinted the leg. Later, he offered me a job. I'm still working for Purcell . . . one of God's great gentlemen."

Redge wanted to question Hank Kutcher about the operation of the Diamond-7; he especially craved to learn more of Stacy Murdock, the foreman to whom he had taken an instant and intense dislike. Yet he decided not to probe, sensing already that here on the plains the best information was that volunteered.

After a time the boy realized that Kutcher was eying him in a speculative way, but it was several minutes before the cowhand spoke. "Son, I like the way you and your dad are pushing to get suitable pens and shelters and a house of sorts ready. Winters can be rough and long on the prairies. You're a stubborn galoot, too. How'd you come by that?"

"Probably from my mother. Mr. Kutcher—excuse me, Hank—my mother was all get up and go. And when she was sure she was going the right way, hell or high water better not try and stop her."

Kutcher, catching the adoration in the boy's words, said softly, "She didn't come with you—and with your dad— from Missouri?"

Redge brushed a fist across his forehead, then gazed beyond the fire and beyond distantly silhouetted peaks. "Hank—sir—my mother died about four months ago. Pneumonia."

"Lad, I'm sorry," the old cowhand whispered.

"I'm over it now, except for a lot of memories," Redge said in a hesitant, uncertain way. "After my mom died,

Dad wanted to make a new start in a new place. I was the one who decided we'd come to Colorado. When I was a little kid my dad's best friend—his partner, Emmett Willoughby—used to tell me—"

As the name spilled from Redge Cardigan's lips, Hank jerked tensely erect. "Wait, boy, wait. Who did you say?"

"Willoughby. Emmett Willoughby," Redge repeated in surprise.

"Godamighty, lad. You mean that Willoughby—the legend of Arizona?"

"I wouldn't know, Hank. He sold out his part of a lead mine to my father when I was about ten. Left Missouri, I guess. But he sure was handy with any sort of gun."

And Hank Kutcher, knowing that many gunfighters of the southwest had fallen second best to Emmett Willoughby, said with awe: *God protect me from one with such skill ever having cause to seek me out!*

31

Chapter 5

By the time when yellowing cottonwoods foretold winter's approach late in September, the Cardigans had managed to haul eight loads of pine poles and house logs from the mountains. Hank Kutcher helped out until the time rolled around for him to return to the Diamond-7. Within a week, other help showed up, in the person of an out-of-luck, out-of-work drifter who claimed Montana as his last stop and no place as home. When not helping on the timber haul, this vagabond proved to be skilled with carpenter tools. He mumbled endlessly in Norwegian, but spoke very few words of English. Redge gathered that the man's consuming concern was to be somewhere south of Taos before the first snowstorm.

Ever mindful of his agreement with the Diamond-7's owner, Andy Purcell, Redge had suggested that the holding pens and shedlike barn for sick and crippled animals take priority in building. Only half a dozen head of stock had so far been driven up from the Diamond-7 and turned over to the Cardigans for care. Among them were a couple of cancer-eyed cows and a badly spavined saddle horse. Treatment of the horse would be difficult, requiring lots of time. Little could be done for the cows. Redge surmised that it had been Stacy Murdock's idea to bring these hopeless cases to him.

He had seen Murdock only once since their clash at the ranch. It happened on a late afternoon when the boy and Hank Kutcher were approaching Crow Creek and the Cardigan's homesite with their second load of house logs. Three riders, moving northward at a brisk trot, came over a knoll and sighted the pole-laden wagon. The three halted for a minute or so and watched; then they reined their mounts directly toward the Cardigan wagon. Presently they came alongside. Stacy Murdock, astride a beautiful black mare, sat with the ease and confidence of a man proud of his authority. Grudgingly, Redge conceded to himself that such a man might be a powerful and efficient foreman for Purcell's sprawling land and the herds that grazed it.

The other two riders lifted their hands in a gesture of greeting and grinned tentatively. There was no greeting from Murdock. His dark eyes examined the house logs and then fastened on Redge as he said, "Kid, you're doing a lot of work in order to get a pen and a shack set up."

As when they had first met, the ranch boss's words and tone sparked resentment in Redge. "Some of us are willing to work for a decent home," the boy answered tersely.

"Just so you keep in mind you and your old man are squatters. Squatters don't stay put long, hereabouts."

Redge bristled, and held himself from leaping off the wagon. His next words were spoken as a flat challenge. The Diamond-7 riders exchanged expectant glances. "Murdock," the boy began. "I don't know what I've done to get you on the prod. If you want a fight, just say so. Otherwise, I'll listen when you own the Diamond-7, or when Mr. Purcell sends word—"

"Damn you, kid," Murdock cut in, "for a nickel I'd—"

Redge's hand was deep in his pocket, searching for a coin, when Hank Kutcher broke in. "Stacy," he said, almost pleasantly, "I've an idea you'd best ride on. Quit baiting the lad."

Murdock acknowledged Kutcher's presence for the first time by saying, "Hank, seems to me you're putting two bits' worth on the wrong side. How come you're traipsing around and hauling poles with a squatter's kid? The ranch gave you a few days off to go to Cheyenne. To get liquored and laid."

Hank Kutcher chuckled as though enjoying the encounter. "Murdock, when the Diamond-7 is paying me, I take your orders. Right now, I'm my own man on my own time. If I help build a pen or a porch it's none of your business."

Murdock remained tensely quiet in the saddle. Then he said softly, "Kutcher, someday I'm going to have my bellyful of you. Then—"

"Forget it, Stacy," Kutcher answered, and there was

33

scorn in his words. "You'll never cut down on me with fists, let alone a six-gun. *And you know why.*"

There was no reply from the Diamond-7 foreman. An angry and somehow baffled sweep of his arm motioned his two companions on their way. He rode off behind them without a backward glance.

Throughout October the weather continued mild, with such an abundance of warm, sunlit hours that Will and Redge were able to accomplish a great deal. They had discovered that the tall grass growing in favored spots along Crow Creek was curing into excellent, nutritious hay. Redge never mastered the scythe's use to where he could equal the long, flowing strokes of his father. Yet between them they managed to harvest and stack hay enough to feed their horses during the storms they knew would soon be upon them. There would be some hay also for what Redge now termed their "hospital stock."

Quite a few more animals were driven up from the Diamond-7 as winter neared. Will Cardigan was glad of Hank Kutcher's aid and of the drifter who had enabled them to get well set for the onslaught of winter. Their cabin, though small, was well built and likely to withstand both snow and wind. The corrals and outbuildings would suffice until warm summer days of another year rolled around.

Redge spent a lot of hours with the sick or injured stock; it was evident that Andy Purcell meant to reap full advantage from his deal. Watching the infinite patience and the growing skill with which his son dealt with his hospital critters, Will pondered how this boy had come by his love and understanding of animals, his almost instinctive knowledge, and his deftly healing touch. He's capable, all right, Will Cardigan summarized to himself, but there's something beyond that. An ingredient that too few of us are blessed with to the degree Redge is. Compassion. Yes, that's it. The suffering of a heifer . . . a mustang . . . even of a broken-winged hawk . . . seems almost his own suffering.

Cardigan's mind swept away time; but still vivid memory remained of his wife, Redge's mother. The boy took after Hazel in so many ways. She'd brave a blizzard if anybody was sick and needed her. God knows how many babies she delivered, or how many old and dying people she comforted. Redge had her touch.

Will Cardigan heaved a lonely sigh. But he followed it with a laugh that rang aloud. But Hazel sure bred something else into this son of hers. Stubbornness. That balky, wonderful, accursed, magnificent ability to see something through even when everyone else says you're whipped.

A trying test of Redge Cardigan's skill and his perseverance came sooner than either he or his father expected. Early in December, a day broke so warm and clear that even the frail edging of ice along Crow Creek disappeared. A faint breeze out of the southwest cascaded over the mountains and whispered its way across the grasslands. Meanwhile vast gray clouds, heavy with moisture, were surging up in the south. That night the weather changed.

The wind whipped around to the northeast. Within an hour the warmth built up during the day gave way to a freezing chill. The moisture blew westward as dense and blinding snow. Within two hours of its coming, a blanket of white about six inches deep lay across northeastern Colorado, the Crow Creek Valley, and around the buildings of the Cardigan camp.

The howling of wind along the cabin's eaves awakened Will Cardigan near midnight. He touched a match to a kerosene lantern and stared at snow that lay thick across their only window. He shook Redge. "Looks like we're in for a real one, Redge. Maybe a blizzard."

Drowsiness left the boy, and his heels hit the floor. "Lord almighty . . . listen to that wind! I gotta get a couple of cows into the barn, the one that got the deep hip gouge and the three-year-old that's due to calve. Outside, they'll both be goners."

Will was pulling on a heavy sheepskin coat and answered, "I'll give you a hand. This is sure a poor time of year for a calving."

"It can happen any time of year, Dad, if the bull breaks out."

"Seems as if, son." Will chuckled. "I've known it to happen with a few people, too."

When they opened the door, there was a swirl of white that hurled them back inside. As Redge slammed the door shut, his father unlooped a long lariat rope from a wall peg. "That Norwegian warned me to keep this handy inside the house." Will explained. "He claimed some of these prairie storms have snow pea-soup thick; people have gotten lost and frozen to death within an arm's length of a building."

With the rope tied firmly to the door handle, they worked their way along it. Presently they came, with snow-matted eyes and cheeks, to the knot marking the rope's end.

"It won't help," Redge called out. "Not long enough."

"It's all right," his dad answered. "We've struck off in the wrong direction. Just hang on and pull it tight. We'll swing an arc to the right."

Moments later they bumped into the log stable, then groped their way to its door. Inside, they were able to relight their lantern. They pushed at the second door, which led into the corral. Cattle had crowded against the outside. It took them half an hour to get their hospital stock inside to special pens. Redge ran concerned eyes over the belly and vaginal area of the calf-heavy heifer. He shook his head and spoke slowly. "Remember, Dad, when Hank Kutcher and another rider hazed these halt, lame, and blind critters up from the Diamond-7 about three weeks ago? He warned me we'd likely have trouble delivering the calf from this one. She's pretty weak, and her bone structure isn't right—hasn't matured."

"Maybe we ought to stay out here with her, Redge."

The boy shook his head. "It won't happen for a few hours. Anyhow, the heifer is sheltered. We'd best get some sleep; tomorrow is gonna be rough."

The rope led them again through white fury, where snow and wind and deepening cold made their every breath a duel with the storm. But inside the cabin, with a length of chopped cottonwood in the flat-topped cookstove, there was an aura of safety and sanctuary.

Daylight revealed nearly a foot of snow, much of which had been whipped into tall drifts. But both the wind and snowfall had lessened, although both continued at a steady rate. As his father prepared breakfast, Redge again tramped his way to the barn; this time he could see and no rope was needed. He found the heifer, a red animal with white patches, lying on the dirt floor of the barn in agonized labor. At Redge's approach she struggled and managed to get her forefeet braced for rising. Then she sank unwillingly back; a despairing sound escaped her.

This caused Redge's dark eyes to reveal the concern and pity within him. "Easy now, old gal. We'll see you through."

An hour later, Will Cardigan came to the barn. He found Redge on his knees behind the heifer, clutching the small and slippery feet of a calf that had not yet passed its way into daylight. The boy had shed his coat; unruly hair lay unnoticed across his forehead. At the heifer's every muscular spasm, Redge pulled cautiously but firmly to deliver the calf.

"Perhaps it's not quite time yet," Will Cardigan suggested.

Redge shook his head, speaking in tense and worried tones. "It's far past time. It's just what I feared; her bone structure won't allow free passage, and she's weak. Far too weak."

"Maybe if we both pulled," Will suggested, and began to roll his sleeves.

But their combined strength was to no avail. Nor was delivery of the calf brought about when they tied a lariat to the protruding feet and used the pulling power of Will Cardigan's saddle horse.

Redge ran exploring fingers into the heifer's birth passage. Part of the calf's nose, and one eye, slid into view. The boy came to his feet with a gesture of despair. "Dad, the little thing is stillborn—dead."

His father looked at the now motionless heifer, noting her tortured breathing. "She's not dead yet, but she's almost certain to die soon. Redge, if you'd like, I'll put an end to the agony. Shoot her."

A sign of stubbornness suddenly marked the thrust of Redge's chin. "No. No . . . by God, I'm gonna save her. The calf doesn't matter now. Somehow, Dad, I'm going to cut it out of her." He paused and stared at his slimy hands, then added, "I'll need the littlest blade of your jackknife, Dad. Honed like a razor. We'd better get some water boiling to sterilize it."

Will Cardigan's face was concerned. "It's a hundred-to-one shot to save the cow, Redge. There's likelihood of infection for the critter—and perhaps for you too, Redge."

"I know that," Redge agreed. "I'll dilute some carbolic acid and wash my hands." For a moment he studied the prone heifer, and the calf's legs and nose protruding from her. "If I can get inside and do some cutting, the calf's bony head, then its shoulders, are apt to slip free."

Will stared at his son with wonder—wonder tinged with apprehension. "Be careful, son. Very careful. There's the possibility of blood poisoning."

"There's also a possibility I can save the cow's life," Redge whispered.

During the next hour, the boy paid little heed to the storm continuing outside, or to other animals voicing their resentment at not being fed. His strokes of the knife were studied and sure as bit by bit he cut free portions of the dead calf's legs and facial hide. Finally the test came. He fashioned a loop of strong, flexible wire and managed to insert it to where it would tighten about the calf's skull. His muscles grew taut and he clenched his teeth as he pulled.

Suddenly the heifer's extended legs moved convulsively. A moment later the bloody remains of a sizable calf lay free of its mother, staining the hay around them with blood and fluids.

A tired sigh escaped Redge. "There's only one thing else I can do for you, old girl." He thrust his hands into a pail of warm water, to which carbolic acid had been added. Then he saturated a clean white rag with the solution and thrust it far up the heifer's bloody uterus.

His father proudly drew Redge to his feet. "I'll take over now, son. Get cleaned up and rest. Barring infection, she may pull through; a range cow is a hard critter to kill."

"I hope she does make it," Redge said wistfully. "We'll know, probably, if she cleans herself just right and gets rid of the afterbirth."

"Redge," the older man asked, "where did you learn so much about these things?"

Redge grinned. "Didn't my mom use to take me along sometimes when she had to deliver a baby? I wasn't even ten years old, but she explained it to me. My mom marveled at birth . . . at life itself."

Twenty-four hours later the heifer lay on the barn floor, practically in the same position, breathing heavily. Staring at her, Redge stifled a frustrated sob. He felt his father's arm across his shoulder and clutched Will's hand in response. "Dad, I guess it was all of no use. Look at those eyes. My heifer has gone into fever—a high fever." He paused, then added, "And I don't have one damned thing that'll fight fever."

The storm, after dropping another five inches of snow, had given way to sunshine that cast a blinding brilliance over the prairies. The stable door was open, and the sun illuminated Redge's pale face.

"Don't take it so hard, Redge. You did everything you possibly could."

"It wasn't enough. Maybe I just killed the heifer."

Will Cardigan's face suddenly lit up with growing excitement. "Redge, wait! Do you know what aconite is?"

"Sure. It's that medicine Mom used to keep handy for dosing me when—" His voice picked up. "For when I had a fever!"

"You're right, son. And I do believe there's nearly a full bottle of aconite in our medicine chest. But . . . but how could we get the stuff down her?"

Redge yelled over his shoulder as he ran toward the house, "We can dilute it. Make what seems a proper dosage for a seven-hundred pound critter. Then I'll twist her head and pry her jaws open. Dad, there's a rubber hose in our storage shed. Cut a length of it. We'll ram it down her throat. Maybe the old gal won't like it. But she's not going to die. We won't let her."

Chapter 6

Within a week, the havoc of the storm had not abated. The snow lay over the prairie buffalo grass as a deep mantle, for there was neither wind nor sunshine enough to clear it. Such a storm in early winter was one of the greatest threats to the cattle industry of the Great Plains. It was the common practice to winter herds on the protein-rich buffalo grass, which cured on the undulating hills and provided adequate winter forage. Usually a hard wind, following in the wake of the snowfall, would sweep much of the snow into deep drifts; this left large expanses of grass exposed and available to hungry animals. Generally the snow from early storms melted before very long and did not endanger the hardy cattle and horses of the plains.

Will Cardigan, surveying the miles of thick snow, wondered how the herds of the Diamond-7, scattered far from the ranch's sheltering buildings, were making out. The cattle rearing and marketing methods of the giant western ranches seemed to be a vast and inefficient gamble—risky and costly as well. Someday, he thought, the method has to change. Hay will be grown and stacked to assure adequate winter feed. Windbreaking pens and sheds will be provided. Selective breeding will have to provide animals capable of better weight gain.

On the Saturday evening following the storm, the Cardigans went to bed aware that the temperature outside was only in the low twenties. The snow outside was still a deep mantle that measured halfway to their knees.

When they awakened to morning light, the world had changed. The dripping of water from the cabin roof brought both father and son to the door to peer out. Warm wind engulfed them as it swept across the hills and down the valley of Crow Creek. Already water was dripping . . . running . . . standing. On the hillsides and along the creekside flats, large patches of bare earth or grass were beginning to appear. There was a soggy grayness of atmosphere, through which the sun was burning a brilliantly warm way. The phenomenon known as a Chinook, the rare, warm wind of winter, had averted disaster.

As he had done every morning since his ordeal with the calving heifer, Redge hastened to the stable. He grinned as he saw the animal standing at a manger with her head lowered to chew a mouthful of hay. She was thin and gaunt, for she had hovered near death for three days. It was only after she had rid herself of the dangerous germ-laden placenta that the boy had gained any assurance she would live. Now, as he walked about the stable, Redge kept a cautious eye on her. Only yesterday she had suddenly lowered her head and charged at him. He had barely sidestepped the thrust of her horns and the crushing blow that would have sent him against the chinked logs. Remembering the incident, he now scowled at the heifer. "So that's how you felt about me, old girl," he mumbled. "Not one consarned bit of gratitude. Just wait. Someday maybe we'll make steak of you. Likely you'll cook out so damned tough—"

Redge's words broke off as he heard the barn door open and close and he wheeled around, startled. A tall, thin, gray-haired man strode through and broke into a laugh. Then he said, "So you're planning to butcher a Diamond-7 beef? Boy, sometimes I wonder about you."

Redge blushed in embarrassment. "I don't plan to eat the critter, Mr. Purcell. Not really. But she's surely been a tribulation." The boy struggled for composure, then added, "It's good to see you again, sir."

The owner of the Diamond-7 Ranch scrutinized this young neighbor with a remnant of military preciseness. He thrust out a hand that was firm and friendly and tanned by the prairie sun. "Redge, it's a treat to see you too. What you've done to save this heifer for me isn't far short of a miracle."

Redge's look was troubled. "I wish I could do as well with every critter you send me. Would you like to see how that spavined saddle horse is doing?"

"Later in the day, son," Andy Purcell agreed. "Perhaps you can show me about your pens and buildings also. Young man, for the last half hour I've been discussing some things with your father. He told me how you saved the heifer by freeing her of a stillborn calf. I'm greatly pleased, and I think it's time the three of us had a talk."

Anxiety rose in Redge. Suddenly he was thinking how dependent the Cardigans were upon the good will of Andy Purcell and the Diamond-7 Ranch. They had come as trespassers, as squatters, onto his graze. Despite their toil, their hopes, and their building, they could remain only through his goodwill. The boy controlled his apprehension, then he asked, "How did your livestock fare during the storm? I sure hope the losses weren't too great."

"We lost about twenty-five head. It'd been ten times that if the Chinook wind hadn't happened along to save us."

"Lord almighty, that many?" Redge whistled in amazement.

"Some ranches have lost fifty percent and more in a killer snowstorm. We never have. We have some pretty good shelter in the timber and brush along Crow Creek. There's some grass there that's tall enough to seldom get entirely snow-covered. Besides, Stacy Murdock is pretty knowledgeable in handling stock in winter. He learned it up Montana way."

Redge had no desire to hear about Murdock, who had so bitterly opposed Purcell's allowing the Cardigans to remain and improve their home. So he asked, "How is Hank Kutcher these days?"

"As fit and cantankerous as ever." Purcell chuckled. "You'll see for yourself in a day or so; he'll be heading up this way with a dozen or more cripples needing your care."

Redge realized that some busy weeks lay ahead. He quickly mulled over the part of his agreement with Purcell that called for his becoming owner of part of the increase. He voiced this factor in a blunt way. "I'll try and pull a goodly part of the sick ones through. And I hope there's a lot of *she* stock, something to provide my dad and me with some calves of our own."

Purcell nodded briskly, then answered, "That percentage-of-increase deal is part of what I want to talk over with you folks—after you provide me with some hot coffee and a meal. It's quite a jaunt up here from our headquarters." Purcell paused, his glance roaming the cabin, the stable and the pens. "Someone here sure knows how to pick

42

lodgepole pine poles—and how to lend permanence to a spread."

The dinner that Will Cardigan provided proved satisfying and unpretentious. It consisted of a canned-tomato stew, an antelope roast, and cornbread. "We'd be able to offer more," Will commented, "if there was a trading post or grocery nearby."

"There is a trading post, a pretty good one, but it is nearly a day's ride off eastward," Purcell said. "It's called Kate's Wagon. Remind me to tell you more about it sometime."

Purcell spread wild-currant jam onto a slice of nicely crusted cornbread before continuing. "Many a time, Cardigan, back there in the '60s, at Shiloh and elsewhere, I'd have been tempted to swap my boots for a feed like you've stirred up today."

"I remember once," Will reminisced, "when my squad got by for three days on stale bread and a tough old rooster we'd swiped."

Andy Purcell grimaced ruefully. "Yes, Cardigan, and I seem to remember I was the party you and that other thieving corporal got the chicken from." Then Purcell smiled as he asked, "That pal of yours—I recall he was uncannily good with a rifle or pistol—what was his name?"

"His name," Will Cardigan answered wistfully, "was Willoughby . . . Emmett Willoughby. We were partners for a long time. We had a lead mine in Missouri. When we sold, he headed for Texas."

Redge was first to note the surprise marking Purcell's face. "Willoughby! Would that be the Emmett Willoughby who's a gunfighter in New Mexico—or Arizona?"

"It may well be," Will Cardigan acknowledged. "I haven't heard from Emmett for a long while, but I knew no one more skilled with firearms."

"You mean you have lost track of so good a friend?" Purcell asked.

"It's the old story, sir—a woman. Emmett was not the marrying kind, but he lived for a time with a grass widow. She couldn't abide his having close friends. Our rift was slow coming on, but had widened when Emmett took off for Texas. Not that we weren't still friends, but neither of us is any great shakes at writing letters."

Andy Purcell touched a match to a short-stemmed pipe and slid his chair a few inches from the table. Momentarily, he was quiet, his mien that of a man struggling to seize and hold something from the mists of memory. "Seems to me," he said finally, "there was something in the paper shortly after the war, about a gunfight or brawl Willoughby was in. Had something to do with a gambling session on a riverboat. One man killed . . . another wounded bad. I don't recall their names."

Redge saw his father grow tense and straighten in his chair. Very deliberately he set his coffee cup on the table. For a moment he was about to speak. Redge was positive Will Cardigan was about to reveal the names. But he shrugged and then with half-smiling eyes he said, "It seems there was something about it in the papers. But so long ago. So hard to remember."

Redge managed to keep all emotion from his face. Yet he was certain. His father had almost spoken the names of the dead and crippled men. And the boy was sure too that Andy Purcell had also realized Will Cardigan had started to reveal his knowledge of the happening, but had chosen not to do so.

The next words from the owner of the Diamond-7 came in a gruff tone meant to conceal deeper emotion. "How about us getting things lined up so that you Cardigans can get title to this squatters' nest? Settle down and stay put?"

Redge let out a whoop that shook the window panes. His father stared at their guest in disbelief, as though unable to fathom the full meaning of Andy Purcell's offer. At last he said, hardly above a whisper, "You mean, sir, we can buy some of this valley land—that you're offering us a corner of—"

"Not exactly." Purcell held up his hands in a forestalling gesture. "I may and may not be in a position to effect a sale—to offer clear title." The questioning faces before him caused Andy Purcell to continue. "Oh, the Diamond-7 Ranch is mine all right, and your setup here is within its limits. But questions remain. When I came west to Colorado, shortly after the war, this area held only buffalo and Indians. The Union Pacific Railroad was moving its westward way up north, but this Crow Creek country, downstream from Cheyenne, was just part of the great American desert. I suppose the government in Washington had claim to it through the Louisiana Purchase."

Purcell paused, deep in reflection. "A claim to land then —an acre or a hundred sections—was something acquired and enforced by driving in a herd, throwing up a headquarters of sorts, and having enough good men and guns to make it clear you meant to stay."

Redge laughed aloud, then challenged the rancher, "Mr. Purcell, you're saying in a sense you're as much a squatter as my dad and me."

"Not exactly, son. I didn't settle on land claimed by anyone else—save maybe a few migrating Arapaho Indians. Besides, there'd be one hell of a ruckus if anyone got brash enough to claim my Diamond-7."

Will Cardigan had listened carefully. Now he asked, "How do you propose, Mr. Purcell, to convey title to us?"

"I'm not going to convey anything," the rancher said firmly. "I am going to write out a letter—we can have Hank Kutcher witness it—saying that I have no objection to your settling on and claiming three full sections—that's nigh onto two thousand acres—immediately adjoining this cabin. Then if I were you, I'd mighty daggoned fast get to a land office; the big one in Denver would likely be best. File a homestead claim on as much of the three sections as you can. The rest you'll probably have to hold something like I hold the Diamond-7—with persuasion. A couple of Winchester rifles are pretty good persuaders."

To halt their astonishment and their words of gratitude, the rancher lifted a hand. "Save the thanks for maybe ten years from now. It may be that by then you'd like to kick my old butt. Stacy Murdock, my foreman, won't take kindly to this."

Minutes later, Purcell gazed sternly into Redge's face from his now rested horse. "Take good care of the critters Hank Kutcher is bringing up; they are springing heifers. You'll likely have more bawling calves about by May or June than you bargained for."

Following the two-day Chinook wind, which swept away much of the snow, the weather continued mild and sundrenched. Hank Kutcher showed up, driving eighteen head of cattle. Redge looked the animals over with amazement. "None of these heifers are crippled or sick," he said in

45

perplexity. "How come you to push healthy springers up here?"

"Just because I've found it wiser and healthier to do what my boss tells me to."

Redge's next words were born of teasing friendship. "You mean your boss, Stacy Murdock?"

"Hell no," Kutcher exploded. "If I'd meant Murdock I'd have said 'strawboss.' Andy Purcell picked these heifers and told me to flag their tails up here. Likely he wants you to midwife them. Anyhow, you've got the critters now, and I'm free of them."

Kutcher threw one leg around the horn of his saddle and put his fingers to fashioning a smoke. Then he asked, "How about riding along with me to pick up the ranch mail, over at Kate's Wagon? We'd be back by noon tomorrow."

"Kate's Wagon?" Redge repeated as a question.

"That's what I said," Kutcher replied testily. "Don't tell me you ain't heard of Kate's Wagon."

"I haven't even heard of Kate herself," Redge admitted with a grin, then added, "Let's talk to my dad. If he will look after the stock a day or so, I'd sure like to ride along to this Kate's Wagon. Has it got wheels?"

"Sometimes, lad, it's nigh to hell on wheels," Kutcher informed him.

Will Cardigan's permission for the trip was readily granted. Save for log-hauling trips, Redge had not been off their home location since arriving the previous spring, and deserved the change.

"Maybe," Cardigan suggested, "you can pick up a few things we're running short of; I've heard there's a trading post of sorts. Besides, son, I'm thinking of going to Denver next week . . . for a touch of civilization."

"You mean because you need a bath in a proper tub, don't you?" Redge prodded, teasing.

"I mean just so I'll be rid of an insolent kid for a spell," Will retorted.

They threw together a quick noon meal, then Redge and Hank said their goodbyes and rode off in a northeasterly direction. "Just how far away is this post office?" Redge asked Kutcher.

"A trifle over twenty miles, Redge. It used to be a good bit farther."

46

"That's crazy," Redge protested. "How can a trading post move?"

Kutcher sighed vastly. "Just so you'll quit pestering me, I'll picture the past of Kate's Wagon. Now listen—and don't butt in."

Kutcher flipped a cigarette aside, then thinking of the dry grass about it, he dismounted and ground it out with his heel. As they rode on he began to talk.

"Back in the late '60s and the '70s a lot of trail herds came up from Texas, heading north to Wyoming and Montana. One of their main trails passed through about twenty miles east of here. Each herd was prodded northward by a sizable crew. And by the time the crews got this far along they were usually short of just about everything.

"A fellow named Dan Andrus knew about the crews. Andrus had worked planting ties and spiking rails for the Union Pacific. He also had a wife, named Kate, who kept him out of the booze tents and gambling halls. Andrus got the idea of buying an assortment of life's necessities—such as plug tobacco, socks, and liniment—at railroad stores and then peddling them to trail crews. He hauled wagonloads of assorted stuff down thisaway, where the trail-herd crews would still be three or four days away from the rails."

"What about the post office?" asked Redge, unable to keep still any longer.

"Men kick off—die—don't they?" Kutcher resumed. "A snakebite put an end to Dan Andrus. But Kate, his widow, kept right on trading with the cowpokes. Figgered she had to, with three youngsters to feed. After a time, the wagon wouldn't hold all of her goods. For a time she had a sort of dugout close to the herds' trail. Business just kept coming. Now there's three or four clapboard buildings. Post office. Store. Horseshoeing shed. A combination restaurant and saloon."

Redge was incredulous as he asked, "You mean there is all that . . . and they still call the whole shebang *Kate's Wagon?*"

"I suppose you're all primed to suggest a better name," Kutcher replied.

"Nope," Redge countered. "I'll settle just to see some faces besides yours."

47

"Soon, right soon, Cardigan," Kutcher vowed.

They came to Kate's Wagon when the sun was still an hour from setting. Redge had pictured a cluster of slovenly buildings standing starkly atop a prairie ridge. Instead, they dropped into a small valley with an ice-edged but flowing stream. There was also an expanse of meadow and a few haystacks.

They rounded the corner of a bluff, and the boy's eyes widened in surprise. There were great cottonwoods and a lot of willows, all standing in the leaflessness of winter. Like sentries, they guarded a row of neatly painted buildings. Close by was a garden plot, and beyond, a series of pole corrals and a shed about which red hens were scratching.

Afront the largest building, there was a plank porch and a hitch rail. Two men lounged on the porch, and Redge noted a woman sweeping a graveled walk. Abruptly he was aware of how long it had been since he had seen the semblance of a settlement, or had heard the voice of a woman. With curiosity he followed Hank Kutcher's lead toward what a sign affirmed to be the post office.

Before they reached it, Redge sensed that he was being watched. He gazed about warily and focused on a clothesline—and on a girl. She was perhaps fifteen years old, and had her coppery hair in pigtails. Her hands moved in an agile manner to pull loose clothespins from the line and drop them into a basket. She seemed to be ignoring Redge, but he was sure it was her stare that had caused him to halt and reconnoiter.

He looked at her, trying to seem disinterested. She dumped some towels into the basket and looked straight at Redge. Then very deliberately she lifted her arm and thumbed her nose at him.

A moment later, Redge heard Hank Kutcher break into a howl of laughter. Then Kutcher swung from his horse and said, "It didn't take her long to put you in your place, lad."

The boy walked quickly toward the post office, his face red and embarrassed. "She doesn't even know me—never saw me before. Why would she do a fool thing like that?"

Precisely at that moment, a woman rushed through the post-office door to clutch Kutcher's hand. Her voice, breaking into words of hearty welcome, brought resurgent memories to Redge; it had been so long since he had heard a woman welcome an old acquaintance. He stood quietly listening, as Hank Kutcher asked her, "Kate, when are you gonna start getting old, like the rest of us?"

She made light of the question, and moved closer to run appraising eyes over Redge. He, in turn, was looking at her. "Ma'am, my name is Cardigan—Redge Cardigan."

Quick but revealing glances passed between Kate Andrus and Kutcher. Then she had both of Redge's hands in hers. "You two wash up for supper. It'll be ready in a few minutes, if . . ." She placed her arms akimbo on the hipline of her gingham dress and finished, "If that girl ever quits gawking, gets those clothes inside, and sets the table."

Within minutes, Redge had scrubbed his face and hands at a back-porch bench. Kutch was already inside the living quarters and in conversation with Kate Andrus. Presently Redge wandered over to the hitch rail, sat down, and studied the tiny settlement, a bit hesitant about joining the others. In the past few months, he had grown used to minimal company—this was a bit awkward for him.

He was still there when the kitchen door opened; the girl came outside and bustled past him with a panful of cracked corn.

Redge got to his feet, then called out, "If you're busy, I can get rid of those for you."

She wheeled about to face him. For an instant he thought she would thrust the pan into his hands. Then she recoiled a little and eyed him in an almost accusing way.

"I don't like you," she said.

"I can't say I'm crazy about you either," he flared. "But just what have I done . . . or said?"

"It's just that you're a boy." Her eyes swept across him, and she stood up taller, as though trying to strengthen her stance. A shaft of late-afternoon sunlight hit her burnished, coppery hair and accentuated her serious hazel eyes. "Boys are a sorry lot," she summarized.

"All of them," he said in mock agreement.

"Every . . . every worthless one. They like to run barefoot and let mud ooze through their toes. Then they try to sneak into bed—between clean sheets—without washing their feet."

Redge would have interrupted, but she went on with her lashing words. "Boys like to hunt and trap and to kill things. They even hold grasshoppers between their fingers, squeeze them and yell some senseless thing like 'Spit tobacco juice or I'll mash you!" And . . . and . . ." Her face flushed. "Every time the wind swishes a girl's dress up, the boys giggle and poke each other and smirk."

She was quiet for a moment, then thrust the pan of corn at him. "Come along; I'll show you how to feed chickens."

His first impulse was to shove the pan aside and to tell her that throwing corn to a bunch of clucking hens was a little kid's job. This was forestalled by her grin, a sort of tentative gesture of mixed curiosity and disdain. Redge noticed the appealing band of freckles across her nose. He surmised from her attitude that she was enjoying his baffled discomfort.

They fed the chickens together, then walked back to the hitch rail.

"You must be new around here," she said after a while. "I've never seen you at Kate's Wagon. What's your name?"

"Redge Cardigan. My dad and I live quite a ways from here, over on Crow Creek."

She swung expertly astride the hitch rail, then asked, "Do you have any brothers or sisters?"

"No," he answered. "We live alone . . . just the two of us." Redge slid onto the opposite end of the pole, letting his heels drag a pattern in the dusty road. "For a mean, spiteful kid," he said, "you sure have a lot of pretty hair."

She flipped the pigtails so that they hung across her chest and explained. "I guess I get all this red hair from my mom."

"You mean Kate. I—I mean, Mrs. Andrus."

"Sure. You can call her Kate. Everyone does."

"So you're Kate's daughter. Well, I sure don't have to ask your name. I'll just call you Carrot Top."

"Like hell you will!" she raged. "My brother tried that. I cracked him a couple of licks with a buggy whip. My name is Audrey—not that it's any of your business."

"I'd sure hate to be your brother," Redge prodded.

He expected another outburst, but instead his words turned her mood to serious anxiety. "I don't need any more brothers," she murmured. "Not like the one I've got. Always getting into some sort of trouble . . . making Kate pace the floor at night."

Redge decided not to pursue this matter of her brother, or of her family. Before he could phrase a suitable reply, the girl spoke again. "I had a sister, too. My big sis, five years older than I. She died two years ago."

Redge dropped from the hitch rail, walked to her side, and waited as she smudged her fist across her tears. "I know, Audrey," he said in quiet but tight voice. "I know. My mom died last year."

Whatever else they might have said was curtailed as Hank Kutcher came from the kitchen door and walked toward them.

"Kate wants to know if either of you had sense enough to gather the eggs," he said, and waited as both shook their heads ruefully. "Well, it's too late now. Supper is being dished up—and we're in for a treat. Ham and greens. And pie—real pie."

The night would be cold, so Kate Andrus insisted the two travelers spread their bedrolls on the counter of her store. Redge was thankful for a spot out of the winter cold, but Hank Kutcher joked about his elegant quarters.

"Kate, there's always one thing I can count on when I mosey up here for the mail or a sack of flour. I know surer than sure that I'll get to sleep on the counter . . . between a sauerkraut keg and the dried prunes."

Kate Andrus had mischief in her eyes. "Which ain't bad, Hank. Not so bad at all—even though I've an idea you've slept next to some *peaches*."

"Oh, my God, Kate. You're terrible." The words ended in an embarrassed screech as Audrey fled from the room, and Redge stood fixedly looking at something a galaxy away.

After making arrangements for Kate to receive the Cardigan mail, Redge and Kutcher headed back home toward midmorning the next day. Before the bluff would cut off their view, Redge turned for a last look at this hamlet called Kate's Wagon. His last glimpse was of a woman and a girl standing on the post-office porch and watching two men ride slowly, almost reluctantly, out of sight.

"That Kate Andrus is sure something," Redge said, finally ending the silence. "But I can't see how she makes a living, with practically nobody about. I don't imagine many trail herds raise a passing dust up this way anymore."

"Not often," Kutcher agreed. "But you'd be surprised how daggoned crowded Kate's Wagon can get at times. Riders from cow outfits nigh onto a hundred miles distant come in for supplies, to celebrate, or just to have a talk fest with Kate. She's a good talker," he added.

"I wonder," Redge said guardedly, "if that freckled kid thumbs her nose at everybody who rides in."

"Nope. She sure doesn't. That's a greeting reserved for those who either interest or irritate her. In your case—"

"In my case," Redge hastened to cut in, "I was one of a species she despises—boys." He spoke casually, but his mind was picturing tossed pigtails and an upturned nose bridged by freckles. "Besides, that spitfire kid is only about a dozen years old," he added.

"So she is," Kutcher agreed with a grin. "And you're such an old man—going on seventeen."

Redge speedily changed the subject, saying, "Wonder how those heifers are doing you drove up from the ranch."

"They'll make out." Kutcher chuckled. "Every last one of them is in top shape for calving."

"I don't understand their being sent upcreek to me," Redge puzzled. "The deal I have with Mr. Purcell is just for critters that are sick or hurt."

"Lad, all I know is you've got 'em. Andy Purcell wants it that way," Kutcher replied. He was quiet for a time, then spoke with thoughtfully chosen words. "Redge, Stacy Murdock hates your innards for some reason. And it sure didn't help things when Purcell told me to trail those healthy springing heifers up to your camp."

"What did old Fat Butt say this time?" Redge's tone was one almost of loathing.

Kutcher eased his horse to a halt, then studied his young companion with serious and uneasy gaze. "Redge, don't spout off too much—and don't underestimate Stacy Murdock. He's a capable cowman. Knows ranching upside down. He's also absolutely ruthless when it comes to dealing with rustlers—Indians or Mexicans—and especially with homesteaders—*nesters*."

"Then why does a fine man like Andy Purcell keep him around?" Redge demanded.

"Because a ranch as big and—and as vulnerable as the Diamond-7 needs a Stacy Murdock, someone willing and eager to see that the outfit doesn't lose one animal or one acre without one hell of a struggle. I heard a gent say once that western cow outfits are built and held by the fire in their owners' eyes. That may have built the Diamond-7 for Purcell, but it's sometimes the fire of fists and guns that keeps out the outlaws, the sneak thieves, the night raiders, and a lot of others seeking to tear down and break up a prime outfit."

Redge had listened with growing anger. "I don't recall anything my dad or me has done to threaten the Diamond-7. I'd eat prairie dog before I'd accept—"

"Wait a minute, son," Kutcher cut in. "Daggone but you're a hotheaded kid. I just want you to know the lay of the land—where you Cardigans stand. Purcell likes you, and trusts you. Sometimes he chuckles about the shrewd deal you made about sick critters. But to Murdock you're a festering threat and irritation—especially since Purcell has tied Stacy's hands."

And Redge, hearing the sincerity and graveness in Kutcher's words, answered in quiet tone, "I won't forget, Hank. I'll be on the lookout. Always."

They had ridden perhaps another mile when Kutcher, groping for words, asked, "Did that little gal, Kate's daughter, tell you about her family?"

Redge glanced at the old cowhand in surprise. "Not very much. She happened to mention she had a brother who's away a lot. She mentioned an older sister too. One who died."

Kutcher's face tightened, and his eyes showed anxiety and pain.

"Did the kid say what brought about her sister's death?" Kutcher's words had become almost inaudible, a questioning whisper.

Something in the older man's face made Redge want to reassure him. "She didn't want to say. I didn't pry. That's the size of it, Hank."

"I believe you, lad. And I wish to God the whole dirty affair had never come about."

They touched spurs to their horses and rode on toward Crow Creek.

54

Chapter 7

On the third morning after Redge's return from Kate's Wagon, Will Cardigan rose early, and by yellow lampglow searched through a seldom-opened trunk. From it he lifted several items of clothing and wrapped them carefully in a canvas-protected roll that could handily be tied behind a saddle. Another item in the trunk caught his attention. He picked it up and silently studied it. The item was one-half of a playing card: the ten of diamonds, roughly torn lengthwise. When Cardigan closed and hasped the trunk, he carefully placed the severed card in his vest pocket.

He prepared a sizable breakfast, then called for Redge to wake up, wash up, and get to the table. "Redge," he said presently, "I'll be riding out, come sunup. Perhaps I can get this trip to Denver out of the way while the weather holds. Think you can make out alone here, son? Say for about five days?"

"There's no reason why I can't," the boy said reassuringly. "Everything is in pretty good shape with the stock. Besides, I'll feel better, come the new year, if we've got those homestead papers started through, like Mr. Purcell mentioned."

Will nodded agreement. "That needs tending to. And being as it's getting close to Christmas, I'd like to fetch home a few things. In an emergency you can likely get hold of Hank Kutcher."

Their meal was almost finished when Will Cardigan lifted the torn playing card from his pocket and laid it carefully on the table, close to Redge's plate. "Son, take a good look at this," Will insisted. "I've been wondering for quite a while when to give it to you. This seems a good time."

Redge's face was puzzled. "But what is it, Dad? Just a worthless bit of torn cardboard."

55

"Redge, it could turn out to be the most important piece of paper in your life. Put it away, son . . . but keep it handy. Protect it."

The boy's face reflected utter bewilderment. "If you say so, Dad." He waited for further explanation.

Will Cardigan rose and laid his hand on his son's shoulder, and said, "Now listen to me, Redge. Listen carefully. That card is a compact. I told you about Emmett Willoughby, partner in that Missouri lead mine, and before that on a riverboat."

"Why did you and he—this Willoughby—split up? After so many years?"

"Emmett was a rover, I guess. We just lived differently —valued different things. About a year before your mother died, Emmett got restless, and tired of lead mining. He liked to traipse about and see the country. The last I heard from him he was in Texas. Before that, a woman had caused a little set-to between us. Nothing too serious."

"So what about this torn card, Dad?"

Cardigan's words were quick and urgent. "Emmett Willoughby has the other half of this ten of diamonds. It's his half of the pledge. We made it long ago, on the day he rode off for Texas. It means just this, Redge. If either Emmett or I ever needs help—be it money, fists, gunfire— all we have to do is see that our half of the card gets to the other party—and matches."

Redge picked up the torn card and turned it slowly in his hand. His father watched for a few seconds, then continued, "That pledge we made covers more than just Emmett and me. Son, we meant it for you too. That's why I'm entrusting it to you. If anything ever happens to me— if you need help—just see that Emmett gets my half of that card."

"I'll keep it handy," Redge said quietly.

An hour later, Will Cardigan was riding a southwesterly course that he surmised would bring him to the Union colony called Greeley. He was curious to see this area of fences, irrigation canals, and farmlands. Here he could put his horse in a livery stable, perhaps find a clean eating house, and then catch a train to Denver. As soon as he was underway, Cardigan acknowledged to himself how eagerly he was anticipating this trip to Denver. Again, for a time, he would mingle with men whose speech and thoughts and mode of dress had once been his during his flush years in business. He had decided to come to Colorado only after his wife's death had made him unable to remain as he was in a life he had shared with her. When he and Redge had started their wagon trek westward, they had been running, running from a vast loneliness.

There was no denying that their months at the little camp on Crow Creek had been good for Redge. He had grown taller and attained a surprising amount of self-reliance. The cooperation that Andy Purcell had given would likely assure a solid and secure future. Perhaps their little array of pens and sheds would someday expand into a full-fledged ranch. And Redge would know just how to handle it. Redge . . . his son . . . still in the midst of boyhood, but boyhood steeled with stubbornness, and with sureness of a great prairie destiny.

Will Cardigan admitted to himself, as his horse's steady gait brought him closer to the South Platte River, that other desires were now stirring within him. After all, he was only in his fifties. How long had it been since he had donned a dinner jacket, had dealt cards onto a green table, or had dined where subdued light, snowy linens, and sterling silver added pleasure to the meal?

And how long—how many centuries—had gone by since he had held a beautiful woman close, knowing the excitement of her presence and her promise?

The day was sunny but crisply cool. Only a slight breeze moved out of the northwest, stirring the sere brown grass, and moving a few white clouds overhead. Cardigan's gaze swept along the great thrust of the Rocky Mountains' Front Range. The clarity of atmosphere brought peaks more than a hundred miles away sharply into view.

It was shortly after noon when he forded the Cache la Poudre River, passed through a barbed-wire gate, and found himself on one of the wide streets of Greeley. He looked about in surprise and admiration. The settlement was less than thirty years old, yet all around him were structures that spoke of permanence and a growing prosperity.

The streets and avenues were already thickly lined with trees. The few business blocks held structures of brick and stone. From this central portion of the settlement, residential areas were spreading out in every direction. Here is something, Cardigan thought, that likely will endure a lot longer than the great, limitless cattle ranches as people flock westward.

On the eastern edge of town, a little beyond the railroad tracks, Will found a livery stable. The man in charge agreed to care for Cardigan's horse, and the condition of other animals in his charge seemed to indicate good feed and good conditions.

"How soon will I be able to catch a train to Denver?" Cardigan asked.

The liveryman drew a heavy nickel-plated watch from a bib pocket of his overalls. "Likely there'll be a mixed train coming down from Cheyenne in about two hours."

"A mixed train," Will Cardigan repeated.

"Yup, a few freight cars, and mebbe a few loads of cattle, with a day coach dragging along behind."

"They haul passengers, don't they?" Cardigan still wasn't sure he understood.

The liveryman shook his head as if pitying this stranger's ignorance, and said finally, "Holy damn, man. Of course they haul passengers—if you can pay for your ride. Why else would they tie on the coach?"

Cardigan sought out the small Denver & Pacific depot and bought a ticket. The agent assured him that he had at least two hours to wait, and mentioned a cafe two blocks away. "The grub isn't fancy, but you can bet it's clean. My wife runs the place."

During his leisurely meal, Cardigan read a copy of the weekly *Greeley Tribune*. The news was mostly local, and of people unknown to him, but an advertisement caught his attention. A local harness show had received a shipment of gent's leather suitcases. The prices seemed reasonable, so Cardigan headed for the shop. Within a few minutes he had selected a case that would be right for the clothing he was carrying in the roll behind his saddle. Will was headed toward the livery stable to repack, when the clerk called him back.

"How would you like your initials—or your brand— stamped on that fine suitcase? We do it free, and it don't take long."

"I've got to get going," Cardigan explained. "Perhaps you could do it as I come back through Greeley in a few days."

"Sure, we'll do it," the clerk agreed. "Nice luggage should be stamped—to help protect it." He paused, then pointed toward a beautiful, expensive set of matched bags. "See those? We ordered them special for a customer that lives way out northeast of town, at the Diamond-7 Ranch." The initials were SM. The clerk studied Cardigan's ranch garb and said, "You look like a cowman—maybe you know the owner of these nice pieces, Mr. Murdock."

"I've heard of him," Cardigan replied in noncommittal tone.

"He'll be coming into town in a day or so. He wants these bags real bad for a trip he takes into Denver every year just before Christmas."

Will Cardigan eased himself away from the talkative clerk and out the door. He hoped to have enough time to get his clothing repacked, take the new suitcase to the depot, then take a stroll about this well-kept town. Murdock, he thought as he walked. Wonder why he's going to Denver.

Because the mixed train from Cheyenne came in half an hour late, Will Cardigan cooled his heels in the small Greeley depot, watching the lengthening shadows of the short December afternoon.

After a while, he heard the sound of a locomotive outside, and of cars passing noisily. When it seemed the train would surely pass him and other waiting passengers by, there was a shudder and clanking that brought a rickety coach to a stop at the depot platform. The waiting passengers boarded speedily—then waited most of an hour while the engine shuttled freight cars about.

Seats in the coach consisted of wooden benches, and above these were racks crammed to overflowing with a variety of luggage and boxes. Toward the rear of the car a loud card game was in progress, while up front a couple of women with small children had arranged coats and a blanket to form a lumpy sleeping space.

With his new suitcase in hand, Will Cardigan walked slowly down the aisle; the crowded confusion of the car caused him to ponder the advisability of seeking out the small gent's room; a few seats were sometimes empty near this area. He hastily discarded the idea, realizing there would be a constant procession from the card table to the toilet area.

Midway through the coach, he noticed a middle-aged woman, clad in a gray serge suit and the strangest hat he had ever seen, staring directly at him. At last his somewhat amused gaze met hers. Almost unaware that he was speaking aloud, Cardigan blurted out, "That's the damnedest excuse for a lady's hat I ever saw."

His words caused her chin to tilt firmly upward and her blue eyes to flash steel. Her hand, with an angry sweep, lowered a copy of *Harper's* magazine onto the fur-collared coat lying beside her.

"How would you know?" she asked witheringly. "I seriously doubt that you would recognize a lady."

The passage of a card player en route to the men's room forced Cardigan to crowd to one side until his knees almost touched hers. He looked again at the woman's clear complexion and the even teeth behind her quivering lip. Then he said, "You may be right; it *has* been long since I saw a lady—especially a beautiful one."

A different passenger, ambling back to the card game, caused Cardigan to again try to clear the aisle. At that same instant the locomotive's engineer chose to butt his steam-powered rig into the string of cars; the jouncing movement caught Cardigan unprepared. His arms flailed out as he attempted to maintain balance. Then suddenly he was sprawled on the floor, wedged between the woman's long-skirted legs and the rear of a forward seat. Something was in his lap, and as he eyed it he knew that disaster had descended. His fingers moved to pick up a hat fashioned of the fur of at least six different animals.

He half expected to see gray or faded or straggling hair where the hat had just been. Instead, the woman's hair, circling her head in intricately plaited strands, flashed burnished chestnut, with only a slight tracery of silver, silver that seemed to add regal highlights. Will caught his breath.

He was wordless as he lifted the hat to her. She was carefully laying it beside the discarded magazine when Cardigan attempted to regain his feet.

"If you'll have the mercy to pardon me," he said haltingly, "I'll get myself and my confounded luggage out of your way."

She eyed him, then laughed. "Men look so childish when they lose their poise." She laid her hand on the loaded seat beside her, then added, "If you can find a decent place for my things, and your suitcase, perhaps you had better sit down here."

Cardigan shifted and straightened a dozen items on the overhead rack, solving the storage problem. Then he sat down quietly and stared straight ahead; his fingers moved restlessly, beating out a nervous rhythm on his knees.

Presently he sensed that his companion was watching, and that an amused smile lurked about her lips.

"It seems," she said presently, "you're too terrified to remember your own name."

He heaved a long sigh of relief. "I was overcome by fear. Fear that you wouldn't speak—and that you surely didn't want me to say one word—even of apology. Ma'am, I'm Will Cardigan, and mighty pleased to make your acquaintance."

She offered him a shapely but firm hand. "I am Carla Dunlop—and I wear unspeakable hats," she informed him. Before he could reply, she glanced in a studied way at his hands. "With fingers such as those—long and tapered, and so cared for—you cannot be a rancher, despite your garb."

"But I am a rancher. I have been for several months, Mrs. Dunlop."

His words brought an amused intensity to her calm gray eyes. "Your assumption is in error, Mr. Cardigan. I am not Mrs. Dunlop . . . merely Carla Dunlop."

"And you live in Denver?"

Her answer was delayed by the jolt and clang with which the train at last got under way. The sparse lights of the Union colony of Greeley were disappearing in space when she moved to ease the uncomfort of the hard bench, faced Cardigan, and said, "No, I used to live in Denver. I'm going there now to spend the holidays with my sister. But I live at Fort Laramie, in Wyoming Territory."

"You . . . you mean the historic Fort Laramie, on the Oregon Trail?" he asked in amazement.

"Yes, the frontier post—where Indians trade and where Indian women make fur hats. Hats that strange men strive to knock from a traveler's head." She ended the accusation with a murmur of laughter.

61

"Which are you," Will demanded, "a teacher or a missionary?"

"Neither one, Mr. Cardigan. It happens that I am the governess of the three children of Captain McIver at the post."

He strove to find a posture to make the seat less of a torture, but it was virtually impossible. Moments sped by before he said, "I've always been fascinated by the Oregon Trail, and by those who moved that way seeking homes and wealth and adventure. I wish you'd oblige me by satisfying the curiosity of a would-be pioneer. What's Fort Laramie like?"

He was, in fact, genuinely interested. But more, he found himself wishing to sit beside this woman, to look into a face that held such animation and beauty, and to listen to the pleasantness of her voice.

Despite a multitude of abrupt and jarring stops and starts, the train reached the Denver station just short of nine o'clock. Cardigan sought out a cab for his companion. Reluctant to lose her to the busy streets, he stood hat in hand beside the vehicle and said, "Thank you for making my trip both shorter and interesting. I dislike the thought of not seeing you again."

"You know more about words than you do about hats," she replied teasingly. "Where will you be staying here in Denver?"

"Probably at the Windsor Hotel," he answered indifferently. "It's the only hotel I know of."

"If you prefer clean and quiet accommodations, plus excellent food, at reasonable prices, to prestige, plus a fancy wine list, I'd suggest the Addison. It happens to be on my way; I could drop you at its door," she offered.

Will Cardigan handed his luggage to the driver and climbed in beside her. As the vehicle moved briskly out, Carla Dunlop spoke of the city and of the buildings they were passing. Meanwhile, Will was striving to phrase what he was determined to say to her. It wasn't until he had alighted at the Addison Hotel that his question found voice. "Would I be insane to hope we might have dinner together tomorrow evening?"

She eyed him in an interested but wary way, so he hastened to add, "At a place of your choosing, of course."

Seemingly indifferent to the driver's impatience, Carla

Dunlop sat quietly studying the man still holding her hand. "Will Cardigan," she breathed finally, "I do wonder about you. Already you know far more about me, and my life, than I know of you or yours. And your shyness . . . is it a clever ploy? Aren't there women in your life?"

"Yes . . . yes, there have been women. Several. And the only one that meant anything to me, my wife, died a year ago."

"You have children?" Her words were an almost inaudible whisper.

"Just one . . . a son, sixteen years old. He's at the ranch, likely wondering what I'll find for our Christmas."

"Perhaps . . . perhaps, Will, I might help you to find something unusual for him—before we dine tomorrow evening." She had signaled the cab into motion before she added, "I will meet you right here. Tomorrow afternoon, then. Four o'clock."

Cardigan stared after the cab until it turned from sight a couple of blocks up Sixteenth Street. Then he picked up the suitcase and handed it to a uniformed doorman. With jaunty step, he entered the Addison Hotel and strode to the registration desk. Something had happened to him—it was undeniable that he felt excitement and desire for the first time in a long time.

He tried to sleep late the next morning, but outside traffic, the strangeness of his room, and the lack of Crow Creek camp routine combined to destroy all hope of luxurious rest. After breakfast he handed a bundle of clothing to a hotel bellhop with a suitable tip and was reassured that the clothes would be pressed and returned before evening.

For a time he strode through the business streets of Denver, noting the vitality and drive of this growing city. Then by midmorning Cardigan found his way to a substantial building on which a sign proclaimed "United States Land Office." It seemed an unusually long time before a clerk, wearing an eyeshade and long black sleeve protectors, motioned him to a chair beside a newly varnished rolltop desk.

"I suppose you're here to file a mining claim," the clerk stated indifferently. "Pretty soon every blasted mountain west of Pike's Peak is gonna be honeycombed."

"I wouldn't know." Cardigan shrugged. "Mining isn't my line." He took a map, drawn in pencil on blue-lined writing paper, from his vest pocket. "I want to register a homestead claim to what's shown here. I'm pretty sure of the legal description; the property lies along Crow Creek, northeast of the Greeley colony, in Weld County."

The clerk made a quick study of the map. "You could have filed this at a local land office. It's usually handled that way. Just take it to—"

Will Cardigan held his steady gaze on the clerk. "I want it filed and recorded and receipted here in Denver. Not at some firetrap shack way hell-and-gone out on the grasslands."

"All of the local office records are sent here, then to Washington," the clerk explained.

"But you can handle it?" Will insisted.

"Oh, sure . . . sure . . . with the proper filing fee." He waited a brief time, studied Cardigan, then said almost reluctantly, "I hope, sir, you're fully aware of the implications, the . . . the risks . . . in what you propose to do. That country, south of the Wyoming border, is rangeland. Grass country claimed and held by big ranching outfits." He drew a finger down Will's map, and asked, "Aren't you claiming land right in the graze area of the Diamond-7 Ranch?"

"As I understand it the ranch has no legal government patent. Nor have they filed."

The clerk seemed taken aback. "Well—you're right there. But if you're intending to dryland it, plow it up . . ."

"Sir," Cardigan cut in with evident impatience, "I've discussed this with Mr. Andy Purcell, owner of the Diamond-7."

"Well, hell, in that case . . ." The clerk shook his head in amazement. "Mr. Cardigan, fill out these homestead application papers. Then I can attest your signature."

Will breathed deeply. Then he asked, "For a suitable fee, say forty dollars, can you arrange immediate recording of my application at the Colorado State House?"

The clerk grinned as two twenty-dollars gold pieces were placed in his palm. "Mr. Cardigan, I'll see to it personally—this afternoon."

Will left the office feeling suddenly his own man. He would have legal claim to Cardigan Camp, as would his son and his grandson after him.

Only a few blocks from the Addison Hotel were several

specialized mercantile establishments. Many of these maintained stocks of diversified goods to be shipped to firms and individual operators in the mountain mining areas. Others were geared to the needs of isolated ranches. From huge stocks of groceries, medicines, clothing, and livestock equipment, shipments could be made that would provide practically all necessities for months to come.

Will Cardigan sought out the Western Rancher's Supply, and spent the early hours of the afternoon selecting goods from a long list that he and Redge had spent several evenings preparing. He did not have sufficient cash to cover the purchases, but the store agreed to draw on an account Cardigan had maintained in St. Louis ever since his lead-mining days. The shipment would be made promptly upon bank verification, with freight charges absorbed by the store.

"We'll notify you when we ship, likely in about ten days, Mr. Cardigan. Just give us your post-office address," the store manager said.

Will suddenly realized that they had not received one piece of mail since settling on Crow Creek. Now they must add to their roots, establish a permanent mailing address. But where? His mind pictured the lonely and vacant grasslands undulating toward horizons far from their camp.

"Just address your letters and catalogs to Kate's Wagon."

"That woman must have an awfully long wagon. Near every rancher and railroad foreman ships things to her," the manager responded, and guffawed at his own joke.

As Cardigan walked back toward the hotel, his mind was already on four o'clock. Why had he not offered to send a team and rig to pick up Carla Dunlop? He had emphatically been away from the company of women too long.

He entered the hotel and glanced at a clock. There was time to bathe, shave, and change to what Redge would surely have termed his "citified" clothing. The bellhop came forward with alacrity. "Mr. Cardigan, you've timed it about right. Your bundle has just been delivered. Right this way, sir. You should make sure we have all items."

Cardigan walked to the desk with the clerk, but his eyes refused to focus on his own items carefully racked before him. His attention had riveted on two new, expensive and shining pieces of luggage—cases he had seen only the previous afternoon in Greeley neatly labeled SM.

SM, Cardigan pondered angrily. SM—for Stacy Murdock. Why in the devil did both of us have to show up at the same hotel?

He became aware of the bellhop's puzzled face when the man asked, "Is there anything wrong, sir? Are your garments—?"

Cardigan regained composure and managed a smile. "Everything seems in order. A nice job." He claimed the clothing, entered the elevator, and was presently in his room.

Later, with a dark topcoat folded across his arm, he stood in the lobby watching the vehicles along the street. It was only a few minutes before the hour of four when he noted a team of matched bay horses, hitched to a black phaeton. This was no livery rig or team for hire. He was sure that the driver, Carla Dunlop, had held the reins to these horses many times. Her actions spoke of skill and experience. And again, the thought struck him that under no circumstances could such a vehicle and horses be bought or maintained on the wages of a governess at Fort Laramie, Wyoming Territory.

He gazed at the woman in the rig who had entered his life so forcefully. She was attired now in a stunning blue dress and a fur jacket. He smiled at the absence of the provocative hat that had brought about their acquaintance.

Had Cardigan gone directly outside to greet her, instead of hovering in the hotel doorway to admire her, events might have proceeded very differently. But as Will watched, he was suddenly aware of the figure of a man approaching on the sidewalk. In an instant Cardigan realized he was watching the ranch foreman of the Diamond-7.

Stacy Murdock's steps brought him toward the Hotel Addison's entrance. He was weaving uncertainly back and forth. Then abruptly he stopped, and with open mouth stared at the attractive woman who was busy controlling the impatient bay horses. He watched for a few seconds, then he directed his course toward the phaeton.

Will Cardigan pushed through the hotel door. A dozen steps brought him into position to block Murdock's progress.

Murdock halted only inches short of a collision. "Who the Almighty do you think you are?" There was an alcoholic thickness about his words. He attempted to sidestep Cardigan, only to find this determined nuisance still directly in his path. "Get out of my way," he growled, then he emphasized the order with a clenched-fist swing meant to destroy half of Will's face. Cardigan ducked clear of the blow. He seized the ranch foreman's shoulder and swung him about until their faces were only inches apart.

"Now, Mr. Murdock," Will said in a nearly sociable tone, "suppose you get along and sober up. The lady is annoyed." As he spoke, Will glanced toward the phaeton and its driver. But Carla Dunlop didn't seem too annoyed. She was half standing in the rig, the reins tightly held, watching the sidewalk encounter with angry fascination.

At the sound of his name, Stacy Murdock took a step back. He studied Cardigan with unbelieving recognition. "Damn my hide if ain't the nester . . . old claim-jumping Cardigan. All decked out . . ." His words trailed off as he turned and again stared at the phaeton. In stupefied wonder, he started a new train of thought and words. "Cardigan, how'd a rat-poor sodbuster like you come up with enough bankroll to sashay around Denver wearing an undertaker's coat?"

Will, aware that an amused crowd was gathering, strode to the vehicle and stepped quickly to the seat beside Carla Dunlop. They were moving into the street, but Cardigan caught some fading words from Murdock. "I'd give a fat yearling or two to be in that bastard's shoes."

The bay team had taken them three blocks up Sixteenth Street toward Broadway when Cardigan favored his companion with a frosty stare. "All right. You can tell me now," he muttered.

"Tell you what?" Carla replied.

"How a nice little governess from Wyoming found a magical lamp. I suppose she rubbed it and two jackrabbits and a tumbleweed turned into a team of blooded bay geldings and a shining coach. Which still doesn't explain that lovely dress. Carla, let's get one thing straight. If you are an heiress, I can't afford you. If you're trying to nab a fortune, you can't afford me."

She eyed him in a half-serious way, then asked, "What makes you think I'm either one?"

The sweep of his hand encompassed the team, the phaeton, and Carla herself. "With such accouterments of prosperity, what else can I believe?"

"Perhaps you are right, Will Cardigan. We must be honest with each other. Now, I am just what I claimed to be, the governess of some small Wyoming Territory children. I get to Denver only once or twice a year." She hesitated, then added in an almost apologetic way, "Can I be blamed for having a sister here in the city who pampers me —an older sister married to a mountain prospector, who took in washing for a brawling mining camp, and who now, because of her late husband's strike, is incredibly rich?

"I am quite a few years younger than Jennifer. As I grew up here in Denver, she was already a businesswoman in Telluride. She wanted me to have the very best of practically everything, for we were the only two children of parents who had acquired little except a home. Jennifer worried about our parents as they aged, and always wanted me close to them."

"Were boys or young men admitted to your restricted schedule?" Will ventured to ask.

"Of course," Carla said, and then her face seemed touched by memories. "Will, there was one special person. Perhaps we would have been married. He went with a party of elk hunters into the wilderness area north of Steamboat Springs. A blizzard came while he was hunting far from camp. His body was found when summer came." She hesitated momentarily and then added, "Will, we are so little the masters of our own destinies. Life makes us what we are."

They were silent as the trotting bays carried them across Broadway. Finally, Will murmured, "I've an idea it would have been better if that drunk, Stacy Murdock, had belted me in the mouth before I spouted off at you."

Her reply was to quickly thrust the reins into his hands. "Don't humble yourself, Will Cardigan. Relax . . . and drive for a while; you'll enjoy this team. Now, aren't we supposed to search out a Christmas present for your boy?"

"That's a problem." Will shook his head. "I just don't know what he'd like."

"What interests him most?"

"A lot of things . . . and every one of them has to do with cattle and trying to build a herd." Cardigan's pride in his son was evident. He continued, "Redge is just sixteen . . . going on seventeen . . . but he's almost uncannily adept at doctoring sick or hurt animals. He even did an operation that saved a Diamond-7 heifer. But this gift problem . . ." He paused, aware of a sudden look of eagerness on his companion's face.

"Perhaps that's it, Will." Her voice was hopeful.

"Perhaps what?"

"His interest in medicine—veterinary medicine. There are supply houses here that specialize in medicines and instruments for livestock. They have the latest books, too."

Cardigan studied the street on which they were continuing eastward. "We're way out in the residential district now. And I haven't the damnedest idea where we're heading."

Carla Dunlop laughed aloud. "You don't have to know. Just let the horses choose direction."

"You mean—?" he answered in confused surprise.

"I mean that tomorrow you take me to a restaurant. Tomorrow we can search out the best veterinary-supply shop. But today—right now—I'm under strict orders to deliver you in person at about the largest and most gingerbreaded mansion on Pennsylvania Avenue. Will, you're to stand inspection before my sister. She wants to pass judgment on you—to know just what sort of railroad traveler would deride a lady's hat, and then stumble into her lap . . . practically."

They swung onto Pennsylvania Street and came presently to a neighborhood where great structures of timber and glass and stone, set in spacious lawns, offered seclusion and spoke of wealth. Suddenly the bay team veered from the street onto a curved and sweeping driveway. Will Cardigan looked at the house they were approaching. It had been built within the last five years, and expense had not been a consideration in either design or materials or workmanship. This home soared three floors above street level, with outer walls of intricately cut gray stone. The slope of its roof and the thrust of great chimneys gave a hint that the architect had drawn heavily on the design of the chateaux of Normandy.

Turning his attention back to Carla Dunlop, Cardigan grinned wryly, then said, "I trust we are merely stopping here to pay our respects to either the governor or King Croesus."

She reined the team to a stop before stone steps that led to a side entrance. A middle-aged man appeared from nowhere and took hold of the bay's bridles. "Unless Jennifer plans to use these beauties, you had best unhitch and stable them, Barney." She turned to Will and explained. "Jennifer is my sister. And Barney's been her carriageman ever since—"

"Ever since she absconded as treasurer of the United States," Cardigan hazarded, as they mounted the steps.

"Jennifer never got to Washington," Carla said, laughing. "But she didn't do badly at that gold and silver town called Telluride."

They entered through a heavy oak door. Carla led the way down a hallway where subdued lights had been expertly set to illuminate colorful prints of mountain animals. They removed their coats, then Carla led the way into a long, high-ceilinged room where books lined most of the walls and a log blazed in a fireplace fashioned from river boulders.

"I like this room, Will," she said. "Somehow it seems to radiate tranquillity. The chairs are comfortable too. Why don't you wait here?" Carla asked. "I'll be back shortly . . . I hope with my big sis in tow."

Cardigan eyed a huge and softly leathered sofa. "Take your time, Carla Dunlop," he replied. "I've got plenty to look at—the wonder-filled commoner within the palace, you know."

"Would a cocktail help, if I send someone to prepare it?"

He shook his head. "Later, perhaps, thank you. I'm just fine now."

Cardigan scoured the bookshelves when she left the room, found a leather-bound copy of the *The Journals of Lewis & Clark*, and idly turned its pages. Suddenly he was caught up in the narrative and hardly aware of the passing of time. Fifteen minutes passed before he sensed that someone had come into the room and was quietly standing close by. Will glanced toward her, then came quickly to his feet. The woman surveying him stood perhaps four inches above five feet. She was wearing a simply cut black afternoon dress; about her throat was a single strand of matched pearls. The whiteness of her hair and the fretwork of lines across her face caused Cardigan to figure her for about sixty. There was both dignity and charm in the smile with which she offered a firm and capable-looking hand.

70

"I apologize for having startled you, Mr. Cardigan."

The calm intenseness of her gray eyes caused Will Cardigan to blurt out, "I'm delighted to meet Carla's sister . . . and . . . and I'm mighty happy she brought me here."

She waved him back into his chair, then seated herself on a nearby sofa. Presently her voice sounded softly across the room. "Yes, Mr. Cardigan. I am Jennifer Waverley. I suggested that Carla let us meet and that we introduce ourselves, without the formality of her presenting you." She peered at him somewhat quizzically, then added, "You see, Mr. Cardigan, I am very fond of my sister—and you are the first man who has aroused her interest since—" Jennifer Waverley seemed about to add to her sentence. Then quickly she reworded it. "The first in a long, long time."

Will Cardigan seemed unaware that his finger was still marking a place in the book as he folded his arms and searched for words of reply. When they came, sounding curtly blunt to his own ears, he was remembering what Carla Dunlop had told him of this woman now sitting opposite him. An older sister who pampered her. Married to a mountain prospector. Took in washing in a brawling mining camp . . . and now was incredibly rich.

"Mrs. Waverley," Cardigan was saying, "I think we can come to understand each other quickly. Through my sheer disregard for courteous speech and my awkwardness, I met your sister on a train only last evening. I found her to be a delightful traveling companion—and a beautiful woman. She has offered to help me choose a Christmas present for my son, and I, in turn, have asked her to have dinner with me. Tomorrow or the following day I shall return to a little cow camp we have up near the Wyoming line. No, Mrs. Waverley, neither your sister nor your fortune is endangered by me."

The older woman broke into peals of laughter. "Oh, my God," she murmured. "You make it all sound as though I was implying something from an Elizabethan tale of intrigue and purported seduction."

Cardigan grinned, then asked, "Did I make it sound that bad?"

Jennifer Waverley rose, walked to Cardigan's side, and laid a reassuring hand on his shoulder. "Come, Will Cardigan. Let's find Carla, then I'd like her to show you through my home. Will . . . did you every try to scrub a miner's

71

socks and winter drawers on a washboard? Believe me, anyone who succeeds in getting them clean deserves a house like this."

They moved along the hallway, coming presently to a wide, gracefully arched doorway where Carla stood awaiting them. "Am I to assume," she asked lightly, "that you two are now acquaintances? Friends? Enemies?"

"That is quite a question, Carla," her sister replied. Seconds later she added, "I'm not going to ease your curiosity by disclosing everything we discussed. But I must tell you, Carla, you are fortunate that Mr. Cardigan chose your lap in which to tumble."

"But I didn't . . . That is, I only . . ." Cardigan began, very embarrassed.

Jennifer Waverley smiled, then interrupted. "Please don't destroy my mind's-eye picture of that train episode. It is fun to imagine such things." She turned toward her sister, and at that moment the family resemblance was striking.

"Carla," the older woman said, "I have so much to do preparing for tomorrow evening. It's an hour until dinner. Suppose you guide Mr. Cardigan through this tremendous heap of wood and stone." She smiled at Cardigan and added, "I hope you won't consider me inhospitable or rude. In just twenty-four hours we're to have a reception for a friend who is in the cattle business."

Jennifer Waverley was silent for a moment, then added in an excited tone, "How stupid of me, Will . . . I hope you don't mind my calling you Will. The reception is for Jeff Masters—do you know him? He was associated with John W. Iliff. We'd be pleased to have you attend, though it's too late for a formal invitation."

"It is thoughtful of you to invite me," Cardigan replied. "I have never met Mr. Masters, but of course I've heard of John W. Iliff, and of his tremendous land and cattle holdings along the South Platte River. He died about ten years ago, if I'm not mistaken. Still, his name and deeds are legend." Cardigan paused reflectively, then added, "Jeff Masters is held in high esteem also."

"Then you'll come?" The eager and excited words broke spontaneously from Carla Dunlop.

Will shook his head. "I'd be out of place among your distinguished guests; I'm not a cattle baron—just a novice at ranching."

"Nonsense, Cardigan," Jennifer responded with irritated firmness, her clenched fists planted on her hips. "If you're going to be in Denver, you get yourself up to this house about six o'clock tomorrow evening. Better yet, Carla can pick you up, or I'll send Barney."

"I'd hate," Will said, "to have been one of those Telluride miners if he incurred your wrath."

Carla smiled and linked her arm through Will's. "Would you believe," she asked proudly, "that this big sister of mine not only has the skill to scrub red flannels—she happens to also hold a degree from an eastern college called *Vassar?*"

Cardigan nodded thoughtfully as Jennifer Waverley hushed her sister and said wistfully, "If only my husband had lived to enjoy these things of which you speak. Up at Telluride, they spoke of him as Lucky Waverley—Lucky, the Midas mine owner. What's so lucky in breaking your back for a fortune . . . and then dying short of your proper time?"

"I've wondered about that too, since my wife died," Will answered, and shook his head.

With no attempt to conceal the tears upon her lashes, Jennifer said, "Will Cardigan, it is a comfort to have a man who understands feelings about this house, even for a short time. Do an old lady a favor. Humor Carla—and me—by coming to our reception."

"How can I refuse?" Cardigan smiled encouragingly. "Expect me just short of six o'clock, if I can locate suitable white tie and tails."

"Thank you, Will," Jennifer Waverley replied. "And don't worry about your necktie. Most of those you'll meet at my shindig live most of their hours with sweaty shirts and with cow dung riding their boots."

Chapter 8

Ever since Will Cardigan's arrival in Denver the weather had been briskly cool but sunny. Now, on the morning following his first visit to the Waverley mansion, there was a change in the wind. Layers of dark and moisture-laden clouds were piling up over the foothills and against the peaks of the Front Range. The feeling that winter was imminent accentuated Christmas decorations on lampposts and in store windows.

Remembering the white fury of the blizzard that had swept across Crow Creek earlier in December, Will studied the gray, sullen sky with growing concern. Had he been a fool to make this trip to Denver, and to leave his son alone at their lonely camp? He pondered the wisdom of cutting short his time in the city, of sending a message of regret to the Waverley home, and of catching the first train home.

Yet, in all likelihood the storm might isolate him in Greeley or make a long horseback ride dangerous. He knew also that Redge wasn't foolhardy or apt to take chances. The livestock would be in good hands, and the supplies on hand would suffice for one person. Besides, a lot of storms blew in and then blew out without dumping much snow. He weighed the possibilities. Foremost in his mind was his son's safety, but he couldn't deny he was looking forward to a party such as Jennifer Waverley would hostess, which would be a welcome respite from monotonous rangeland days. Then too, Carla would be at the reception. Perhaps she might even again come for him with the spirited bay team. He would again know the exhilaration of her touch and her words and the smile that danced within her eyes. Cardigan could not believe that he had become infatuated, that he might be about to fall in love. Yet, long slumbering emotions stirred within him. How would it be to again hold a lovely and responsive woman in close embrace? Tonight's reception would mean postponement of their dinner together. But postponement until when? Of a certainty, he must leave tomorrow for the return trip home.

Toward midmorning, Cardigan sought out a men's apparel shop and bought the items he surmised would be proper for the evening event. He paid for the garments with inward ruefulness, thinking of the additional supplies this money could buy for the Crow Creek camp. It occurred to him too that after tonight this city wardrobe might remain unused for months—or even years.

After a leisurely lunch at the Addison Hotel, he settled down with a stack of past issues of the *Rocky Mountain News*. An hour later, with tired eyes, Will Cardigan dozed off in the most comfortable chair of his room. Outside, the wind had changed, coming now from due east. A scattering of snowflakes raced the streets, then thickened into a mantle of white which lay across the city.

The snow fell heavily across the plains. Along Crow Creek it was preceded by a gale which howled through the naked cottonwood boughs. Redge Cardigan hastened with every precautionary measure. He judged that it would be wise to stable the horses and corral the springing heifers that Andy Purcell had put in his care. A sizable stack of the scythed native hay still remained. He made sure enough of it was handy to the mangers.

As the afternoon wore on, the boy peered time and again far up the creek through the scattered timber. Redge was becoming worried about Hank Kutcher. Less than an hour after Will Cardigan had ridden off for Greeley and Denver, Kutcher had showed up at the Cardigan camp. He had stayed only a few minutes, gulping hot coffee and assuring himself that Redge was making out all right. Then he left, heading upstream to a point where he would swing onto a fast, direct route to Cheyenne, carrying business papers for the Diamond-7. And now Kutcher's return was already overdue.

As darkness came on, three to four inches of snow lay across the valley slopes; more continued to fall, although the wind had slackened.

After a time the boy fixed a meal for himself. He ate very little, then paced about the cabin. The urge came upon him to saddle a horse and ride upstream to meet Hank. He flung open the outer door, only to stare into a thick wall of whiteness. Any search would be futile. Likely, not knowing the country farther north, he would be quickly lost if he attempted a night ride.

About nine o'clock Redge touched flame to a kerosene lantern, then trod out to the barn and corral. Everything seemed secure, so he trudged back toward the cabin. He looked past the barrier of tumbling snow in the direction from which Kutcher should have appeared. The snowfall no longer seemed as dense, but perhaps it was merely his eyes tricking him.

He started to enter the cabin, then he turned and sought out a nearby fence post. He slipped the wire handle of the lantern over it. The lantern's beam cut a meager swath, but its light was visible from the north.

Redge entered the cabin, stomped snow from his feet, and, by a small glow from the kitchen stove, pulled off his clothes and fell into bed. He tossed about for at least two hours before he dozed in a restless and troubled way.

He awakened with a sudden startled jerk. Instantly it seemed that his every sense was attuned to sound and movement beyond the cabin walls, somewhere in the stormy night.

Redge sat up, placed his feet on the floor, and listened. He caught faint, muffled sounds, like those of a rider in his saddle. Surely no one except Kutcher was likely to be nearing the cabin. But Kutcher would by now have either called aloud or rapped on the bolted door. The cabin had one window not boarded up for winter, but it was on the opposite side from which he had hung the lantern. He remained silent. Cautious. Listening.

Abruptly there was a low but discernible creaking, a sound Redge could identify. Someone had pulled open the door to the horse barn.

Quickly the boy slid into pants and shoes. Then he felt along the cabin wall and lifted a short-muzzled rifle from its pegs. Redge made sure it was loaded, and that one shell was in the firing chamber. He crept to the door, unbolted it, and very slowly pushed it a few inches ajar.

There was no lantern glow, and at first the yard appeared to be empty. The snow had stopped falling; ragged clouds struggled to obscure a first-quarter moon. The boy's eyes, sharpened by the cabin darkness, caught sight of the lantern lying in the snow, as though snuffed and flung aside. Fifty feet beyond, near to the corral fence, was the indistinct figure of a stranger sitting aside a horse which pawed and shifted restlessly under its rider.

Suddenly a rift in the clouds poured light into the yard. For perhaps three seconds the horseman was more clearly revealed. He was squat and bulky, with the collar of a heavy coat cutting the light from his face. His seat in the saddle was awkward; he held both the bridle reins and a drawn revolver in his left hand as it hovered above the saddle's pommel. His right, briefly revealed by moon and snow light, hung useless, seemingly paralyzed, from a misshapen arm.

Redge's attention was torn away by sounds cutting through the cold night. Again there was the squeaking of a barn-door hinge. It was followed at once by footfalls of horses, almost imperceptible upon the snow within the corral. The boy was well aware that within seconds, the Cardigan horses would be driven through the corral gate to disappear into the night. Without them, he and his father would be helpless and stranded.

Despite the cold, he slipped through the cabin door. There were deep shadows beneath the eaves of the cabin, so he hastened into them. From here, he could see the corral gate. It was still closed, a sure sign that the thief leading the horses had entered the barn by the one door not leading into the corral.

Redge lifted the rifle and waited only momentarily. The form of a thinner man moved toward the gate, his arm lifting to open it. Quickly Redge lined his sights on that arm—and squeezed the rifle's trigger.

The flash and the following sound of the boy's shot tore a vast hole in the darkness. He jumped toward deeper darkness near the cabin's end, at the same time pumping another shell into the rifle's chamber.

The camp erupted into frenzied action. The intruder with the crippled arm reacted by pumping revolver shots into the cabin logs near which Redge had first fired. The gunfire sent terrorized horses circling in a gallop within the corral. A yell of fear and pain told Redge that his shot had found its mark. Now there were excited cries and curses from the corral. The boy knew instantly that two men were freeing the horses. Again a man's form neared the gate. With an icy calmness, Redge drew bead and fired a second shot. Then he threw himself flat on the snow-covered ground and crawled around the cabin's corner.

He was none too soon, for even as he was struggling to his feet, another burst of revolver shots thudded into the wall. He pumped the lever action of his weapon and raced around the cabin to its far end. His next target would have to be the mounted and revolver-toting raider. Redge knew there was barely light enough; with luck, he could place a lead slug in this one's chest.

"Damn it, Slick," the crippled horseman roared. "Forget that gate. Tear down the corral poles behind the barn. I'll fetch your mounts around there. Hurry it up. Let's get going."

Redge took a shallow breath. Of a certainty, he could pick off this one-handed fellow who was shouting orders. But there was an alternative. By running the brief distance across the yard, he could position himself behind a cottonwood tree. This would enable him to shoot at any portion of the corral, to perhaps forestall the tearing down of poles and escape of his horses. Only two or three bullets remained in the rifle; he had brought no others from the cabin. He would have to place his shots perfectly.

He ducked low, and headed in a crouched run for the cottonwood. He had covered half the distance when a yell came from the crippled leader. Then a bullet sang too close to Redge's right ear.

"Seems there's just one nester doing the shooting. I'll pin him down. Ain't you got them horses out yet?"

Redge would have made it to the solid and protecting shelter of the tree, but snow was his undoing. His next leap ended in a sickening, skidding fall as one foot shot from beneath him. He rolled quickly over, fearful that his rifle would be choked with snow. He saw that the boss rider was reining his horse into movement and carefully lifting and aiming his revolver.

Redge flung himself into another quick roll. This time, as he came to a stop, his rifle was lined directly toward this approaching stranger's heart. He must wait. Sight. Be sure. Kill.

There was the instant crack of a shot. Then another. Momentarily, Redge believed that he had used his rifle and missed. Or had it been the cripple who had failed to send a bullet home? The boy's senses cleared . . . sharpened. Abruptly the one-armed rustler swerved his horse and sought to spur free of the yard. Redge crawled toward the cottonwood on his belly. Likely the three would get the Cardigan horses—but at a price. With two or three shells he was pretty sure to rid Crow Creek of at least one bastardly horse thief.

He struggled toward the tree, slid behind it, then gasped in utter wonder and relief. Behind the tree, wearing a sheepskin coat, with a saddle gun pointed at the corral, stood Hank Kutcher. For the first time, Redge realized that he was miserably cold. His teeth were chattering and his feet were numb. He waited as Kutcher took deliberate aim and fired.

A lurid string of oaths came from the direction of the corral. Then a young and frightened voice yelled, "For chrissake, get our saddle horses over here. There's maybe a dozen lousy homesteaders plugging at us. Slick is bleeding like a stuck hog."

"Get the corral poles down," the leader roared.

"To hell with poles and horses and you," the scared, boyish reply came. "I'm cutting out. So is Slick. Pick us up pronto—down in that willow thicket."

Redge wiped snow from his weapon with fumbling fingers. He would have fired again, but Kutcher's firm hand restrained him.

"Let 'em go, son," the ranch hand muttered.

"But they're rustlers," Redge protested.

"So they are. But let's give someone else a chance to string the damn fools up. You're too young to have a killing notch on your gun."

Hank swung about and faced Redge. The boy's eyes flew wider in concern. "Hank, what . . . what happened to you? Lord Almighty!"

"You mean this jaw of mine?"

Redge gulped, then asked, "Is that big lump a jaw? It's red and blue and—"

"I know all about that," Kutcher cut in testily. "And how it hurts like fired up hell."

"But what—?" Redge persisted.

"Kid," Kutcher growled at him, "get into that cabin and stoke up a fire. I'll mosey in pretty quick. After I make sure your midnight company skedaddles out."

"We could have hanged them," Redge spat out as he moved away.

"Mebbe so. Mebbe not. Besides, I know who they are. You don't."

The cabin blazed with cheery warmth and Redge was brewing coffee when Kutcher finally came in. "Had to put my horse in your stable. Checked to see that them corral poles were still solid enough to keep your animals in."

As his words ended, Hank Kutcher slumped in a chair and cautiously cupped his palm over his swollen jaw. Redge was struck by the haggard, pained grayness about Kutcher's closed lips and eyes.

"Hank, out with it," he demanded. "What's wrong? What happened to you?"

"It's my tooth. A jaw one," Kutcher groaned. "It got to acting up on my way to Cheyenne. Now it's about to do me in." Kutcher slumped farther into the chair, and back-handed beads of sweat from his forehead.

Redge shook his head, then asked, "Why didn't you have it patched up or pulled in Cheyenne?"

"I was a mind to," Kutcher mumbled. "Even set up a time with a doc. Then that damned passel of horse thieves got in my way of doing it. I found out what they might be up to. A bartender I know told me some things he heard. So I trailed pretty close behind them coming down Crow Creek."

Redge laid his hand on Hank Kutcher's shoulder. "It's lucky for me you did." Then he added, simply, "Thanks for my life, Hank."

The boy turned abruptly, poured hot water into a bowl and scrubbed his hands. Then he stood in front of Kutcher. "Sit up a bit, Hank, and open your mouth. I'm going to take a look at that tooth."

Kutcher recoiled, with widening, wary eyes. "You ain't gonna touch it, are you?"

With firm, gentle fingers, the boy pulled his friend's jaws apart and studied the teeth and gum tissue.

"Hank," he said, "it has to come out. I'm going to pull that tooth."

The old cowhand snapped his teeth into a clench, let out a roar of pain, and then said, "The hell you are, boy. Not a chance. You ain't gonna go farting and fumbling around in my mouth." He calmed, then asked, almost piteously,

"Redge, can't you just slap on some hot or cold compresses? Get this branding-iron thing to let up?"

"You'd only be delaying things—and it would likely get even worse."

"Maybe you've got something—say some whiskey—I can hold in my mouth, Redge," Kutcher persisted.

Redge's mind worked quickly, seeking a reply. A very faint smile was on his lips as he answered, "Hank, perhaps there is something. I remember that when I was a little kid I used to have terrible earaches. Once, when we ran out of medicine during the night, my mother used an old pioneer remedy. She went to the barn, came back with a bottle of horse urine, and heated it. Then she poured it in my ear. It worked. It killed the pain."

Redge waited for Kutcher to absorb his words, then went on, "The nerves of the teeth aren't much different than those inside the ears. I've an idea if we'd fix a cup—"

The words were blotted by Hank Kutcher's sudden bolting upright in the chair, his eyes blazing. "Cardigan," he roared, "dammit, you listen to me. Just listen one sheep-diddlin minute. You're sure as Satan not gonna pour no cup of hot stud piss into my mouth."

"Oh, shut up, Hank," the boy shouted with exaggerated anger. "You can hang onto all that poison and pain if you want. But you'd better flag your hind end back to Cheyenne for help . . . while you're still able."

Hank Kutcher listened in silence, then lowered himself into the chair, defeated. "Redge," he said hoarsely, "pull the damned tooth."

"Good. Now you're showing sense," Redge replied. "It'll take me a few minutes to get ready. Just stay put and take it easy, Hank."

The boy went into the cabin's lean-to storage shed and dug into a tool box. There was a pair of fence-mending pliers, and some blacksmith's tongs. No good for any mouth measuring less than a foot across. Farther down among the tools, he found a pair of slim pointed pliers, almost needle-nosed. He studied them, wishing that their point was curved. There was no possibility of bending them, but he could file ridges across the biting surfaces of the points. Maybe this would keep them from slipping off a tooth's slick surface.

Minutes later, when he returned to the cabin, he found

Kutcher grumbling in increasing pain. Redge thrust the pliers into boiling water, then laid them on a clean towel. He went to a corner cupboard and poured half a water glass of whiskey from a bottle his father had kept since their coming to Crow Creek. He was ready to begin; then he shook his head and went back to the lean-to. When he returned, he had a four-inch piece of rounded wood, cut from the end of a mop handle.

He washed his hands again, picked up the whiskey and shook Kutcher awake. Despite his inward doubt and anxiety, the boy's hands remained completely steady. "Drink this, Hank," he said and held up the glass.

"What's it from?" Kutcher muttered through the lethargy of his pain. "Probably your bay mare." He sniffed the glass, then grabbed it and with fast gulps downed its entire contents. "Redge, you tricked me. Fill 'er up again."

Redge shook his head, waited for the inevitable alcoholic stupor, then thrust the short length of mop stick into one side of Kutcher's mouth. "That'll keep you from chomping down on my fingers," Redge muttered. He pushed Kutcher's passive form lower in the chair, twisted his face to the best light, and fixed his gaze on the offending tooth. This would call for fast and ruthless action.

Seconds later he had clamped the slim-nosed pincers onto Kutcher's tooth. He pulled slightly to make sure of their grip. In one quick, coordinated movement, Redge's knee came onto Kutcher's chest, while the boy's hands doubled up on the plier handles with a sudden and powerful pull. Suddenly Redge was dodging a fist swing that would have smashed him against the wall. Kutcher fell back and gave forth a groan, then strained to rise against the pressure of Redge's restraining knee. It was then he saw the tooth, long-rooted and bloody, lying on the floor.

"Hank!" Redge shouted. "We did it. The tooth is out."

Comprehension and the wisp of a grin broke on the old cowhand's face. "Redge," his voice sounded thickly, "how about me having another swig of that hoss pee. It ain't bad."

"Sure . . . in a little while, Hank." The boy's voice betrayed his relief. "Right now let's pack some cloth strips into that hole to stop the bleeding. We'll get you washed up —then you sleep."

Sunlight was beginning to sift through the cabin windows. For the first time in an hour, Redge thought of the night's events. The raiders; Hank Kutcher's timely appearance; his own deadly ordeal. "Hank," he asked abruptly, "Who were those horse thieves? You said you know."

It was a long time before Kutcher's guarded answer came. The cowhand spoke reluctantly.

"Redge," he muttered, "does the name Devlin mean anything to you?"

The boy stood in quiet perplexity. "Devlin . . . Devlin," he repeated. "No, Hank, can't say I recall ever hearing it."

"Then likely I'd best wait until your dad gets home. Talk to both of you together." Kutcher rose, swaying on unsteady legs. "Get my horse, lad. I gotta . . ."

Redge led him to a bed, pushed him onto it, then threw a blanket across the sprawled form. "Right there you stay, Hank. All today. Maybe until tomorrow. I'm going to get that swelling under compresses."

"You tricked me," Kutcher's voice was trailing off sleepily. "Tricked me with horse . . . horse . . ."

Chapter 9

An insistent rapping on the door of his room at the Addison Hotel brought Will Cardigan awake and to his feet. He peered out of a window and noticed that darkness was gathering across the city. He had napped for hours. The rap was repeated, so he called aloud, "Just a moment," then strode in stocking feet to the locked door. "Who is it?" he asked cautiously.

"The bellhop, sir. There's a lady in the lobby waiting for you. She said tell you she is Miss Dunlop."

Cardigan sucked in his breath in expectation. He opened the door and laid a coin in the hand of a young, red-headed boy in striped uniform.

"Thank you, Mr. Cardigan."

Cardigan nodded. "See that she has a comfortable seat, and tell her I'll be down within fifteen minutes." He re-entered his room and touched a light switch. The speed with which he plied his straight-edge razor was nothing short of astounding. He managed to shave with only a minor chin nick, then quickly changed into the dress suit which the harberdasher had affirmed would be correct for Jennifer Waverley's party. After a final, critical glance into a mirror, and tug at his necktie, he left the room and hurried downstairs to the lobby.

She was waiting for him near a window that framed the snowy street and a few late-hour shoppers hurrying by. Cardigan hurried to her, blurting out, "I'm a hopeless case, Carla . . . snoring time away and causing you to wait." His gaze swept the street, and he asked, "Your team? The bays? Didn't you drive them?"

"Good evening, sleepyhead," she greeted him. "The door-man found someone to tend the horses; they're waiting close by." The tantalizing smile again lurked about her lips and danced within her eyes.

An instant impulse seized Will Cardigan to put his arms about her, and to kiss the mystery of her lips. Instead, he linked his arm into hers and said, "Carla, do you realize how bewitchingly beautiful you are?" Before she could answer, he added, in reproving tone, "Except for that godawful fur teepee you erroneously term a hat."

"Will, how nice of you to notice my apparel." She laughed.

They had reclaimed the phaeton and were on the snowslushed street going toward Jennifer's when Carla wheeled the bay team in another direction.

"We've got just time enough, Will. I found it this afternoon—the perfect Christmas present for your boy. It's at a stockman's supply house on Blake Street."

They reached the store so near to its closing time that the manager was already preparing to lock up. He let them in, his impatience giving way to eager service at the thought of a substantial sale. Carla moved quickly to a glass-topped showcase, then pointed to its upper shelf. "Will, wouldn't that be perfect for any promising young animal doctor?"

Cardigan's face mingled both admiration and a tinge of disappointment. Before them was a chest of rubbed oak with its hinged lid raised to reveal a gleaming array of metal tools and instruments that ranged from suturing needles to complex devices for internal probing and operating.

"You will find it an excellent value," the clerk urged.

Will studied the glistening metal array, then with reluctant eyes turned to the woman beside him. "Carla, it is wonderful—a livestock man's dream. But I can't afford it."

As though she had not heard him, she asked quickly, "Would your boy, your Redge, like such a set, Will?"

"He would treasure it throughout his life. But there's no way I—" His words died as her gloved finger touched his lips.

"Will, I'm under strict orders from my sister to see that this goes home to your boy. Jennifer would have my skin if I failed her. It is a joy of hers to buy things for boys at Christmastime."

Will Cardigan's face turned from hesitation to excitement. "This is too much—I really shouldn't . . . at least, Carla, let me pay part."

"I've a better idea, Will," she countered. "I noticed an

excellent book on veterinary medicine over there. Your son would likely find it invaluable."

"Of course," Cardigan agreed, then asked the clerk, "Can you supply Christmas wrapping, and deliver these parcels to the Addison Hotel?"

Will was glad that no other customers were in the store, and that the clerk, with his back turned, was searching a shelf for the book. No longer could Cardigan deny himself the inevitable. His arms reached out, with power and eagerness, to encircle his companion and draw her close. The press of her body, and the quickening of her breath, seemed to justify his impulsiveness and to promise more. His caress touched the cool smoothness of her cheek, then with passionate firmness moved on to the exhilaration of her lips.

Few words passed between them when they were again behind the bay team and heading at a brisk trot for the Waverley mansion. The snowfall had stopped, after dropping a three-inch blanket, and a first-quarter moon was attempting to cast light through broken clouds.

The night was turning colder, so Cardigan tucked the heavy woolen lap robe about Carla Dunlop and himself. Now, with his arm about this entrancing woman, the tiny sleigh bells on the harness of the bay team seemed to sound in the elated rhythm of his own heartbeat.

They had crossed Broadway and were nearing Pennsylvania Street when Carla's head dropped happily on his shoulder. "Will, I'm glad you boarded that train—even glad you knocked my hat off."

He was a little slow in replying, basking in the radiance of her nearness, but also uncommonly aware of the way the fur of her headpiece was tickling his cheek.

He drew her closer, then said, almost in a whisper, "You've made these Denver hours memorable, something I wish could go on and on."

"Will, do you believe in lives being controlled by fate? Like our being literally thrown together on a train? It seems so strange . . . yet so inevitable . . . one day I'm at Fort Laramie, teaching the three Rs to a few children. That same day, you were out on the Colorado plains. Then suddenly fate smiles—or smirks—and we're here together in Denver . . . you deciding to kiss me . . . and me hoping you will."

He shook his head, then said, "I've learned not to question Providence too closely. Just to draw every ounce of happiness from today. And, Carla, you are indeed happiness."

"Time rushes so, Will. In just a few days I have to return to the orderly drills and the routine of my real life."

He was quiet for a moment, then said thoughtfully, "Carla, perhaps I'm rude or snoopy to ask, but why do you hold such a job, and live at a lonely outpost, when your sister has . . ."

"You mean when Jennifer is very rich, has no family, and rules such a mansion?"

"In blunt terms, that sums up my curiosity," Will answered.

"Oh, Will," she began, "I adore my sister. She is thoughtful and charming, and vastly devoted to my achieving happiness. And perhaps that's just where the problem lies. Jennifer, as you know—or suspect—is a powerful personality. Sometimes a bit overpowering. She put herself through an elite college, by doing laundry for students. Then she scorned the teachings of that school to marry a penniless prospector. Perhaps she sensed his shrewdness, his intelligence, and his business acumen. Jennifer performed about every menial task in a raw mining camp in order to give her man his chance. He won. Won what many consider an incredible fortune."

Carla paused, busy with the task of getting the rig onto Pennsylvania Street. Then she laughed, and said, "How I run on. But, Will, my reasons for working are very different from Jennifer's. I work in order to be my own person with my own self-respect. When one of my students—my kids—masters something, I have a feeling of being useful." They were swinging into the driveway of the Waverley mansion when she hastily concluded, as she said, "That's quite a dull statement of fact and purpose. With me, Fort Laramie is for serious. Denver is for fun. And, Will Cardigan, what can be more fun than Christmas?"

He reached out, quickly pulling the fur hat from her head, and allowing her hair to brush against his lips. "Christmas is glorious, Carla. And so is my sureness of being utterly under the charm of a vacationing Wyoming governess."

"Will," she answered in a quiet way, "I'm having a

wonderful time." Her eyes, revealed in a driveway light, said far more.

The rooms of Jennifer Waverley's vastly sprawling home were aglow with light; from an inconspicuous corner of the drawing room a string quartet played with melodic appeal.

Carla and Will had scarcely entered the house when Jennifer sought them out. She was wearing a gown of pale-green hue in a classic Grecian design. It was accentuated by a silver-chained necklace supporting a small, flawless emerald.

Jennifer extended a hand toward Cardigan, then said, "Welcome again. This time to a couple of hours of mixed sobriety and booze . . . if also to mingled intelligence and boorishness." She turned to Carla, urging, "Change as quickly as you can. Already many are asking the whereabouts of my vivacious sister."

Will edged away, intent on giving the sisters a few moments for confidential words. Jennifer Waverley called him back. "Will, I'll soon have to flit about to make sure no one feels snubbed or neglected. But right now I want you to meet several of my friends—including the honored one, Jeff Masters."

As he was led from group to group, Cardigan tried to tie the names with the faces of these strangers. Much of the conversation of these men in evening dress, and of the expensively gowned and jeweled women, would be alien to him, touching upon subjects a world removed from the camp on Crow Creek. Yet, acquaintances might be formed, even friendships initiated.

After a time, Jennifer Waverley was called away to deal with some foulup in the kitchen. Cardigan finished a cocktail, then made his way toward the book-lined room that had so greatly appealed to him the previous day. Now, three men were in the room, with comfortable chairs drawn close together, and animated conversation under way. Will was about to turn away to avoid interrupting, when one of the men waved for him to join them.

It was Jeff Masters. He said in a deep but friendly voice, "We're just discussing cattle-range conditions. We could use another opinion of what summer is apt to bring. Here . . . this sofa looks inviting," and there was friendly insistence that Cardigan should stay.

Will dropped thankfully onto the sofa, aware that his

feet were hurting in the highly polished shoes for which he had earlier discarded his ranch boots.

"I'm Will Cardigan," he said, "and I'm plenty ready to sit down." Then he added, with a smile and open candor, "My feet are killing me . . . and this collar pinches like the devil. Out on a ranch one loses the feel of city clothing in a hurry."

Jeff Masters laughed aloud, then said, "Those remarks brand you as country lad—just as I am. Mr. Cardigan, meet Adolph Brinner and Tom Foxley. Adolph's job is to endanger a bank's solvency by making loans to cowmen. And Tom? Well, I'll be charitable and just say Foxley is a cattle buyer out of Omaha."

When the introductions were completed, Jeff Masters said modestly, "I try to manage a cow spread that's up north along the Platte River."

Cardigan liked what he saw in Masters' face. He judged the man to be about thirty-five years old. His face was weathered, covered with a full black beard. His brown eyes were steady and clear. There was about him an air of self-confidence, but nothing of assumed superiority. He laughed often, and had an infectious sense of humor.

"Judging from what I've heard," Cardigan said, "Mr. Brinner's bank will never close its doors because of loans to you. But Mr. Foxley may find himself outdealt at shipping time."

Masters waved an unlit cigar in a self-deprecatory manner, then asked with a grin, "Cardigan—excuse me for dropping the stuffy 'Mister' formality—but by whom was I so overrated?"

"My neighbor, Andy Purcell, had a few words to say; so did one of his riders, Hank Kutcher."

Jeff Masters's eyes sharpened with interest. "So your holdings are close to the Diamond-7. You're lucky. Andy Purcell is a credit to our business."

Will Cardigan quickly corrected the man's false impression, saying frankly, "My holdings consist of only a small camp that is located about twenty miles above the Diamond-7 headquarters on Crow Creek. My son and I have lived there several months in modest quarters we built with Mr. Purcell's consent."

Of the three listeners, only Jeff Masters evidenced no great surprise. His eyes roved over Cardigan, sharply appraising a man who would so openly disclaim wealth and prestige. He then said, as though thinking aloud, "Andy Purcell has a way of making his own decisions. Sometimes he's a hard man to figure out, but there aren't a dozen cowmen on the plains who've built and operated an outfit as successful as Purcell's Diamond-7."

Both the banker and livestock buyer had listened quietly in order to let Jeff Masters establish the degree of acceptance and cordiality Will Cardigan should be shown. Now, Tom Foxley, the buyer, said, "I know the Diamond-7 crew pretty well. I can't see the foreman, Stacy Murdock, having much use for any sort of camp—or as you put it, Mr. Cardigan, 'modest quarters'—anywhere on the Diamond-7 holdings."

Before Cardigan could reply, Masters said, "Stacy Murdock doesn't own the Diamond-7. He'd like to, and he hopes to. I know Stacy pretty darned well. There's not a better hand with cattle." He paused, then added in a wry voice, "Nor an uglier-tempered damned fool when he's liquored up."

Brinner, the banker, leaned forward. The words he spoke brought surprise to all others in the room.

"You're aware, aren't you, Jeff, that Stacy Murdock is here tonight, attending this reception? Mrs. Waverley invited him—out of respect for the Diamond-7, I would presume."

Jeff Masters again waved his unfired cigar. "Well, whether he's here or elsewhere, my assessment of the man stands."

Cardigan rose to his feet. "Perhaps it would be best for me to express regrets to Mrs. Waverley, our hostess, and leave. Stacy Murdock and I have an aversion for each other. I wouldn't wish to mar this reception by a chance encounter with him."

Masters shook his head disapprovingly. "Cardigan, I'd suggest you stay. Have an enjoyable evening. Usually, after the niceties have been observed, Tom and Adolph and I make these functions bearable by finagling a few other guests into a card game. That time of evening has come."

Masters took Will's elbow and was walking with him into the hall when his voice lowered, and he said softly, "Besides, if you leave now, Murdock is sure to find out about it;

likely he would go about saying you were too cowardly to meet him."

For a brief moment, Cardigan caught sight of Carla. She was standing beside a fireplace that was bordered by red brick and rubbed cherrywood. The leaping flames mingled firelight and shadows across her white gown, giving it hues that varied from pink to deep rose. She looked absolutely ravishing. She glanced about, and her gaze picked out Cardigan in the hallway. She waved, then spread her hands in a gesture that indicated the impossibility of deserting three elderly women grouped about her. Will Cardigan felt long-pent desires resurgent within him. He clenched his teeth in frustration. Tomorrow he must leave Denver, and return to the windswept world along Crow Creek. But how many nights ahead, he wondered, would be spent lying awake with a restlessness born of unfulfilled desires?

Making their way slowly through the crowd, with several stops for handshakes and bits of conversation, Masters and Cardigan came finally into a room offering discreet silence. There were three circular card tables, a sideboard with liquor decanters, and an array of highly polished cuspidors, giving evidence that Jennifer Waverley assuredly had studied the furnishings of some Telluride gambling establishment. A screen had been set to baffle the draft from a window left open to siphon cigar smoke toward the outer night.

The four men chose a table, moved it a trifle to assure better light, and settled into comfortably padded chairs. There were already boxed poker chips and sealed decks of cards stacked on the green-velveted surface. Jeff Masters shoved them toward Brinner, saying, "Adolph, why don't you dole out the red, white, and blue?"

Values were set on the chips, and Cardigan was relieved that he could buy into the game modestly, without too great a cash outlay. One by one, a few other men appeared in the card room, and presently a white-coated servant went about the business of pouring drinks as they were requested.

The game was draw poker: jacks or better were required to open. Foxley won the cut for deal, shuffled, and, after the cut, dealt the four hands. Will Cardigan's cards offered nothing to build on, so he laid them down. He peered about the room, which was already a bit thick with cigar smoke. The faces around him became unrevealing. The

91

men bandied about the friendly, yet challenging, thrusts of game comment. Suddenly the vividly familiar scenes from the riverboat—from the long ago—flooded to Cardigan's mind. Since the shooting that had caused him and Emmett Willoughby to desert the gambling tables, Will had played cards sparingly, and then only in friendly games with readily controllable limits. But he knew that the talent had never deserted his hands and his mind; once mastered, the techniques and the skills and the odds of poker are with a man for good.

It was Cardigan's turn to deal. He knew that his fingering of the cards would immediately reveal a degree of expertise, but any staged fumbling or awkwardness would be immediately spotted and arouse distrust.

His fingers snapped the cards onto the green table top with his old, familiar rhythm and speed. He saw the banker and Tom Foxley exchange quick glances. Masters gave him an appraising glance.

"Cardigan, you've handled the cardboards before," he said.

Will answered as he kept a level gaze on the cowman's face, "I learned poker playing in the army camps. Later, the game earned me a living for a time on the boats between New Orleans and St. Louis." He waited, then added, in a soft but deliberate tone, "Gentlemen, I play to win, but I play fair. Would you prefer that I vacate my place?"

"Hell, no!" Tom Foxley answered. "Maybe for the price of a few cow critters I can pick up some pointers."

Jeff Masters grinned and nodded. "I've always had a yen to face off against a riverboat gambler." He looked at Brinner, and added dolefully, "Adolph, if you take a trimming, and have to dig into the bank's assets, I can hide you out along the Platte."

The comments had drawn about a dozen men into a circle about the table, and Masters waved to two empty chairs at the table. "Sit down at your peril, gentlemen. Losses are more bearable when shared by a maximum group. Besides, with Lady Luck caressing me, maybe I'll trim the whole caboodle."

Half an hour later, Will Cardigan was fully aware that there were skilled players besides himself at the table. Poker was a game to which most of them had given hour upon hour of spare time. Of the players, Adolph Brinner

92

and a middle-aged man with an Italian accent were best able to read and play their hands. Will was only about three hundred dollars ahead of the game, and that amount was of no great significance among these players.

He knew also that those about the table were feeling him out. Presently, with a locked-in or superior hand, someone would make the inevitable move, a bet that would challenge all opponents. Nothing had been said of table stakes; a hand could be bet to any limit within the bettor's financial means.

Cardigan had chosen a seat facing the room's doorway. It was an instinctive gesture, carried over from the days when caution had been a rule of life for him.

Foxley again dealt, and Will found himself holding a four-card club flush. All players at the table pushed in the one-dollar ante and stayed for the draw. The first bettor opened cautiously for two dollars, and the second was content to call. Cardigan glanced coolly about the table, and then shoved in his two dollars. His face was noncommittal. One of the remaining players chose to pay and stay, but Brinner folded his hand and dropped out.

Foxley chose to pass, and it was Jeff Masters's turn. He grinned, then said, "There comes a time of inflation. The price of poker has just gone up, gentlemen . . . by one hundred dollars."

The player to Masters's left heaved a sigh of resignation and tossed his cards onto the velvet. Then it was Cardigan's turn. He waited a little, then shrugged. "I've always been one to live dangerously," he said, "so, Mr. Masters, I'll raise you two hundred."

Masters stared into Cardigan's unrevealing face. Then he said, "I've got a gut feeling about this. I'm going to call."

Will laid down five clubs and raked in the money. Masters looked perplexed and shook his head. "Cardigan, it's hard to figure. You drew one card, drew it to a four-card straight flush. The odds are forty-six to one against filling such a hand." His voice conveyed amazement that a skilled gambler would take such risks.

Before Will could answer, Adolph Brinner broke in. "Jeff, you overlooked one point. It cost Mr. Cardigan very little to see his fifth card . . . and to know he had you in a squeeze. Then there's the matter of pot odds against drawing odds. The pot offered five-to-one odds, while the odds on making a flush are only four to one. His drawing to a straight flush was so much icing on his cake."

Masters laughed ruefully. "What am I doing in a game with a couple of financial analysts?" he demanded.

Before anyone could answer him, the door was pushed open. Distant voices in the next room overrode the strains of a Viennese waltz. A breeze blew the curtain at the open window—and Stacy Murdock stood in the doorway.

Will Cardigan stared fixedly at the newcomer's face and form. He had seen Murdock only once at the Diamond-7, when Redge had made his deal with Andy Purcell, but the foreman's opposition to the Cardigan's presence was enough. Then too there had been the encounter at the Addison Hotel. A hatred had been born between them.

Clad in formal attire, Murdock now seemed younger, taller and more handsome than he had seemed at the ranch. Yet the arrogance was still about him. Cardigan saw instantly that the man was half drunk.

Murdock strode close to the table. "Jeff Masters, I've been looking in every part of this half mile hacienda for you," he said. "I promised the boss, Andy Purcell, I'd find out—"

Murdock's words broke sharply off as he recognized Will Cardigan. When he spoke again, his voice was filled with loathing. "God almighty, if it ain't the nester. Have I got to put up with seeing your face everywhere in Denver?"

Will's determination to remain unprovoked was a bit shaken by the insolent question. "Murdock," he retorted, "I can't say the pleasure is mine either."

Jeff Masters rose to his feet and placed his hand on Murdock's arm. "Stacy, why don't you and I find a quiet place to talk . . . somewhere we'll not disturb this game?"

Murdock shook himself free. "Hell, Jeff, that can wait. I'm of a mind to sit in on the game. Find out if old Cardigan . . ."

With a signal of apology to those about the table, Masters again tried to lead the intruder from the room. Then he listened in speechless disbelief as Stacy Murdock leaned over the table to confront Cardigan. "When I get home," he said with venom, "I'll see if the Diamond-7 heifers are still up at that miserable camp you and that smart-assed son of yours set up. Likely they won't be. Likely you've

94

already sold them. That money . . ." He paused, pointing at the chips on the table in front of Will Cardigan.

There was an uncomfortable silence around the poker table. Stacy Murdock's breathing sounded loud in the room.

Cardigan felt a coldness he had not experienced since the days of his infantry service. No man could tolerate such an accusation and maintain a semblance of honor or dignity. He pushed back his chair and rose. "You filthy, lying son of a bitch, Murdock," he said in an all too quiet tone. "I'm a guest here. I don't propose to embarrass Mrs. Waverley. If you have any decency—which I doubt—I'll meet you off these premises now or later. Fists or guns—Murdock, it's your choice."

Under the lash of Cardigan's words, Murdock had turned ugly. He stood sweaty, panting, and oblivious of everyone else but Cardigan.

"Shit, homesteader," he growled. "You talk big. Wait till I tell Andy Purcell I learned up at the State House that you sneaked down here to Denver and filed homestead claim to nigh onto a thousand acres."

"Inasmuch as you don't have claim to an acre," Will said carefully, "I'd say the matter is between Mr. Purcell and me. Now . . . are we going outside?"

Murdock stared down at the cards and the chips. A mirthless grin swept his face. "I'll take my time nailing your hide, Cardigan. Right now I'm primed to beat hell out of you with poker cards. Get back that heifer money—"

Jeff Masters seized Murdock's arm again, this time with no-nonsense firmness. "You're a drunk mess, Stacy. I'm going to find someone to take you—"

"That won't be necessary, Mr. Masters!" The words rang out in a clear and angry voice, causing everyone to turn toward the door. Jennifer Waverley stood with her back to the door, which she had closed behind her. As she walked to Stacy Murdock, her hands were clenched and the knuckles white. Her face was flushed, and her eyes narrowed in contempt.

"Mr. Murdock," she began. "Will you do me the honor of leaving my house immediately? Leave—and never return. What you've done in this room is inexcusable and . . . and downright loathsome."

She let the import of what she had said sink in. Then she turned to face the other men about her. "In a few minutes, my carriageman will have a rig at the side door. I trust you gentlemen will make sure Mr. Murdock takes his departure."

Jennifer Waverley swung about to face Murdock once more. "I trust you understand what I've said. It will spare me having to reword it in the blunt terms of a Telluride miner."

Will Cardigan walked to a side of the room and stood in half-relieved and half-frustrated silence. The matter had been taken out of his hands—or had it, actually?

Half a dozen men formed an escort for Murdock, but the ranch foreman broke loose and brought his face within inches of Will's.

A calmness and a deadliness marked his voice. "Cardigan," he said, "either take your kid and get off the Diamond-7—or wait and you'll wish to eternal God you had."

The following morning came to Denver with clearing skies that foretold a sunny but cold day. Will Cardigan awakened shortly after sunup, and stood for a long while at a westward-facing window of the Addison Hotel. The storm's rapid passing had left only three or four inches of snow across the city and foothills that climbed in dazzling whiteness toward the high peaks. The clarity of the air, in strengthening sunshine, lent a deceiving nearness to valleys and hills. The foothills seemed but a few minutes' walk away; in reality, their distance from the city was almost twenty miles.

Will's thoughts were sober and reflective as he recalled the unpleasant encounter with Stacy Murdock. It had put an end to the poker game, and also had had disastrous effects on Jennifer Waverley's party. In order to relieve the awkward situation, Cardigan had quickly expressed both his thanks and his regrets to Jennifer, and quickly left the mansion. The urge had come to him to seek out Carla, but Jennifer Waverley had spoken words that forestalled this.

"Will, she is upstairs in her room, crying, devastated. Come and see us tomorrow, before you leave the city." Her hand sought his, and lingered in a reassuring way.

It was Adolph Brinner, the banker, who gave Cardigan a ride back to the hotel. On the drive, neither had spoken of the nasty ending of the card game. But now, with morning light pouring across the city's activity, Cardigan smiled as he remembered Brinner's parting words. "Will Cardigan, when you are in Denver again, I trust we can have dinner together."

Cardigan sought out the hotel's coffee shop and spent almost an hour over a light breakfast and a copy of the *Rocky Mountain News*. Study of his Union Pacific timetable revealed that a mixed train would be leaving for Greeley and Cheyenne shortly before noon. He remembered Jennifer Waverley asking him to again come to the house on Pennsylvania Street. He mulled over the idea for a couple of minutes, then shook his head.

What good could possibly come of it? he asked himself. I've visited the mansion once too often. Because of me, a carefully planned party turned to havoc.

Along with these thoughts, Will was conscious of an even greater reason for his reluctance and his decision. Why subject Carla to a goodbye that surely and inevitably would be final and enduring?

This morning Will realized he was in love with Carla Dunlop. During the relatively few hours since he had knocked a crazy-quilted fur hat from the loveliness of her hair, and had peered into her startled eyes, a tenderness and a longing had grown within him, a need for a woman's love and nearness. This he had known—for the first time since his wife's death.

And so Will came to acknowledge his greatest reason for remaining away from the Waverley mansion. He was not sure that he himself could withstand the bittersweetness of a final word . . . a final embrace.

Will returned to his room to begin packing. He eyed the clothing he had bought for the reception wryly and then began folding each garment with care. He wondered what Redge's comment would be upon seeing such a coat and shirt and tie. And what would salty old Hank Kutcher say if he should spot evening attire dangling from a roof pole of the shack on Crow Creek? Likely it would be best to leave such fancy duds in his new suitcase, together with a handful of mothballs.

He walked to his dresser, then slowly picked up other objects, the new set of shining veterinary tools and the book he had chosen for his son. He laid them into the bag, and glanced at a calendar lying on the room's small desk.

December 23. I'll be home with my boy, home with Redge, all day Christmas.

By midmorning, his quiet room seemed like a prison. With the aid of a bellhop, Cardigan got his belongings downstairs. Ten minutes later, he had checked out and was seated in a cab on his way to the Union train station. A hotel room can seem so warmly inviting upon one's arrival, he mused, then turn cold and depressing when time of departure is near.

Traffic about the depot was light; little time was required to check his luggage, and he had the round-trip ticket he had bought at Greeley. The hard benches of the waiting room seemed scarcely inviting, but he settled onto one of them. There was an hour to train time, so Cardigan drew a livestock journal from his coat pocket and settled in to read it.

He had nearly finished the first article when the sound of nearing footsteps and the rustle of a coat caused him to glance up. He stared with disbelief into Carla Dunlop's agitated face.

"Will . . . thank goodness I made it here before the train. They told me at your hotel . . ." She paused, extending a hand that seemed to need the assurance of touching him.

"Carla . . . Carla . . . sit down," he interrupted, concerned by the paleness of her face.

She reached out her other hand to capture his. "Why, Will? Why were you leaving like this—without even a word—or a farewell?"

Cardigan's gaze roved her troubled and questioning face; then it lifted, and he forced a grin. "Maybe," he said, "I just couldn't bear another look at that damned maze of fur bits you persist in cramming onto your head."

Her expression vacillated—he couldn't tell whether she was about to laugh or cry. Then she said, "Will, you're using my bonnet as an evasive tactic." She added, "It was awful—what you endured at that card game. Jennifer is furious. She's letting it be known that she will never knowingly attend a function in Denver where that Murdock man has been invited. Even our respect for Mr. Purcell and his Diamond-7 Ranch cannot change that."

Cardigan murmured slowly, "But Carla, that means he will be ostracized. Your sister's social prestige will assure it."

"He brought it upon himself, Will."

They sat quietly side by side, and Will Cardigan was
aware that her hands were still snuggled into his. Presently
he said, "It's better than half an hour until my train leaves.
That's time for the bite of breakfast I'm sure you haven't
had." He rose and tugged at her hand. "Come along."

She shook her head, then hesitated, before saying, "I am
hungry, Will. But I have a better idea. Listen. I have the
bay team outside, and they need to be exercised. There's
an evening train. Why don't . . ." Her words trailed off and
a flush livened her cheeks.

Carla gazed with determination into his face. "Dammit,
Will Cardigan, I am going to say it: Why don't we go for
a long drive, stop for breakfast, and then drive again. Perhaps to Golden . . . or Morrison. Then we'll make sure
you're here on time for that evening train."

Oblivious of an old lady and two youngsters who were
watching them, Cardigan's fingers tilted her chin so that his
lips could touch hers. "May I drive those beautiful bay
horses?" he asked, then added, in an almost timid way, "I
can take care of them, Carla, my dear, and have one arm
free."

She tilted her face toward him again, ignoring the disapproving scowl of the old lady and the tittering laugh of
the children.

Minutes later, they were seated behind the bay team, with
a lap robe tucked around them, and tiny harness bells
sounding in rhythm to the smooth and even-paced trot of
the horses. Will guided the team across the railroad tracks,
across a bridge spanning the South Platte River, and up a
snow-mantled road that climbed a bluff and then led westward to Golden.

They came, after a time, to an attractive restaurant with
stone fronting and perhaps a dozen blue spruce trees facing
the road. Cardigan tethered the bays to a hitchrail, and
carefully strapped warm horse cloths about them. They
tossed their silky necks as if grateful for the rest.

There was a pre-noon lull inside the restaurant. Holly
wreaths and a decorated spruce tree spoke of the Christmas
season. The massive stone fireplace cast warmth and light
and a sense of tranquillity across the tables of the spacious
dining room.

They tarried a long time in the restaurant, pleased by

both the service and the food. For Will Cardigan, it seemed enough to be able to reach out and touch Carla's hand, to know the softness of her smile, and the lilt of her words that said little and yet conveyed so much.

After their meal, they strolled out of the restaurant and into the sunshine. Cardigan peered at the angle of the sun, then toward the sharp rise of mountains off westward. Then he asked, "Carla, would we really have enough time to drive to Golden, and get back before train time? It's several miles . . . on snowy roads."

"Probably not, Will. I wanted to make sure of having you with me every possible moment." She squeezed his arm, then asked, "What would you rather do?"

He had untied the horses and was climbing to the seat beside her. Abruptly, her question, her nearness, and the surge of his own aroused emotions, formed his answer. It came out with honest boldness. "There's only one thing, Carla, I want to do—this afternoon—right this moment. Carla, I want to make love to you."

Her answer came as she reached out to take the reins from his hands. "Will, I need you too. Your love. Your arms." She was quiet, except for her quick breathing, as she maneuvered the horses onto the roadway. Then she moved on the seat, pressing unabashedly close to him. "There is a small house about three miles from here, down in the Barnum section of town. Jennifer and I own it—and just now it is available."

His arm went about her possessively. "Carla," he said, with a boyish grin, "I'd love to see another Waverley house, if you'll conduct the guided tour. Can't these horses move any faster?"

Later, when he had spotted a small corral, and thrown hay to the unhitched bays, Will walked to the small frame house, which was painted white and trimmed with brown. There was no fireplace, but Carla had already fed a base-burning stove, and already its warmth was spreading through the rooms. He was surprised to find the cottage fully furnished with attractive pieces. Carla, standing beside him within the heater's ring of warmth, seemed to read his thoughts.

"This used to be my home, Will. Before that, it belonged to my mother. Jennifer and I keep it largely out of sentiment. Besides, when pressure builds at the Waverley mansion, it's a hideaway for either of us." She hesitated a while, then asked, "Will, is it terrible to bring you here? Am I a hussy? A strumpet?"

Will Cardigan's answer was to draw her into his arms, and to press his cheek to hers. "Carla, you could never be those things. You're a beautiful and maybe sometimes a lonesome woman. And lovelier than an old prairie dog of a widower deserves."

Her fingers tightened about his neck and lifted to stroke his graying hair.

"Carla." He spoke her name in a hushed, adoring tone. "Carla, we have only three or four hours. Can we make of it a lifetime of love . . . of happiness . . . of all our bodies promise . . . and offer?"

For a moment her lips and her breasts were crushed against him in ecstasy. Then she drew away reluctantly. "Next week, Will, I will be the restrained and proper governess at a fort in Wyoming Territory. But this day belongs to us." She blew a kiss toward him, then walked toward a portiered door. "Will, my own, give me five minutes—then come to me."

Chapter 10

Spring comes to the Crow Creek Valley in diverse and unpredictable ways. There are years when the grasslands seem reluctant to shed their protective cover of snow, and to allow even hardy flowers and grasses to yield to the alchemy of warming days. There are other years when the season of greening is ushered in by soft rains. These are the springs when the wind, coming steady and humid off the Gulf of Mexico, piles dark, heavy clouds against the mountains. Baffled by the peaks, these thickening clouds vent their frustration by releasing a steady downpour across the grassland stretches of the high plains.

To Redge Cardigan, continually busy with ailing and crippled livestock and with his newborn calves, the coming of spring was a miracle somehow wrought within a few days. There was both warmth and subtle promise in the sunshine that followed the April rains. It was good to move about without the restriction of a heavy coat, and to plunge into the still-frigid waters of a Crow Creek pool for an invigorating swim.

Several times he had had use for the gleaming veterinary instruments which his father had brought home from Denver on Christmas day. Already the boy had read completely through the book that had accompanied the set. Now he was rereading, chapter by chapter, pausing to consider the means by which he might apply the different medical techniques to his own animals and their problems.

He had received the expensive set of steel instruments with a cry of amazement and delight. Will Cardigan had handed it to him, then searched awkwardly for words.

"This is meant to make your Christmas a happy one, son. The book is from me. The case of instruments is from two women who live in Denver . . . Jennifer Waverley and Carla Dunlop."

Redge removed the wrappings, opened the case, then gave out a whoop. "Dad! They're beautiful—and must have cost a fortune." He stared at Will Cardigan, then said in eager delight, "Who are these wonderful women?"

"Two good friends, Redge. I'll give you an address for your note of thanks."

Redge peered curiously at his father. The words had been spoken in a civil but entirely impersonal way. And Redge saw no indication in his father's face or his manner that any further information would be forthcoming.

The boy found reason to wonder, however, and then to grow concerned at a change that little by little came over Will Cardigan. The understanding and the closeness was still between them. The older man worked even harder than before, and spoke often of the ranch and the herd that Andy Purcell might someday help the Cardigans to establish.

But there were the unfathomable times, those periods of quiet, when the older Cardigan seemed lost in reverie, somewhere in a world of his own.

As the days warmed, and greening grass caused the livestock to graze farther from the camp, Redge became increasingly aware that his father now made it a point to ride with a rifle as his constant companion. There was a wariness about Will nowadays. He often stopped to scan the horizon, or grew watchful upon the few occasions that a stranger hove in sight.

Finally, the boy worded his perplexity. It came about toward dusk one day in early May, when the two of them, weary from a long day's activity, sat quietly resting on a fallen tree. Presently Redge caught sight of a lone horseman riding in from the east. The stranger's form was indistinct in the deepening shadows. "Whoever that is," Redge said, pointing, "is riding a mighty tuckered-out horse."

The words and the gesture brought Will Cardigan instantly to his feet. His arm snaked out to retrieve the rifle he had leaned against the tree's trunk. He moved the weapon into level readiness. "Redge, be careful," he demanded. "Keep in shadows and shelter until we find out who—"

"Good Lord, Dad," the boy gasped. "What's wrong with you? You're as skittish as a gunshy antelope." He grew silent, peering into the distance. "Whoever it was must

103

have turned downcreek. Likely just some Diamond-7 employee who's been over to Kate's Wagon."

His father remained tense, but turned to face Redge.

"Son, I guess I'd better tell you something. I have been putting it off . . . didn't want to worry you. I had one hell of a run-in with Stacy Murdock in Denver. It happened at a party. Murdock got drunk and loud . . . and ugly. Then he mouthed off an insult against us Cardigans. One that no man could ignore and still respect himself. I called him. Now Murdock is more set than ever to have us off Crow Creek and the Diamond-7 graze."

"If you ask me, Dad," Redge answered, with a careless shrug, "I think Stacy Murdock is big on words and mighty small on follow-through."

"I hope you're right, son," Will muttered. "Just watch out and play it safe. The law doesn't amount to much this side of Greeley—a long ride away."

For a time they sat silent. The lone rider was nowhere in sight. A cow was bawling anxiously for her calf. The chirping of a cricket sounded nearby. And a slight breeze rustled through the bud-laden branches of the cottonwoods.

They were about to go back inside the cabin, when Redge spoke again. "I'm glad you told me, Dad. Perhaps we both wanted to protect each other too much. Something happened while you were in Denver." And then Redge told of the stormy night when he and Hank had scared off a trio of horse thieves.

"Crucified Christ!" Will Cardigan breathed aloud at the finish of the account. "Son, you should have told me. That's what I get for leaving you here by yourself and traipsing off to Denver. What if the sleazy rustling bastards had come back?"

Redge grinned. "Probably they felt lucky to get away with only one shot up. Anyhow, Hank had to stay all the next day. I'd pulled a big jaw tooth of his."

"You what?" Will howled.

"I yanked a tooth. Old Kutcher's jaw was like he had three plugs of chewing tobacco in it."

"I wonder who those rustlers were?" Will pondered. Already his mind was exploring the possibility that the horse raid might be linked to the Diamond-7 foreman. He discarded the idea with a shake of his head. Stacy Murdock had been in Denver, and he had no henchman who would do his work for him.

Redge had touched a match to a kerosene lamp and was opening his veterinary book when he remembered Kutcher's enigmatic words. He stared into his father's face. "Dad, I just recalled—Hank knows who the horse thieves were. At least he said he did. He wants to talk to you about them." Redge was lost in thought for a while, then he asked abruptly, "Dad, what does the name Devlin mean to you? Who is he?"

It was as though the years had spun backward and Will were again catching the blow of pistol behind his ear . . . watching a hulking blond giant slump to the floor, crumple to the gambling boat's carpet . . . then seeing Hollis Devlin, knife in hand, spin about from the impact of the bullet with which Emmett Willoughby had destroyed his elbow. And here in the silent cabin on Crow Creek, with his son staring expectantly toward him, Cardigan again remembered Hollis Devlin's venomous words: *You bastard! I vow I'll kill you if it takes me the rest of my life. Willoughby won't always be by your side.*

And now, with Devlin's name sounding as an echo and a specter from the past, Cardigan knew the inevitability of the choice he must make. He must either lie to his son or reveal a resurgent menace springing from that night of gunfire and blood on a riverboat. Will's gaze again swept Redge's tense—and now worried—face. In that moment a father saw his son in a new and revealing way. Redge was no longer a child to be constantly watched over and protected. There was now a maturity and capability about him, born of the challenge and the labor and the promise that their start of a homeplace had instilled within the boy. Redge, in the pale lamplight, seemed almost a man. Yes, regardless of the past, the future was something that father and son must now face together. Redge must be told.

Will Cardigan threw another length of cottonwood into the stove, poked at it thoughtfully, then sat down at the scrubbed table facing his son.

"Yes, Redge," he began, "the name Devlin—Hollis Devlin—isn't new to me. Once, a long time ago, it meant a challenge for me at the gambling tables. And now? Now, it's apt to mean trouble. I had hoped that the damnable affair was over and done. I've heard of Devlin over the years," Will continued. "He kept telling everyone how he'd cut me down like a mongrel dog. That sort of talk gets around fast. And usually that's just it—windy talk. The last definite word I ever had was that Devlin and a new partner he'd teamed with were heading out for the Nevada gold fields."

"I wish Hank Kutcher would show up again," Redge commented. "He said those horse thieves got in his way somehow in Cheyenne, and that he trailed behind them that night. I bet he knows more about them, and about your old, crooked-elbowed friend, Devlin."

"Likely then," Will suggested, "we ought to ride down to the Diamond-7 again and have a talk with Kutcher."

For a time there was silence between them, with each wrapped in his own thoughts. It was broken finally, as Will said, "I'd be a fool not to tell you we're sitting on a keg of dynamite. First, I get Stacy Murdock riled up to run us off the Diamond-7. And now we've got to wonder what brought Devlin to this part of the country, and what he's up to." He sighed, then he asked flatly, "Son, am I letting you risk too much by staying here on Crow Creek? How would you feel about calling it quits with this camp and heading out?"

Redge's eyes hardened and he thrust out his chin in the stubborn manner his father had come to know so well. "Dad, you're thinking of me . . . afraid for me. Otherwise, you wouldn't turn tail and run."

Will Cardigan's hand went out to clutch his son's shoulder.

"Redge, life wouldn't be worth a plugged nickel if my enemies, or my doings, brought harm to you."

For a moment the boy stared into the lamp's mellow glow. Then he said, "This place is ours, or will be when we get full homestead title. We've got our horses and cattle. We've got some good friends. Mr. Purcell. Hank Kutcher." And although he didn't voice their names, Redge was mentally including Kate Andrus, over at Kate's Wagon—and her fiery and freckled daughter Audrey, who might just possibly be counted as a friend.

Will's voice was firm and decisive. "Son, when we first topped the ridge, and you wanted to build here in this creek valley, I said it was your future we're after. It still is. If you say stay that's what we will do. If there comes a time when it's needed, son, we'll fight to have . . . and fight to hold."

Redge nodded in a determined way, then grinned. "Thanks, Dad. Troublemakers are gonna find two Cardigans a handful." He hesitated, then added, in a slyly teasing way, "It's too bad you can't fan a six-shooter like you can a deck of playing cards."

The older man's face became suddenly serious, and he said, "Redge, speaking of cards . . . did you put that torn half of the ten of diamonds in a safe place?"

Redge had placed the card safely beneath the velvet lining of his prized veterinary-tool case that day his father had returned from Denver.

"The very safest place, Dad," he assured.

For a moment his father's face was somber. But all he said was, "Remember where it should go, son, should you need help—to Emmett Willoughby, in Arizona." He cut off questions Redge might have asked as he added, with finality, "Let's get to bed. Perhaps we can get things in shape in a day or so to take time for a ride downcreek to see Hank Kutcher."

In the grayness of dawn, they awakened to the steady murmur of rain on the cabin roof. There were a couple of spots where the downpour was trickling through the roughly hewn boards, so they set a large tin can and a bucket to catch drips. Daylight brought a brisk wind out of the southeast, together with heavier rain.

After a while, Redge put on their only oilskin raincoat and headed for the corrals and the stable. He found a drenched world outside, with every small ditch a muddy, flowing stream. The surrounding hills were veiled by low-hanging clouds and wind-blown rain. There was little to be done, except to feed his hospital animals in the stable. Much of the stock had taken shelter under a lean-to shed. Redge sniffed the freshness of the washed air and noted how the creekside grass and shrubs had already taken on more luxuriant shades of green. The usually quiet flow of Crow Creek was wider and more hurried, attempting to carry off the water pouring in from surrounding hills.

The day wore on without any letup in the steady downpour. Will Cardigan prepared their breakfast, then later wrote some letters, while Redge read and reread chapters

107

of his book on veterinary science. Occasionally they would stride to the cabin door, open it, and study the continuing rain. Such abundant moisture would mean a fine spring for the grasslands. Warm days would soon bring the green and verdant grass to a considerable height; under summer winds it would stir and billow as an endless vista of livestock feed.

By late afternoon, both Redge and Will were congratulating themselves for having built their cabin and the outbuildings on the cottonwood-studded knoll that rose about thirty feet above the flow of the creek. Had the log structures been placed at streamside level, they would now be inundated. Somewhat farther down the creek, where its course came into a meadow, the turgid and rapidly moving water had already spread out to a width of several hundred feet.

During the afternoon, Redge grew tired of the cabin's restricted space. He shed his shoes and socks, then rolled his trousers to his knees. He left the cabin and walked up the creek, although it was slippery and his feet were chilled. The wind had slackened, but above him there were still the heavy, rain-laden clouds.

An hour later he was somewhat over a mile upstream. He came presently to a place where the creek's valley narrowed into a deep, narrow gorge. Water was now roaring, angry and turbulent, through this obstructing course. As he drew nearer, keeping to higher ground, Redge saw that the hillsides, drawing quickly in, rose steeply above him. He climbed to a better viewpoint—and then gasped. Upstream, the wide valley had become a lake, a broad, stretching body of water held back by this natural dam. Even if the rain were to immediately cease, it would require hours for the sizable body of water to drain through the only outlet, which was the narrow, spume-filled chasm beneath him.

Redge stood for a long time in entranced wonder. He judged that the backed-up water already reached a mile up the creek. How could placid Crow Creek possibly have created this reservoir of water so soon? The creek, coming down from those Wyoming Territory mountains, would have to drain hundreds of square miles . . . dozens of gently sloping prairie hills. And now the rain must be widespread across the seemingly endless prairie reaches.

What would happen, Redge wondered, if the confining hillside walls were to wash loose, and allow the pent-up acres of deep water to plunge downstream? Without a doubt, the Cardigans' camp would be swept away—buildings, livestock, corral posts, and poles. And the Diamond-7 Ranch buildings, far downstream! Such a flood would overwhelm the ranch.

The boy ground his heel into the wet dirt. The grass-matted sod, sprinkled with clumps of sagebrush, cast an aroma of freshness into the damp air. Likely these abutting hills had stood for thousands of years and through ages of recurring floods. They would continue to stand as a slit dam, holding back the flood waters, with the narrow chasm serving as a safety device.

He stared quietly about, his gaze moving over the obstructing heights. What if the slit . . . the ravine . . . was piled full of rocks? There would be a dam—flood waters channeled for irrigation. He eyed the sweep of backed-up water in a calculating way. Excitement stirred within him, and he stood looking upstream, oblivous of the rain still pouring across his face.

A dam like that, with the gorge plugged and a spillway built, could irrigate a hundred—maybe a thousand—acres of valley land. Hay meadows. Winter feed for the cattle that in summer grazed these undulating hills.

Redge turned, and in his excitement practically ran back to the cabin. He had scarcely cleared the door when he yelled excitedly at his father, "Get a coat on and come with me, Dad. You'll have to see it to believe it. It's already a mile long. Deep as—"

"Whoa up, son," Will Cardigan managed to cut in. He pulled on a sheepskin coat, buttoning it tight. "I'm coming. Boy, when you get fired up, it's downright infectious. Now, tell me what all this is about."

Two hours passed before they returned, soaking wet, to the shelter of the cabin. The darkness of evening merged with the darkness of the storm. Redge fed his livestock, then stood for a time in the stable doorway watching the flow of the creek. The dark water, in which floating debris appeared from time to time, was now swirling almost half-way up the knoll to the corrals. He knew that barring an utter catastrophe, the Cardigan camp buildings were safe, but likely downstream the situation was more serious.

He smiled in appreciation at the aroma of his father's cooking; now the scent of a venison roast mingled with

109

that of a pie fashioned from canned peaches. As he watched his father baste the roast, he said, "You know, all we need here is a big dam and we can have all this creek bottom-land under irrigation ditches."

"You may have a great idea, son." Will Cardigan nodded. "How come you stumbled on this notion?"

"That's the way Brigham Young and his Mormons are building their empire," Redge answered with assurance. "Their new Jerusalem, out in Utah. I read a book about it, back home in Missouri."

The following morning they awakened later than usual. The rain had stopped. Small rivulets were still hurrying down the knoll; the creek was still a broad and muddy watercourse—too swollen to permit crossing by foot or horseback. Toward noon, the blanket of clouds began breaking up, and shafts of warm sunlight filtered through. Redge opened the corral gates to allow his stock to feed upon the hillside grasses. Barring the possibility of more rain, things would return to normal within a day or two.

It was midafternoon when they spotted a horseman coming slowly toward the camp. Because of the creek's flooded width he kept well above it. Redge recognized the rider and quickly called his father from the lean-to, where he had been sharpening a crosscut saw.

"Dad, there's Hank Kutcher. And his horse looks just about on his last legs."

Will nodded, and remarked, "It's a good thing old Hank is on our side of the creek. He looks about as beat out as his gelding."

Hank Kutcher's face was haggard and weary as he gratefully eased his horse to a halt. He clutched the saddle's pommel to keep from swaying. Redge and Will went quickly to his side.

"Kutcher. Climb down. Come in," Will said in a concerned voice. "Take care of his horse, Redge. I'll get him inside."

As if in a trance, Kutcher swung himself from the saddle and onto the ground. He peered at the two men. When he spoke there was vast weariness in his tired voice.

"He's dead. Andy Purcell is dead. He drowned in the creek last night."

The impact of Kutcher's words did not immediately register. Then Redge asked, "The ranch? Were others trapped?"

The boy threw an arm about Kutcher, whose knees were close to buckling.

"The headquarters buildings are safe—or were when I rode out. Andy had put in some dikes a few years ago. Everybody else is high and dry."

Redge quickly knotted the gelding's reins to a sapling. Together, father and son kept Kutcher erect as they got him to the cabin and eased him onto Redge's bunk.

Kutcher stared past them, then drew an unsteady hand across his forehead. "Lad," he said to Redge, "this is a damned sight awful thing. Andy Purcell wasn't just my boss. He was my best friend. For short of twenty years my best . . ." For perhaps a minute Kutcher's eyes were closed, then with a sudden jerk he tried to sit up. Words rushed from him again, and his voice broke as he tried to control his feelings. "I saw him go under. Tried to get a rope around him. There just wasn't time. Andy died trying to save a stove-up old steer that wasn't worth two whoops in hell."

They resisted the urge to question him—that could come later. Kutcher was soon asleep, no longer able to fight off his utter fatigue. Will Cardigan drew a blanket about their friend, and Redge pulled off his soggy boots and set them in the sunshine to dry.

Redge squatted down in silence on the cabin's outer step. His father came to him and dropped down worriedly beside him.

Redge picked up a rock and flung it fiercely toward a pool of rainwater. "Why . . . Dad . . . why does it always have to be the decent people who die? My mom. Mr. Purcell." The boy thumbed a tear from his cheek, then asked, "Dad, I'm sure glad you took care of the homestead filing, in Denver, like Mr. Purcell said we should."

"Yes, one of these days we'll have clear title to our land." Will gazed at his son's stricken face, then added, "And I am pretty sure Mr. Purcell meant for you to have that bunch of springer heifers. If I knew Andy Purcell, he would have worked out a means for you to buy those heifers from him. Likely Kutcher will know something about that."

Redge rose, thrust his hands in his pockets, then looked gravely into his father's face. "From now on, Dad, we're going to have to be careful . . . be ready for bad trouble any hour of the day or night. Mr. Purcell was our friend. Our protection. And now there isn't one blessed thing can keep Stacy Murdock from trying to run us off the Diamond-7—and maybe hound us clean to hell 'n' gone."

"That's just what I rode up here to warn you about."

The words coming from Hank Kutcher caused the Cardigans to swing about and gaze at the old cowhand, who was standing in his socks in the doorway. His legs seemed steadier now, and his nap had driven some of the wild desperation from his face.

"You ought to rest some more," Redge urged.

"Later I can," Kutcher said. "Right now I'd appreciate a few swigs of your horse piss, lad. Then some coffee to drink while I tell you the worst. That thieving son of a bitch—that crooked-armed horse rustler, Devlin—has been snooping around the Diamond-7. Somehow he's wormed his way into a setup with Stacy Murdock."

Will Cardigan listened, then slowly folded his arms. His face became inscrutable, and his voice a thoughtful whisper. "Willoughby handled Devlin that time on the river. Now it's my turn."

Redge stepped closer to his father. "At least we know who we're up against," he said.

"But do we?" his father asked. "You said there were three night raiders tried to rustle our horses. We know that one of them—probably the leader—was Hollis Devlin. But the other two—how about them?"

"It was too dark to see faces," Redge said. "One of them was a tall fellow, sort of thin. I heard his voice when he yelled—sounded like he was pretty young."

Hank Kutcher walked unsteadily toward the Cardigans. He came through the cabin door and propped an arm against the log wall. "All right. I guess you have to know. That skinny one is the fool kid that guided Devlin and his sidekick down from Cheyenne. Redge, I sort of hoped the horse-stealing affair would blow over and I wouldn't have to tell you. That young hellion is Bert Andrus, Kate's son—of Kate's Wagon. He's a brother of that freckled little gal you met."

Redge gazed stolidly at Kutcher, shaking his head as though unwilling to accept what he had just heard. Then he sighed aloud. "Audrey told me her brother causes Kate no end of worry and heartaches." He paused, as his mind reviewed the tense minutes of the raid. "I was pretty sure I plugged a shot into that one when he tried to open the corral gate. That yell he let out made it seem he was in a lot of pain."

"You hit the young idiot, all right," Kutcher affirmed. "I found out about his shot-up arm when I got back to the ranch. That was the day after you used them fence pliers and tore out half of my jawbone. Andy Purcell told me what had happened there at the Diamond-7 headquarters. Devlin and the Andrus kid rode in. There was a gimlet-eyed character with them that they called Slick. They had one hell of a story rigged up to tell Purcell. Something about Devlin and Slick being laid off by a cow outfit up by Buffalo, Wyoming. They claimed they'd run across the Andrus kid a few miles upcreek from the Diamond-7, and that Bert Andrus had offered to buy one of their revolvers. Then he'd accidentally shot himself while examining it. The wound was in the kid's left upper arm, so it could have happened that way."

Redge snorted. "Hank, do you mean Mr. Purcell was taken in by all that bullshit?"

"Easy now, lad." Kutcher grinned wryly. "What they didn't take into consideration was that Andy Purcell had known Bert Andrus since he was ankle high to a piss ant. All he had to do was look at the kid's nervous, twitching face to figure out that the accident story was hot air and lies."

Kutcher pared off a liberal slice of chewing tobacco and thrust it into his cheek before continuing. "Likely you'll be interested in what they offered to swap in exchange for getting Andrus's arm patched up. They told Andy just to say the word and they'd rid Crow Creek of the nesters that had squatted upstream on his graze."

"What did Mr. Purcell think of that—an offer to do us in?" Redge asked.

"He didn't cotton to it at all." Kutcher half smiled, but he was numb with the grief of losing Andy Purcell, and suddenly the mention of his name made it difficult for him to go on. He fought to control his voice, and continued, "Purcell patched up the kid's arm himself. Then he made it daggoned clear to all three—Devlin and Slick and young Andrus—that there would be no jobs or deals or anything else for them on the Diamond-7. He recommended that they get off his ranch pronto—and not come back."

Will Cardigan rubbed his chin thoughtfully and commented, "I've a hunch they didn't go very far. Hank, do you suppose they've been in touch with Stacy Murdock, and hatching up trouble, ever since he got back from that trip he took to Denver? He and I had one hell of a run-in that week."

Kutcher spat tobacco juice on the ground. "I gathered, from a few words Murdock let drop, that there had been some sort of ruckus, and he'd come out on the short end."

Redge had been sitting in the sun's warmth, thinking and forming his own ideas. Now he commented, "It's Murdock, that big tub of mutton, I think we have to be on guard against. He seems to have brains—even Mr. Purcell mentioned that once. I only met up with Hollis Devlin for that short time when you kept him from shooting me, Hank. But I don't think he's as smart as Murdock."

Will Cardigan shook his head. "Don't discount Devlin, Redge. I remember the days when he practically controlled gambling on the Missouri River run of the steamboats. Bitterness and rancor have had a lot of years to build in this man. Besides, a snake isn't apt to become less deadly with the passing of time."

Redge entered the cabin and soon emerged with steaming mugs of coffee. He pressed one into Kutcher's hands. "Dad brews this so it's as strong as horse liniment and blacker than an Angus bull. Now tell me, Hank. Just how did you get on the trail of Hollis Devlin and that Slick character in Cheyenne?"

Kutcher's hand moved in exasperation, and he muttered, "Didn't I tell you about that? No? Well, maybe I just wanted to forget that Bert Andrus and his way of singling out worthless characters to chum around with. Bert had been in Cheyenne maybe a week when Mr. Purcell sent me up to that hell-on-wheels cowtown with some legal papers. I met the kid on the street. He was riled up at first to see me, accused me of being in Cheyenne to spy on him for his mother." Kutcher clucked his tongue and added, "I wasn't no spy, but I hadn't talked to the kid five minutes when I wished Kate Andrus was in town to kick some sense into her kid. Bert had met up with Devlin and some other riffraff in a saloon. Somehow the kid hap-

114

pened to mention that a young fellow named Cardigan had been at Kate's Wagon. That name, Cardigan, brought about a curious change in Devlin. He let the Andrus kid win a couple of poker hands, bought some drinks, and even offered to finance a visit to Cheyenne's lousiest whorehouse. All Devlin asked for in return was all the information he could get about you Cardigans—plus the number and quality of any horses you might have."

"So Bert Andrus told where we live . . . what stock is about . . . the whole works," Redge commented angrily.

"That he did." Kutcher nodded. "But I managed it so he was also blabbing everything about Devlin and Slick to *me*. I think I knew what those thieving bastards were up to even before the stupid kid agreed to show the way down Crow Creek to this camp. They left Cheyenne kinda hurried and on the sly. That's why I had to skip my date with an honest-to-God dentist and traipse back here behind some outlaws."

The men were silent for a moment. Then Redge got quietly to his feet and strode toward the corral that held the hospital critters. Will sat somberly studying the sun now dropping with shafted glory toward the white and thrusting peaks off westward.

"I wonder why, when Devlin knows where we live—my boy and I—that he hasn't made that play of revenge he's nursed through the years," Will said.

"Likely there's two reasons," Kutcher replied. "Up to now the boss, Mr. Purcell, was at the Diamond-7. Devlin and the others weren't hankering for a second run-in with him. Then too, your boy and me poured a lot of bullets at them that night they were after your horses. It's possible they aren't entirely sure just how many guns they'd face if they came riding at this camp. I remember that the Andrus kid yelled out that he was sure a dozen homesteaders were shooting at him."

"But they'll come, Hank," Will Cardigan said, in a flat and determined tone.

"Yes, Cardigan, they'll come. Maybe tonight. Maybe six months from now. But they'll come calling on you. Murdock. Devlin. Slick. And maybe Bert Andrus."

After a long time, Cardigan asked softly, "What's your future now, Hank . . . with Mr. Purcell gone?" He groped for the right words, and added, "I'm sure Redge would be happy for you to throw in with us and build a herd. It would please me too."

"Thanks, Will," the cowhand said. "That's an offer I'd have been proud to accept, under other circumstances. But I'd best hang on at the Diamond-7, that's what Mr. Purcell would want. I'll ride back tomorrow, in time for the services."

"He was a big man, as big as the land he ranched," Cardigan said. Then he asked, "Who will take over the ranch now—as legal owner?"

Kutcher shook his head. "That's something that'll need looking into. He has a niece living back east, in Virginia, I believe." His tone suggested he had decided not to pursue the subject.

They sat for a while in the gathering darkness, needing no further words to anchor the bonds of understanding between them. Presently there was the whooshing sound of a night hawk's flight, the persistent call of a cricket, and the slamming of the barn door after Redge had finished his chores.

"I'll scrape together some sort of supper," Will said, and started into the cabin. "You bunk here tonight, Hank; we've plenty of blankets."

Kutcher's thanks were unspoken, but they shone from his face. "That boy of yours is a natural cowman," he said. "He'll make out. Someday, he'll make it big. He could be another Andy Purcell, you know . . ." His voice choked with emotion.

Will Cardigan turned impulsively, and grasped the old rider's hand. "Hank, if things come to the worst—and I'm not around—make sure my boy gets in touch with Emmett Willoughby—Willoughby of Arizona."

Chapter 11

After the short season of heavy rains, the days became much warmer. Soon the branches of cottonwoods and willows along Crow Creek formed a rim of green against the soft cloudless sky. Rose thickets became a riot of pink, and cast off a fragrance that carried on the breeze far onto the creek-bordering meadows. Grass became tall and plentiful, offering refuge for a dozen species of prairie birds and small animals.

By early summer, the creek had receded to the normal flow provided by the far-off mountain watershed. The hill-bordered basin, over which Redge had gazed when it became a lake of flood water, was now a dry and silted expanse. In all directions from the Cardigan camp, the rolling hills reached out verdantly green and rich with the natural high protein known as buffalo grass.

Ever since the day of Hank Kutcher's return to the Diamond-7 Ranch, Redge and his father had established a careful routine for their days. They were never out of calling distance of each other. They kept all livestock within a short ride of their camp, and now they went about their work and their leisure moments with loaded firearms, both revolvers and rifles, always within reach. Twice they saw a horseman pause on a distant hill to reconnoiter the camp and its surrounding acres, but they had no visitors.

Most of what had once been Redge's hospital stock had now recovered and was growing fat on the abundance of grass. The majority of the eighteen heifers had already calved, but there had been no word that Diamond-7 riders would arrive to reclaim the stock that Andy Purcell had put in Redge's care.

By mid-June, the Cardigans had a few new worries. No more rain had come; it appeared probable that this would be a summer of drought and searing heat. Watching the herd of heifers, now with fast-growing calves at their sides, Redge experienced a growing frustration. It was time that these young cows should be bred again. Many were coming into heat, and moving restlessly to greater distances across the grasslands.

There was a problem, too, of supplies. Items of clothing and of staple groceries were used up or running out. They must be replenished, even though it meant sparing a man from urgent ranch work. From day to day, they delayed making a trip to Kate's Wagon for the badly needed supplies. For either Will Cardigan or the boy to go would leave the other alone, and perhaps in danger. For both of them to go might well mean returning to a destroyed home and to empty livestock pens.

Perhaps, Redge hoped, Hank Kutcher might show up again, bound for a supply point, and they could ask him to fetch back the most desperately needed items.

On the last day of June, a real scorcher, Redge glanced out the window onto the small meadow downcreek from the cabin where the heifers usually bedded down during the night.

His eyes widened, then he let out a loud whistle of surprise. "Dad, take a look at this," he urged. "There's a bull—one damned big, beautiful, red bull—down there with the young cows. Maybe they'll be contented for one day."

"Some of them are apt to be contented for at least nine months," Will said and laughed.

"I'm going to sashay down there and see if the old boy is branded," Redge said.

With the wariness that had become part of their lives, Will Cardigan handed his son a loaded rifle. Then he cautioned, "You'd best ride a horse, son. That way, you can get closer before you spook the bull. Besides, if the old fellow gets on the prod, a horse can get you out of his way a lot quicker."

Redge threw a saddle on his mare and rode slowly away from the buildings. He could see his father standing in the cabin doorway with a rifle cradled in his arms. He was certain he would remain there, watchful, until his return. The sun had now climbed well above the eastern rim of hills and was causing the heat to intensify. Today the livestock would no doubt keep close along the cottonwood shaded areas and near to water.

The boy swung his head about, hoping for clouds that might build into an afternoon thunderstorm. The prairie grasses, which had grown rapidly after the early spring rain stood dry and sere. A breeze had sprung up from the northwest; likely it would strengthen to a hard wind before noon—a despised early-summer wind of drought. It would whip as a hot blast down the valley, swaying tree branches into wild gyrations and flattening the dry grass into a twisted mat.

Redge had only to ride within a hundred feet of the big red-and-white bull to confirm its ownership. On its left side, midway between front and rear flanks, was a brand, which the boy surmised to be at least two years old. It read ◊ 7. This had to be an animal that had wandered in from one of the ranch's grazing herds. It was apparently of good stock, and was healthy in appearance. If only this stray bull would remain for three or four weeks, most of the eighteen heifers would become with calf.

For nearly half an hour, he lingered in the shade close to the small herd. He remained mounted, but eased on his reins and allowed the horse to nibble at choice clumps of grass. Presently Redge was idly calculating how fast eighteen head of healthy heifers might become a sizable and profitable herd. Despite the sweeping wind, which sometimes blew steadily for many hours, these high plains of eastern Colorado provided almost ideal conditions for the growing of cattle. Only a winter blizzard, one that combined violent wind with deep snow, could prove an effective deterrent to producing good beef animals. If only there were some means whereby the Cardigan stock could be grazed over a wider area than the homestead offered.

Suddenly an alarmed yell from his father caused the boy to jerk about in his saddle. Will Cardigan was pointing out toward the west. In that same instant, Redge caught an acrid scent of smoke that now rode the air. He sat bolt upright. Along the valley's westward rim, and perhaps half a mile beyond the cabin, a far-spreading fringe of flames was topping the hills' crest. Then, driven by the wind, it began eating the dry grass in a downward-sloping course which would eventually lead to the camp . . . the stable . . . the corrals . . . and the cabin.

Redge spurred the mare into a run that brought him quickly back to the camp yard and to Will Cardigan's side.

"Prairie fire. With the buffalo grass dried out, and this wind, it'll be down here in a hurry."

Redge eyed the line of leaping flames that showered sparks into the hot air and formed a black cloud of wind-blown smoke. He could see the fire literally jumping ahead as wind-borne particles of flames were carried far in advance of the main wall of burning grass.

"We've got to stop it somehow!" the boy shouted. "Maybe we can hitch our work team to that old plow and—"

"We haven't time for that, Redge. Maybe when the fire hits the greener meadow grasses it'll be slowed."

Redge touched his heels to the mare, putting her into a gallop. Then he shouted back to Will, "Open the corral gates so my hospital cattle and the horses can get out. Get them across the creek. I'm gonna look for a ridge where we can slow this mess by backfiring." He headed his mount upstream, angling from it to gain higher ground and approach the menacing fire line. He was heedless of the alarmed, and then frightened, shouts with which his father sought to call him back.

Nor did he see Hank Kutcher, riding at top speed, break from a willow thicket a mile below the camp, spur his horse past the restlessly moving heifers and bull, and speed past Will Cardigan. "Get your guns and take cover, Cardigan," the old cowhand howled. "I'll go after the boy. Murdock and Devlin set that blaze."

Even as he heard Kutcher's words, Will felt a sickening pang of despair. Despite the careful planning he and Redge had done, and although they were constantly armed, their position was now critical—perhaps perilous. Rifle in hand, he ran to the corral, flung open the gate, and shouted and waved three head of crippled stock through it toward freedom. He quickly managed to untie two of their own horses and then slap them into a gallop that would take them across the creek.

He felt impelled to run in the direction Redge had taken toward the distant fire line—to get where he could use his rifle to protect the boy. He gave up the idea, knowing that Redge was already too far away. If harm should threaten the boy, it would have to be Hank Kutcher's job to help him. Will started toward the cabin for their

120

revolver and extra ammunition. He gathered the weapons from their wall pegs, and with deft fingers made sure that each was fully loaded.

Suddenly a calmness came upon him; his mind analyzed what was happening. Knowing we were prepared, Murdock and Devlin decided to burn us out instead of risking a ride-in against whoever might be here. But they've gained more than they probably hoped. The fire has split our defense . . . with Redge and me separated by maybe a mile.

Perhaps it was well the showdown had finally come. They could not have continued to live in a normal way knowing fury and fighting and hell would sooner or later have to be faced. In a methodical way, Cardigan strapped a revolver belt about him and slid his own weapon into the holster. He left the second loaded revolver on the cabin table, then picked up his rifle and stepped through the door and onto the small mud-stained platform that served as a porch.

He looked quickly about—and was horrified by what he saw. To the northwest, riding in from toward the dancing line of flames and the darkly swirling smoke, he could now see four horsemen. Two of them were strangers, and between them, as a captive on his own mount, rode Redge. The boy sat upright in the saddle. He looked angry, stubbornly defiant.

Will Cardigan's mind was suddenly extremely clear. He saw everything as though in a gigantic pattern with the pieces all set together. They were approaching the cabin with his son as a prisoner. Off to the side a few rods, Hank Kutcher was riding by himself. For an instant Will Cardigan's gaze went beyond the riders, and searched the distant line of prairie fire. There had been a slight change of the wind to the west. Should it continue, the flames' progress might move more directly eastward toward Crow Creek. Possibly the camp buildings might be spared.

A sort of sixth sense caused Will Cardigan to swing about and stare downcreek. It was then he realized the full hopelessness of Redge's situation—and of his own. Six more riders were approaching. Moving at an unhurried pace, they seemed to be timing themselves to reach the Cardigan camp at the same time those guarding Redge would come into the yard. Even before he could discern forms and faces with certainty, Will knew beyond doubt who two of

121

the horsemen would be. He would soon be face to face with Stacy Murdock and Hollis Devlin.

Will knew that he could speedily knock two or more of the riders from their saddles with his rifle, send bullets tearing through those who were riding toward him in brazen and seemingly fearless fashion. But if I do, he thought, they can take vengeance upon my boy. They know that I won't shoot. I can't.

He stood motionless and watchful against the cabin wall. The stifling heat of the day, and the heavy smell of grass smoke, pressed in upon him. The rifle lay across his arm in a manner that would allow him to ready it for instant use. He made sure too that the handgun could easily be drawn from the holster at his thigh. Then abruptly the yard filled with unsmiling men and restlessly moving horses. Will Cardigan glanced at them, then for an instant looked upstream. He was almost sure now that the fire would move due eastward, burning itself out after reaching the barrier formed by the damper grasses and the waters of Crow Creek. But, there would be no diverting the havoc sure to be wrought by this overpowering number of men that Murdock had brought upon the Cardigans.

Murdock and the two men flanking him reined their horses to a halt fifty feet from the cabin. Coming in from the opposite direction, two strangers, astride sweating horses, led Redge to a spot where he would be facing Murdock and his riders. Will could see that the boy's hands had been drawn behind him and tied; he could also see the anger and desperation with which Redge was staring at his enemies. Hank Kutcher had ridden in too, keeping a dozen yards distant. For a moment Will Cardigan was perplexed by Kutcher's seeming acquiescence to what was happening. Would the old ranch hand's sympathy lie with the Diamond-7 gang in this showdown? The thought quickly vanished. Had it not been Kutcher who had ridden in only minutes before with a warning? Apparently there had been no action against Kutcher during Redge's capture. But against such odds, even the tough old ranch hand would have to wait for the right moment—for an opportunity.

Stacy Murdock broke the tense silence with a chuckle, then with words that sounded almost sociable. He glanced toward his older companion, who had reined close on his left side. "Hollis, it was almost too easy. Here we sit with both the old man and his cub rounded up without a struggle or a shot."

With his mind tense as a steel spring, Will Cardigan ran his gaze over this man with a crooked and stiffly extended arm. Changes, wrought by time and suffering and the outlaw trail, had come upon Devlin since their last meeting. That long-ago night, on the riverboat, the man had stood tall, like a proud and ruthless Slavic prince. Now, Devlin was seated uncomfortably in a saddle that seemed to scarcely provide room for his protruding belly. His voice, when he answered Murdock's gloating words, came in a tone and cadence distorted by long-pent-up hatred.

"Do as you want with the kid, Stacy," he said. "Just so you leave the old bastard for me. I've waited a heap too long already."

Murdock swung about to look directly at Redge, then said, "Kid, we're here to straighten out a few things. One of them being to drive home that bull you stole from the Diamond-7."

Perhaps five seconds passed as Redge's mind caught the full impact of Murdock's accusing words. Then in a voice no louder than Murdock's he answered, "Murdock, you're a two-bit, lying spawn of a whore and a coward." The boy threw himself from the saddle, jerking desperately to free his hands. His mare, frightened by the actions, spun about, seeking to free herself of the bridle reins clutched by a dour-faced rider to her left.

Then instantly, the unexpected happened. Redge, moving away from his prancing mare, struggled toward his father's side. He was within a dozen feet of the cabin porch when there was movement by the rider seated at Murdock's right. Murdock gave a quick command: "Not now . . . don't. Damn it, Slick!"

Murdock's rough words went unheeded. The rider called Slick got his six-gun free of its holster—but never raised it. Will, sensing that the rider's bullet was meant for Redge, lined his rifle by slight movement and fired without raising the weapon. The heavy slug caught Slick in the chest, tearing a hole through his lung and blasting him backward off his saddle.

An enraged yell broke from Hollis Devlin, and he tugged his gun free. There was a melee of frightened, plunging horses, as Devlin sought to take aim. He finally got the shot off, only to have it thud into the cabin wall. Another shot was fired off as Stacy Murdock took calculated aim. Will Cardigan was slammed against the wall by its force. Then he doubled up and slid lifeless from the porch.

Redge dropped to his knees at his father's side. Devlin's wildly furious words sounded across the yard. "Damn it, Murdock. You stole that shot from me . . . killed the bastard after I'd waited . . ." The words broke off as he fought to control his fear-crazed horse. Then Devlin managed to yank the animal about and try for a second aim, this time at the kneeling, dazed boy.

A clear and cold voice, sounding above the confusion, caused Hollis Devlin to falter. From the spot where he had been silently watching, Hank Kutcher had spurred close to the red-faced, breathless Devlin.

"Put that gun down, Devlin," Kutcher commanded. "Just one shot at that lad and whoever fires it is a dead man."

Despite the warning, Devlin might have gotten off a shot, had not Stacy Murdock prevented it, as he reached out and grasped Devlin's arm. "Leave the kid be," he growled. "We don't shoot babies on the Diamond-7. Besides, I've got something better in mind for him." Murdock then turned angrily toward Hank Kutcher. "You meddling old fool," he snarled. "Someday I'm going to drill daylight through you."

Hank Kutcher swung his gaze about the circle of horsemen. For a little while his eyes, laden with contempt, were upon Hollis Devlin. Then, seeming to dismiss Devlin as of no consequence, he rode close to Stacy Murdock, their faces a scant yard apart. "So someday you're going to drill me, Stacy. Just remember. That same day a certain letter will be mailed—and you'll be preparing for a date with the hangman down at Canyon City." Kutcher swung slowly down from his horse. As he moved toward Redge, his mutter of scorn was clearly heard across the yard: "Someday you'll shoot me, eh? Stacy, put that threat in one hand . . . and shit in the other. See which fills up first."

He came quickly alongside Will Cardigan's sprawled form. Then he swept his battered hat from his head. With gentle care, he laid it across Cardigan's face, to hide the line of blood that had trickled a staining path into the grass.

A few seconds passed, then Kutcher extended his arms to Redge, who was still kneeling beside his father, white-faced and vacant-eyed. Presently the old cowhand's weathered but agile fingers began working at the knotted rope binding the boy's arms. Already a few of Murdock's riders were moving their horses farther from the spot, as though impatient to be away from the dead man, the boy, and the scene of what they had allowed to happen.

Murdock snarled at Kutcher with rage and resentment. "Leave him tied," he commanded, then turned to riders close at hand. "I want that interfering old homestead lover watched. If he tries anything, knock him cold." He turned toward Kutcher. "I'm not going to shoot you. We'll just make damn sure you watch. I've an idea you'll wish to Christ you were dead." He flung an arm in impatient signal, and added, "Let's get on with it."

Suddenly there were half a dozen Diamond-7 riders crowding their horses about Redge and his old friend. The moment of possibility for Kutcher to draw his gun was gone. Then Redge was half led and half dragged from the porch and Hank was firmly held by several brutal men.

Murdock pointed toward the Cardigan lumber wagon that stood alongside the stable. "Get him over there. Spread-eagle him on the wheel." As he spoke, the Diamond-7 range boss reached to the side of his saddle to untie a long leather whip.

On his way to the wagon, they led Redge Cardigan within arm's length of Murdock. For a moment the boy stood still in his tracks. As he peered into Murdock's face, there was no trace of shock or grief. He spoke in a level voice and his eyes were twin glints of ice. He nodded at the whip. "Stacy, you'd better put me out of the way for good with that. I'll be remembering every touch—when I look you up to kill you—within a year."

They tore his shirt off him and bound his wrists to the top of the tall wagon wheel, with his belly to the spokes and his bared back to the torrid sun.

Hollis Devlin thrust forward. "Let me handle that bull-whip, Murdock," he insisted.

"The hell with you." Murdock pushed him aside. "This smart-assed kid needs something to always remind him of

125

the Diamond-7. I'll give our brand to him neat as if I'd done it with a running iron."

His words, and his vengeful grasp of the whip's butt, caused Hank Kutcher to try to wrest himself free, but rough hands held him powerless.

Then there was the arcing anger of the lash. With its first slashing descent, a streak of dotted red and white appeared on the boy's naked back. He gasped, then stiffened in anticipation of the next blow. It came, leaving a second streak. Then there was a third . . . and a fourth. The streaks had joined now, to form a diamond that was already marked by raw flesh and oozing blood.

Suddenly Redge's knees buckled, giving way. He hung unconscious from the wheel.

The sight brought a grin to Stacy Murdock's face, as he stood with his legs spread in the hot yard and flicked the slender lash of the whip behind him. "Now for an artistic 7 to finish the job."

One of the riders, a squat and powerfully built man, walked over to Murdock and grasped his arm. "There'll be no 7, Stacy. You could kill the boy."

Murdock flung the whip into the grass. "Maybe you're right." He wiped sweat from his neck, then added, "I want that kid to remember. No one tampers with the range and the critters where I'm boss."

Hank Kutcher's guards had again let go of him. Now he dodged them and strode forward to eye the ranch boss. "Stacy," he said softly, "I'm glad you did that—lashed the lad."

Murdock looked surprised, but his expression vanished as Kutcher continued, "Stacy, you poor, stupid fool. You just signed your death warrant." He paused to jerk a disparaging thumb toward Hollis Devlin, then added, "And his too."

"So we're supposed to tremble because of an insolent kid?"

"No, Stacy," Kutcher said slowly. "Likely you don't have to fear the kid. But if I was either you, or that crooked-armed horse thief you've palled up with, I'd thank God and his angels for every sunrise I would live to see. There won't be many of them for you now. From this hour—from the minute you killed Will Cardigan—you've been doomed. *Both of you are looking straight down the barrels of the guns of Willoughby."*

There was a stunned and awful silence across the camp yard. For a second or so, it seemed that Stacy Murdock would strike Kutcher. Then he picked up the whip and slowly began rolling it. Hollis Devlin stared unbelievingly at Kutcher. He cursed violently, attempting to hide the fear that had come to linger in his eyes.

No one moved a hand toward him, or uttered protest, as Kutcher strode to the wagon wheel, dug out a knife, and cut the ropes from Redge's wrists. He eased the boy onto the ground and into a spot of shade, then he glared at those ringed about.

"Why don't you sons of bitches get on your way? You've done your killing . . . and likely you're right proud. I'll take care of the lad and bury a better man than any of you."

Stacy Murdock gestured toward Redge's unmoving form. "You can get him out of here now, if you're set on it. Don't bother to slink back to the ranch; you don't ride for the Diamond-7 anymore."

A strange smile spread across Hank Kutcher's face. "I couldn't take the stink of what you've done to Mr. Purcell's place by hiring the scum of the earth since his niece made you manager, Murdock. Now suppose you ride the hell 'n' gone out of here."

Murdock stepped closer, thrusting out his chin in a belligerent manner. "Here's something to chew on, Hank. Before we ride out of here, we're going to burn these sorry shacks to the ground. And we'll be driving all the stock ahead of us."

Hank Kutcher faced the younger man stolidly. Some of the onlookers moved hastily aside, for the old ranch hand's posture was suddenly that of the ready gunman. "Stacy," he said with finality, "I can't keep you from touching a match to Cardigan camp. But get this straight. There are things here belonging to me—and you'd better not touch them. Inside, there's a box with some veterinary tools. They're mine. Just like those eighteen heifers I bought from Andy Purcell, and have a bill of sale for them stashed away."

"Someday, Kutcher . . ." Stacy Murdock muttered.

127

"Hell, Stacy! Why someday? How about making your move right now?"

Redness surged across Stacy Murdock's face. The cords of his arms stood out, as did the white knuckles of his clutched fists.

"Get the damned kid and the heifers off my graze before sunup. We'll be back tomorrow to set another blaze."

Kutcher's loud and raucous laughter sounded in the air. Then he asked, "Your graze, your ranch, your Diamond-7, Stacy? Don't you wish it was?"

Chapter 12

The band of Diamond-7 riders turned their horses downstream and left the Cardigan camp. There were somber faces among them, men just now realizing the futility of what they had allowed Murdock and Devlin to do. Hank Kutcher stood and watched until the last rider had disappeared beyond the screening willows. Word of this fracas would spread, for news travels on a speedy mount across the grasslands. For more than twenty years, Andy Purcell's ranch had been one of pride and honor and big-hearted hospitality. Had this morning's harsh and vengeful acts brought an era of esteem to a close for the powerful Diamond-7? Kutcher shook his head sadly, sensing that it had.

He shrugged the premonition aside and turned quickly to the urgent tasks to be done. Redge still lay, face down, in the shade. He was beginning to stir a little, and was moaning softly. Kutcher found a bucket, filled it full of creek water, and began dipping cool handfuls onto the boy's forehead. Presently, Redge's eyelids lifted, and he stared at Kutcher with returning realization.

"Hank," the boy muttered in a lifeless way, "my dad is dead. They killed my dad." He struggled to sit up, but Kutcher pushed him firmly back on the grass. "Lie still, lad. They're gone. If there's some salve about, I'm going to get some of the sting out of your back."

Redge's gaze traveled across the yard and rested for a long while on his father's body. He was quiet for a while, seeking to quell the tumult of his thoughts. He watched Kutcher enter the cabin and then return with clean cloths and a medicine jar. Then he said, with the first hint of acceptance in his voice, "My dad would have wanted to be buried close by, Hank. Up the creek a way, there's a slope, with some young cottonwoods and wild-rose bushes. Dad can rest—" His voice broke, and abruptly Redge Cardigan, with his face buried in his hands, was sobbing out his loneliness and his anguish.

Hours later, in the cool of sunset, a breeze stirred in from the distant peaks. They left Crow Creek Valley with the few head of Cardigan horses and Kutcher's saddle mount and headed toward the east. When they came to the crest of the hill sloping up from the tree-fringed creek, Redge halted his horse and turned to look back. "This is about where we stopped, my dad and I, when we saw the valley for the first time. It was my idea to settle down here and build." A slight shudder passed over the boy. "And tomorrow they'll burn every stick—and every hope."

Kutcher swept sharply appraising eyes over the boy. Then he slapped Redge's horse into motion. "Let's be getting on. Redge, you've got a fever setting in. I'm taking you to Kate's Wagon just as fast as we can make it."

The hours went by as they kept up a steady pace across the grasslands. There were few words spoken, and Redge sat huddled in his saddle with a heavy coat about him. Kutcher took the lead, finding his course by memory, and with the aid of a star cluster that held steady in the northeast sky. A very different sort of journey from the one the two men had taken to Kate's Wagon only a few months before.

They paused about midway of their trip for Kutcher to examine and tighten the ropes holding a pack of possessions from the Cardigan cabin. It consisted of necessities, the veterinary kit, and a few family papers and photos. Kutcher eyed the pack pensively. How little they had been able to salvage. How little there remained to show of the brave attempt of a father and son to establish a means of security, a means of livelihood, and a homeplace.

Redge had insisted they take the filing papers by which Will Cardigan had laid claim to certain sections of the Diamond-7 cattle range. Now Will Cardigan lay buried on a grassy Crow Creek slope, and his badly beaten son was forced to flee. Only time would reveal the result of the Cardigans' legal claim to land.

Of more immediate importance was a slip of torn cardboard, also resting safely within the pack. Will Cardigan had never made but one request of Kutcher: *Hank, if things come to the worst—and I'm not around—make sure my boy gets in touch with Emmett Willoughby—Willoughby of Arizona.*

And now the torn half of a playing card, a ten of diamonds, would be called upon to fulfill its mission. Kutcher let his hand move over the roped pack until it searched out the square firmness of the veterinary-instrument case from which the ripped card had not been removed. It had been the first item that Hank Kutcher had carefully packed before their trip from Cardigan Camp began.

Dawn was beginning to flame the east, and they were within five miles of the valley where Kate's Wagon nestled, when Redge sat suddenly erect and listening. There was a silence in which he drew his horse to a halt, then waited momentarily in expectant silence. The sound came again—the far-off and anxious bawling of a range cow.

The boy started to dismount, but Kutcher threw a restraining arm about him. "Easy, lad, it's only a cow that's got separated from her calf."

"It's one of the heifers. One of Mr. Purcell's heifers. I've got to help her."

The manner of Redge's speech caused Kutcher to look into the boy's face. Even by starglow his sweaty forehead and uncertain gaze were easily discernible. Redge Cardigan would soon be delirious. Kutcher abruptly pulled Redge's bridle reins from his hands, and arranged them for leading the boy's horse. Then he crisply yelled the string of animals into a fast pace. The sun had barely topped a ridge to the east when they drew up before the store and living quarters of Kate Andrus. Hank Kutcher cut loose with a loud and urgent yell; then he dropped to the ground and carefully pulled the swaying and vacant-eyed boy from his saddle.

Forty hours later, Redge awakened to rational thought, and to an itching that made him want to claw off the bandages across his back. He rolled over and opened his eyes. The room spun about him. He closed his eyes again and dozed off. When he awakened, the spinning had stopped. A coal-oil lamp was burning on a table beside the bed, and someone was standing in the door. His eyes focused into a stare, then a sort of grin tugged at his mouth. Very deliberately, he lifted his hand from the patchwork quilt with which he was covered. Mimicking the gesture that his memory had held for months, he thumbed his nose at the pig-tailed, solemn-eyed girl about to enter the room.

She took two steps toward him, then halted. Redge became aware of the coppery glow of her hair, and of two large tears coursing down her cheeks. When it seemed that she was about to turn and flee, the boy spoke, his voice cracked and weak.

"Hello, Audrey. Going to give me some more pointers on feeding chickens?"

She used a trembling fist to dash away the tears, then said, with feigned scorn, "Too late for that, silly. It's after nine o'clock."

Surprise mounted on Redge's face, and he struggled to rise to his elbow. The movement caused the quilt and sheet to slip from his shoulders; for a moment his back, and the expanse of bandages, lay revealed. "You mean," he demanded, "I've been asleep all day?"

"You've been here almost two days," she answered. Abruptly her eyes became wide and horrified as the full significance of the cotton dressings grew upon her. Her face whitened. "What have they done?" she murmured. "Oh, God, what have they done?"

Fifteen minutes later, Kate Andrus, with Hank Kutcher close behind her, came to check on Redge's condition. They found him asleep, with the traces of his agony beginning to vanish from his face. His hand lay upon the color-splashed quilt, clutched by a girl—a girl who, for the first time in her life, had no lively comment with which to greet them.

Two days later, Kate Andrus removed the bandages for the last time. Where those of the past several days had been bloody messes, they now carried but a few brownish stains and no sign of infection. Kate assured Redge that tomorrow, if the fever continued to clear, he could be up and about. She did not mention the obvious—that he would carry a huge, diamond-shaped scar for the rest of his life.

Three more days passed, and Redge's healing progressed splendidly. He was soon on his feet, and began spending much of his time in Kate Andrus's trading post. The variety of goods sold, and the manner of payment, amazed him. The customers, coming to Kate's Wagon from the far reaches of the grasslands, bought in quantities meant to last for several months. Sometimes, furs and cowhides were hauled in to be bartered for such items as canned tomatoes, sugar, coffee, work boots, harness straps, plug tobacco, and liniment. The larger outfits maintained charge accounts, to be settled upon payment of cattle or horses. When cash payment was made, it was almost always in gold or silver coins.

During the busy hours, Redge found ways to help in the store, hoping to repay Kate Andrus for the hours that had been devoted to his care. He tackled harder jobs, although sometimes the lifting of sacks and boxes and crates caused jabs of pain across his tender back.

Usually the talk at the store was of back-east happenings. There was also lively discussion of the Klondike gold rush, and of ships putting in at San Francisco with hundreds of thousands of dollars in gold. There was always talk of the weather and of cattle-market conditions.

Among those who visited Kate's Wagon during July, there were those who looked at Redge with open curiosity. It was widely known that the Cardigans had been cleared out of Crow Creek Valley. On two occasions men rode in from the range astride horses carrying the Diamond-7 brand. Redge studied them as he went about his work, but he could not identify them as members of the Murdock-Devlin raiders. They bought a variety of small items, picked up some mail, and immediately left the trading post. Redge suspected they had been sent primarily to find out his whereabouts and just how well he had recovered.

Hank Kutcher had ridden out of Kate's Wagon the day after Redge was allowed out of bed. He crisply informed the boy that there was a matter needing his attention, saying, "You're on the mend, lad. It's time I get a few things straightened out. Don't worry about your horses; they're pastured with Kate's stock, and will be safe."

The old cowman also handed Redge an awkwardly wrapped square package. "Son, here's your veterinary-tool box. I figured you would want . . ."

Redge was eying the package in an eager and joyous way, and interrupted, "Hank . . . thank you." He tucked the box under his arm, and added, "There's something else in this box too, Hank. It's just an old and torn playing card . . . but my dad . . ."

Kutcher nodded his understanding. "Yes, son. Will . . . your father . . . told me about it, what it is and where it should go."

"It's about time I deliver that card," Redge replied. "It's a long way to Arizona, to wherever I'll find Emmett Willoughby."

The old ranch hand pressed the boy's hand for a long time, then simply said, "Son, if you're gone when I get back here to Kate's Wagon, take care of yourself. I ain't gonna say goodbye, Redge. I've got a feeling you'll be riding back into Cardigan Camp one of these days."

On an evening in late July, Redge sought out Kate Andrus during an evening lull in the store business. She was seated at a rolltop desk between the partitioned-off post office and a rack holding half a dozen new saddles.

"Kate," he asked, "can you spare a few minutes?"

She looked up, smiled, and waved him to a chair. Kate Andrus's level and penetrating gaze spoke of the determination, and the shrewd business ability that had held the trading post together through the years since her husband's death. She was of medium build with auburn hair streaked with gray, which she coiled in a no-nonsense way about her head.

In the evening light splashing through the window, Redge noticed deep etchings of weariness on her face. "Kate, you're tired," he blurted out. "All of this store work, and taking care of me. You lost a lot of sleep."

"I don't require much," she answered. "And you have helped me out so much lately."

"I guess some chores have agreed with me, Kate. I feel strong now. Ready to be on my way . . . thanks to your care and hefty meals."

"What are your plans, Redge?" she asked quickly.

"Right now, Kate, all the plan I've got is to get to Arizona." He stared out the window, seeing the westward prairie, beyond which was Crow Creek. Then he went on, in a choked voice, "An old friend of my dad's is somewhere in Arizona. Once my dad told me that if anything should happen to him I should look up his friend. His name is Emmett Willoughby."

"I have heard of him," Kate Andrus answered in a noncommittal way, and sat as though searching for words. When she spoke again, her voice was filled with concern.

"Redge, can you put Arizona off for a few weeks?"

"Why, Kate? I've been a burden on you too long as it is."

She reached out and placed a firm hand on his knee. "Nonsense, Redge. Anyone who works like you do is never a burden. Besides . . . besides, I . . . I need you. Redge, I haven't even told Audrey this yet. The last time I was in Cheyenne I went to a doctor. He said I have to have an operation." She grinned reassuringly at Redge's troubled face. "Oh, don't look so stricken. It's not that serious. But the sooner the better. So, now you know. I need someone to watch after the store. It can't be my kids. Audrey is too young. And . . . and my son, Bert—but I've an idea Hank Kutcher has told you about Bert—is never around when I need him."

For a couple of seconds, Redge wondered if this woman, who had taken him in, and cared for him, knew or suspected that her son had ridden with raiders against the Cardigans.

"Kate, get yourself up to Cheyenne. Then get well," he said. "I'll be here every day until you're back and healthy." Redge paused, smiled at her, and added, "But I'm just a kid too . . . not all that much older than Audrey."

Kate Andrus rose, then looked down to study him. "Just the same, I'll rest better knowing you're watching after things."

She turned to meet the dust-caked rider who had entered the store. Redge walked outside and stood leaning against the hitch rail. He was studying the dust of the roadway, then kicking stray pebbles with a scuffed boot. Surely his father would have urged his son to help friends in need, even though it meant delay in getting a ripped ten of diamonds to Arizona.

He paused, looked up, and stopped beside the hitch rail, and the girl sitting angrily upon it. With a gesture that carried both disdain and dismissal, she tossed coppery strands of hair behind her. Her eyes were large and remote and troubled. At last she spoke.

"Go ahead. Pack your belongings. Then you'll ride away again. Only this time it's likely you won't come back here to Kate's Wagon."

Redge drew nearer and hoisted himself onto the hitching rail to sit beside her. "Now, Miss Andrus," he said in perplexity, "suppose you tell me just what you're talking about."

"You know what," she flared. "You're about well, and now you have been talking to Kate. And there's a map in your room; it is marked with a red trail all the way to Arizona." She paused, then beat helplessly on the hitch rail with her fist. "So . . . ride off again, you . . . you big nincompoop. See if I care!"

"Audrey, whoa up. Listen." Redge lifted a hand in protest. "Look . . . I'm not going anywhere. Not yet. Your mom wants me to sort of help her hired people look after the store while she's in Cheyenne."

"I know. I'm going with her. She'll need me," the girl answered anxiously.

"Of course, Audrey." He placed his hands on his hips and grinned at her insolently. "You know what?" he asked. "Every morning I'll be telling myself how great Kate's Wagon is without that daggoned kid around." He waited a few seconds, then added, "But then I'll turn around and tell myself how much I miss you, Audrey."

He peered at her expectantly, sure that his jest would rouse her instant wrath. Instead, she leaned toward him, tilted her face, and almost let her lips touch his cheek. In a practically inaudible voice, she echoed, "I'll miss you too." A moment passed. Then she straightened and glared at Redge with the scorn that only someone going on fifteen can muster.

"You're still a sorry sort of person," she declared. "But maybe while I'm gone you'll learn to gather eggs, and to stop fumbling when you sack dried apples."

With both Kate Andrus and her impetuous daughter away from the trading post, the routine at Kate's Wagon became one of work and wait. It seemed odd and dull for an entire day to pass without either Kate's bustling about or the laugh-provoking antics of the girl whom Redge had once called Carrot Top.

Weeks passed, and it became apparent that the doctor in Cheyenne had been overly optimistic about the date of Kate's return home. August passed, and then September. Frost touched the grasslands, and lent hues of saffron and gold to the cottonwood trees about the tiny, isolated hamlet. October came in with a light snowfall; it mantled the ground with an inch of white, but it took only one day of warm sunshine to cause it to vanish. Suddenly the haze of Indian summer settled on those serene days. Yet the chilliness of the nights foretold bitter, snowbound days ahead.

It was on a day of blue sky and autumn smoke that Kate Andrus came back to her trading post. The caravan crested a northern ridge just after the noon hour, and moved toward the cluster of clapboard buildings. Redge was surrounded by the store help and a couple of customers as he stood on the porch and watched the rigs approach. There were two heavily laden wagons, each drawn by two spans of mules. Behind these freighting outfits, keeping well back to avoid the dust plumes stirred up by wagon wheels, came a sumptuous carriage unlike anything Redge had ever seen. It was black and polished and tassle-topped, and drawn by a pair of sleek white mules.

The carriage drew steadily closer, and Redge peered at those seated inside. Two men, both in ranch garb, were up front. Kate Andrus was sitting alone in back. No mischievous-eyed, coppery-haired girl sat beside her. Audrey had not come home.

The cumbersome freight wagons rattled by the store and drew up in front of a storage shed at the rear. Then, moments later, the carriage driver maneuvered his mules to a spot where Kate Andrus could easily step down to the store porch.

Redge waited for others to greet her first, giving way to those who had worked for her a long time. At last, he moved forward to take her hand, and a long glance at her face reassured him. She had regained much of the healthy, glowing appearance she had had when they had first met, months before. He stared again at the vacant seat, upset and frustrated.

Kate seemed to read his mind and said immediately, "Audrey is in school now—in Denver."

"Kate," he answered in a subdued tone, "you always surprise me. But you sure look in top shape."

"I'm pretty chipper for an old gal," she assured him, and gave him an unabashed and hearty hug.

137

Redge eyed the mules and the expensive rig. "Well, Kate, you really rode home in style."

She waved a hand toward the two men who were climbing down from the front seat and explained, "These are the Farnum brothers from Kimball, Nebraska, up on the Union Pacific Ralroad. They deal in livestock and vehicles, and they insisted that I ride home in this luxurious chariot. Likely they'll try to sell it to me."

Minutes later, Redge left the porch, aware of a sudden need to be alone. Kate had returned. Likely she could now take over the business of the trading post, and would not need him. It would be best, he thought, to leave Kate's Wagon quickly. Without the enlivening laughter and insults of a freckled girl, loneliness would creep upon him. That dratted kid sure got under my skin, he mused, realizing how much he had looked forward to her return.

His mood grew somber, and he thought, as he often had in the past months, of Cardigan Camp. What would likely be there now? Cottonwoods yielding their sere leaves to the wind. The ashes of a stable and a cabin. And the quiet grave of his father, marked only by the rough stone he had placed there instead of a headstone.

No doubt there were cattle grazing the meadows of Crow Creek and the slopes above. Cattle bearing the brand of the Diamond-7 Ranch. And what of the eighteen heifers? Had they been driven back toward the ranch headquarters, to mingle with the Diamond-7 herds?

Many weeks had passed since Redge had last seen his old friend Hank Kutcher. Could it be that the ranch hand had managed to thwart Stacy Murdock and to hang onto his job? Or had he left for good, seeking work on some cattle outfit in Wyoming or Montana or Texas?

Suddenly Redge realized he had to do what his father had urged—make the trip to Arizona, and place in the hands of Emmett Willoughby half of a torn ten of diamonds. The time had come to ride out of Kate's Wagon. His days here had brought strength and health. He was ready.

An hour after supper, he found Kate at her desk in the store and asked if he might speak with her. He pulled up a chair and sat facing her. "Kate," he said firmly, "it's time for me to be on my way . . . to take care of this Arizona matter."

She tapped a pencil against her chin and looked at him thoughtfully. "Thank you for helping me out, Redge. I could use you permanently, you know."

He grinned at her and said, "Maybe I'll come moseying back, come green-grass time."

Kate chuckled aloud and said teasingly, "You mean about the time school is out in Denver."

Her remark caused him to redden, but then he became very businesslike. "Kate, there's something I need to discuss," he hurriedly changed the subject. "I have two saddle horses and a work team . . . and owe you for their pasture."

"Nonsense, Redge, you don't owe me one cent. But I would like to keep the work team here and use them."

"I hoped you'd say that."

"Well, it makes more sense having a good work team about than giving those Farnum brothers a hefty price for two white mules and a fringed carriage that I've no damn use for."

Redge nodded agreement, then seemed at a loss for words. Finally, he blurted out, in a frantic way, "About my two saddle horses. I'll need one for getting on my way. And . . . and, Kate, I want Audrey to have the other one."

"She'd love that, Redge . . . and she'll be too proud for me to live with." Kate Andrus turned, spun the dial of a huge old safe, and removed a leather pouch. Then she placed five gold coins in his hand.

"What's this for?" Redge demanded.

"Your wages for the weeks you put in keeping this shebang of mine operating." When she sensed his reluctance to take the money, she said with finality, "You earned every penny, and down in Arizona, among strangers, you'll need it."

"Kate," the boy said in a stunned but thankful way, "it seems you're always about when I need help . . . I'll be riding out come sunup." He was silent awhile, then added, "I sure wish I could have seen Hank Kutcher again, or found out what he's up to these days."

Surprise came to Kate Andrus's face. "Why, Redge, don't you know?"

"Not a single thing, Kate. Old Hank just rode off . . . and the prairie swallowed him."

"Not quite. He left here in a hurry just as soon as I could assure him you'd get well. After all, he had to find a place to pasture a bunch of heifers . . . eighteen of them, I think."

Incredulity marked Redge Cardigan's face. You mean that the Diamond-7 Ranch—and Stacy Murdock—let old Hank drive off those heifers I had been tending for Mr. Purcell?"

Kate Andrus leaned back in her chair and nodded. "There wasn't one blasted thing Stacy Murdock or anyone else could do, Redge. Hank Kutcher had a bill of sale in his pocket for those heifers. So he herded them off the Diamond-7 range, taking time enough to allow a range bull to service most of the heifers. Kutcher found a job working on another ranch, far south of the Diamond-7, where they were delighted to have him, and to let him turn those heifers loose. His new place is down along the South Platte River—one of the John Iliff properties, but now it's owned and operated by a man named Jeff Masters."

Redge's eyes were bright as he exclaimed, "So old Kutcher is gonna have a cow herd of his own."

Kate Andrus shook her head. "No, now, I didn't say that. Kutcher has the bill of sale to the heifers . . . a bill of sale signed by Andrew Purcell transferring the heifers' ownership to someone named Redge Cardigan!"

Chapter 13

It was a briskly cool morning when Redge started, with mellow sunlight that fanned out across the grasslands. Far ahead of him, he could discern the white, upward-thrust peaks gleaming in the sunshine. The Cardigan Camp was so close it was tempting to ride in that direction, but he curbed his nostalgic longing and veered sharply to the north. Prudence warned him not to allow himself to be caught riding, alone and unarmed, on the reaches of the Diamond-7 domain. He allowed his horse to choose a gait that could be held for the long hours ahead so that he could cover many miles before evening. Redge's thoughts reverted time and again to what Kate Andrus had told him about Hank Kutcher. Could it really be true that Andy Purcell had signed a bill of sale giving Redge ownership of the eighteen heifers before his death? If it was, something unusual must have happened, and Kutcher somehow must have had a hand in it.

The thought led Redge to ponder, for a long time, the strange relationship between Hank Kutcher and Stacy Murdock. As he rode on, the boy recalled the day on which Stacy Murdock had come upon Kutcher and Redge as they hauled poles from the mountains for building the camp on Crow Creek. He recalled Murdock's threat: *Kutcher, someday I'm going to have my bellyful of you. Then—"*

And the scornful answer of the old cowhand: *Forget it, Stacy. You'll never cut down on me with fists, let alone a six-gun. And you know why!*

Redge remembered too, that in the terrible hour before his father's death, that Stacy Murdock and his riders had made no move of any kind against Hank Kutcher.

Redge shook his head and muttered aloud, "It's a mystery, too deep for me."

Throughout his ride from Kate's Wagon, the sawtoothed

ranges of mountains off westward seemed to rise steadily higher, as the miles to them decreased. Toward evening, Redge crested a prairie knoll and drew his horse to a halt. He held to the line of telegraph poles and the two steel rails that Kutcher had long ago told him formed the Denver and Pacific Railroad, linking Denver to Cheyenne.

Redge coaxed his horse acoss the rails and wooden ties. He reasoned that by now he was well off the Diamond-7 holdings, and could turn his course south toward Denver in the direction of the more settled farming area.

He rode for half an hour, as the air became chilly and the sun dropped behind the barrier of peaks. After a time, he came to a dry creek, with bordering trees and intermittent waterholes. He looked carefully about before dismounting. It was time to picket his horse and set up his first trail camp.

Toward noon of the next day, Redge, moving ever southward, rode down the long north slope of what he surmised was the valley of a stream flowing from the mountains. The stream was shallow with the barrenness of autumn, and he forded it with ease. Then he reined his mount to a halt and allowed the animal to munch at the streamside grass. Redge had to admit that he too was hungry. Kate Andrus had supplied him with sandwiches, but he had eaten the last one at midmorning.

He gazed up and down the creek, wondering if there might be a pool containing a trout he might try to bring to shore. He paused, then sat upright when he caught sight of a log cabin, a fenced yard, and just beyond, the figure of a man working with a team of horses about half a mile to the east.

Redge rode downstream, skirted the buildings, and approached the stranger. He kept a slow enough pace to allow the man to look him over.

Finally, the man motioned him closer. As he drew near, Redge could see that the stranger's team was hitched to a V-shaped device with which he was trenching out a ditch which would lead from the stream onto a flat expanse of plowed ground. After studying the boy for a time, the stranger, a bearded, middle-aged man, said, "Light down a spell, lad." He wrapped his reins about the plow handle and squatted close to the stream.

"Thanks, mister," Redge answered and swung from the

saddle. "I was wondering if there's a place about where I might buy something to eat."

"Which way are you headed, boy?" the bearded man asked.

"South," Redge answered, and included a lot of territory in the direction of his hand's sweep.

The stranger shook his head, then said slowly, "It's a long ride to any store thataway. Tell you what. I've got a rump of deer and some sourdough fixings up at the cabin. Why don't we take a break and eat a bite?"

Redge was quiet for a time, weighing the offer. This man was a total stranger, and the boy was keenly conscious of a little over three hundred dollars which Kate had given him. "A slab of venison sounds mighty tempting," he acknowledged. Then he pointed at the homemade implement and asked, "What do you call that thing?"

The stanger chuckled. "Stumps you, eh? Well, its a homemade ditcher. All that patch of plowed ground needs is plenty of water during the summer. This ditcher ought to help me to get the creek water from here to there . . . through a lateral."

"There's not much water in this creek," Redge said dubiously.

"Not this time of year. And, kid, this ain't a creek. It's the Big Thompson River. Comes all the way down from the Longs Peak country. In spring, it can get high, wide, and muddy." He paused, then asked bluntly, "Are you gonna eat with me? I'd sort of like some company; don't get much here along the Thompson."

Redge intuitively knew this was someone he could trust. He stepped closer to the stranger and thrust out his hand. "My name is Cardigan—Redge Cardigan. And I'm hungry enough to eat that whole deer."

"Everyone calls me Lester," the stranger answered with a grin and a shrug. "Lester the *nester* . . . ever since I started plowing. It doesn't matter, though; there's plenty more homesteaders pouring into this neck of the woods."

They unhitched the team and led all the horses toward the cabin. Redge bent down and let a handful of dark, moist earth sift through his fingers. "This is rich soil, pretty much like river bottomland in Missouri. It should grow anything."

"Maybe so . . . and maybe not," Lester answered. "Out

here it's not the land that's so important. There's plenty of it, all right—it's fertile and it's cheap. It's the water that counts. There's scant rainfall, and you can't depend on it."

"You mean everything has to be watered by ditch to grow?" Redge asked.

"Just about everything. Almost every year, it's irrigation makes a crop. Without the water, boy, this here Colorado land just ain't worth a whoop in hell."

Redge was quiet for a long time, lost in thought, as they entered the small, one-room shack and Lester went about preparing a meal. They were stowing away slabs of venison and bread when Redge suddenly looked up and asked pointedly, "If everyone takes water from the creek—I mean, the river—isn't there a whale of a ruckus and dispute when water runs low?"

Lester nodded, and explained, "It can lead to bad feelings and sometimes a killing. But nowadays the state of Colorado is beginning to get it organized. Decrees are issued to set up priorities of claim and ownership of the stream flow."

"Have *you* got a decree?" Redge queried, with interest.

Lester pushed back from the small table with a burp of satisfaction, then wiped the back of his hand across his mouth. "Have I got a decree?" he repeated. "I sure have, son. Two of them. One's a paper setting forth how much water I'm entitled to take out of this here Big Thompson River—and the other decree is a Colt .45 revolver to persuade some fellows to let go of what's mine."

An hour later, Redge rode on toward Denver. The settler had been loath to see the boy leave, and had waved off his offer to leave money for his meal. Redge surmised that Lester's way of life was a lonely one, and that this isolated land imbued men with a need for companionship and conversation. The homesteader had told him that he still had about fifty miles to Denver. It was too far for an afternoon's ride; he would have one more night of pitching camp before reaching the city.

Redge spent much of his time studying the lay of the land. Always there was the vast and thrusting escarpment rising above him a few miles to the west. The foothills were closest, then growing tier on tier were the mountains with the blue-green slopes of their forests. Higher still rose the white-mantled peaks, already wrapped in the deep ermine of winter.

Several streams, pouring down from the mountains over eons of time, had fashioned wide, deep-soiled valleys that led onto the prairies and toward the South Platte River. Redge considered how vast an area this eastward-sloping plains country was. Streams meandered through it, yet, in reality, they offered scant water for the seemingly endless stretches of grasslands. He mulled over Lester's plight. Here was a homesteader who was striving to make a path for riverwater to his few acres of tilled land. *There's plenty of land, all right. . . . It's the water that counts.* If that was true here, close to Denver, it must be doubly true along the vast valley of Crow Creek. Water could be the determining factor for success or failure—domestic water, stock water, water for irrigation. In the years of growth and development ahead, water would surely be a means of securing and holding control—of attaining power. He recalled with extraordinary clarity the way the downpour that day months ago had created the far-reaching expanse of water that had formed behind a natural barrier on Crow Creek.

The lake had been formed by rainwater, draining from upstream slopes. Yet, it had held water—life-giving and powerful water. An earthen dam, provided with a headgate and a spillway, could provide abundant water for the acres to which his father had filed homestead claim.

Then it came to him, entering his mind with clarity and sureness and urgency. He knew what must be done immediately. Redge touched his heels to his horse's flanks impatiently to urge the animal toward the distant crest, and Denver just beyond it.

He made camp that night on the northwest fringe of the city. Shortly after sunup, he was in the saddle again and riding along a dusty street that led into Denver's business section. His first task would be to search out a livery stable at which he could leave his horse, saddle, and gear for a few hours.

Toward midmorning, Redge trudged a few blocks from the barn where his horse had been fed and watered; his steps carried him onto lower Sixteenth Street and into an area of prosperous stores and office buildings. He hesitated, peering about. There was an impressive stone structure just

145

across the street; above its door, and on its plate-glass windows, were the words "Stockgrowers' Bank of Denver."

"They sure ought to know one," Redge muttered, then crossed the street to enter the bank. Off to one side of the room was a marble-topped counter. Behind it were three men sitting at desks, looking properly busy and dignified. Redge strode to the counter, placed his hands on the marble, and spoke to the man closest to him. The employee, a middle-aged man, whose neatly clipped mustache matched his white hair, looked up, smiled professionally, and asked, "Young man, may I help you?"

"I hope you can," Redge answered. "I need a good, honest lawyer. One that doesn't charge a fortune. I thought maybe a big bank like this could tell me where to find one."

"Ordinarily, we don't . . ." the banker began. He stopped himself and then asked, "Are you a customer of the bank, Mr. . . ."

"Cardigan. Redge Cardigan. No, I don't have an account here; I'm a stranger in Denver." Redge was aware of the close scrutiny he was undergoing as the older man jotted his name onto a pad. It led him to add, in a mildly irritated way, "I'm not in trouble, if that's what you're thinking." He turned to leave and said, "I'm sorry to have bothered you."

"Hold on a moment, Mr. Cardigan." The banker's tone was suddenly more friendly. "My, my, the impatience of youth." He held out a hand, in which there was a small piece of printed cardboard. "Here's the name and address of a law firm that frequently handles minor affairs for our bank. They are both capable and trustworthy. You'll find their offices two blocks up the street."

"Thank you, sir," Redge said, as he accepted the card and moved to the outer door.

If he had looked back, he would have seen a man rise from a desk and stride to that of his white-mustachioed assistant. The assistant came to alert attention, then commented, "That young fellow certainly had a no-nonsense way about him. Don't you agree, Mr. Brinner?"

It was quite a while before Adolph Brinner replied. He picked up the note pad from the desk, then said seriously, "Cardigan. I wonder if . . . yes, it has to be."

"Then you know the boy, Mr. Brinner?" the assistant queried.

"No, Tom. But I'm quite sure I met his father—a quite remarkable man." Adolph Brinner had torn the name from the pad and was carefully folding it. "Redge Cardigan," he repeated. Then he asked, thoughtfully, "You sent him to the Van Cleve firm, I assume?"

"Yes, I gave the young man a Van Cleve business card, Mr. Brinner."

Adolph Brinner walked back to his desk. For a few minutes he sat staring out onto Sixteenth Street, but saw little of the downtown activity. Instead, his mind's eye was picturing the card room of the Waverley mansion and a gala pre-Christmas reception honoring Jeff Masters. Words came clearly back to Adolph Brinner. The impassioned threat of a drunken Stacy Murdock: *Either take your kid and get off the Diamond-7—or wait and you'll wish to eternal God you had.*

Then, mingled with these remembered words, Adolph Brinner had another thought. There was the copy of the *Rocky Mountain News* which many weeks ago he had read, then put away in his desk at home. He had read and re-read the short news story reporting hostilities on a ranch in northern Weld County. Word was circulating about the range country that a claim jumper on Crow Creek had been killed after shooting down a Diamond-7 Ranch employee. No verification had been forthcoming from the Diamond-7 Ranch management, but it was believed the nester's name was Will Cardigan.

Adolph Brinner reached out for his appointment schedule. He wrote a reminder to himself to make certain inquiries at the Van Cleve law offices.

Redge Cardigan was ushered into a book-lined room, to a seat beside the desk of a man wearing a gray tweed suit. The lawyer had probing blue-gray eyes, a thatch of startlingly red hair, plus a smile apt to put new clients quickly at ease.

"How do you do, Cardigan," he was saying. "I'm Allen Van Cleve. Now . . . you must have some sort of problem. What is it?"

Van Cleve's approach was brisk, but it did save time.

Redge got down to business with a comparable sparse number of words.

"Sir, I can only be in Denver a day or so. What I need is someone to explain . . . to help me . . . to show me . . . how I can claim ownership of a sizable part of a creek's water flow—to irrigate land, and for livestock."

The lawyer studied his visitor's seriously eager face, then commented, "You're pretty young to have landholdings."

"It's for homestead land my father filed on." He added determinedly, "My father died last June."

Allen Van Cleve stroked thoughtfully at his unruly red hair.

"It's quite an undertaking. Where is the stream—and the land—located?"

"Up on Crow Creek, northeast of Greeley. Here's the section and township numbers; I copied them from my father's homestead applications." Redge laid a paper on the edge of the lawyer's desk.

Van Cleve studied the legal descriptions, then rose and checked them against a large map hanging from a rack. Then he said, "That's right out on the prairies. Is there water enough coming down the creek to make it worthwhile?"

Redge nodded. "Crow Creek runs some the year round. You should see it after a hard rain—maybe half a mile wide. And there's a natural reservoir site."

"But isn't that area in the grazing territory of one of the big ranches?"

"It sure is," Redge answered firmly. "Smack on the graze of the Diamond-7 outfit."

Van Cleve whistled in a startled and unbelieving way. "You mean, boy, that your father filed homestead claim to some Diamond-7 range? That was Andrew Purcell's territory."

"I know," Redge acknowledged. "It was Mr. Purcell who told my dad and me we ought to homestead right there where we'd established our camp. It was a sort of handshake agreement. That was a few months before Mr. Purcell drowned in a flood on Crow Creek."

"And now you want to request rights to a portion of the creek's flow?"

The set of Redge's chin was stubborn and firm. "I don't just *want* to claim that water, Mr. Van Cleve. I'm going

148

to. Surer than hell, I'm going to—somehow." He waited a bit, then with a tone of finality, asked, "How can I go about it? How much will it cost?"

Van Cleve scrutinized his visitor again with a growing respect. Then he explained, "The cost will be dependent on several things, Redge. We will have to determine what portion of the stream flow should be requested to fill your present and future needs. A sort of title search will have to be conducted to make sure there aren't prior decrees that would invalidate your claims. The fees for filing have to be paid to the Secretary of State's office."

"How much?" Redge asked insistently. "How much will it cost for the whole shebang—for everything?"

"If we can undertake the action for you," Van Cleve answered, "our fee will be five hundred dollars. But there is another obstacle, Redge. I'm certain you are not of legal age—twenty-one."

Redge rose and tensely clutched his weatherbeaten hat. "It looks as though I've been building some air castles, and wasting your time, Mr. Van Cleve. You're right, sir. I'm not of age—and I only have three hundred dollars. Now . . . I want to pay you for setting me straight on this."

The lawyer was quiet as he studied Redge Cardigan's face, and his decisive manner. He again ran his fingers through his red hair. Then, with a grin, he waved the boy back to the deskside chair.

"Listen to me, Cardigan," the lawyer said, with enthusiasm. "I got money to pay for law schooling by running a coal chute for the D&RGW Railroad. Believe me, I know how terribly important an idea—even a dream idea—can be during growing-up years. Besides, it's very unusual for the bank to make a recommendation of attorneys."

Redge's gaze held level on the lawyer's face, and he spoke with conviction. "That dam up there on Crow Creek would hold enough water to take care of mighty big meadows. Winter hay for scads of range cows."

Van Cleve smiled in his excitement. "Let's try to find out just how right you may be, Redge. Is there someone, perhaps a relative, whom we could get to sign as a trustee—a sort of guardian of the water decree until you reach legal age?"

Redge's thoughts flashed about, searching the past. Then

149

he grinned. "Hank Kutcher would do it. I'm sure he would. He used to ride for Mr. Andy Purcell, for the Diamond-7."

Allen Van Cleve nodded, and asked, "Where could we get in touch with this Mr. Kutcher? We'll have to send legal papers to him for signature."

Redge looked perplexed for a brief moment. Then he heaved a relieved sigh. "Just send them to Kate's Wagon."

"Kate's Wagon. I've heard of a place called that. Never met anyone who'd been there, though."

Redge laughed aloud, then answered, "Well, you're looking straight at me—and I've spent a lot of time there. It's a pretty busy trading post, maybe a day's ride south of Kimball, Nebraska. But it's in Colorado. It's operated by a fine lady, named Kate Andrus. Kate will know where Hank Kutcher is, and get the papers to him."

The lawyer leaned far back in his chair and clasped his hands behind his head. He stared in admiration at the boy. "Redge Cardigan, I bet you could make a dream come true." Then he became businesslike. "I'll need a lot of data, figures and information. So . . . what say we get down to details?"

An hour later, with the preliminary paperwork underway, Redge rose, thrust his hand into an inner pocket, and pulled out a leather pouch. He counted its entire contents onto Van Cleve's desk—three hundred dollars in gold pieces, the money Kate Andrus had insisted on paying him.

"I'll give you a receipt for this," Van Cleve said. Then he added, "Perhaps I should have told you sooner. This covers attorney fees. But there will be filing fees to be paid at the Secretary of State's office. Likely fifty dollars. You can pay me for that later."

Momentary concern clouded Redge's face, then it was replaced by a look of confidence. "Mr. Van Cleve, I will pay the fifty dollars to you sometime this afternoon." The tone was that of someone who had just decided the exact course he must follow. Redge knew he would sell his horse.

"But why, Redge? I told you the payment could wait."

The boy shook his head. "It can't wait, sir. With one exception, this water application is the most important thing in my life. I can raise the fifty dollars now. Maybe later I couldn't. Besides, I'll be leaving Denver this evening —heading for Arizona to find somebody."

When Redge Cardigan had disappeared through the office

door, lawyer Allen Van Cleve sat for a long time assessing just how he had happened to take a case—a case that might have far-reaching ramifications and consequences. But presently some of the boy's words came back to hound the attorney.

"He said," Van Cleve muttered aloud, "that the water application is the most important thing in his life—with one exception. *Damned if I wouldn't like to know just what that exception is!*

Chapter 14

Two days later, Redge Cardigan stood in the Santa Fe Railroad freight yards at Albuquerque, New Mexico. He was cold. He was hungry. He was broke. But he had kept his pledge to immediately pay fifty dollars to Van Cleve. To accomplish it, Redge had sold his horse and saddle, and dug from his pockets all but two dollars of the money with which he had started this long trek.

A streak of good luck had brought him into Albuquerque at noon of the second day out of Denver. After paying Van Cleve and bidding the lawyer goodbye, he went to the stockyards. There he had wangled a job helping to tend a shipment of bulls to Albuquerque.

And now, dodging a persistent Santa Fe yard detective, Redge climbed aboard a freight train bound westward toward Los Angeles.

Throughout the afternoon the string of freight cars rattled westward. Several times the engine drew to a stop beside a coal chute or a water tower. Then it again searched its way around long, sweeping curves, or labored loudly, as it spat black smoke against the sullen sky and fought determinedly toward the crest of a long, sloping ridge.

Hours passed, and darkness began to encompass the desert; a chill wind lent urgent speed to intermittent snow flurries. Once more the train came to a halt. Redge squatted in the corner of the empty boxcar. He pulled his mackinaw coat about him and pondered the wisdom of continuing this illicit ride as night came on.

The decision was made for him. Suddenly the car door was pushed open; an arm holding a lantern was thrust into the car, and a brakeman in overalls stared at the boy. The trainman climbed through the car door, stood up and confronted Redge.

"I had an idea you'd be holed up in here. Saw you slip

152

on board back in Albuquerque." He looked closer, surprise marking his face. " 'Sakes alive! You're just a kid."

Redge clambered to his feet, then answered, "I'm trying to get to Flagstaff . . . then maybe down to Prescott."

"Not on this train. Not tonight," the brakeman said firmly. "We'll be climbing into mountains pretty soon, where you would freeze to death. Flagstaff is better than seven thousand feet high. Probably has a foot of snow on the ground."

"Couldn't I help you?" Redge asked. "Maybe then I could ride in the caboose."

"Not a chance, kid. We're carrying a trainmaster. If I let you into the crummy to ride, he'd have me fired and afoot." The brakeman paused a bit, scrutinizing Redge. "Tell you what. I'm gonna put you off here. But after we pull out you keep walking. There's a little town, a town named Grants, about half a mile ahead. There's a small sawmill close to the tracks. Likely you can sleep in the shed where they keep a fire under the boiler. Tomorrow you can—" His words were cut short by the howl of a distant whistle. "Hurry up and hit the ground; we're set to pull out."

As Redge dropped from the car into the windswept cold, the train was already in motion.

Minutes later, when the red lights of the Santa Fe caboose faded from view, the tracks seemed desolate and unfriendly. Redge picked his way along them, worried and aimless. Presently, he saw a few lights ahead, those of a small depot, and of buildings set along a short street facing the tracks. Before the buildings were pretty sizable stockyards. Cattle were penned within, probably waiting for loading. The bawling of cows was a sound from his past, bringing a resurgence of bitter memories.

One pen of the stockyards held perhaps a dozen saddle horses. Nearby, a campfire had been built. Men crowded close to it and stretched their hands to the warmth. Two others were unpacking supplies for an evening meal.

The scent of strong coffee drifted to Redge. Potatoes and meat were cooking, and their smell reminded him how hungry he was. The riders seemed somber and rough-hewn, with tiredness stamped across them. All wore the wrinkled, soiled garb of range riders, along with holstered six-guns. Tarped and tied bedrolls lay strewn about, and Redge knew

153

that later these riders would bunk down for a few hours of rest.

The boy stood watching, reluctant to leave. Where would he spend this night that would doubtless turn bitter cold?

His thoughts were interrupted by a tall man, past middle age, who glanced at him from the fireside's ring of warmth. Moments later, the stranger strode close and looked straight at Redge. Both hope and concern surged over Redge. Would this stranger mean trouble, or could he possibly offer a meal in exchange for a chore that needed to be done?

He kept his gaze steady upon this man, who appeared to be the outfit's foreman. Dark-complexioned, perhaps in his early fifties, he was clad in boots, Levi's, a blue woolen shirt, and a worn leather jacket. His broad-rimmed hat was black and old and sweated. On each of this stranger's hips hung a well-used leather holster that nestled serviceable-looking weapons. Redge noted the deep-set, dark eyes as they scrutinized him from a face carved by sun and wind. A dark mustache spilled to either side of a strong mouth.

"Kid," the stranger asked finally, "where are you heading?"

He decided to tell the truth; he said simply, "I got kicked off that last westbound freight when it stopped. I'm trying to get to Arizona."

"And you're broke and hungry."

Redge nodded, then said, "I'll work for a meal."

"Come along." The man motioned him to follow. They reached the fire, where the boy was quickly the object of everyone's curious glances. The older man gathered up a plate and cup, to thrust them at Redge. "Feed this boy, Sam," he said to the cook. "And you'd better rustle up a couple of blankets for him."

Redge would have uttered his thanks, but the stranger had already stridden away, dismissing the boy. It was evident now who was boss of the crew, whose word would be strictly followed, and who would not take kindly to anyone who questioned his decision.

Later, the foreman rejoined the circle for his meal. Little was said except in regard to the work that tomorrow would bring. The desert cowman who had provided for Redge's needs squatted a little apart from the others, rolled a cigarette, and stared into the fire. His thoughts seemed to rise upward with the smoke.

All except two of the crew crawled into their bedrolls early. From the hushed words of those lingering over coffee, Redge learned that the crew boss was Dade Sutherland, a rancher whose cattle grazed a large portion of the eastern Arizona mountains. Just as soon as this shipment could be loaded, Sutherland and his outfit would head for the Show Low country of the White Mountains.

The crew was up and stirring about early, in the dark and chilly dawn. Breakfast was dished out to Redge along with the riders. He ate, then sought out Sutherland. "I want to help with the loading, sir. Maybe I can square up a bit for the blankets and meals."

"Did you ever handle cattle?" Sutherland asked doubtfully.

With a pang of memory, Redge answered, "Yes. Quite a lot—back in Colorado."

"We need help prodding critters up the loading chute," Sutherland said, then walked away.

Near midmorning, a potentially dangerous incident occurred. A few head of steers jammed against a pen gate, causing it to give way and collapse. The cattle broke from the corral and gathered on the railroad tracks. Dade Sutherland rode to drive them back. Seconds later, his horse wheeled to escape the lowered horns of a scared and angry steer, but fell because his footing was unsure on the rails and ties. Sutherland was pinned by his fallen horse across a rail just as a switch engine was backing a string of empty cars toward the stockyards.

Redge was the nearest person; he ran in desperate haste to the scene. The nearness of switching cars filled him with terror—he knew he would have to act quickly. There was a stacked pile of railroad ties close by. He managed to drag one to the track and laid it across one rail at an angle which he hoped would be sufficient to derail the first car and stop the switch engine's movement.

Other men were running toward him now, shouting, but Redge knew that only the tilted tie could save Dade Sutherland. And the tie must be held to an angle that would cause the cattle car to derail. He dug his boots into the dirt and fiercely set himself to hold. He was only a couple of car lengths uptrack from Sutherland and his sprawled, struggling horse.

He heard the old cowman yell for him to get himself

155

clear of the track. Ignoring the order, he held to the tie
with a firm grip and taut muscles. Then a car wheel hit it.
Redge was flung about, almost under the cattle car. In an
instant he sensed that a wheel had jumped the rail. It
knocked him unconscious. He was not aware of men lifting
him from the site.

It was night when he again knew reality, dimly realizing
that he was in a warm bed, and that someone was sitting
nearby with dusty boots propped onto a white commode.
The boy's eyes opened and he saw a kerosene lamp. The
flame seemed to swirl strangely about, then darkness closed
in on him again.

Dawn was lighting the room when he roused himself
again. This time he could look about with clear vision; at
the same time, he became aware of a headache such as he
had never before known.

The scuffed boots still topped the commode, and now the
watchful eyes of an old, white-whiskered man fastened
upon Redge. "So you're coming around at last, son." The
words were followed by a sigh of relief. Then he added,
"I'm Ben Bohlin, a cowhand for Dade Sutherland."

"What happened?" Redge muttered drowsily. "Where am
I?"

He struggled to sit up, but the old man thrust out a restraining hand and said, "Take it easy, youngster. The doc
says you'll be all right in a day or so."

Memory was seeping back to Redge. "But the crew
boss . . . was he . . . did he get . . ."

"Dade Sutherland, right. He's okay—thanks to your
hanging onto that railroad tie. Dade told me to stay with
you a day or so until you're up and about. He had to get
back to headquarters, up Show Low way. Said to tell you
there's a steady job waiting iffen you should want it."

The oldster's recital was cut short by entrance of another
man, clad in a white shirt and a baggy suit. With a competent air, he moved to Redge's bedside, removed a bandage
from the boy's head, and studied what lay beneath. "You're
a lucky young whippersnapper," he growled, "Just a little
harder, or off to the side, and that rail would have put you
out of commission for a long time."

Redge grinned weakly. "I'm pretty hungry." Then, remembering, he added hastily, "But I'm also broke."

The bewhiskered gent put in a few words. "That's all the

lad knows about it, Doc. Dade Sutherland left money for his care."

The doctor cocked his head toward Redge. "You picked the right man to rescue. Dade Sutherland has more land and cattle in eastern Arizona than even the rustlers can keep track of."

On the third day, Redge rose early, dressed, and began a restless walking tour of the small town of Grants. It was a desert settlement, close to the vast Indian lands, with an altitude that brought cool summer nights and heavy winter snowfalls. The Navajo tribesmen journeyed here to trade their turquoise and silver, their woven blankets and piñon nuts, for the goods the town's traders offered.

Entranced by the town's activity, and the vast and lonely distances beyond, Redge walked for two hours before returning to his room. His white-whiskered guardian sat by a window, puffing an odorous pipe. He eyed Redge's condition with approval and said, "Iffen you're well enough to gad about half the morning, likely we'd best head for Flagstaff."

"But you told me Mr. Sutherland headquarters at some place called Show Low."

"That he does, but he's taking some steers to Flagstaff come the end of this week. Beef for a logging crew. We can ride the passenger train to Flagstaff, and meet the crew there. But right now we're going to pack our bellies full," the old man vowed. "I've starved better than an hour waiting for you."

Sunset was near when the westbound passenger train left Redge and Ben Bohlin on the station platform at Flagstaff. For nearly an hour the engine had been laboring ever higher into timber country where ponderosa pine spread across rolling hills, and where the high altitude brought heavy winter snows and almost ample summer rain. The air was fresh and already crisply cold.

Peering northward across the small frontier town, Redge marveled at the bold upthrust of the San Francisco peaks. They seemed to rise just behind town, their distance of several miles belied by the clear, cold air.

A small business district, mostly false-fronted stores and saloons and hotels, bordered the Santa Fe tracks, which severed the town in two. South of the tracks lay stockyards,

157

lumber mills, and a parklike area dotted by a couple of small lakes.

"I didn't know there were so many trees west of Missouri!" Redge said with wonder.

"It's quite a pine forest—some say the largest of its kind in the world," Bohlin explained. He waited as the boy swung about for a view in each direction. After a while he urged, "Let's get over to the Weatherford Hotel. Dade Sutherland puts up there. Maybe he's in town already."

They trod a rutted path from the station, across the fronting street, and onto a broad sidewalk.

They found that Sutherland had checked into the hotel earlier in the day, and had made provision for them to have a room with two beds. But, the clerk informed them, he had already gone out. Knowledge of his foreman's usual routine in town enabled Ben Bohlin to find Sutherland without much delay in a cafe facing the railroad.

The rancher greeted them warmly, then motioned for them to join him at the dinner table. "The food is reasonably good here. The place has the fewest kitchen rats and roaches in town, I'm told."

Ben Bohlin chuckled. "Thanks, boss. Just let me turn the hassle of caring for this hobo sightseeing kid over to you. I need to look up the crew and catch up on a couple of details."

Redge sensed that Bohlin was getting out of the way on purpose, that he wanted to allow Dade Sutherland to be able to talk freely. "Thanks, friend Ben." Redge grinned. "I'll see you later at the hotel."

"And keep me awake all night with your snorin'," Ben grumbled as he left.

"I'd recommend the special steak with trimmings here," Sutherland said. His appraising gaze swept Redge as he went on. "Son, I don't even know your name. Just that you're from Colorado and that you were broke. Another little thing. You saved my life."

"You sort of saved mine too," Redge murmured. "Likely I'd have froze to death that night if you hadn't offered me grub and a bed."

"I like men who can use their wits—do the right thing perhaps instinctively in a hurry. Now. How's your banged-up head?"

"Just some black and blue, as you see. A mite of swell-

158

ing. It'll be gone in a day or so." Redge added, "My name is Redge Cardigan. I know cattle pretty well, especially how to doctor sick critters."

Dade Sutherland's gaze bored into Redge. "Redge, are you running from the law?"

"No, sir."

"Then what brought you to Arizona on the bum?"

"I'm looking for a man," Redge answered in civil but unrevealing tone.

"I'll not pry. But if I can help, I'll be proud to do so. Meanwhile, I'd suggest you hire out to the Slash-8—that's my brand—and get acquainted with the Show Low country." As an afterthought he added, "A lot of men pass through Show Low—both good and bad."

"It's a fine offer," Redge said. "I appreciate what you've done. Let me think the job over until morning, sir." He eyed the huge steaks being set before them. "Likely we'll still be eating these come sunup."

Sutherland's answering laugh was warm and sincere.

Ben Bohlin didn't show up at the hotel room until dawn was sifting through an eastern window. Then he noisily kicked off his boots and pulled the blankets up around his chin. Redge awakened, looked over at his companion, and wondered if old Ben Bohlin always went to bed with his clothes on. He braced himself to hear Ben snore mightily.

Instead, Bohlin sat abruptly up, drew a worn deck of cards from his pocket, then dealt five of them face up. "The law of averages says it shouldn't have happened," he muttered. "It ain't natural—not for that Mormon bishop to draw out on me after my two aces were showing, and I had another in the hole. His coming up with that spade flush . . . he bet 'em as though the Lord was a dealin' for him. Plucked me clean, he did."

Now wide awake, Redge laughed aloud. "Ben, likely it's the sinful way you live. You ought to join the same church . . . and remember to divvy up to the collection plate."

"You're full of bullshit," Bohlin roared. "Don't go handing out either credit or blame to the bishop's creed . . . or to old Brigham Young. There's someone else to blame, and I should have known it. I ought to keep clear of any card player that associates with Emmett Willoughby."

As he heard the name, Redge Cardigan gasped, aware that his every sense was suddenly honed to alert expectancy.

159

A silence ensued, in which he remained tense, but strove to display a calm and scant curiosity. "Did you say Emmett Willoughby?" he asked with seeming indifference.

Bohlin cast a glare of utter scorn upon the boy. "Dammit, kid, you're dumber than I feared. Of course I said Emmett Willoughby. He's a legend to some and a terror to others."

"Right here in Flagstaff?" Redge queried.

"Hell no. Willoughby's from here, there, and everywhere. Just now he ramrods the freighter line from here in Flag; it goes from hereabouts north to Kanab . . . and other points in Mormon country."

"You mean a cardsharp owns a freighting outfit?" Redge asked doubtfully.

Bohlin scowled. "I didn't say anything of the kind. Dade Sutherland owns the outfit. He needed someone to straighten things out—called in Willoughby."

"Seems an unlikely job for a gambler," Redge observed carefully.

Bohlin's response came with a baleful glare. "Boy, you've a lot to learn. He plays expert cards, but that's not why Sutherland wanted him. He needed an expert with men—and guns—and that's Willoughby."

"Where does this gun-fanning gambler headquarter?" Redge was striving to show but passing interest. Caution, born of the pain and travail through which he had already passed, decreed that few men if any should know of his mission. News had a way of drifting from state to state. And Stacy Murdock must not know—not yet.

"There's stations here in Flag and at Kanab. Others all along the way. One or two of them are in Navajo hogans out on the reservation," Bohlin explained. "But I guess the real headquarters are those of Dade Sutherland at Show Low."

Bohlin was slowly giving way to his need for sleep. He shoved the cards back in his pocket and gave forth a sorrowful sigh. A minute later he was stretched out and snoring.

Sunup came. Redge rose, quietly left the room, and washed with buckets of incredibly cold water which brought him fully awake. Then he searched out Dade Sutherland at the Weatherford Hotel coffee shop.

The rancher's face lit up as Redge approached. "You're

facing the day early," he commented. "Either that is ranch training or you couldn't stand any more of my man Ben."

"He's pretty doleful just now," Redge said.

Sutherland showed no surprise but commented, "Which is the state he gets into every time we come to Flagstaff. He's unbeatable as a cowhand, but dismal with women, liquor, and cards." Dismissing his errant jack-of-all-jobs, Sutherland asked briskly, "Have you made up your mind, Redge? I hope you'll be riding home to Show Low with us today."

Redge lifted a steaming cup of coffee, then said bluntly, "I want to work for you, sir—but not at Show Low."

"What do you mean?" Sutherland made a perplexed gesture.

"Mr. Sutherland, you own a freight line . . . from here north into Utah country, don't you?"

Sutherland grimaced. "It owns me, in a way—and so far has paid precious little."

"I want a job on that freight route. As a hostler maybe . . . or freight handler. Something that'll get me about the desert country."

An expression of understanding crossed Dade Sutherland's face, and he sat erect as his dark, thoughtful eyes searched Redge Cardigan. "On your search, right? You wouldn't be one to give up easily." The rancher drew a notepad from his breast pocket and wrote rapidly. "Take this down to the Canyonlands Freight Office on Front Street. As a new hire, they're apt to send you to the most godforsaken outpost." He drew a couple of banknotes from his wallet and thrust them at Redge. "This is just an advance on wages. You'll need several things." When Redge saw the amount, his eyes widened. He would have protested had not Sutherland said, "Don't be a fool; I know you'll square your bill."

Redge finished his meal with few words. As he rose to leave, he looked with admiration at Dade Sutherland and said, "My dad would have liked you, sir."

When the boy had left the coffee shop, Sutherland sat staring after him. He'll make out, the rancher thought. I have a feeling that someday . . . somewhere . . . that boy is going to bust all hell loose.

* * *

Just short of 120 miles north of Flagstaff, the freighting waystation of Bitter Springs sat in sun-baked or blizzard-raked isolation. Here men and livestock rested on the northward trips, knowing that the treacherous crossing of the Colorado River at Lee's Ferry was but a two-day journey ahead. Men were prudent not to stray far from their weapons at Bitter Springs. Nor was it deemed healthy to climb the vastly sweeping escarpment that lifted only a mile to the east. This clifflike barrier marked the actual boundary of Navajo country, and the beginning of a remote wilderness land known to only a handful of white men. On the west lay the twisting and multicolored depths of Marble Canyon. Hereabouts, rainstorms were infrequent, but sometimes came with a savage downpour that could quickly turn a dry wash into a raging and devastating torrent.

Redge's first freight-line assignment was to Bitter Springs. On the ride from Flagstaff, which took the better part of a week, he had his first lesson in the diplomacy of desert commerce. Northward, across the Colorado River, lay the mountains and valleys of Utah's "Dixie." It was Mormon country, the land of Brigham Young, a man whose story had intrigued Redge. Here Mormon settlements had been made, wherever stream flow might afford irrigation for crops, and water for people and livestock. The dwellers of farms and hamlets and budding towns knew allegiance only to the church and its governing leaders at Salt Lake City. In Latter-Day Saint country, visitors were discouraged, and intruders pointedly told to get out.

Yet, the Mormon settlers were shrewdly practical. Many of the goods they needed were produced in the industrial east and came to them via rail to Flagstaff and on wagon hauls across the desolate stretches of northern Arizona. Supplies and building materials and farm tools came more speedily—and cheaper—this way than any other. And so a freighting business such as that of Dade Sutherland was tolerated.

Also, Sutherland was fair in his dealings. He could sense the needs of the Mormon settlers and have the goods to their trading centers quickly. He scrupulously avoided voicing any opinion of Mormon doctrine. His men were ordered to do likewise, and to offer all available help to the scattered Saints in any emergency.

To assure that his policies were carried out, Sutherland

hired several of the restless breed of men who carried their frontier justice in a holster. Emmett Willoughby was one of them. It was inevitable that Willoughby would sooner or later show up at Bitter Springs.

Work at the freight station came in erratic spurts. When a long drag of wagons arrived, plodding dustily in either direction, there was a flurry of activity. Work horses and mules had to be tended, wagons put in serviceable condition, and some cargo unloaded or new sacks, bales, and boxes loaded for outgoing.

A great deal of this labor fell to Redge, for it was customary for the newest member of the crew to be dealt hard and distasteful tasks by other hands.

Of his diverse duties, Redge naturally preferred the doctoring of ailing animals. The hard pull of heavily laden wagons through desert brush and sand washes brought some horses and mules to Bitter Springs in lamed condition or with raw and festered collar sores.

Toward midmorning of a November day, Redge was squatted beside the foreleg of a powerful dun-hued mule. Some road hazard had caused the animal's hock to split, bleed, and swell. Redge bathed it up. His only bandage material came from an old cotton work shirt he had salvaged and washed.

A sudden shadow across his work caused him to glance up—squarely into the dark and intensely interested face of a boy near his own age. The newcomer wore tattered overalls and a black sateen shirt, and was barefooted. His hair, long and black, was held back by a band encircling his head. His features carried the strength and dignity of the Navajo, but he spoke a clearly understandable English.

"Needs plenty of air so it will heal quick."

With quick fingers Redge showed the looseness of the cloth wrapping the mule's hock. "Yes," he answered, "enough air, but wrapping to keep out dirt and flies. I'll clean it every day. Change the bandage."

The Navajo dropped to his haunches and sniffed the scent clinging about the mule's leg. "What did you use for medicine?" he asked.

"Carbolic acid. It's . . . it's all I got."

A wisp of breeze stirred the stranger's dark, tousled hair as he came to his feet. "My mother has a riding horse with such a wound. Likely the horse will die. The Navajo have

163

no medicine, no carbolic acid." His face was blankly stolid as he added, "There are many things my people do not have."

Redge's gaze swept over the Bitter Creek yard and searched the horizon. "Where is your mother's horse?" he asked.

A wave of the Indian's hand indicated the sweep of high battlementlike ridges to the east. "Our hogans are over there about five miles. There are trees and a spring. The horse cannot travel."

Redge studied his visitor with increasing interest. "You speak our language well, much better than other Navajo who have come here."

Bitterness clouded the Indian boy's face and added remoteness to his dark eyes as he answered. "Five years I spent in a mission school at Albuquerque learning the language of white men. The religion of the padres. Skills I find useless here among my people."

Redge looked at the boy. "My name is Redge . . . Redge Cardigan. What is yours?"

Amusement showed for the first time in the Navajo's dark features. "You mean the name the Catholic padres at Albuquerque called me . . . or my real name, that given to me by the Navajo, my people?"

"Whichever you prefer," Redge said quietly, then waited.

"I am Hosteen . . . Hosteen Begay. Before we were penned like sheep on this reservation, my fathers held power over much of the north mountains." He turned, and would have run off had not Redge called in a low but urgent voice.

"Wait, Hosteen. Come here." Redge was gathering his medical supplies into a small box. He thrust them out to the hesitating boy. "Take these, Hosteen. There are dressings and the carbolic acid for killing germs. Clean the sores of your mother's horse. Dress them with cloths so flies are kept out. Then return these things to me."

Hosteen Begay reached for the box with an eager hand. Disbelief was written across his face as he said, "You would trust a Navajo with medicines . . . with the healing powers of the white man?"

Redge nodded. "I think we are going to be friends. Come back when the horse is cared for." Redge was still watching in silence when Hosteen Begay reached the high ridge's summit and disappeared beyond.

During the next two days, Redge often scanned the eastern horizon and the precipitous slopes leading into Bitter Springs from the east. There was only one other person, a middle-aged, surly individual, stationed at this remote trail stop. He spoke mostly Spanish, and he gave almost endless hours to braiding lariat ropes that were perfect both to look upon and to use.

The tedium of this practically forgotten outpost bothered Redge. Despite the element of danger and the necessity of carrying firearms, he began ranging farther from the station buildings, to study this desert land and its vegetation. On the evening of the second day after the brief meeting with Hosteen Begay, Redge walked about two miles down the trail meandering south toward Flagstaff. There was an arroyo off the trail and a little to the west; there a tracery of green told of a spring or an intermittently flowing stream.

He had scarcely reached the patch of grass, surrounded by a few willows, when two things caught his attention. Close by were some piled rocks, with the dead ashes of a campfire. Small bits of trash—white man's trash—lay scattered about. On one rock was a tin of baking powder, which had apparently been forgotten by whoever had made camp here.

Redge was within a few yards of the can when he stopped abruptly to listen to distant sounds, coming from the south, where the trail crested a rocky divide. Over the ridge spilled a cloud of dust and a line of freighting wagons. In front of the wagons, two men rode steadily toward the spot where Redge stood waiting.

The mounted men had already sighted him. But it caused him no concern. Undoubtedly this was one of Dade Sutherland's freight caravans heading north toward Lee's Ferry and the Mormon settlements beyond. The wagons were slow moving and would not be able to reach Bitter Springs before dark. Likely the approaching riders were scouting out a suitable place for overnight camp.

Eager anticipation swept Redge. People to talk to. News of the outside. He could spend a couple of hours with these wagon people and then walk the moonlit trail home to Bitter Springs.

He strode to the charred camp embers, stirred them indifferently, then thrust the almost-new can of baking powder into his pocket. The wagon-train cook could make good use of it.

And now the two riders closed in toward him. One was dressed in a dark coat and black, flattened hat, giving clear indication that this stocky graying stranger was a Mormon, possibly the guide and business agent for the wagon train.

Redge studied the second man, perplexed. He rode tall and erect in the saddle, despite the years evidenced by his whitened locks of hair and weathered face. There was a free-flowing, rhythmic grace about his movements, his gestures, and his manner of turning often to scan and assess his surroundings. His garb was that of a working cowhand, different only in the skillfully arranged placement of his gun belt and two polished weapons it supported.

The heavy-set Mormon spoke directly to Redge. "How are you, young fellow? We didn't expect to see a living soul this side of Bitter Springs." He looked searchingly about, then added, "Are you camped here—alone?"

Redge, shaking his head, would have explained, but he fell silent under the scrutiny of the taller horseman. The man's gaze swept him from head to foot. His gray eyes livened, yet held both wonder and disbelief—as though he was seeing a ghost. "Boy," he asked softly, eagerly, "what is your name?"

"Cardigan, sir," the boy said. "I am Redge Cardigan."

The stranger slid easily from his sweat-stained horse, to grasp Redge's hand and to place an arm about the boy. "I knew it, son. It had to be . . . to be Will Cardigan or his phantom. Just as I remember him standing back in '65, in Tennessee."

Redge knew that tears had come, coursing down his cheeks. He stood comfortably beside this tall, lithe man who should be a stranger but somehow was not.

"And you," he said with surety, "are Emmett Willoughby."

The half-dozen freight wagons were close now. The Mormon rider sized up their progress. "I'll get them located and settled," he said to Willoughby. He seemed to understand that these two needed some time alone.

Willoughby tossed his bridle reins to the Mormon. "Elder, thank you. And would you see to this dusty, trail-tired old gelding?

"Now, son," Willoughby asked, turning back to Redge, "where have you come from? And what of my old partner, Will?"

"My dad is dead, sir. We had a little cattle spread in Colorado, out on the prairies. I'm here because Dad asked me to look you up—to give you this." Redge drew a small piece of oilskin from his pocket, and with trembling fingers unwrapped it. One half of a torn playing card lay revealed.

Emmett Willoughby reached out; there was tenderness in his face as well as mingled anguish and awe. "Redge, boy. I have the other half. Do you know what this card means . . . why it was sent by your father?"

"Not really . . . not completely."

"I'll explain, then. But first tell me about your father. And your mother. And about that ranch in Colorado."

For a long time, as the sun dropped behind a far mesa, and as a campfire sprang to flickering brilliance near the wagons, Redge's voice held Willoughby in rapt attention.

The retelling of the day of Stacy Murdock's vengeance, and of a future suddenly shattered by gunfire and a bullwhip, drained the color from Redge Cardigan's face. Memories of a little ranch and of his smiling, quiet father overwhelmed him. He had thought about it many times since, of course, but actually saying the words aloud brought everything back in a flood of emotions. He had been stoic about losing his father, but now, in front of this man, he knew he could let his feelings out. His words became a tortured sob, then trailed off into silence. With fists clenched, the boy sat on a small rock ledge and stared unseeingly at the grass below him.

Emmett Willoughby sat silently beside him, with an arm flung about Redge's shoulders. He sensed that futile words of comfort would be neither helpful nor wanted. The emotional storm would pass; Redge would lift himself from this grief and despondency.

After a while Willoughby rose. "They'll have something ready to eat soon. I'd be pleased to have you join us, Redge. We've much to talk about—decisions to make. But not tonight."

Redge got up slowly, strode a few steps from Willoughby, then lifted his face toward the final flame of sunset. When he turned back, calmness and an utterly bleak and determined firmness held about his strong chin, his tightened lips, and eyes so sternly cold they startled Willoughby.

"I'll not be a burden to you, Mr. Emmett. There's just one thing I want—that I must have."

"What is it, son?" Willoughby asked.

Redge stepped closer and laid softly exploring fingers on one polished revolver. "Teach me to use a six-gun. To be as fast as my dad said you were. Fast enough to kill Stacy Murdock!"

Whatever answer Emmett Willoughby would have made was cut off by sudden excited yells from the teamsters who had gathered about the campfire. Two other teamsters approached the fire from a clump of shadowed willows, holding a slight form between them. Their prisoner did not struggle or even raise his voice. Instead, as they drew him closer to the wagons and the freighters, he walked proudly, fearlessly, ridden not by fear but by scornful anger.

Redge drew his breath in sharply. Suddenly he broke into a run and trotted speedily to the campfire. Avoiding those who would have grabbed him, he stepped to the prisoner's side and yelled aloud, "This is Hosteen Begay. My friend. There must be a mistake. Why is he a prisoner?"

"He's a thief. A stinkin' Navajo thief," blurted out a teamster, whose face was livid with rage.

"Did he steal from you?" Redge demanded.

"He surer 'n hell did. A can of baking powder. I'd just found it sitting on a rock. Precious little of it used up."

Redge dug into his pocket, drawing out the can he had found on a rock. He eyed it, then glanced at the Navajo boy. Sight of the can in Redge's hand seemed to bring instant frenzy to Hosteen Begay. With a lightninglike surge of power he broke free of his guards. A few steps brought him to Redge's side. His hand shot out, and he grabbed the can. The Navajo's face was distorted with anger as he twisted off the lid, flung the can's white contents into the dust, then kicked it about.

"Hosteen . . . Hosteen, are you crazy?" Redge cried out, startled.

Before answering, the Navajo boy retraced his steps to stand between his captors. "Redge, you tell them. Make them believe. It is not baking powder in the cans. It is poison . . . arsenic."

"He's lying," the irate teamster persisted.

168

"Hosteen, how do you know?" The question came softly from Emmett Willoughby.

Hosteen Begay folded his arms. "Many such cans are left on the reservation, in spots where my people will find them. It is meant to be so."

"Wait a minute," the Mormon leader interrupted. "I'm familiar with poisons. If it's arsenic, I'll know." He retrieved the can Hosteen had thrown aside and rubbed a finger lightly around its inside. Then he lifted his finger to his nostrils and whiffed lightly. For an instant he placed a white-tinged finger across his lip. Then he spat forcefully. "It's arsenic, all right. Bring a canteen so I can rinse off my hand and face." He turned, signaling the guards to move away from Hosteen. "How did you know, boy?" he asked thoughtfully.

The Navajo was aware that the men were staring at him, awaiting his reply. "Death brought knowledge of the poisoned cans to my people. The mother of two children in our village found such a can and used the powder. The children are dead."

The Mormon shook his head in a worried way. "I heard a little of something like this. A mad killer loose on the reservation. I thought it was just an Indian rumor."

The belligerent teamster eyed Hosteen with continuing suspicion and distrust. "None of this explains why the Indian was prowling around here in the first place. They're born thieves, them Navvies."

With temper flaring, Redge squared off before him. "You're grateful as hell, aren't you?" he jeered. "Hosteen likely saved your life. Besides, mister, right now your feet are planted on reservation ground. Any Navajo has more right here than you!"

The teamster's face reddened with rage. "I can't see as this is any of your business, kid. If you were, say, a couple years older I'd . . ."

Redge became absolutely calm. Suddenly he was on guard, and there was a coldness about his face and his eyes that caused older men to glance at each other and shake their heads.

"There's no use waiting a couple of years to settle this," Redge said crisply. "I'm ready now—if you've the guts to try me."

For a few moments the teamster stood fuming, legs apart.

Then he turned and walked silently into the twilight shadows.

The Mormon leader glanced at Emmett Willoughby. "Likely he was smart not to tangle with your young friend."

"There are others, a long way from here, who will also do well to turn tail when their time comes," Willoughby answered.

He was not overheard by Redge, who was standing with Hosteen Begay, listening to the Navajo intently. "Redge. My mother's horse. His leg is much better. I returned your medicines; they are in the stable at Bitter Springs." He waited for Redge's nod, then added, "I'll go now; the trail to my mother's place is long."

"Wait, Hosteen. I've got to hurry back to Bitter Springs. We can travel together."

Emmett Willoughby had been standing quietly nearby. Now he grinned and asked, "Mind if I trek along with you boys? The bishop won't need my help this side of the stage station."

"How did you know I was hoping you'd come along?" Redge managed. Now there would be a chance to get acquainted with this man from Will Cardigan's life and time. And maybe he could learn more about those guns which had made of Emmett Willoughby a legend across the west.

Willoughby chose to lead his horse and walk the distance to Bitter Springs with Redge on one side of him and Hosteen on the other. The desert night was about them, as was an errant breeze that spoke mysteriously of the Kaibab Plateau off westward. Occasionally there were the soft sounds of animals that slept by day and sought food in darkness.

Their leisurely pace brought them, within half an hour, to a place where the trail angled its way up a sand-blown ridge. There was a short climb, and then they discerned the shadowy forms of the stable and station at Bitter Springs. There was a pinpoint of light cast by a smoky kitchen lamp. Redge suddenly remembered that he had not eaten since noon. In a rueful voice he said to Willoughby, "I can stir up something for us to eat, but likely you'd have done better to wait for your meal with the teamsters."

"Their grub isn't so tempting," Willoughby replied. "Mostly it's tough beef, some sort of bread, and canned tomatoes . . . washed down with some of the concoctions Mormons substitute for coffee." Willoughby fell quiet for a time, then added, "I remember your father as being right handy with a skillet, son."

"He was a real good cook," Redge agreed. "My dad could have been successful at just about anything. It was my stubbornness that kept us at Cardigan Camp after Stacy Murdock had warned us to leave . . . and after that damned horse-stealing Hollis Devlin showed up at the Diamond-7."

"Devlin!" The word exploded from Willoughby. "Boy— say that again. Was Hollis Devlin somehow responsible for your pa's death?"

Redge nodded numbly, and said, in a slow-worded whisper, "Devlin is a big man, physically. But he's lower than a rattlesnake."

Emmett Willoughby stopped, threw his arm across his horse's mane, and quietly stared up at the distant clusters of stars. A cold firmness came into his face and his words. "So now Will's half of the torn playing card has come to me. It's time that the task be done—that which I should have finished that night, long ago, on the riverboat." He paused, then turned toward Redge. His face was ruthless. "You asked, boy, if I would teach you to use the six-gun. To draw . . . to fire . . . to kill. There is no need. I had a compact of both care and retribution with Will Cardigan. My pledge will be kept, Redge." Willoughby struck his open palm with slashing blows of his bridle reins. Then he added, in a warmer tone, "Besides, you're too young to become a killer. Leave that to me, and to guns that have already spoken too often."

Redge Cardigan whirled about, as though stunned and enraged by the enormity of Willoughby's decision.

"You can't go after Stacy Murdock. That's my job, my future, and maybe my life. Side with me, Emmett . . . Uncle Emmett. Take old Hollis Devlin out of my way—or anyone else. But for God's sake let me be the one you make ready . . . and train. Make me good enough to put one bullet between the eyes of Stacy Murdock."

"Why, Redge? Why should I teach you something you may always carry—a gunfighter's reputation and loneliness?"

Distant starlight illuminated the boy's steely eyes.

171

Suddenly his hands grasped his coarse work shirt and yanked it free of his encircling belt. Then he pulled it over his head, to let it dangle at his side in a careless way. He turned then, so that his naked back would be revealed to both the starlight and to the amazed stare of Emmett Willoughby.

"Now . . . can you see it? Sure you can. It was put there with a rawhide lash . . . for people to see for the rest of my life. Know what it is, Uncle Emmett? It's a diamond. A red and seared and vicious diamond—because I'm supposed to carry the brand of the ranch where Stacy Murdock is boss. The Diamond-7 Ranch. It'll stop shaming me someday. On the day I've gunned that monster down . . . to rot in a Diamond-7 grave!"

Hosteen Begay had witnessed the scene, listening in utter silence. Now he stepped forward, and his darker hand lay for an instant on Redge's arm. Then he took hold of the shirt hanging unnoticed at Redge's side. With deft movements, he straightened it, then helped the branded boy to slip into it.

Redge's breathing had slowed to normal, and he had turned toward the beckoning freight-station light, when Emmet Willoughby pulled gently on the reins of the horse he was leading. He came quickly into stride with Redge, then said, in a brisk and matter-of-fact way, "It will take several weeks, boy, if it can be done at all. We'll need a quiet, out-of-the-way place, and endless hours. I have to go on with the wagons as far as Kanab. Then I'll double back, and we will get to work."

He had scarcely finished when the Indian youth spoke in a strangely musical way. "There are things of the Navajo way that I can reveal to a friend."

They turned to look toward Hosteen, and to acknowledge his words. But suddenly there was only silence about them. He had vanished.

The following two weeks passed slowly for Redge. He had hardly met Willoughby, and the compelling, taciturn man was already gone, riding north to help provide protection for the freight wagons bound for Kanab and points beyond. A change in the weather brought deep snow to the forested uplands; cold winds blew continually across the open reaches of the desert. During the warmer hours of the day, Redge busied himself patching and repairing the freight station's corral and living quarters. After considerable dickering, he managed to buy one of the expertly braided lariats that were fashioned by the station's Spanish caretaker. The rope seemed at times to be almost alive and ready to leap at Redge's directive motions. Soon he was able to cast loops easily over the posts and the rocks of the station yard.

Emmett Willoughby was gone fifteen days. He returned to Bitter Springs just after noon on a day when darkening skies and a rawness of the air foretold the approach of another snowstorm.

Redge met him in the station yard and took the reins of Willoughby's tired horse. "I'm sure glad you made it here ahead of the snow," he said with a broad, welcoming smile.

"I am too, Redge. There's not much shelter this side of the river crossing." Willoughby gave Redge an appraising glance. Then he asked, "Well, lad, are you still of a mind to study firearms?"

The words brought a bleakness to Redge Cardigan's eyes, and the old stubbornness returned to his lips and chin. "I've been ready a long time. Can we start tomorrow?"

"Ease down, Redge. It ain't as simple as picking up a rock and flinging it at a badger."

"You haven't decided not to teach me, have you?" Redge demanded anxiously.

"Of course not," Willoughby answered a bit testily. "The arrangements are made. That's why I was gone so long. I got in touch with Dade Sutherland. You and me will be heading south in the morning—or just as soon as this storm plays itself out. Away from this cold that chills a man's trigger finger and stiffens his arm."

"Where are we going, Uncle Emmett? Flagstaff? Show Low?"

"Neither, Redge. We're going down into the Verde River Valley. Most of the time, it's warm there; besides, Dade Sutherland has a camp where we can put up and not be bothered for a few weeks."

"You know best," Redge agreed, and then added, "but I have sort of hoped that Hosteen could be around when we . . ." Redge paused and shrugged. "I can't imagine where he went to."

"The boy will know soon enough when we leave here,"

173

Willoughby said. "Between here and Flagstaff we'll be traveling across many miles of reservation land. There are small trading posts. Red Lake. Kayenta. Moenkopi. We will be watched . . . and word of strangers travels fast across this Navajo land."

The word must have indeed ridden the wind, for Hosteen Begay did appear. It was at the camp that Willoughby and Redge made on the south bank of the Little Colorado River, some sixty miles north of Flagstaff. When they bedded down for the night, the place was deserted. When they awoke to the chill and the cloudiness of winter dawn, the Indian boy was squatted over the ashes of their campfire, wrapped in a multicolored blanket. He maintained the stolid patience of one accustomed to waiting.

Redge crawled quickly from his warm blanket roll, threw more fuel on the handful of embers, then shivered as he awaited the fire's warmth. "Hosteen, I'm glad you are here," Redge said in greeting. "You must have ridden all night." He looked about for his friend's horse, but saw none.

Hosteen leaned his head sidewise and smiled as he said, "Redge, you will find only the traces of my moccasins. My feet brought me here . . . swiftly."

"We better eat," Redge said. "You must be hungry, and tired out."

"The trail toward a friend is not tiring," Hosteen answered with quiet dignity.

There was a silence between them as Redge fed the flames and brought them to a dancing glow. Emmett Willoughby propped his head on his arm as he studied the two boys. "I've an idea we could find plenty for your friend Hosteen to keep busy with if he's of a mind to traipse down to the Verde Valley with us."

The glow of eagerness suffused Redge's face. "Would you, Hosteen? Could you go with us? You said once that there were things you could teach me. And I'd really like your companionship."

Hosteen Begay rose to his feet, let the blanket slip loosely onto his arm, and then stood in quiet study of the distant, snow-robed San Francisco peaks to the south. "Perhaps I am needed, Redge," he said finally. "We will come soon to the trader's place at Gray Mountain. There I will leave word for my mother that I have gone with my friends to the River Verde."

174

They came, the following day, into the timbered area that leads ever upward toward the mountains and the town of Flagstaff. At first the trail wound through endless thickets of brush and dwarfed piñon pine. As their elevation increased the piñon stands became taller and more verdant; after a few miles, a scattering of tall and regal ponderosa pine stood sentinel above the lesser trees. Presently the timber took on more height and density as they rode into the vast and virgin forests that reach from the Kaibab Plateau southward to the isolated Tonto Rim.

Their stay in Flagstaff was brief. Redge hoped to find Dade Sutherland in town, but was given word that he had gone southward toward Tucson on business.

Willoughby visited the Babbit Brothers Trading Post and put together a pack of supplies they would likely need during their stay in the Verde Valley. Redge had determined on one purchase, and quietly slipped away from both Willoughby and Hosteen. He came back to their campsite a couple of hours later, riding a smooth-coated, frisky pinto gelding. He swung from the saddle, held the reins out to Hosteen Begay, and said quietly, "I hope you like this paint horse. He's yours, Hosteen. I only had enough for the bridle and a blanket. No way could I talk them out of a saddle."

With wordless wonder and excited eyes, the Indian boy seized the pinto's mane and leaped to the animal's back. His heels touched the horse's flanks; then he rode off, made a wide circle through the snow-laden trees, and then pulled to a stop beside Redge.

"He is a fine pony, Redge. Mindful of the reins."

Southward from Flagstaff, they followed a trail that wound through small, open parks and again into the dense stands of timber. They rode, when the sun was marking noon, around a jutting ridge of rock. A sudden shout of wonder broke from Redge, and he drew his mount to an abrupt stop. Almost at his feet, the forest land dropped off, giving way to a vast and deep canyon. Although the upper slopes and timbered ridges were heavily mantled with snow, the valley far below seemed a place to which summer had escaped. There was a flowing stream, and a hint of green.

As Redge sat staring, Willoughby pulled up alongside. "What is this . . . this beautiful place?" Redge demanded, and then added, "It's endless, falling off there to the end of the earth."

"It's Oak Creek Canyon, son. Our gateway to the valley of the Verde River."

"How do we get down there? It's miles below us."

"There's a trail of sorts that zigzags down along the north and west canyon walls." Willoughby flicked a thumb past Hosteen, who was already urging his horse between the clustered pines that grew on steep slopes. "Leave it to an Indian to somehow know every right step to take." He urged his horse into the pine cluster, motioned for Redge to follow close behind him, and then said, "About thirty miles down south, Oak Creek dumps into the Verde River. About there is where we'll set up camp."

In the broad and warm valley of the Verde River, where Emmett Willoughby, Redge Cardigan, and Hosteen Begay went about the grim business of preparation, December was marked by short, cool days. Here, the blizzards, blown in from the northern uplands, lost their urgency and their fury. They dwindled into occasional rain showers that brought a fresh greenness to the desert and swelled the river's flow. The camp was marked by a purpose and a routine. There were times when Emmett Willoughby's voice sounded time and again with patient and detailed instructions. There were other times when a sudden burst of gunfire sounded across the secluded glen they had chosen for their deadly practice. From it, a young and determined gunfighter might come forth.

Chapter 15

Christmas of that year, 1898, drew near. In Denver, the holiday lights, laden store windows, and the sound of the old carols spurred on the shoppers who milled about the streets. Early winter had been mild upon the plains this year. Both the grasslands and the city expectantly awaited the coming of Christmas and a heavy fall of snow.

Shortly after seven o'clock, on December 22, a carriage drew up to the side entrance to the Waverley mansion on Pennsylvania Street. As though expecting the rig, the carriageman approached, then touched his fingers respectfully to his cap.

"Good evening, Mr. Brinner. I haven't seen you since last Christmas. I'll take right good care of your team."

"You always do, Barney. Thank you . . . and have a jolly Christmas."

The banker stepped from the carriage, thrust the reins into Barney's hands, and turned toward the doorway, where a recessed light poured a warm glow onto a wreath of holly, fir branches, and scarlet ribbon. Before reaching for the doorknob, Adolph Brinner stood for a few moments in silent reverie. His thoughts were upon the holidays a year past, and the drama between Murdock and Cardigan that had unfolded in Jennifer's Waverley's card room. His thoughts turned to the determined-faced boy who, weeks before, had come into Brinner's bank seeking directions to a lawyer.

Adolph Brinner opened the door and stood in the subdued light of the hallway. He had scarcely had time to remove his overcoat when voices sounded a greeting and Jennifer Waverley and her quietly composed sister, Carla Dunlop, came to meet him.

In the moment when the banker's hand touched Jennifer's, he hoped desperately that his thoughts were not written across his face—for he was noticing that Jennifer was aging fast these days. There was little left of her bounce and vitality and eagerness.

"I'm glad you asked me to come by, Jennifer," he said. "This home always seems to spread an aura of the Christmas season, whatever month it happens to be."

"Thank you, Adolph," she answered simply, and then nodded toward the woman standing beside her. "Carla, you remember Mr. Brinner, don't you?"

"Of course." Carla Dunlop smiled, then added, "I'd be foolish not to remember your banker, Jennifer. Someday I might need a loan."

Brinner's shrewd eyes swept her countenance. She also has changed, he thought. Not from either age or illness. It's . . . it's a barrier. A sort of reserve . . . a retreat into self, as though she has been deeply hurt, and is on guard so that she will never again be vulnerable.

The banker's gaze remained unrevealing, but abruptly a thought and a memory was upon him. This house. At Christmas. A year ago. And Carla Dunlop radiantly alert and happy—and with eyes that took on softness when she was near Will Cardigan.

They had entered the living room, chosen their favorite seats, and were sipping Tom & Jerrys, when Jennifer tugged nervously at an earlobe and asked, "Adolph, are you aware that Will Cardigan, the man whom Stacy Murdock insulted here in my home, was killed last summer?"

Brinner was conscious of Carla's restrained gasp and the tight anguish with which she twisted the pendant at her throat.

"I read of Mr. Cardigan's death; it was a rather sketchy and incomplete account in the *Rocky Mountain News*. Early last July, I believe."

"Of course it was sketchy," Carla said, in a flat and toneless voice. "The vast, ruthless Diamond-7 Ranch has a way of suppressing news of its actions—and its murders."

A silence fell on the room, then Adolph Brinner said, "I met Cardigan's boy last fall. He happened to come into our bank."

"When?" As the word escaped her, Carla rose to her feet and moved closer to the banker. "Mr. Brinner, when was Redge—Redge Cardigan—in Denver?"

"It was in October. They boy came in one morning—by

178

chance—and asked one of our officers if he could recommend a good lawyer. Something about the boy and his manner impressed the officer. We gave him the address of Allen Van Cleve." Adolph Brinner paused, then, seeing the urgency in Carla's face, he went on. "Later, I asked Van Cleve about the boy. It seems he broke himself by paying Van Cleve a three-hundred-dollar retainer."

"A retainer? For what?" Jennifer questioned.

"To enable Van Cleve to file with the Secretary of State for some water rights. Part of the flow of Crow Creek, in Weld County. It seems that the boy's father had homesteaded quite a bit of land along the creek."

Carla Dunlop had been pacing across the room. Now she dropped into a chair nearer to Brinner and said firmly, "Mr. Brinner, I believe I should explain. It isn't my nature to be either demure or coy. And I must be truthful. I was deeply in love with Will Cardigan . . . and he with me." Carla Dunlop lifted her head proudly, and her eyes shone. "It is likely that Will and I could never have married. But he was important to me. And so is his son.

"It was a long time after Will's death that I heard of it at Fort Laramie. I requested time off from my work, and came to Weld County. I encountered a stone wall of conspiracy and silence. There were those who knew nothing. Those who might have helped seemed afraid to speak. My only break came when I happened to meet two brothers, the Farnums, from Kimball, Nebraska. They'd come on a trading trip to Kate's Wagon. I asked them if they knew anyone named Cardigan. One of them remembered there had been a boy named Cardigan at a place they called Kate's Wagon.

"In early November, I made a long and slow trip to that trading post. But I was too late. The owner, a wonderful lady named Kate Andrus, told me Redge Cardigan had been brought to her in early summer. Whipped. Branded. In critical condition. Stacy Murdock hadn't limited his vengeance to the father—to my beloved Will."

Her reserve shattered, Carla Dunlop slumped in the chair and uttered broken sobs.

Then she calmed herself and continued, "Will's boy, Redge, had left Kate's Wagon before I arrived. I was told he would go to Arizona."

Brinner nodded. "That would tie in with what Allen Van

Cleve told me. The boy left Denver in a hurry. Because of his not being of age, Van Cleve was to send the papers to someone at Kate's Wagon." Brinner halted, probing his memory and striving to get incidents into logical order. Then he added, "Something that Tom Foxley told me last week may throw some light onto this. Foxley had been up along the South Platte River on a cattle-buying trip. He stopped to visit with Jeff Masters. Jeff was telling what happened when Stacy Murdock and a couple of his riders showed up in real friendly fashion at Masters's headquarters. Stacy explained that old Mr. Purcell, the owner, had drowned, and that Murdock was now full manager— and hoped to presently be owner—of the Diamond-7."

Jennifer Waverley straightened, her eyes flashing contempt. "I trust that Jeff Masters had the common sense to send that cur slinking off his property," she declared.

Adolph Brinner smiled, then lifted his hand. "Wait, Jennifer. Stacy Murdock left Masters's ranch sort of quickly. But it wasn't Jeff who sent him. It was an old hired hand of Masters. A grim, salty-tongued fellow named Hank Kutcher."

"What did he do?" Carla leaned forward expectantly.

Brinner drained the last drops of his Tom & Jerry, ran a handkerchief across his white mustache, then settled back to tell the story.

"It seems Stacy Murdock made a mistake. While riding into Jeff Masters's headquarters, he'd spotted some heifers. Springers due to calve in late March or April. They carried a brand unknown to Stacy Murdock, but he flatly told Jeff Masters that on one of the heifers he'd seen the Diamond-7 brand worked over."

"My God," Jennifer half shouted. "The fool was accusing Jeff of rustling! What did Jeff do—knock hell out of him?"

"He did not." Adolph Brinner was savoring the drama of his words. "Jeff just gave Stacy Murdock a long, frosty stare. Then Jeff shouted to the bunkhouse. It was this feisty fellow, Hank Kutcher, that came strolling out toward Masters and Stacy Murdock. Before Murdock could say a word, Jeff Masters laid it out for Kutcher.

" 'Those heifers of yours. Murdock claims they're Diamond-7 stock, and carry that brand—tampered with.'

" 'And the dirty, murdering son of a bitch is lying!'

180

Kutcher hissed, clear for everyone to hear. 'The heifers belong to a family named Cardigan, by Andy Purcell's hand.'

"Stacy Murdock turned white, let his arm move just a trifle toward his holster. 'Kutcher,' he howled. 'I'll cut down on you. Surer than hell I'll do it, one of these days!'

" 'Crucified Christ,' Kutcher answered, with scorn. 'You'll never do that. There's that mess you've been in a long while up at Kate's Wagon. If I'm shot—you hang. Ain't that simple, Stacy?' Then Kutcher just pointed toward the sun, and stared hard at Murdock. 'You've seen the old sun rise again, Stacy. Time grows shorter. Every sunrise. Every noon. Every sunset. It's about time, Stacy. Time for you and that crooked-clawed horse thief Hollis Devlin to glimpse eternity—to face the guns of Willoughby.' "

"How strange," Carla whispered. "What did he mean, Mr. Brinner?"

"I'm not sure. Foxley tells me there is a Texas gunslinger who carries the name Willoughby."

The room was hushed for a moment. Carla rose again, moved behind her chair, and gripped its leathered back. When she spoke, there was sureness and purpose in her words.

"Mr. Brinner, I am so glad you could come this evening. What you have told changes my plans—and perhaps my life. I will give due notice to my employer at Fort Laramie, then come back here to Denver. I'm not wealthy, but then I'm not penniless either. Will you do something for me? Get in touch with that lawyer, Van Cleve. Tell him to follow up on the boy's . . . on Redge's . . . water application. Also, he's to find out the legal status of the Will Cardigan homestead claims. Keep me fully advised. If more money is needed, my savings should cover the expense."

Jennifer Waverley stood up, holding her empty glass aloft, and banged a small bell. "We'll drink to that," she said, and animation brought color back to her wrinkled cheeks. Then she predicted, "We're in for excitement, Carla. Maybe a real fight—something I've missed ever since leaving Telluride. We'll find out just what it takes to make Will Cardigan's dream come true. A homeplace for his son. A ranch with plenty of grasslands and water . . . right smack where that bastard Murdock doesn't want it." She fell silent for a moment as a butler appeared and served another round of drinks.

Adolph Brinner, Jennifer, and Carla raised their glasses in tribute to the season, to the man who had shared the holiday with them a year ago, and to his son and his future.

"God rest Will Cardigan," Jennifer said softly. Then she lowered her glass and murmured, "It would be interesting to know just who does hold title to that damnable, sprawling, profitable Diamond-7 Ranch."

Chapter 16

Spring comes early to the Verde Valley of Arizona. It lies, broad and sheltered, between the upthrust of the Coconino Plateau and the true desert, off southward, that pioneers named the Valley of the Sun. The days grew warmer, bringing the roar of spring runoff to the river and its tributary creeks. The branches of cottonwoods became a riotous spread of swelling buds. Occasionally, the rains of spring poured down from dark clouds that hovered above the timbered canyons and hit the snow-speckled tips of the distant San Francisco peaks.

By the end of February, a restlessness was growing within Redge Cardigan. In late afternoon, when Emmett Willoughby's set hours of studied practice were over for the day, the boy would saddle his horse and ride across the grass-and-brush-mantled valley slopes. His mind turned often to the vastly undulating grasslands of eastern Colorado . . . to Crow Creek Valley . . . to the pleasant hamlet known as Kate's Wagon . . . to freckle-faced and impish Audrey Andrus . . . to volatile old Hank Kutcher . . . to the quiet creekside grove where Will Cardigan would forever rest . . . and inevitably to the hate-torn faces of Hollis Devlin and Stacy Murdock.

Redge was aware that blizzards could still be sweeping the Colorado plains as March and early April warmth and greening affirmed the arrival of spring in the secluded canyon country of central Arizona. Waiting was a hard and tedious thing, but inevitably the day must come to return to the ruins of Cardigan Camp—and to let those of the Diamond-7 know that another day of decision was at hand.

The routine that Willoughby insisted they maintain at the camp was a rigorous one. The periods given to actual handling of weapons were brief. Redge was being conditioned both mentally and physically.

On an afternoon in late April, Willoughby watched as Redge went through an intense session of target practice. Then, for the first time since they had begun the lessons, he voiced an appraisal. "Redge, I don't know. I just flat don't know. You're in top condition . . . and you're a pretty tough kid. You've the guts and the drive and the determination. You've got sharp eye and a steady hand."

"Am I ready?" Redge demanded.

Willoughby pulled thoughtfully at his mustache and said reluctantly, "There's an element, son, that neither you nor I have much control over. It's a combination of coordination, agility, and speed. Maybe it is hereditary . . . or just instinctive. But it's hardly ever acquired." Willoughby paused, reached out to clutch Redge's shoulder, then spoke brusquely. "Dammit, Redge, what I'm saying is that when you come up against an experienced gunman you're going to need a particular break."

"You mean I'm not good enough—fast enough on the draw?" Redge's voice wavered with concern and frustration.

"Oh, you're good, all right. Stance. Hands. Nerves. Eyes. It's just that you need that split second of advantage." As he spoke, Emmett Willoughby whirled, his hands a claw-like blur as they sought the holstered guns at his sides. The yanking of the weapons upward, the lining of them, and fingering of triggers was a symphony of blended actions, of smooth and instantaneous reaction.

They were standing near a fallen log on the edge of their practice range. As the roar of gunfire subsided, Redge did not have to examine the white square of paper on a tree some thirty paces from where Willoughby stood. He had seen this before, and knew the incredibly small area into which his companion's lead slugs had found their way.

Hosteen Begay walked quickly to Redge's side and said softly, "He is right, Redge. There will always be those who are faster with a six-gun."

"I don't care about others—just one man, and just one time," Redge said, his voice mingling irritation and anxiety. "I only need to be fast once—to gun down Stacy Murdock. After that I'll hang up my revolvers . . . and hope to hell to forget them."

Hosteen Begay squatted on the ground, grasped a pebble, and skimmed it onto the swollen expanse of the river. Presently he turned his face toward Emmett Willoughby. There was an intensity in his eyes and voice as he spoke.

"Long ago, when we were on the trail to Bitter Springs, I said perhaps knowing the ways of the Navajo might help my friend. When he faces a gunfighter, he will be . . . will be . . . what is the phrase? In a spot. My people have learned that an enemy—either a bear or a wolf or a man—can be distracted by a sudden cry—a yell—"

Willoughby nodded. "The element of surprise. Something that offers that important instant of advantage. Maybe not a yell, but something unexpected, maddening. Hosteen could be right. We'll try to come up with something."

On a sun-drenched morning in late April, Redge awakened early, prepared breakfast, and then sought out Willoughby at their horse corral. He had been thinking about what he had to say all night long. "Emmett, have you got time for a bit of talk?"

"Sure thing, Redge. What's on your mind?"

"The time has come for me to pull out . . . head back to Colorado. I'm not getting any handier with a six-gun. Maybe now I'm just wasting time. Mine and yours."

Willoughby nodded gravely, then said, "I've been waiting for you to assess your own progress. There's such a thing as trying to hone a razor—or a gun draw—too fine. Likely you're as fast with the sidearms as you'll ever be. And don't mistake what I'm saying, boy. You're pretty fast and dangerous."

"If I am, I owe it to you. I'll be tested before too long. My dad was shot down just before the fourth of July last summer. I promised myself that Stacy Murdock wasn't to live a year."

"When do you plan to take off?" Willoughby asked.

"How about today? Hosteen says there's an old Indian trail that runs from the Navajo Reservation up into the Colorado mountains. Plenty of grass and fish and game most of the way. I can mosey along, see a lot of country. Maybe I'll toughen up a little more."

"That trail, Redge—nowadays some pretty desperate characters, men on the dodge, use parts of it. You'd be taking a big chance up that way alone."

"I've been hoping that Hosteen might agree to going with me, at least part of the way."

"Then there would be three of us, Redge." Willoughby's words were quietly spoken but decisive.

Redge Cardigan looked up with a smile. This was a man who kept his promises, and renewed them daily.

Willoughby nodded confirmation of his words, then walked to the fence to watch Hosteen Begay, as he worked tirelessly with the pinto gelding that Redge had bought for him in Flagstaff. Hosteen sat astride his horse toward one edge of a small, circular clearing, where grass and brush had been trodden down by the pinto's hoofs. He spoke a low command that halted the animal, then he quickly dismounted and ran across the clearing, a distance of about sixty steps. Then he stopped, picked up an egg-sized rock, and threw it where it would fall only a few feet in front of the motionless pinto gelding. The only sound was the thud of the rock hitting the ground.

Instantly the spotted horse threw back his head. Then, breaking into a charging gallop, he moved in a direct line to the spot where Hosteen stood alertly waiting. It seemed at first that the horse would crash into the boy, but suddenly he came to a sliding halt that brought his muzzle within three feet of Hosteen's upraised hand.

Redge shook his head in disbelief. "I didn't believe any horse could be trained to do that. I never heard of such."

"I remember hearing, a long time ago, down in Texas, about a woman who'd taught a big, blooded mare that same trick. When anybody would pester the woman, she'd scare hell out of him by having the mare charge while she was standing beside whoever was annoying her. It seems that any horse trained that way will run over anyone who gets in its way, but it'll practically sit on its haunches to stop when its trainer lifts a hand."

Redge gazed out at the far western horizon of the Verde River Valley. "Maybe," he murmured, "if I'd practiced gunplay as hard as Hosteen worked with that pinto, I'd be faster—"

"Shut up, Redge!" Willoughby said sharply. "You worked hard, and I'm proud of what you've done. Forget doubt. Put doubt in the same place you've put fear, son—out of your mind and out of range."

As though triggered by Willoughby's suggestion, Redge whirled to face their target tree. He crouched down, and sent three shots, almost as a single and blended action, into the paper. They were true shots; any one of them would have dealt death had the target been a man.

Willoughby nodded his satisfaction. "How come you didn't shoot that good yesterday . . . or this morning?"

Redge reholstered his weapon, then grinned. "How come you hadn't fired me up by letting me know you're going along with me to Colorado?"

When Emmett Willoughby failed to answer, Redge rose, peered keenly into the older man's face, then asked, "How about your job? Emmett, you've given practically the whole winter to me, and paid practically all the grub and ammunition expense. Won't you have to hire out somewhere? Maybe go back to guarding Mr. Sutherland's freight wagons?"

"Likely someday I will," Willoughby said. "But not for a while. When I took on the chore of making you fast with a six-gun, Dade Sutherland laid down the law to me. He was madder than all get out because I hadn't talked you out of the idea of a showdown with Stacy Murdock."

"You couldn't have changed my mind." Redge's voice and the thrust of his chin indicated his deep determination.

"I know that, Redge. You're like your father. Both stubborn as a wolf hanging onto an old cow's snout. I told Dade that neither him nor me nor the good Lord could head you off. Sutherland hesitated, then agreed that probably I was right. He thinks a lot of you, Redge. And your quick thinking that kept him from being run over by those cattle cars, last fall at Grants."

"He has been a fine man to work for," Redge said. There was admiration in his voice.

"Well, I still am working for him," Willoughby informed him. "When I asked Dade to pay me off so I could work with you, he just grinned and told me to go to hell. Then he said my new job was to beat some gun sense into you—and stay with you—back your hand and your play—in whatever lies ahead on that Crow Creek range you're always spouting about."

They left their camp in the Verde Valley the following morning. The wary-eyed and leanly erect Emmett Willoughby. An Indian boy whose deeply bronzed knees touched the spotted sides of his spirited but trained pinto gelding. A boy who was carrying back to Colorado a diamond-shaped brand upon his back, and his unwavering determination to face the brutal foreman of the Diamond-7 Ranch in the combat that must mean death for one of them.

Creeks were chuckling with the runoff of spring as the three, moving in a leisurely but steady way, followed a canyon trail that brought them up over the Mogollon Rim. In the higher country, in the great and virgin pine forest, there were still snowbanks in shaded spots. The nights were cold, but the days held clear and warm with the assurance of coming summer.

They dropped down from the timbered Coconino Plateau onto the arid and multihued reaches of the desert, and the beginning of the Navajo Reservation. There were place names that imbedded their sounds in Redge's memory. Wupatki. Moenkopi. Tonalea. Kayenta. Teec Nos Pos. At a Navajo village that was very small and without name, Redge and Willoughby pitched camp and waited three days while Hosteen Begay rode off to visit his mother. When he returned, the Indian boy's only mention of the visit was spoken to Redge.

"My mother's horse—the one you gave me medicine for —is well and strong again. My mother wishes you a successful journey."

"What does she think of your traipsing along to Colorado?" Willoughby demanded.

"She hopes that before another winter I will return to her hogan."

A trace of concern appeared on Redge's face, and he asked, "Hosteen, are you sure it's all right for you to go to Colorado with me? It's a long way—and what if your mother needs you?"

Hosteen shook his head, then stared steadily at Redge. "It is best I go. I have brothers and a sister at home who help with our few sheep and a corn patch. For them, I would like to do something, Redge. The mission school taught me many things about white men and their ways. I wasn't taught how I could make life better—and healthier —on our beautiful land of desert and canyons and mesas. I will go with you now, Redge. Maybe I will learn a better way of providing food and shelter and medicine." It was an unusually long speech for Hosteen Begay. As it ended, he fingered a hard clod, then threw it to a spot before his

188

pinto. The horse wheeled and bolted quickly to where the Indian boy was holding up one commanding hand.

Redge watched in a reflective way. I wonder, he thought, if Hosteen could find one single thing worth learning . . . there along Crow Creek . . . there on those undulating grasslands of a ranch I mean to rid of its foreman? His eyes widened in a startled way. The thought had brought to mind a face and a voice that seemed of his distant past. The upturned and mischievous face at Kate's Wagon. And Audrey Andrus's words—*You're still a sorry sort of person. But maybe while I'm gone you'll learn to gather eggs, and to stop fumbling when you sack dried apples.*

"Audrey," Redge Cardigan whispered, "just so I don't fumble when I am face to face with Stacy Murdock."

189

Chapter 17

They entered Colorado by way of the ranching and mining town of Durango. They would have pushed on eastward, but a grocery store owner convinced them to make camp alongside the Animas River and wait. "The last stage in from over Alamosa way reported it's snowing hard and steady on Wolf Creek Pass. You Arizona sunshine boys wouldn't last very long up on Wolf Creek. It's mean— sometimes downright deadly. In a few days, after the storm, they'll clear the trail so freighters and the stage can get through. But right now, boys, the snow is probably belly high to a Rocky Mountain canary—that's a braying jackass, in Durango lingo."

It was four days before Redge and his companions resumed their eastward ride. On the high surrounding mountains, the snowfields were deep and of a dazzling whiteness. But lower down, in the warming valleys, the alchemy of spring was breaking ice from the creeks and allowing an occasional wild flower to break cautiously above ground.

They reached Pagosa Springs, arousing the curiosity of a few residents who rarely saw visitors from the Arizona country and its Navajo Reservation. They were told that the headwater reaches of the San Juan River would bring them to the zigzagging upward climb of Wolf Creek Pass.

From the 11,000-foot summit of Wolf Creek Pass, the great mountain barrier drops swiftly toward the level expanse of the San Luis Valley. The crest was still snowbound, except where the trail had been cleared. Redge stood for many minutes on a lofty outthrust of rock and studied the white peaks and dark forests as they marched, range upon range, from south to north.

Presently he was remembering how his father had suggested, so long ago, that they find land and a future in the mountain vastness instead of tarrying on the plains, along Crow Creek Valley. Momentary remorse gnawed within Redge's mind. Perhaps, he thought, if I had listened, had agreed to go on, I would still have my dad. . . . He brushed away the regret, realizing its futility.

Redge Cardigan swept pensive eyes across the vista of peaks. The harsh grandeur of this high country was something he would always remember, yet it would never call overwhelmingly to him as did the flatlands lying off eastward. His was a nature that called for a gentle rise of plains reaching to far and level horizons . . . a domain where the sun rose early above an eastern rim, and many hours later dropped behind a silhouette of the distant front range. A broken skyline was fine—as long as it reared many miles westward from the short-grass country.

He thought of how, a year previous, he had watched the magic of spring's return to the vicinity of Cardigan Camp. And suddenly Redge knew his thoughts for what they were—homesickness for Cardigan Camp, or the tragic little that remained of it. Within a week or so he would again ride down Crow Creek. He sensed the inevitability and the desperation of his return to the acres claimed by the Diamond-7 Ranch. His future would surely depend on the outcome of the next weeks.

He jerked erect, then shrugged. In a few hundred more miles of travel he would see such places as Kate's Wagon and a Denver law office. And his ultimate reality would lie in wait for him: that of standing, six-gun in readiness, and wording the challenge following which either Stacy Murdock or he himself must crumple lifeless in the grass.

From the hour the three travelers came over the summit of Wolf Creek Pass and wended their way slowly toward the far-spread San Luis Valley, spring seemed to travel with them. Free of the stinging snow, their horses could travel at a faster and surer pace. Within a few days, they were over Poncho Pass, at the far-northern end of the San Luis Valley. At noon on a warm day, they came to the banks of a river that surged from high snowfields and traveled through canyons and well-grassed valleys, flowing eastward. They had come onto the Arkansas River; it brought them, a week later, onto the plains and into the town of Pueblo. Now they had to strike northward across the greening expanse of plains. Redge noted the similarity

191

of this area, through which they rode northward, to the Crow Creek Valley. The creeks that brought snow water down from the high mountains were studded with cottonwoods and screened by willows and rose thickets. Cattle grazed the unfenced reaches, and frequently they spotted antelope gazing curiously at them from atop a grassy ridge.

Just before noon of a cloudy and rain-cooled day, they rode up a long slope, came to a crest, and abruptly halted. Denver's outskirts were only ten miles away. Emmett Willoughby looked out ahead. "It has been almost ten years since I was in old Denver town. It has grown . . . and my God, look at that plume of smoke up yonder."

Hosteen Begay sat erect and quiet as he followed the direction in which Willoughby was pointing. Wonder and bewilderment crossed his bronzed face, and he said slowly, "I've never been in so large a town. Perhaps it would not be safe for me—a Navajo—to be seen so far from the reservation."

"Don't worry, Hosteen," Willoughby assured the boy. "Just don't get separated from us, or lose your way. We'll make out all right."

Redge Cardigan scanned the city with mixed emotions. He felt an urge to push hurriedly on toward the spot that had only last year been Cardigan Camp. But he had to acknowledge, there were things about this city on the South Platte River that drew him. He could possibly visit Allen Van Cleve's Office and learn if any progress had been made on his request for an adjudication of Crow Creek water. Then too, it would be a downright relief to leave their horses at a livery stable, sign in at a hotel, and once again have an honest-to-goodness bath in a tub. He had one change of clothing carefully tucked among his gear. After a scrubbing, a hair trim, and a change of outfits he would feel civilized again.

But there was something else charming him irresistibly toward the streets of Denver. Very clearly, he was recalling the autumn day when he had eagerly awaited the return of Kate Andrus from Cheyenne. She had told him, to his immense disappointment, that Audrey was in school—in Denver.

Redge caught his breath, fighting an almost unendurable hope and anticipation. School shouldn't be out out for the summer this early. Memory brought to him the name of the school Kate had mentioned. Likely she was still here. He bit his lip, attempting to keep calm. Just a kid, he mumbled. A spunky, nose-thumbing kid with freckles across her nose. Suddenly he realized what he was feeling with a sense of disbelief. Audrey Andrus. A girl with wind-tousled hair, and eyes that held the levelness of a prairie horizon. And he was on the verge of falling in love with her memory.

In late afternoon, when he judged classes would be dismissed for the day, he changed clothes and struck out on foot for the school. Luckily, there was a trolley route in the right direction. He scrambled aboard a car, then watched the blocks of the city's residential area slide by.

The school, a boarding establishment for young ladies, finally came into view; it was a sizable red brick structure with dormered windows, a steep roof, and a broad sweep of green lawn. Redge walked bashfully up a curving sidewalk and a dozen stone steps. A dozen or more girls, clad in navy-blue skirts and white blouses, were seated under the trees and on the steps.

Finally, he found himself, with hat in hand, before the desk of a middle-aged, portly woman in the school's office. She assessed him in silence, then asked, "Yes, young man, may I help you?" Her tone was politely impersonal, and perhaps a trifle disapproving of his having entered the room without formal permission.

"Do you have a Miss Audrey Andrus enrolled as a student here?" Redge asked.

The woman acknowledged his question with a crisp nod, and the tapping of a pencil on a notepad. Then she asked, "Are you a member of Miss Andrus's family?"

He shook his head. "Audrey is a friend of mine. So is her mother, Kate Andrus."

The woman's face thawed slightly to permit a smile as she asked, "What is your name, young man?"

"The name is Redge Cardigan, ma'am. I am passing through Denver from Arizona."

She rang a small bell, and one of the older students entered the room. Then she said, "Laura, kindly find Audrey Andrus; tell her that a Redge Cardigan is waiting to see her."

"But she's not here," the young woman said. "She left an hour ago."

"To go where?"

"Don't you remember? This is her evening to work at Mrs. Waverley's home."

The older woman peered silently for a moment at a suddenly crestfallen and unsmiling Redge. Then abruptly she said, "Young man, I need a message taken to Miss Carla Dunlop—she's Mrs. Waverley's sister. Would you care to deliver it?"

Eagerness surged to Redge's face, and for a moment the lingo of old Hank Kutcher touched his tongue. "Oh, ma'am . . . I'll carry the word for you . . . be glad to. Plumb to hell and gone."

Redge recovered his wits and a bit of prudence, and stared at the floor in consternation. The student had fled the room with a gasp and a giggle. The older woman, with her face turned from him, was rapidly writing. Presently she finished, sealed the message in an envelope, and wrote an address upon it. Her face was composed as she thrust it toward Redge but a glimmer of mirth danced within her eyes.

"Mr. Cardigan, I'm asking that you deliver this to Carla Dunlop in person. You may inquire of her regarding Audrey Andrus." She hesitated, and then with a chuckle added words that were almost a whisper. "Now—in your own words, young man—get the hell and gone on your way."

Redge strode hurriedly from the school grounds, aware of the curious glances of more girls than he had ever seen before.

At a corner pharmacy, he inquired about the most direct and fastest means of reaching the address on the envelope. An elderly clerk raised his eyebrows in surprise. "You must be a stranger here. Well, let's see—there's a trolley line out that way . . . into the part of town those rich people live in. Otherwise, if you want to walk, it's a hike of maybe twenty blocks to the Waverley mansion."

Redge uttered his thanks, then struck out on foot. His mind was in a turmoil. Pretty soon he would see Audrey. But the clerk had called the place "the Waverley mansion." Maybe they wouldn't let him inside. Then abruptly he stopped short in his tracks, as memory stirred amazement. The Waverley mansion. Waverley! Long ago, he had written a thank-you letter for his case of veterinary tools—to Carla Dunlop and Jennifer Waverley.

His mind was still upon the gift and his father's reticence to discuss the donors as he turned onto Pennsylvania Street. With astonishment he stared at the grandeur of the homes and the vastly sweeping grounds upon which they stood. He studied a house number, then began walking south. He felt like one about to enter Camelot.

Redge had turned from the street and was standing uncertainly in the driveway of the Waverley mansion when an elderly, white-haired man strode to his side and asked, "Howdy, son, are you looking for someone here?" The coachman was studying him closely.

"I'm supposed to deliver a letter—if this is the home of Mrs. Jennifer Waverley."

"You've a letter for Mrs. Waverley?" Barney asked.

"No, the letter is for a Miss Carla Dunlop. And I'm supposed to deliver it in person."

The coachman grinned. "Simmer down, lad. I wasn't trying to run you off. Just the same, I'd like to know your name."

"My name is Cardigan—Redge Cardigan."

"Come along then," Barney urged. "Just ring the bell on that side door. Miss Carla is inside." He turned and ambled toward the carriage house.

Redge squared his shoulders, ran an unsteady hand through his thatch of hair, then turned the knob of the doorbell. He was standing rigidly erect and expectant when the door swung quickly open—and he was looking into the surprised face of Audrey Andrus. Her hand flew to her throat in astonishment and her eyes danced.

Redge had rehearsed this moment a hundred times in his mind, choosing and discarding and then groping again for words with which he would counter the thrust of disparaging wit that would surely be her greeting. But now as she lifted her face, and her eyes widened in surprise, he could only murmur, "God, how I have missed you, Audrey. It's been so long since—" His words were halted and he felt a sudden surge of elation as her arms encircled his neck and she placed her lips firmly upon his for a moment.

Then she thrust him away and held him at arms' length. She said, almost angrily, "Redge Cardigan, you big dolt, where have you been? Everybody's been worrying about you."

195

"I'll tell you later. Just let me look at you for a while, Audrey. Before you decide to favor me with your favorite gesture."

Her chin tilted upward, a stray lock of hair fell forward, and she mischievously brought her thumb to her nose. "So you still remember." She laughed.

Redge held tightly to her hand and glanced down the long and beautifully furnished hallway. "This house . . . it's incredible," he stated aloud.

"It is a lovely place, Redge—wait till you see it all. But how did you manage to find me here?"

"I have a letter for a Miss Carla Dunlop. The lady in charge at your school suggested I deliver it for her."

Audrey led him down the hall and into the library. "Wait here, Redge. I'll find Miss Dunlop." She turned to leave, and reluctantly she freed his hand.

After a moment, he dropped into a comfortable chair; his eyes roamed the walls of the room, upon which were oak shelves holding more books than he had ever seen. Then he closed his eyes and allowed a mental image of Audrey Andrus to fill his mind. She had seemed so much a teasing child . . . a brat . . . when he had last seen her, and he had listened in irritated silence to her sarcastic gibes. Now, after many months, here in the quiet grandeur of the Waverley mansion, Audrey Andrus seemed sophisticated, graceful . . . and utterly lovely.

Minutes later, her well-remembered giggle brought him to reality. He sat bolt upright.

"You fell asleep, right there in that chair," she accused.

"You're crazy," he defended himself. "I was just daydreaming." Redge came to his feet as he looked beyond Audrey to the two women standing behind her.

The girl turned to them, saying, "Mrs. Waverley and Miss Dunlop, this is a friend of mine. His name is Redge Cardigan—and sometimes he is a trial. Maybe when he grows up . . ."

Redge was unprepared for the change that mention of his name brought to the faces of the two women. The younger of the two gasped, and for a moment she buried her face in her hands. The older one, whose face showed both strength and suffering, and now excitement, gathered Redge's hand into both of hers. "Of course. Of course . . .

I should have known. There's much of Will Cardigan about you."

"And my father told me about the two of you," Redge exclaimed. "You sent me those wonderful instruments at Christmas."

Jennifer caught both of the boy's hands in hers. She released them as her sister stepped forward and looked in silence toward this visitor who had so suddenly brought the bittersweet past back to her. "Redge," Carla said finally, "I've looked just about everywhere for you. Will spoke so proudly of you." Her soft but firm hands lay for a time on his shoulders, and she allowed him to gaze searchingly into her eyes.

And somehow, at that moment, Redge Cardigan knew, without further words, that this woman had been deeply in love with his father, and that her affections had been reciprocated. "Those instruments," he murmured. "I'll treasure them . . . always." He was quiet for a little time, then said briskly, "Miss Dunlop . . . I'm supposed to deliver this note from the lady at the school. It's for you."

Carla opened the envelope and quickly scanned the short handwritten note. After a soft laugh, she said, "The note was just a means of making sure we would see you —and I understand the *we* should include Audrey."

Audrey smiled, a bit impishly. "I told you he is a friend of mine—and tried to warn you. He's a grievous trial. A . . . a fumbler."

Her thrust brought laughter that dispelled Redge's sense of unease. He felt relaxed and comfortable in this enormous and intriguing home. Then Jennifer Waverley said firmly, "You must stay with us while you're in town, Redge. There are so many things we'd like to know." She turned to Carla, after she had indicated they all be seated with a sweep of her hand. "This house has been so . . . so damned quiet, almost desolate. Carla, won't it be fun to have this young man about? We can . . ." Jennifer Waverley paused as she noted the seriousness of Redge's face.

He was shaking his head as he answered. "It would be wonderful. But I can't. I've others waiting for me. We'll be heading on north in the morning."

"North!" The word broke from Audrey Andrus almost as a cry of alarm.

197

Redge turned to her in a plea for understanding. "Yes Audrey, back to Crow Creek Valley . . . and Cardigar Camp."

"But Stacy Murdock is still managing the Diamond-7. He and that Hollis Devlin have some sort of partnership."

"They won't have it much longer." Redge's tone was cold, and bleakness crossed his face. After a while he spoke again, slowly and almost inaudibly. "Dead men don't need partners."

Abruptly a gasp of realization broke from Audrey Andrus. "Redge," she cried out. "Oh God . . . no, Redge. You mustn't . . . you can't . . . ride in on them alone."

"I won't be alone, Audrey," he answered sharply. "I have friends I can trust. A man named Emmett Willoughby And Hosteen Begay, a Navajo."

Jennifer Waverley reacted instantly. "Redge," she asked in wonder, "did you say Emmett Willoughby is with you here in Denver?"

He nodded. "Emmett was a friend of my father's. I looked him up in Arizona." He paused, stared at her briefly, then asked, "Why? Do you know him?"

"Mostly by reputation, although I did meet him years ago in Telluride."

Carla Dunlop stood and said briskly, "Then why don't. you bring your friends here so we can meet them?"

Audrey looked at him expectantly.

"I want to bring them here. Emmett. Hosteen. But not tonight. We're heading for Crow Creek about sunrise." He paused, then added, "This thing with Stacy Murdock and with Hollis Devlin . . . let me get it out of the way. Then I'll be proud to bring my friends here to meet you."

There was a moment of silence. Carla moved nearer to the boy, and it seemed that her arms might encircle him as though to hold him from the menace of what she knew lay miles away, along Crow Creek.

A different reaction came from Audrey Andrus. Her eyes widened, and Redge was aware of the bridge of freckles that stood boldly from the whiteness of her face. Her voice was tense, and hardly audible, as she said, "I had better be getting about my work. I'll be folding linens upstairs if you should need me, Mrs. Waverley." She turned, then hesitated and looked back over her shoulder. For hardly an instant her thumb touched her nose and her fingers wiggled at Redge. "I'll . . . I'll show you how—one of these days—to gather eggs—you crazy, brave homesteader."

Then she vanished through the hallway door.

Jennifer Waverley had watched in silence, aware of the tension and the despair affecting both her sister and the spirited girl she surmised was somewhere by herself shedding tears of worry.

"I will accompany you to the door, Redge," Jennifer Waverley said as she laid her hand on Redge's shoulder. When they were alone in the hallway, she added, "We scarcely got to meet you, Redge Cardigan."

"I'm sorry. But it's best I . . ." he answered haltingly.

She laid a firm hand on his shoulder, and in the subdued hallway light, looked steadily into his troubled but stubborn face. "I'm perhaps old enough to be your grandmother, Redge. But for years I lived and worked and fought alongside miners. I know something of men. When a man is driven, as you are, it is best not to interfere with him. It's a strange thing. A man denied his chance for a showdown —for revenge—is never as complete and as strong as the one who meets his challenge. Somehow the encounter is a cleansing and strengthening thing." Then she added, "You'll emerge from this. Perhaps not unscathed, but you'll reap your vengeance." She opened the door, then touched his forehead with her lips.

"Come back to us, to two lonely women, and to a lively girl who has fallen in love with you."

She closed the door behind him, and stood for several minutes in thought. Then she sought out her sister. "Carla. Send Audrey to help me pack a bag. Then tell Barney to get the team of bays hitched and ready to go. You and I are going on a trip."

"Where?" Carla demanded in surprise.

"Down along the South Platte River—all the way to old John Iliff's headquarters. That's where we're pretty sure to find Jeff Masters. And if we're lucky, we'll also run into that Hank Kutcher."

Carla Dunlop stared at her older sister in admiration. "You don't waste time, do you, Jennifer?" Not waiting for a reply, she asked, "But what about Audrey? Do you think we should drop her off at the school?"

"Audrey can go with us, if she wishes. For sure, she won't be worth a damn in school until this affair on Crow Creek is over . . . one way or the other."

Chapter 18

The cool showers and the greening of late May lingered across the high plains. On a cloudy morning, two days after his trip to Waverley mansion, Redge and his two companions left the irrigated area bordering the railroad running north from Greeley toward the Wyoming border. They turned east, roughly retracing the trail by which Redge had ridden from Cardigan Camp and the Crow Creek Valley, months before.

Now they rode spaced apart, forming a triangle with Redge in the lead. Occasionally Hosteen Begay spoke in wonder at sight of the seemingly endless green hills that undulated toward every horizon. But mostly his eyes, trained to distance and movement, kept watch for sight of any riders who might suddenly crest a far-off hill.

Emmett Willoughby rode a scant two rods from Hosteen. A casual observer might have mistaken Willoughby for a middle-aged rancher urging his horse along in search of strayed stock. He found this area to his liking. Although summer had not set in, clumps of sand grass and a variety of budding prairie flowers were already tall enough to stir in the occasional breeze that swept broadening stretches of cattle country.

Despite the pleasure he took in the creek-etched grassland, Willoughby's mood was one of seriousness. Before many days, or possibly within hours, the quiet serenity of these virgin acres would inevitably give way to the harshness of men's voices and the roar of gunfire. He had seen such showdowns too many times not to be aware of their brevity and their devastation. Men met. Men fought. And usually at least one man died. It had become a pattern, a way of life, for Emmett Willoughby. For him, it would end only when someone with either greater skill or luck with a six-gun would decree and provide the ending.

As the sun rose higher, and Willoughby followed Redge Cardigan ever eastward, he pondered the wisdom of preparing this son of his old friend, Will Cardigan, for the showdown they were riding relentlessly to bring about. He had done his best throughout the winter, there in Arizona's Verde Valley, to prepare Redge for the gunplay in which the boy must either kill or be killed. There had been no other choice than to school Redge in the art of gunfighting. Had Emmett Willoughby refused Redge's plea for instruction, the stubborn kid would have dared Stacy Murdock to meet him in a contest that could have had but one result.

If only there were some way to give Redge that split-second advantage. Something that would break Murdock's rhythm and concentration . . . his intensity as he went for his weapon. The miles and the hours fell silently behind them.

The sun had broken through rain clouds, and stood an hour above the western prairie rim, when they rode wearily up a long, greening slope. At its crest, Redge halted his mount and waited for the others to come alongside. Now the land to the east fell gently away to a long line of trees that marked the course of a flowing creek. There were meadows and parklike areas studded with tall cottonwood trees.

Redge swept his hand in a gesture that encompassed the valley from north to south. "There it is," he said in a tone that was excited and proud. "That is Crow Creek Valley. It starts somewhere west of Cheyenne, and finally dumps into the South Platte River. We're just about a mile from where our cabin and our barn stood—and from the circle of trees where my dad is buried."

"You mean the cabin isn't there now?" Willoughby asked softly.

Redge averted his face, turning toward the distant peaks now visible through a rent in the rain clouds. "They burned our cabin," he murmured. "Our barn. Even our corrals, probably."

Hosteen Begay had been silently gazing down into the valley. "There is someone there, Redge. Among those willows, close to the water. A horse has been hobbled—and there is a man squatting on a stump. I don't think he has seen us yet."

"Redge! Hosteen! Get back over the crest and out of sight from the creek." Emmett Willoughby was speaking as he spurred his horse sharply and led the way from the hilltop. "You boys stay here," he continued. "I'll mosey down and size things up. Nobody knows me short of five hundred miles from here." Before they could protest, he rode in an easy trot to disappear over the ridge and from their sight.

Ten minutes later he was back, with a broad grin across his face. "Come along," he urged. "It's a friend."

The boys followed him down the slope. When they had ridden within fifty rods of the stranger, Redge yelled aloud, "Good God almighty—it's Hank Kutcher."

With his eager face aglow, he rode toward the spot where the old range rider stood waiting. Then he eyed Kutcher, and shouted, "Hank . . . damn, but it's good to see you again; you haven't changed a bit."

Kutcher's eyes were bright as he gathered the boy into a bone-crushing hug. "The only reason I ain't changed, boy, is because you haven't been about to spoil my face with what you mistakenly call dentistry." He paused to size Redge up, then added, "About one more winter and you'll be as husky as a full-fledged man. I've missed you, son. Where in creation have you been?"

As he answered, Redge was aware that both Willoughby and Hosteen had stopped a short distance away and were studying the valley's slopes for sign of riders aprowl. "We left Arizona a few days ago," he explained. "Came over the mountains, then up by way of Denver. But how about you, Hank? Where do you spread your bedroll these days? And how come you're here at Cardigan Camp?"

"I was waiting." Kutcher chuckled. "I've been here since midmorning." Seeing the utter bewilderment on Redge's face, he explained, "Yesterday morning two women—and a little gal we both know—drove in from Denver to Jeff Masters's headquarters down on the Platte. Plumb tuckered they was, after driving hell-bent all the way."

"But how did you happen . . ." Redge muttered in amazement.

"If you'd just not interrupt," Kutcher growled, "I'll set it straight in your mind. I work for Jeff Masters now on his spread south of the Platte. Anyway, after them women got through talking to Jeff Masters, nothing was to do but

203

for me to saddle up and ride all night. And I'm here—tired and hungry—and daggoned happy to see you, boy."

Willoughby and Hosteen were slowly approaching, and Kutcher remarked, "Is that tall, middle-aged fellow, with the hawklike eyes, who I'm thinking it is?"

Redge nodded. "That's Willoughby, the one and only, Hank. My other friend is Hosteen Begay, from the Navajo Reservation. He's got eyes that can see halfway into tomorrow. He knows horse-training tricks too; some of them you'd never believe."

Introductions were made, and quickly there was a friendly acceptance among the four. Kutcher eyed the two holstered handguns that Emmett Willoughby was laying aside and commented, "The fame of those sure got up this way a long time before you showed up, Mr. Willoughby."

Willoughby shrugged. "Mostly, such tales that fly about are either dreamed up or exaggerated out of all reason." He waited until Redge and Hosteen had moved away to care for their horses, then asked, "You got wind of our coming in a hurry. Is it likely that others in the area already know?"

Kutcher shook his head and answered, "If you mean Murdock and Devlin and the rest, I doubt they know any of us are here on what they claim is their graze." He stared at the charred ruins that had once been the Cardigan cabin and added slowly, "I reckon Redge has come here to take on Stacy Murdock. I always knew it was just a matter of time." He hesitated, then looked with a level and searching stare into Willoughby's face. "Is the lad ready for gunplay? Has he got a chance?"

"I'd rate it about fifty-fifty—but he'll need the right conditions, and a good break. But for damn sure there's no stopping him. The sooner the better, now."

"It'll come mighty soon," Kutcher answered flatly. "Well, I'm gonna stick around to help see that Redge gets a fair chance." Kutcher squatted and ran his fingers through a clump of grass. "I'd say offhand, Mr. Willoughby, that a crooked-armed bastard named Devlin will already have figured a way to protect his crony, Murdock."

At the mention of Devlin's name, Willoughby's body grew tight. For a moment he was silent, then he said, "Devlin's the real reason I'm up here. We had a disagreement back on a Missouri River boat shortly after Lee surrendered at Appomattox in '65. Almost thirty-five years ago. I reckon it's time to settle with Devlin once and for all."

The boys returned, and the four of them sat and rested among the greening cottonwoods, until evening stole across the quiet width of Crow Creek Valley. The sun dropped toward peaks that were still snow-tipped. Myriad rays of crimson and gold streaked upward, reflecting on the now scattered rain clouds. Hank Kutcher pointed to a pile of dried wood and cottonwood bark. "I gathered that while I was waiting this afternoon. If you pilgrims are as hungry as I am, we can get a fire going. If Hosteen will give me a hand, and you've brought some extra supplies, I'll throw some grub together so we can eat before dark." He paused, noting that Redge was gazing upstream toward the knoll that held his father's grave. He poked a thumb at the boy. "Why don't you make sure the horses are hobbled firm, then show Emmett here that dam site you've had in mind up the crick?"

"Come along," Redge urged Willoughby. "You should see where Dad is buried."

At the gravesite, a few prairie flowers and a clutter of weeds marked earth that had already sunk. Redge knelt in silence; the plaintive call of a night bird sounded in the stillness. Then he rose and banged a fist against a huge spreading willow. "Within a few days, Dad," he whispered, "I'll start rebuilding Cardigan Camp." He straightened, and there was an absolute certainty about him as he motioned Willoughby to follow. "Let's get back to the others, Emmett. Tomorrow I'll show you where the dam could be built. But right now I think we should get back. It was our getting split up that let Stacy Murdock get control of things."

At midmorning of the following day, the four men had their first glimpse of a stranger. Willoughby had insisted that Redge again go through his gun practice routine. Hosteen Begay was again at work with his horse. Half a dozen times he dismounted, ran about fifty steps from the gelding, then whirled about. His arm arched and let fly an egg-sized stone he had been carrying. It struck the ground and thudded just short of the horse's forefeet. As though struck by a whip, the gelding leaped forward in a direct line toward Hosteen. He was only a few feet away from Hosteen's upraised hand when he halted.

Hank Kutcher watched in amazement. After the horse's final run, the old range rider went over to Hosteen. "I'll be damned," he muttered. "Boy, I thought I knew about every hoss-training trick. But that . . ." He broke off, seeing that the Navajo boy was not listening. He was busy scrutinizing the western rim of the valley. He stood for a time, his eyes narrowed, quietly appraising. Then he uttered a quick call that brought Redge and Willoughby to his side. "There's someone up there on horseback. He's in the shadows, up that little gully a way." Kutcher strode closer and squinted in the direction Hosteen had indicated. Presently he swore softly, then said, "It's Bert Andrus. I'd know that roan he's astride anywhere."

"Probably he's spying for the Diamond-7," Redge answered.

Kutcher slowly shook his head. "I'm not so sure. Bert is a pretty undependable kid." He paused, spat tobacco juice into the dust, then added, "Likely Bert has been admiring the way the Indian lad put his horse through that trick. Bert was always crazy about horses."

Redge vividly remembered Bert Andrus's role in the attempted theft of Cardigan horses, when he had ridden with Hollis Devlin. He was more suspicious than Hank Kutcher, who had already mounted his horse and said firmly, "I'll mosey out and have a few words with Bert. Find out what's on his mind."

The distant rider did not attempt to ride off as Kutcher approached him. For a brief time they could be seen facing each other. Minutes later both Kutcher and young Andrus rode within a hundred yards of the watching group. Then Bert waited behind and Kutcher came on by himself. "Bert wants to know if he can come in and watch Hosteen's horse perform a time or so."

"How do we know he ain't just snooping for Stacy Murdock or Devlin?" Redge demanded, still wary.

"We don't," Kutcher admitted. "He admits he's still pretty thick with the Diamond-7. He even tried to warn me that Murdock will have my hide for showing up again at what Bert calls 'this damned nester's camp.' But he claims he hasn't been at the Diamond-7 headquarters for days."

Redge stared undecidedly toward the distant figure. He couldn't even remember Bert's face or his voice. But he had taken part in that horserustling affair. Still . . . he was young, just about Redge's age. And the son of Kate Andrus. A quick breath escaped Redge as he thought: Bert is the brother of Audrey Andrus. What would she think if I . . .

Emmett Willoughby made his decision for him, his voice thoughtful and firm. "Let the young fellow ride on in. We'll keep an eye on him. We need to know the faces and the facts about everyone who might have a mind to cut themselves into the fracas we're heading for."

With a sweep of his arm, Hank Kutcher motioned Bert Andrus into the area where the four waited. As he drew close, Redge swept carefully appraising eyes over him. Bert's face carried an undeniable resemblance to both Kate and Audrey Andrus. Yet it lacked the strength and the spunk of the women Redge had come to know . . . and yes, to love.

"Hello, Bert," Redge said aloud, and his voice made Bert lower his head and look about in discomfort.

"Cardigan," he acknowledged quietly, and said no more.

"Bert, don't look so stung. You—and a few others— should have known I'd be back." Redge turned to Hosteen Begay. "This fellow wants to see what a real horse trainer can do. Want to show him?"

The Navajo nodded, then handed his mount's bridle reins to Hank Kutcher. "Would you lead him over there by the creek, among those willows? Then fasten the reins loose to the saddle horn."

As Kutcher moved off, Redge glanced again at Bert Andrus. "Light down and be comfortable if you want."

Bert's face hardened with distrust and suspicion. "You're not going to get me afoot and into any trap." He waited and then added, "You're a damn fool, Redge Cardigan. An idiot about to cut his own throat. Wait till Stacy Murdock finds out you're back on Diamond-7 graze."

"I'm depending on you to ride downcreek right away and tell him," Redge replied coldly.

Andrus did not immediately reply. He was fidgeting with his reins and staring at Emmett Willoughby. It was plain he could not evaluate this stranger who stood nearby looking imposing with two dark-handled guns slung low in the holsters at his hips. Suddenly Willoughby stooped, picked up a rock, and handed it to Redge. "Here, Redge, you fling it. You ought to learn how it's done."

Without comment, Redge glanced at Hosteen and saw his nod of agreement. Then, arcing his arm backward, he sent the rock sailing, and howled out the command he had so often heard Hosteen voice. The stone fell three paces short of the horse, then skidded almost to the animal's hooves. True to his training, the animal leaped forward and broke into a run across the area that had once been the yard of Cardigan Camp. When it seemed that his course would cause him to smash into Redge, he slowed, then plowed to a stop with forefeet outthrust.

"Jesus! I wouldn'ta believed it," Bert Andrus said excitedly. He turned to Hosteen Begay. "Can any horse be taught to do that?"

Hosteen assured his questioner in a disinterested way. "Not all horses. Just a few. You have to start when the horse is young, and hope."

Redge, suddenly softening toward this boy—Audrey's brother—heard himself saying, "Bert, if you'd stick around a few days, maybe Hosteen would help you get the hang of how to train a horse for the trick."

There was a silence, a short time in which the offer seemed to entice Bert Andrus. Then his voice was desperate and savage as he yelled, "You go to hell . . . all of you. You haven't even a shit-thin chance against the Diamond-7. Stacy and Hollis and the others—a bunch of others—will come riding in hell-bent to smoke every one of you into hell." His voice was wild and out of control as he wheeled his mount to ride off, but he hesitated and quieted when Hank Kutcher spoke softly to him.

"Bert, you've a mighty fine mother and sister. Your mom needs you to help run that shebang at Kate's Wagon. Boy, why . . . why, in the name of crucified Christ, did you get mixed in with varmints like Hollis Devlin and Stacy Murdock?"

Young Andrus ignored Kutcher's words and turned to Hosteen Begay. "Indian, I'd buy that trained horse. Pay a good price."

Hosteen's reply was distant, almost scornful. "My horse is not for sale. Now or ever."

Hank Kutcher wiped a hand across his mustache in

frustration. His voice was almost a whisper, but carried across the sudden silence of the group. "Bert. You've made your decision. Now you'd better ride out—hit the trail to the Diamond-7 and spill all you know to Stacy Murdock." He paused, and his voice rose with a flat deadliness. "Just tell Murdock one thing. *Tell him that the time has come for him to look into the guns of Willoughby.*"

They made camp, prepared their meal, then spread bedrolls for a night's rest. Two would keep watch for half the night, then the other two would take over. The precaution proved needless, for when sunrise came there was no sign of approaching riders or other danger.

The day wore on toward noon, and a quiet, almost of expectancy, hovered about them. It was broken when Hosteen Begay saw, a couple of miles southward, a band of antelope grazing the crest of a hill. He pointed out the white-tailed animals to his companions.

"One of those would taste mighty fine in a skillet," Emmett Willoughby commented.

"It'd best be a buck," Kutcher said. "This time of year the female pronghorn are either giving birth or nursing their young."

"If Hank will lend me his rifle," Hosteen said, "I can have a fat buck for you. Very soon."

Willoughby considered the matter. "I don't like the idea of our splitting up, even for a little while. Still . . . we sure could use fresh meat." He turned to Kutcher and asked, "How does the idea strike you?"

"I could go along with the boy," Kutcher offered. "Sit on a knoll and scan the prairie for any riders closing in."

The old ranch hand's words stirred uneasiness in Redge. It was splitting up that had been partially responsible for the death of his father and the whiplash scars Murdock had inflicted. He would have voiced a protest, but already Hosteen Begay was shaking his head. "It is best I go alone. The antelope are easily frightened away. There is a way I can approach them, and then cause them to come close." He paused, seeing the anxiety in their faces, and then went on, "My horse is trained. If danger comes, he can have me here . . . fast."

"Go ahead then," Emmett Willoughby acceded. "But, damn it, Hosteen, just don't get more than five minutes' ride from us. If you see anyone, fire two quick shots to signal us."

Hank Kutcher drew a short-barreled rifle from his saddle scabbard. He worked its lever action to throw a shell into firing position, then handed the weapon to Hosteen. "Sight just a mite low with this; it ought to knock over a pronghorn up to, say, three hundred yards."

They watched tensely as the Indian boy rode out, guiding his pinto gelding due east. They surmised that his intent would be to get behind a ridge, out of sight of the antelope herd, and then work stealthily toward them. When Hosteen was out of sight, Emmett Willoughby muttered, "Likely the lad will dismount, crawl a bit, and wave something to attract the pronghorn. They're creatures of curiosity."

Time crawled at an interminably slow pace. They scanned the hillsides off to the southwest, but the antelope had grazed over a crest and beyond their sight. Nearly half an hour had passed when the sound of a shot reached them, its sharpness dimmed by distance. They waited momentarily, but there was no second shot. Hank Kutcher scowled, then spoke. "That didn't sound like my rifle." He waited half a minute, with concern growing in his face. "Something's wrong out there." He turned toward his grazing horse and added, "I'm saddling up to go find out."

"What—?" Redge began.

"Son, I gotta find out."

"I'm riding with you," Redge said with certainty.

"Listen to me!" Emmett Willoughby interjected. "If one goes we all go—together."

The sun stood slightly past midday and the spring sunlight was warm across the grasslands when the three swung into their saddles and rode away from the charred remains of Cardigan Camp. Their course took them directly toward where the antelope band had last been sighted. They rode closely bunched together, each with a growing concern that he kept to himself.

They came to a small draw, the sides of which were grassy and the channel wet from recent runoff. From here, the hoofprints of a dozen antelope led them southward toward a knoll where a few slabs of sandstone rock marked the crest.

Amid these prairie rocks they found the body of Hosteen

Begay. He was lying face-down, with arms outflung, and the bunch grass was stained by his blood.

Redge uttered a cry of agony and rage. Then he threw himself down from his horse and held his friend in his arms as he turned the lifeless face toward the sun. Emmett Willoughby came near and examined the dead boy. "He was shot through the belly. It would take something damned near as big as a buffalo gun to tear a hole like that."

Hank Kutcher walked carefully about, his wrinkled, brown face a study in suspicious anger. He knelt in several places to peer at and then touch clumps of grass and the imprints where footprints of men and of a horse had left a few discernible marks.

The rifle that Hosteen had carried lay propped against a rock. Willoughby picked it up and jerked the lever to open it. Then he said, "It hasn't been fired. He must have had a bead on a pronghorn when something caused him to turn and stand up."

"But his horse. Where's Hosteen's horse?" Redge asked suddenly. He gently laid the form of his Indian companion on the grass and came to his feet to gaze somewhat wildly about.

"Redge, you will not spot the boy's pinto. He's gone—stolen." Finishing the words, Hank Kutcher clamped a firm hand on Redge's shoulder.

"But who could have gotten close enough to Hosteen to—"

"Just one person, Redge. It had to be someone your Indian friend trusted a bit."

Redge's eyes darkened. "You mean—?"

"Yes, son. It had to be Bert Andrus."

"That doesn't tally somehow," Emmett Willoughby put in. "That kid—Andrus didn't have a big rifle when he left our camp."

Kutcher shrugged resignedly. "I said Bert was the one who could get close to Hosteen—and later probably stole the pinto. But he wasn't the one who killed our friend."

"Seems so. Bert came up close. The other one stayed off a piece. Probably came close after he'd shot the boy. But who in hell could it be?" Willoughby snapped coldly.

Hank Kutcher had been pacing watchfully among the rocks. Finally he bent down to retrieve an object from the ground. It was the chewed butt of a cigar, still damp and odorous. He thrust it toward Emmett Willoughby. "Does this mean anything to you?" the old rider asked.

"No. I can't say it does."

"It should," Kutcher said, and smiled in a satisfied way. "Someone you used to know chews 'em up this way."

"Who?" asked Willoughby.

"Hollis Devlin—that's who!"

Willoughby's face did not change. But his reply, too softly spoken, carried the sureness of vengeance. "I'll be looking them up—Devlin and the horse-swiping kid. Right shortly I'll be calling and paying my respects to the Diamond-7."

The shock of death and grief gave Redge's movements a dull, numbed quality as he took the blanket from beneath his saddle and wrapped it about Hosteen Begay. Then he turned to Kutcher and Willoughby. "I'll need your help this afternoon. I want to bury Hosteen in the grove—close to my father."

Their slow trek back to camp came to an abrupt halt when they crested a hill that gave view of the creek and the knoll that had been Cardigan Camp. They had left the camp deserted, save for some of their heavier gear. Now there were half a dozen horses picketed about, and a light spring wagon stood in the yard. Smoke lifted lazily from a campfire; men could be seen driving stakes to erect a tent.

"Who the hell ever it is sure plans on staying awhile," Willoughby commented testily. Then he added, "Dammit . . . my bedroll and a bottle of drinking whiskey are down there."

They rode cautiously forward, unsure of what sort of reception awaited them on the banks of Crow Creek. Redge was quiet, his thoughts dwelling on the quietly dignified friend who would never return to his hogan in Arizona. Would he have to fight . . . even for the right to place Hosteen beneath the grass above Cardigan Camp?

The answer came as Hank recognized the men who had taken their campsite. "Well! I'll be a ring-tailed raticoo," Kutcher exploded happily. "That's Jeff Masters and his crew squatted down there. We can ride on in, boys."

Masters was waiting for them beside the tent—a lithe, bronzed cowman, with a look of authority about him.

"Hello, Hank," he greeted Kutcher. "We surmised from your gear strung about that you'd be back—and wouldn't mind having a few friends from down on the Platte join you." Masters was suddenly silent as his gaze fell upon the blanket-shrouded form lying across the saddle of the horse Redge Cardigan was leading. Masters studied the boy's face and then said, "No need to ask. It's stamped about you. You're Will Cardigan's son."

"You knew my father?" Redge asked, stunned.

"Briefly. Too briefly." Masters thrust out his hand. "You're Redge, aren't you?"

Even as Redge was nodding, Hank Kutcher broke in, "Jeff, what in tarnation are you doing up here more than halfway to Wyoming?"

"We made an unexpected trip to Kate's Wagon. Those three women from Denver decided to stay at Kate's until . . ." Masters let his eyes convey the rest of his thought to Hank Kutcher. Then he added, "We were heading home, but got the idea to swing over and have a look-see at Crow Creek." Masters turned back to Redge and said gently, "I'll have my men do the digging . . . wherever you'd like."

Redge nodded upstream. "There's a place up there a little ways. It's where my father is buried."

They returned from the gravesite and the simple service at midafternoon. Immediately Emmett Willoughby began selecting parts of his gear and fashioning a saddle roll. He turned to those about him and said, "I'll be riding down to the Diamond-7 now."

Jeff Masters, who had heard of the day's happenings, answered, "I thought you would. Just remember that Stacy Murdock will be expecting someone—and he plays for keeps."

The words brought a mirthless grin to Willoughby's face. "I'm not going for a call on Mr. Murdock. I'll just be after a strayed pinto horse—and a son of a bitch called Devlin."

Hank Kutcher scratched thoughtfully at his graying mustache. "You'll need someone who knows the lay of the land. I'm riding along." His words left no room for argument.

"Have it your own way, Hank," Willoughby answered. His voice was indifferent, but there was no mistaking the gratitude in his face.

Jeff Masters walked over to Redge. "If you're of a mind to see the Diamond-7 with them, I'd mosey along."

Redge grinned wryly, then shook his head. "Thanks, but no thanks, Mr. Masters. I intend to stay right here, right among these ashes of Cardigan Camp—and make Stacy Murdock come hunting me. This was where he killed my father and whipped hell out of me. It started here—and here it will end."

Jeff Masters nodded, then told Hank, "Don't worry about this boy while you're gone. We'll be here—me and my men—until you get back. Yes, by God, until Murdock comes calling. There's going to be an even chance and no bushwhacking this time around."

Without another word, Emmett Willoughby and Hank Kutcher reined their horses down Crow Creek for the long ride that lay ahead. The slanting rays of sunset told that darkness would overtake the two riders an hour or so before they could reach the Diamond-7.

Chapter 19

Earlier in the day, Tom Foxley had ridden unexpectedly into the Diamond-7 headquarters. Although the months of late summer and autumn were Foxley's time for heavy cattle buying, he was apt to show up at any time of year. Foxley prided himself on knowing well in advance the size and quality and possible weights of herds for which he would be dealing as the summer grasses browned at winter's approach.

Now, as he headed toward the ranch house and the prospect of a hot supper, Foxley from time to time scrutinized the man riding alongside him—and used every bit of his restraint to keep from showing his surprise, even shock, at the change that a few months had wrought upon Stacy Murdock, manager of the widely sprawling Diamond-7.

They rode silently for a while, having exhausted the usual topics of livestock and grass conditions. While Murdock had never been a close friend, Foxley had come to respect the man's ability to handle cattle and land so as to protect the herds and to make sure that the pastures did not deteriorate from overgrazing. He knew that Andrew Purcell had valued Murdock's hard-working drive and his knowledge of ranch management. But had Purcell, in the years before his death, recognized other facets of the man? Had he known of, or even suspected, the insane anger, the ruthlessness, and the utter lack of compassion that mingled to make up Stacy Murdock? What must a man be like to let such hatred fester within him, to become capable of gunning down a homesteader and then horsewhipping the man's son?

Murdock's true personality had somehow emerged in his physical presence. There was no longer the neatness of dress, or the pride of his former erect postures. He had put on weight, too. No man has a right to change that much within a few months, Foxley told himself silently.

Murdock broke his train of thought with a harsh laugh. "There's some booze about the ranch house, if you'd like a shot before we eat. But likely it'll be inferior to what old banker Brinner and some others can provide in Denver."

Foxley nodded. "They seem to know how to charm and dazzle a rancher . . . or a tired old cow buyer. By the way, Stacy . . . speaking of happenings in Denver, how is the loss of so much of the water in Crow Creek going to affect your operations?"

Murdock stared at him blankly, then asked, "What are you talking about, Tom? There hasn't been any change in the flow of old Crow Creek."

"But there will be. Haven't you heard? The Colorado Secretary of State, in Denver, has adjudicated a good percentage of the creek's flow to the Cardigan holdings."

Murdock grinned mirthlessly. "Now ain't that swell? Especially when there's no Cardigan Camp. No Cardigan land—and no Cardigans."

In a way, Tom Foxley could not help savoring his next words. "Don't be too sure, Stacy. The water was adjudicated to the estate of Will Cardigan. The officials wouldn't have done that without knowing there was land for it to be used on."

Anger swept Murdock's face. "Cardigan's kid—damn him. I should have let Devlin shoot him last year. But soft-hearted me, I let him off with a good hiding. I'll have to look the kid up for another go-round."

"Maybe not," Tom Foxley said in a noncommittal voice. "I hear rumors, Stacy."

"Like what?"

"Like that someone named Cardigan, and fitting the boy's description, put up at a livery stable in Denver a few nights ago. There was an Indian boy—Navajo—with him, and an older man that the liveryman surer than hell thought was Emmett Willoughby, the Arizona gunfighter."

"You sure seem to hear everything," Murdock jeered. His words were an effort to make light of the news Tom Foxley had imparted. But within the Diamond-7 foreman's mind was the unsettling echo of a name. *Willoughby.* He repeated the name within the silent recesses of his mind. Yes, it was the same. The name old Hank Kutcher had repeatedly thrown at him. And now some of Hank Kutcher's words came starkly back to Stacy Murdock. *It's about time for you to glimpse eternity, Stacy—to face the guns of Willoughby.*

How come I remember a stupid thing like that? Murdock thought fretfully. I need some time away from cowshit and horse sweat. Go to Denver and . . .

He cursed in baffled fury. For many months now, the doors of Denver society had been closed to him. Jennifer Waverley, the domineering slut, had seen to that.

The quiet of dusk was about them, with each wrapped in his thoughts, as they broke over a prairie rim and saw the silhouetted outline of the Diamond-7 buildings.

A dog's barking told of their coming, and when they dismounted at the horse corral gate, a lanky cowhand was already hurrying toward them. Murdock slipped the saddle and bridle from his mount, then tossed them over a corral pole. He motioned for Foxley to do the same and turn his horse into the corral. It wasn't until they opened the gate that Murdock noticed the pinto gelding in the pen. "I wonder who rode in atop that critter; I never saw it around here before."

Bert Andrus had come out from the barn and spoke in hasty excitement. "That pinto belongs to me—that is, to Hollis and me. He's a trick horse. Worth a bundle."

"Where did you get him?" Murdock demanded. When Bert hesitated, Murdock demanded, "Bert, I asked where that horse came from."

"We . . . we sort of lifted him from an Indian."

"You mean you and Devlin stole the horse? Where?"

"Up the creek a ways," Bert Andrus answered evasively.

With an unexpected brutal jerk, Murdock seized the Andrus boy and spun him around until Bert's face was within inches of his own furious eyes. "Damn you, Bert, if you and that crooked-armed fool stole a horse you'd better spill the whole story. Besides, I haven't seen an Indian hereabouts for five years."

There was a moment of silence, in which Bert Andrus stared toward the bunkhouse as though willing Hollis Devlin to appear to share the questioning. Then he blurted out, "The Indian was camped up there where the Cardigans used to have that nester shack. There's others up there too.

217

I saw them. That feisty Redge Cardigan. And some stranger."

"God almighty," Foxley exclaimed, quickly realizing what Bert had implied, "you mean you swiped a horse from that Navajo kid and Emmett Willoughby—that Arizona gunslinger?"

The words seemed to break down all Bert Andrus's restraint as his face went ashen. "I didn't kill the Indian. Hollis shot him . . . while I was trying to talk him out of the pinto."

"Heaven have mercy," Tom Foxley said slowly. "There'll be blood on the grass right pronto. Plenty of it."

For a moment Stacy Murdock's troubled gaze swept the rim of the yard, as though anxious that there might be men lurking in the darkness. Then he said, to Bert, in a strangely dispassionate voice, "I want to see you and Devlin up at the ranch office in just an hour. Be there." He turned to Foxley, saying, "I'll have to clear Cardigan's young'un out. No ranch can let claim jumpers and nesters nibble at it and survive. Let's see if we can round up a drink and something to eat."

The ranch cook served them a satisfying supper, but Stacy Murdock ate very little, preferring to replenish his glass with generous amounts of whiskey. Before an hour had passed, Foxley excused himself, saying it was his usual practice to walk around a bit before going to bed. As he left the ranch house, he knew that he was avoiding overhearing the pent-up fury that Murdock would unleash upon Hollis Devlin and young Andrus. Murdock had seeded the wind; now his companions were hastening the coming whirlwind.

Foxley was walking briskly toward the willow-bordered edge of Crow Creek when he noted the bunkhouse door open. A slim young figure with unruly blond hair stepped out, followed by a heavy-set individual whose slower movements indicated might be of middle age. Foxley was unable to distinguish the features of either man, but he was sure that Bert Andrus and Hollis Devlin, reluctant and angry, were on their way to meet with the ranch boss.

Tom Foxley had gone about fifty steps along the log and stone bridge arching the creek, which marked the path of extensive corrals and a large open-fronted shed, when he became aware that he was not alone. A figure was moving

218

toward him, and although the stranger's pace was un-hurried, they would come face to face within seconds.

Foxley stopped to watch and to wait. He breathed a relieved sigh when he saw who it was: "Hank," he said. "What in hell? You're the last man I'd expect to meet here on the Diamond-7."

Kutcher raised his hand to hush the other man. Then he answered, almost in a whisper, "Howdy, Foxley. At least there's one man on this damned spread I won't have to keep an eye on."

"I thought you went to work for Jeff Masters." Foxley's words were puzzled.

Hank Kutcher ignored the cattle buyer's perplexity. "Is Murdock up at the house?" he asked tensely.

"He was five minutes ago. And right now he has com-pany—Bert Andrus and that stiff-armed hombre, Hollis Devlin."

"So the bastards are here. I thought they would be." Kutcher rubbed his gray whiskers thoughtfully. "At least we know where they are. Which will make it easier to be set when all hell breaks loose in the morning."

Foxley stared at him and muttered, "Hank, what are you talking about? Speak plain."

Kutcher drew a deep breath, and then said in a low, angry voice. "Tom, listen. Them two—the Andrus kid and Devlin—stole a pinto gelding. It's out there in the corral right now. Then one of them, probably that son of a bitch, Devlin, killed the Indian boy the hoss belonged to." The old rider paused, shook his head, then went on. "Now the murdering hoss thieves are in trouble up to their asses. Redge Cardigan is back here on Crow Creek—up at the old ruins of Cardigan Camp. He brought the Navajo boy and Emmett Willoughby, the Arizona gunslinger, with him."

Foxley absorbed Kutcher's words, then he said, "But Hank, all that doesn't answer why you came here."

Kutcher grinned wryly. "Maybe you'd call my being back on the Diamond-7 an act of mercy. Emmett Willough-by is less than two miles from here, waiting for me to rejoin him. Come light enough, and he'll be riding in. But not for trouble with Murdock, unless he's unwise enough to interfere. Willoughby is comin' to take back the stolen pinto, and to settle with whoever killed the Navajo lad. I'm gonna advise Stacy to keep out of it—and stay alive."

Tom Foxley shook his head admiringly. "You're riding into a ranch you were fired from and kicked off—in order to hand Murdock advice that likely could save his life?"

"Don't build me up for no hero," Kutcher growled. "More likely I'm a meddling damn fool. There's reasons, Tom. First, Redge Cardigan demands to be the one to try gunning Stacy Murdock down. God knows he's earned the right."

Hank paused, then he continued reluctantly, "The other reason, Tom, is that until a couple of years ago Stacy Murdock was as decent a ranch foreman as you'll run across—and Tom, maybe it's time someone knows. *Stacy Murdock is my nephew.*"

Foxley was silent in his amazed surprise.

"Old Andy Purcell knew it," Kutcher was continuing. "When a rattlesnake's bite killed my brother-in-law, Purcell proved a good friend to my sister. He practically raised Stacy."

Hank Kutcher's words broke off abruptly as the ranchhouse door swung open and Murdock's visitors emerged. When Bert Andrus and Devlin were a prudent distance from the house, the older man vented his anger with a lurid string of oaths, then said, in a piercing tone that was audible through the quiet night, "Someday I'll have a bellyful of Murdock's orders. Maybe I'll cut down on him myself. I only hung around the Diamond-7 in order to get a chance at Cardigan."

"Hell, Devlin," was Bert's caustic reply, "with Murdock's speed, you'd be dead before your hand got near a holster."

The two walked in sulking silence toward the bunkhouse, then entered and slammed the door behind them.

Tom Foxley turned to the old rider who was squatted beside him. "Hank, what the hell got into Stacy Murdock to make him change so? I used to be proud to call him a friend."

Kutcher's answer was slow in coming. "Tom, maybe Stacy didn't change. Maybe all along he was a born killer, but keeping it in check, thinking Andy Purcell would leave the Diamond-7 to him. His trouble began a couple of years ago when he was stud-hot and too impatient. Went on the prowl for a woman. Any young and pretty woman. That did something to the rest of him."

"So then . . . ?" Foxley was caught up in this revelation.

"So then," Kutcher echoed, "Murdock got to calling at Kate's Wagon. Shining up to Kate Andrus's daughter."

"Wait a bit," Foxley interjected. "I know Audrey Andrus; she's much too young . . . even now."

"It wasn't Audrey," Kutcher said savagely. "It was Kate's other daughter—the older one. Her name was Karen."

"Karen Andrus," Foxley murmured. "I have never met her."

"Nor will you ever," Hank Kutcher answered in a dull tone. "Karen Andrus died a couple of years ago." With a gesture that indicated he had told as much of his story as he could, Kutcher rose to his feet, pulled at his hat, and held out his hand to Tom Foxley.

Foxley didn't take it immediately. "Hank," he asked, "why don't you let me tell Murdock that Willoughby will be riding in to demand the horse, the Andrus boy, and Hollis Devlin?"

"Thanks, Tom, but I'll do it. And don't worry about old Hank Kutcher. Murdock don't dast draw on me—and nobody else on this ranch has a damned bit of reason to!"

A little more than two miles upstream from the Diamond-7 headquarters, a small tributary creek merges with Crow Creek. For most of the year its winding course is dry and its channel but a scrawling trail of sand. During rainy springs, it flows for a while and leaves several pools that offer water for thirsty men and horses. Emmett Willoughby chose one of these spots for a night camp. The contour of the surrounding land would make it difficult for anyone to approach the campsite without being seen or heard. As an added precaution, he would not light a fire, and his horse was picketed within easy reach.

Midnight approached, and the air became briskly cool. A wind had come up, bearing in from the southeast. There were broken clouds and the hint of a brewing rainstorm.

Emmett Willoughby sat on his bedroll and peered quietly off to the southeast where Hank Kutcher had ridden off a couple of hours earlier. It was an extraordinary thing for Willoughby to allow his coming to be announced in advance. But now there seemed to be valid reasons. He, personally, had no feud with the boss of the Diamond-7. If there was even a vestige of honesty or reason about Stacy Murdock, he would offer no protection or help to the men who had committed the intolerable crimes of the west —horse thievery and murder. Murdock would face his own showdown before long, but it would be with Redge Cardigan.

Again Willoughby's mind reviewed the weeks and months of preparation young Cardigan had undergone for the test. I've given him all the advice and teaching I can, Willoughby thought. He is fast. But is he fast enough? Speed is an instinct. Something that a man either has or doesn't. If only Redge could have that split second . . . that crucial edge! Willoughby shrugged. There was no way that he could implant that ability. The Navajo boy had displayed such instinct—he had come to mean a lot to Willoughby. And now the Indian boy lay buried beside Will Cardigan at a quiet spot near the ruins of a rudely built camp far upstream.

Another hour passed, one in which Emmett Willoughby's thoughts covered much of the spectrum of his life. He had grown up on an isolated Indiana farm, where his parents were striving to wring a living for too large a family. Almost since his first remembrance, he had been left to do what best suited him. An elderly neighbor had given him a hunting rifle, but had in turn demanded two months of heavy land clearing. It had been a tedious indenture, but when it at last came to an end, young Emmett was free to roam the Indiana woods and swamps in search of wild game that would help provide food for the family. He became an expert shot . . . and he became a taciturn and thoughtful loner.

His first real companionship was when the war brought him together with young Will Cardigan. They hit it off well from the first, and as time swept by, they managed to bind their lives together. Despite his feelings for Will, restlessness had always been his truest partner. It had led him to Arizona by way of Oklahoma and Texas. It had caused him to acquire and master handguns. Now, he prided himself that they had never been used except in the cause of justice or self-defense. The brace of meticulously kept pistols that he almost constantly wore had taken lives. This was a way of life that Willoughby had coldly learned to live with. And he prided himself that the guns had thundered only on the side of borderland law, or to save himself from the deadly breed of men whose greatest pride was in attaining skill in order to best and kill any fabled gunslinger.

A slice of moon had descended close to the ground far to the west when the slow-paced thump of a horse's hooves brought him erect and alert. Seconds later he relaxed as Hank Kutcher rode up beside the little pool.

"It took you quite a spell," Willoughby commented.

Kutcher dropped from his horse, then flopped belly down to drink from the pool. Afterward, he sat up and wiped the back of his hand across his mustache. "Emmett," he said thoughtfully, "it don't add up. There's something missing. Something wrong."

Willoughby did not respond. Kutcher lit his pipe, puffed a couple of times, then spoke as though thinking aloud. "The pinto gelding was there . . . in the Diamond-7 corral. Just as I got close to the ranch house, Murdock was having some sort of talk inside with Hollis Devlin and young Bert Andrus. I ran into a chap I know, a cattle buyer named Tom Foxley. Visited with him a spell out by the creek. Then I went up to the ranch house. I can't say Murdock was delighted to see me. When I told him I'd come to offer a mite of advice, he got pretty salty. Said any advice from me wasn't worth two whoops in hell, and that I'd best be off the ranch before his riders got wind of my whereabouts."

"Did you get to tell him it's a horse, a kid, and a card-shark I'm after?"

"Sure I did. But Stacy didn't bat an eye. Just said it would be settled come morning. I got an idea he's already been tipped off to our coming, and sort of looks forward to it. Almost as though he thinks he has some ace in the hole."

Willoughby yawned, pulled off his boots, and climbed into his bedroll. Then he said placidly, "The hole in which quite a few men tuck an ace somehow turns out to be their grave."

It was drizzling when the two awoke. With damp grass and twigs they started a fire and prepared a sparse breakfast. They saddled their horses, checked their weapons, and then rode determinedly to the creek junction and then on toward the buildings that presently came into view. They drew to a halt near the corral in which half a dozen saddle horses were nosing forkfuls of hay. Hosteen Begay's pinto was not among them.

With a single smooth movement, Emmett Willoughby slid from his horse and handed the reins to Kutcher. "Move the horses and yourself back out of here. They're set to welcome us—and this ain't your fight."

Three men stood guarding the corral gate. As Hank maneuvered the horses off to one side, he gave the three quick scrutiny, then dismissed them. They were Diamond-7 riders, but they rode for wages and not to back Murdock's hand when trouble came.

Kutcher wheeled around when he noticed Hollis Devlin standing near the corral corner post. The hand of his crooked arm was on a corral pole, and the angle of his stance was such that the bad arm could be used as a lever for the gun he seemed eager to draw. Off to the other side about thirty paces, Stacy Murdock was also waiting.

Willoughby went to Murdock and spoke to him in a soft, unhurried, and almost sociable way. "I won't waste time saying why I'm here, Mr. Murdock. You already know. Do you hand over what I want—or do I take it?"

The abrupt words seemed to lift a bit of the confident smile from Murdock's face. Then he recovered. "If it's that pinto nag . . . he's just coming in."

And at that moment, from out of the small meadow close to the creek Bert Andrus was approaching at a sauntering walk, leading the pinto by the reins.

Murdock saw him and called sharply, "That's far enough, Bert. Stop there."

And then Hank Kutcher saw through it. The pinto had been deliberately positioned to hide the approach of a third man, now coming through the bunkhouse door. Abruptly Kutcher abandoned all caution and yelled out, "Bert, get that hoss the hell out of there. You're being used. Bert . . . I'll tell you now. It was Stacy who killed your sister. Raped her, then panicked and killed her."

Throughout this, Emmett Willoughby had stood still, his hands hovering close at his sides. But it was Hollis Devlin, straining with anxiety to even an old score, who precipitated hell across the yard. His good hand snaked toward his holster. Willoughby watched the reaction of young Andrus. But even as Bert dropped the pinto's reins and broke into a

224

run toward Hank Kutcher, and Hollis Devlin was steadying his revolver onto his bracing arm, Willoughby's left arm lifted and a heavy handgun belched lead and flame. The bullet caught Devlin high in the chest and flung him against the corral poles. He clawed at one of them, then slumped already lifeless to the ground.

The crash of the shot caused the pinto to shy nervously aside. For the first time Emmett Willoughby had a clear look at the man who had been coming cautiously closer. "Well, I'll be damned. So it's you, Slick. Last I heard of you, you were killing off Navajo women and children."

There was hatred and near insanity glittering in this new-comer's eyes. Emmett Willoughby recognized that old, ruth-less craving some sick men have to kill a noted gunman and somehow assume his mantle.

For perhaps ten seconds there was absolute silence across the yard. Willoughby waited, in seemingly frozen stance. The pinto horse dropped his head to again nibble grass, and the course of his grazing put him in a direct line between Willoughby and Stacy Murdock. Emmett Willoughby's mind noted the fact and its potential hazard. He instantly relegated this new development to secondary importance. To the others watching, it seemed as though the speed with which the stranger, Slick, slapped for the worn handle of his right-hand weapon was lightning-fast.

Only Emmett Willoughby, so long schooled in the neces-sities of survival, was aware of another movement, the minute movement of his opponent's finger to form the trigger hook before the draw. With a grunt that was savage with anticipated triumph, Slick got his shot off. His single and only shot. The leaden slug sang a wild and off-course way toward the open-faced shed. For Willoughby had also drawn and fired. This shot, unlike the one that had killed Hollis Devlin, tore through its target's belly. With the impact of the heavy slug reeling him backward, Slick tried in des-peration for a second shot.

He was stumbling upon sagging knees as another shot tore the morning calm apart. But Slick, with death rushing in, never knew that another, and fatal, shot would mark the end of this bloody melee.

As Slick, upon whose accuracy and hatred Stacy Mur-dock had banked to win, caught the heavy, tearing slug in his midsection, Stacy Murdock tore a pistol from his belt.

As he drew, he meant the bullet for Bert. But at that moment, the nervous pinto moved just enough to reveal Emmett Willoughby, standing with his side toward Murdock and his eyes focused on the falling Slick.

Murdock's shot was timed and aimed with skill. It caught Emmett Willoughby just in front of the right armpit and tore through to his heart. Willoughby was never aware of the last shot of his last gunfight. His body hit the dust and he lay sprawled, with morning sunlight falling upon his face and upon the blood that stained the well-trodden dirt about him.

A subtle release from fear crossed Stacy Murdock's face. "The guns of Willoughby—shit!" he said aloud.

Then abruptly Murdock motioned Bert Andrus toward him. "Come on, you yellow-tailed little bastard . . . it's time for you to get yours now."

Andrus, scared and white-faced, started to stumble forward. Then he stopped and stared. Two men were already moving with rapid stride toward Murdock. One was Hank Kutcher. The other was an individual who had stood aside during the showdown. The cattle buyer, Tom Foxley.

There was a grim intensity of purpose upon Hank Kutcher's face. His voice was near a snarl as he said, "Stacy, if you harm this kid, by holy God I'll kill you myself. Kate Andrus ain't going to lose another."

Tom Foxley interjected, "Three men are dead here, Murdock. It's enough. Too many."

Foxley paused, studying Murdock's face, and seeing upon it a craving for more bloodshed. Then he said harshly, "You didn't do yourself proud, Stacy. You never gave the Arizona gunman a chance. Now . . . if you use a gun on Bert here . . . if you harm him . . . I'll see that you swing for murder."

Stacy Murdock stood in shocked silence and gazed about the yard of the Diamond-7. There was Devlin, lying dead with his stiff arm grotesquely lifted. And Slick, the strange man of hatred and ambition. And Emmett Willoughby, whom he, Stacy Murdock, had feared to give an even chance. Then finally he looked about at the faces of the others in the yard, and realized there was not one real ally among them.

"Take the kid—and get the hell out of here. Out of my sight. Off the Diamond-7." He waited as both Kutcher and

226

Foxley stood contemptuously silent. Then he added, in a strangely abandoned and naked voice, "Tell that bastardly Redge Cardigan that I'll be up Crow Creek in just forty-eight hours . . . to take care of him." He stared again about the yard, and when he spoke again, his voice was touched with a plaintive whisper of regret. "It was that Cardigan kid who started this whole fracas. I've got to put an end to it—and to him."

Hank Kutcher strode to Willoughby's body, unstrapped the worn gun belt, and hung it across the horn of his own saddle. With the help of a stunned ranch hand, he lifted the body onto Willoughby's horse and roped it tight.

Tom Foxley, without even a glance at Murdock, caught up the reins of the pinto gelding and handed them to Bert Andrus. "Take this horse up to Redge Cardigan. I'll be riding with you as soon as I get my saddle mare from the corral."

Presently Kutcher and Foxley and a very subdued Bert Andrus were riding in single file toward Cardigan Camp. The next task would be to break the news to Redge Cardigan that another of his friends would soon join his father and the Navajo boy in the quiet creekside burying ground.

Chapter 20

Shortly after noon of the following day, Redge Cardigan wandered aimlessly up Crow Creek. The full green of summer would soon be upon the prairie; already the buds of streamside rose clumps were impatient to become a riot of pink and crimson. The air was softly quiet and sundrenched. It seemed incredible to Redge that all this could be so. He had just spent half an hour of anguish saying a final and empty farewell to the two friends who had ridden northward from Arizona alongside him.

His steps brought him after a time to a place where the creek's valley narrowed to become a deep, narrow gorge. Soon he was standing on a well-remembered spot. Beyond this point, at a time that now seemed like something remembered from a dream, he had glimpsed the flooded lake —and daydreamed the challenge of creating a vastly sprawling reservoir. He recalled the eagerness with which he had sketched the idea . . . and his father's enthusiastic receptions of his ambitious plans.

And now. Now the dreams and plans and ideas were as much charred rubble as the ruins of Cardigan Camp. His insistence on setting up camp on Crow Creek—on Diamond-7 graze—had led to his father's death. His steady pursuit of revenge upon Stacy Murdock had caused both his Navajo friend and Emmett Willoughby to lose their lives.

Redge's mind probed the future. Perhaps for him it lay far from Crow Creek Valley. He knew that the offer of Dade Sutherland, whose ranches and freighting lines covered northern Arizona, would still hold good. Perhaps in Arizona, somewhere between the White Mountains and the brooding and mysterious Grand Canyon uplift, there would be a time and a place for forgetting.

Then his mind turned to Audrey Andrus. Jeff Masters

had reported that she was at Kate's Wagon. He could still best picture her there, sitting astride the store hitch rail, with sunlight highlighting that bridge of freckles across her nose.

The sound of footfalls caused him to turn. It was Hank Kutcher. "Wait up, lad," he called. "I need to talk with you."

Redge lifted a hand in acknowledgment. He stared fixedly at the objects in the old rider's hands—the dark leather gunbelt, the smooth leather holsters, and the two heavy weapons that had been a way of life for Emmett Willoughby.

Kutcher came alongside and halted. "I needed to talk a spell with you alone, Redge." He thrust the holstered weapons and the buckled belt forward. "These belong to you, son. Willoughby was your friend; he'd want it that way."

Redge Cardigan took the guns and their accessories into his hands with eager acceptance. "Emmett was touchy about their care," he murmured. "Used to shine and polish and oil these to perfection. He let me use them some—in practice."

Kutcher nodded. "The guns of Willoughby. He used them to perfection yesterday." Then he added quietly, "What ought we to do about that pinto hoss of Hosteen's? Foxley and me fetched him up from the Diamond-7."

Redge thought for a moment. "What is Bert Andrus going to do?"

"Right now his mind is too muddled for him to figure anything out. It tore him apart when I spilled that about Murdock being the one that killed his sister."

"Is it true, Hank? Did Murdock do that?"

"Hell yes. I happened to be the one that found Karen after Stacy had panicked and left her dead." Kutcher lowered his head and stared at the ground. "I know, lad. I should have turned him over to the law. But Stacy was my kin—my sister's boy. Besides, would dragging it through a trial, and maybe a hanging, have made things easier for Kate, or for Audrey?"

When Redge voiced no criticism, Kutcher said, in brighter tones, "Say, boy. Them heifers—the batch that Andy Purcell sent up to you—are doing fine. They're on Jeff Masters's ranch, down the Platte. Quite a few calves trotting at their sides too."

Redge's answer was a smile of thanks, but his voice sounded preoccupied. "Keep them, Hank. They're more yours than mine. At least you have a safe place for them."

"We can talk it over later," Kutcher said. Then, sensing Redge's mood, he turned again downcreek. "I've gotta help scare up something to eat, lad." Then he moved briskly away.

For many minutes after he left, Redge stared at the guns in his hands, his only remaining link with the man who had become a legend in Arizona, but had not hesitated to fulfill the pledge he had made to Will Cardigan. Then, with deliberateness and infinite care, he strapped the gunbelt about him and adjusted the holsters to his side.

The guns of Willoughby, he considered, as with smooth and steady movements he brought the guns into his hands and sent twin shots speeding toward the stump. And he repeated the act . . . again . . . and again . . .

In keeping with his word, Stacy Murdock approached Cardigan Camp as the sun was seeking its way above an eastern ridge. Four ranch hands rode with him, but he had scoffed at their suggestion that some precautionary scouting be done. "Scout for what? Nobody's there but doddering old Kutcher and that damned Cardigan kid. And maybe yellow-livered Bert Andrus . . . but likely Bert has tucked his tail and headed out."

They crested the valley rim, then drew abruptly to a halt. Cardigan Camp lay clearly before them, and there were far too many horses and bedrolls and waiting men about.

Before the Diamond-7 riders or Murdock could alter their course, a solitary rider, unarmed, left a small ravine and approached them. The stranger, astride a rangy roan mare, rode up quickly to talk to Stacy Murdock. His words were short and to the point. "I ride for Jeff Masters. He and some others are expecting you. Jeff sent word that all of you can ride in—but there'll be no tricks. No bushwhacking!" As quickly as he had appeared, the rider wheeled his horse and moved toward Cardigan Camp.

An irritated Stacy Murdock led his four hands on a direct trot into the camp yard. His eyes swept over Kutcher and Bert Andrus, lingered a moment on Redge Cardigan, then sought out Jeff Masters. "What's the idea, Jeff?" he

230

demanded. "This is sure one hell of a way to greet a neighbor."

"So?" Jeff Masters responded with unperturbed face. "Stacy, it's a bit friendlier than the setup you had for Kutcher and Willoughby."

For a moment Murdock looked as if he was going to argue, then he shrugged and looked again toward Redge Cardigan. The boy was standing quietly beside a cottonwood tree, with holstered guns at his thighs. Murdock sensed something different about him—a maturity, a confidence, a sort of determination that he had not expected. For the first time, Stacy Murdock felt a sobering uneasiness.

Murdock swung from his horse and slapped the animal aside.

"I don't see the need for all this crowd and ruckus, Masters," he said.

"There'll be no ruckus—if you keep it on the level, Stacy. The boy gets a chance, an even break. Understand?"

Murdock grunted acknowledgment, and the men moved aside to leave an open expanse between him and the boy standing so quietly alongside the cottonwood. Murdock felt a resurgence of confidence. This had best be done quickly and cleanly. This kid had started it by defying the law of the Diamond-7 and squatting on the ranch's grazing area. There could be but one ending—with Cardigan Camp the burial place of the boy and a permanent warning to others who would encroach upon the ranch's grasslands.

The distance between them was still a little long for accuracy, so Stacy Murdock took a few measured steps forward. He noticed Redge shift slightly, but keep unwavering eyes upon him.

"Kid, are you ready for it?" Murdock called mockingly. In his mind he was coolly remembering the effect that taunting sometimes had on opponents. When there was no answer, save for the steady, boring scrutiny of Redge Cardigan's cold eyes, Murdock hunched a little, his arms loose at his sides. His right hand was hovering, just ready to begin its clawing descent, when Redge's voice sounded. "Look, Murdock—*into the guns of Willoughby!*"

A split second of shock . . . of old and ghostlike memories . . . and of hesitation slowed Stacy Murdock's hand. This was his last moment of full consciousness. A heavy, gleaming and fire-spouting weapon had leapt into Redge

231

Cardigan's hand. And the .45-caliber bullet entered Murdock's neck just below the chin, then tore upward to blast most of the back of his head away.

There was no cry from Murdock. No staggering. No attempt to complete a death-moment draw. He was thrown backward onto the grass, to lie limp and sprawled and lifeless.

With the muzzle of his weapon still marked by a fading curl of smoke, Redge walked forward, his steps dragging and his face trancelike. For a few seconds he stared down upon the object that moments before had been a live and conscious man. Blood had gushed out of the neck wound, and its raw edges gaped open.

A shudder escaped Redge Cardigan, followed by a small and tormented cry. His mind was suddenly recalling the times when he had tended wounds and used the tools of veterinary surgery in an attempt to save life. The waste and the futility of all gunfighting, of all violent lifetaking, crowded in about him.

Oblivious of the concern on the faces about him, he turned, avoided hands thrust out in an effort to help, and staggered to the edge of Crow Creek. With lifeless fingers he fumbled at the buckle of the heavy belt. When he was at last free of the belt and the holsters and the weapons, he stared almost unheedingly at them. Then with a savage swing of his arm, he sent the guns of Willoughby splashing into the depths of Crow Creek.

He turned back to those about him. "We're going to Kate's Wagon!" he sobbed.

232

PART II

THE VENTURE

PART III

THE VENTURE

Chapter 21

Mark Cardigan was four years old in 1911 when he awakened in his small bedroom off the ranch kitchen in the darkness of an early-spring night. He heard someone singing, and accompanying the voice other sounds, the most beautiful he had ever heard. He got out of bed, padded barefooted across the kitchen, and cautiously pushed open the door to the living room.

His eyes widened with wonder. Aunt Carla stood across the room; she was wearing a white blouse and a blue skirt. Just now the song pouring from her had something to do with "endearing young charms." The words mixed with the melody born of the black and white keys his mother was fingering. The sounds of the new parlor organ delighted him.

Redge Cardigan spied his son creeping into the room and noted the wonder-struck way in which the boy was peering at the new instrument. He went to him and lifted him into his arms. The leaping flames from a stone fireplace cast restless patterns across the faces of both.

"Where did we get that?" Mark asked, and thrust a small finger toward the organ.

Redge ran a proud hand across his son's sleep-tousled hair. "It came up from Denver, Mark, on the railroad. Your Aunt Carla came too. I hitched the roans to a spring wagon and drove into Hawk Bend to fetch them . . . and surprise you."

The child stared sleepily into Redge's face, trying to make sense of the words. For Mark, the railroad meant two things: the long scar of graded and fenced right-of-way upon which steel rails were thrusting up Crow Creek Valley, and the black, smoking monster that rattled along on the rails and sometimes let out a loud and frightening whistle. His mind now pictured the parlor organ atop the locomotive, close to the smoking stack, and tied down with lariats such as old Hank Kutcher spent so much time braiding. His Aunt Carla—almost as old, it seemed, as Hank—must have ridden a saddle cinched to that coal car behind the engine.

Mark was sound asleep when his mother rose from the organ, moved close, and held out her arms. "I'll tuck him in again, Redge. But I'm warning you . . . the new organ means that he'll be up and about at the crack of daylight."

As Audrey Cardigan spoke, the room's subdued light was ample to reveal the love and the pride within her. It seemed to add emphasis to the liveliness of her eyes and the band of freckles bridging her nose. On sudden impulse, Redge bent and placed a firm kiss on her earlobe. He was handing the boy to her as he said, "Audrey, do you realize it has been more than thirteen years since I first showed up at Kate's Wagon, and you quick-like told me you didn't like me? Said I was a sorry lot."

"I'm not so sure yet," she teased. "That's why I have Mark keep an eye on you when you feed the chickens."

He followed her into his son's bedroom and watched as she drew a patchwork quilt up to the boy's chin. Presently he said thoughtfully, "He'll grow up in a different sort of world, Audrey—with a railroad, the grasslands ripped up for corn and wheat fields, and the confounded barbed-wire fences separating about every half section of land."

"I'm not at all sure I'll like it, Redge my dear," she answered, and moved to let her upswept but still coppery-hued hair touch his cheek. "It's these newcomers—the drylanders—who will become desperate during the years of scant rainfall. Crops take a lot more moisture than buffalo grass needs."

"We're lucky to have the dam to provide irrigation for the meadows," he agreed. "But that isn't going to help the upland pastures, miles from the creek." Redge paused, his mind sweeping back to the days when there had been nothing except open grazing country on this north side of the South Platte River. But, he recalled, there had been hardships then; those who make a living from the soil are bound to encounter hardships. The cattle barons had defied the westward thrust of those hungry for land and adventure. Ranches like the once highly profitable Diamond-7, which Andy Purcell . . .

With a shrug, Redge made an effort to rid himself of

memories of this kind. They inevitably brought vivid recall of gunplay and of graves.

Sensing his mood, Audrey took him by the arm and moved with him toward the living room. "Don't, Redge. Don't torture yourself. It all happened years ago." Moments later, she brightened and urged, "Get Carla into a pinochle game while I fix a snack. She will think we've forgotten her."

Through the remainder of that night, and for many ensuing nights, Mark Cardigan slept peacefully and securely in the comfortable ranch house on that gentle knoll that was less than a stone's throw from the now controlled and steady and clear flow of Crow Creek. At four years old, he was too young to have or seek much knowledge of the past life of his father and mother. He did vaguely realize that before his own birth his father had spent several years at a faraway place, a school in Iowa. There he had studied to become something called a *veterinarian*. The child did not yet associate the word with the tools and the medicines and the care Redge Cardigan employed for doctoring animals.

One of the things that Mark liked most about his mother was her way of taking him onto her lap and rocking him, as she used one free hand to work the dasher of a butter churn. He sought the softness of her bosom for his tired or sleepy head. And he remembered, vaguely, how his mother's shoulders had heaved in torment as she told him that his two-year-old sister had died of pneumonia.

Mark had not yet learned to equate the youthfulness of his parents' faces and their zest for living with their ages. To him the fact that in this year of 1911 his father was thirty years old and his mother twenty-five had little meaning. He realized only that Redge and Audrey Cardigan were grown-ups. Just like Aunt Carla, who sometimes came from Denver to visit, and Hank Kutcher, who had always lived with the Cardigans, were old people. Old people were the ones whose movements were slower, and who had more time for a boy's problems.

Time sped by, bringing to Mark greater awareness of the house, the ranch yard, and the surrounding touches of outer world. His world expanded to include the garden, the hay meadows, the livestock, and even the fascinating expanse of reservoir water behind the earth-fill dam upstream. He had been sternly told never to go near the big lake by himself.

Chores were assigned to him by the middle of his fifth year; they gradually became more complex and carried ever-increasing responsibility. Pull weeds in the garden. Take care of his dogs and the ranch cats. See that grain was put in the stall feeders for all work and saddle horses. Drive in the cows from pasture.

The organ melodies, played by his mother, as her feet pumped air into the instrument, were moments to which the boy looked forward. Then there were the storybooks from which Audrey, and sometimes Redge, read to him after the day's work.

Most enjoyable of all were the summer hours when he was free to roam along the tree-fringed creek. The clear and shallow reaches held little danger, and seemed made for wading and for forming dikes and ditches to bring water onto a sand bar. The boy tarried here, under the spell of meadow scents and of wild flowers that nodded a greeting his way. There were also the birds and the rabbits, to whom he remained an intruder.

Sometimes he found unfamiliar and surprising things about the yard. There were a few empty gun cartridges that made good whistles. Sometimes he came across bits of wood, charred and crumbling; at a later time, he would know them to be remnants of the buildings that had been Cardigan Camp before it vanished in blood and flame.

Upstream a way, and surrounded by a neat picket fence, was a spot of which the young boy had little comprehension. It was a small square of grass and flowers, with a few graves marked by the sandstone slabs that Redge Cardigan had arranged to have hauled, given chiseled inscriptions, and then set on edge. He knew that the markings on these rocks were writing, but not that they spoke of birth and death.

Slightly downstream from the ranch house stood one special tree. Mark cherished it above all others, for this was a cottonwood that seemed to spread and to tower in enormous size. Both the windmill tower and the peaked roof of the barn were dwarfed by the upper branches thrusting toward the sun.

By the time Mark was seven years old, and slim and agile, he was able to climb to the highest and springiest branches. From them a far and sweeping vista offered awe and excitement. Only a drifting cloud, or a circling hawk, might reach a point assuring more distant horizons. The lowest branches diverged high above the trunk. They spread cool summer shade in a large circle, while the thick green foliage was a haven for nesting birds. The cold winds of winter tossed the naked boughs with deeply resonant sighs.

The tree held another delight for Mark. One summer day when Hank Kutcher had been helping Redge turn loose some sick-list critters to feed upon the lush creekbank grasses, Kutcher had leaned down from his horse and had lifted the boy onto the saddle behind him. Presently Hank uncoiled a lariat rope and with a flick of his wrist sent a loop outward to encircle a stump.

Mark, with his arms about the old cowboy's waist, pointed aloft at the towering cottonwood, then challenged him. "Hank, I betcha can't toss your loop over that tree."

Kutcher eased his horse to a stop, then let his gaze run up and down the huge branches. After a bit, he said, "Nope, lad, I can't. But I can do a lot better. How would you like to have a swing? An honest-to-goodness bag swing?"

Redge came alongside and also appraised the cottonwood. "I suppose I'll get hooked into this. You two will expect me to furnish a rope that's long enough. Then I'll have to shinny up the tree and fasten the swing rope to a high branch."

Kutcher grinned agreement, while Mark's eyes danced with expectation. Then Hank pointed to a huge branch that projected from the tree trunk practically at a right angle. Slightly above and behind the branch was another one with a similar slant. The old range rider scratched the whitening disarray of hair at his temple. "Iffen we tie the rope high enough, and just right, Redge, the kid will be able to swing off that top branch, sail out over the creek, and glide back to drop off the bag of straw onto the lower branch. He could keep that up all day."

"Which he probably will," Redge answered ruefully, then added, "Which might not be so bad. That way he won't keep pestering Audrey and me—and you—to push him."

And so the swing came into being, and more than ever the vastly spreading cottonwood became Mark's favorite retreat. For weeks after his swing was strung up, he could hardly wait to finish breakfast each morning and to get his chores out of the way. Then he would race out to the tree and swing out over the creek. He had learned that by clinging tightly to the rope and unstraddling from the sack of hay he could dangle his bare feet in the cool flow of Crow Creek. Someday, making sure his mother was not about, he might strip off all his clothes, sail naked on the bag swing, and drop into the water. The daring of it brought a determined grin to Mark's face.

One early August, there came a morning when eight-year-old Mark Cardigan forgot his pets, the swing, and half his breakfast. Today the county road crew would come. He was awake and outdoors to watch the summer sunrise. Presently he strode to the north-south tracery of wheel marks left by wagons that lately had been using this course for the journey to the newborn village of Hawk Bend, on the railroad. As the boy waited, a touch of morning wind stirred the grass, promising that the heat of summer might soon slacken.

The wheel traces across the native grass would disappear today. Tandem-hitched mules and the long, sharp blade of a road grader would transform the wagon trail into a real road. Soon there would be a wide right-of-way, for which his father and mother had granted an easement. The new road would be guarded on either side by barbed wire strung along cedar posts. For about half a mile, this new road would border the creek and the Cardigan home acres, and a driveway would give access to the corrals and the barn and the house that Redge Cardigan had built a few years previous. Mark did not yet realize that the first rough buildings built here, known as Cardigan Camp, had been laid waste by burning. His father had returned to build anew . . . this time to hold.

As the sun rose higher, the boy's view also encompassed the row of poplar trees and the lilac hedge his mother prized so highly. Already a small iron-framed gate stood at the road's edge; toward it, from the ranch house, Audrey had planted multihued flowers. The flowers bloomed throughout the summer, and were his mother's means of transporting to Crow Creek a touch of the garden she had known in childhood at a place called Kate's Wagon.

The sound of creaking steel wheels brought an abrupt end to the boy's waiting. It was accompanied by hoof falls and an occasional loud and authoritative mule-skinning command. Mark stared toward the approaching rig. He sensed that the voice was that of a lean man, past middle age, sitting on a spring-steel seat up front of the grader. From his knotted and dark fists, leather reins reached out to the bridle bits of eight mules, hitched two abreast. The driver was clad in riding boots, bibbed overalls, and a greasy black hat.

The grader blade, now lifted and reflecting sunlight from its burnished steel curve, was suspended from an arched steel frame. Its design allowed an operator to lift or lower it by spinning two giant geared control wheels.

The outfit was still a dozen rods from Mark when it came momentarily to a halt. The driver tilted his hat to a rakish angle, sent a stream of tobacco juice spraying into the grass, then squinted along a series of survey stakes. When the grader moved again, the blade was lowered, slanted to a calculated angle, and locked in place. And now there was a supple smoothness about the laboring mules; their pull had become even . . . hard . . . steady.

The deep and fertile prairie loam gave readily before the blade; the grassy sod was folded upside down, to be buried under moist and pungent-smelling soil. The grading crew had gone but a few yards when blackbirds began alighting on the upturned ridges of earth. Worms twisted frantically in an effort to regain a dark hiding place.

It was nearly noon before the first mile of road took on a leveled shape suitable to the crew. Mark trudged along after them spellbound until they stopped for lunch in the shade of a willow tree. He knew his mother would be expecting him home for the noon meal, so he tore himself reluctantly from the crew; he ran barefooted along the new road, then down the path to the ranch kitchen. His mother's firm instruction sent him toward a wash bench with its water pail and basin.

He bolted bits of food, all the while telling her of the marvelous workmen he had met, and of the magic wrought by a string of mules and a huge steel blade. "Can I go back and watch them this afternoon? Can I . . . please?"

Audrey reached out to brush dark, unruly hair from his forehead. Then she sighed. "Only if you are very careful not to get in the men's way—or to get hurt. You'll have to be back home in plenty of time to get your chores done before sundown."

He was nodding agreement as he slid from his chair and cleared the outer door at a run.

Mark approached the four resting crewmen, who had finished their lunch and were talking. They spoke of surveys, of drainage, of bridge materials, and of their mules and the grading machine. Two of them mentioned other jobs waiting for them miles away.

He listened in awe. If only he could go with them and learn to handle the mysterious control wheels, or guide those sleek and heavily muscled mules. His wistful dreams remained unspoken, but his consuming desire shone on his eight-year-old face.

When the mules were rehitched and the men moved toward their work positions, Mark was suddenly lifted by a workman and placed on a platform beside the control-wheel operator.

"Lad," the man said, smiling, "how about a little help with these infernal wheels?" He winked at the mule skinner. "Nothing like having a husky fellow to spell us off a bit."

Mark squared his shoulders and thrust out a determined chin. It had happened! Now he was a working member of the county grading crew—a road builder.

His companion spun one of the blade-control wheels and asked, "What's your name, kid?"

"Mark. Mark Cardigan, sir."

"A good Scotch name," the operator affirmed. "Now me . . . I'm Irish. Tim O'Connor. And the mule skinner is Sandy Beetham."

Mark glanced at Beetham, who had gathered all eight reins into one hand while delving with the other into an overall pocket to pull forth a square of chewing tobacco. He bit off a hefty quid, then held the plug very still as the words of a wide-eyed boy, of Mark Cardigan, the road builder, came to him.

"Sandy . . . Mr. Sandy. Can . . . can I have a chaw? Just enough to cut this damned dust."

Before noon of the next day, the road crew had finished and were gone. Their smoothly finished work remained, for a wide and straight road had come into being. It would offer easier and quicker access to the far outside. And it

242

would call as firmly for young Mark to go as the clustered buildings of the homeplace urged him to stay.

Unknowingly, the road crew had left something less tangible than the contoured earth of the roadway. They had given a boy his first inkling of an urge and a challenge. Surely these skilled men who built roads must be a select and powerful group, bringing to an isolated, almost virgin land the roads, the dams, and the railroads' paths. These . . . and also the buildings by which civilization marks its upward course.

I will do this work—I surely will, the boy affirmed to himself. This dazzling glimpse of the world of building was just a beginning; someday, somehow, Mark Cardigan would be known as a great builder.

His first solo effort met with disaster. He fashioned a rope harness for the two ranch dogs and hooked them to a discarded plowshare. He had fashioned a pitchfork handle to guide the share, in an attempt to invent an implement that would cut a new irrigation ditch for his mother's garden.

The dogs scented a fleeing rabbit and took after it with excited yelps. Their pursuit led through the thickest stand of garden vegetables, amid growing beets and onions and peas. Much of the green growth fell uprooted and was dragged out by Mark's ingenious tool.

When he managed to halt the dogs and get them untangled and unhitched, he yelled in dismay, echoing the mule skinner's words.

"You . . . you crazy bastards," Mark panted. "How am I gonna get a lateral built with you mutts runnin' to hell and gone?"

He glanced about—and fell silent as his mother came from the house with a disapproving expression on her face. She surveyed the damage with growing dismay. Even more upsetting was the echoing through her mind of the boy's mule-skinning words, his off-color tirade.

"Mark Cardigan, where did you hear such language?"

"You gotta use it to skin dumb old mules—or dogs—if you expect to get a grading job done," he defended himself.

Audrey managed to stifle the smile aching to break across her face. "From now on," she said sternly, "we'll use shovels or a hoe to make garden ditches. Right now, young man, you have your choice. Either I wash out your mouth with yellow tub soap, or we cut a willow switch for your father to lay across your behind."

For a time he mulled the choice of evils. Then he bargained. "Suppose I hoe out every damn . . . darned weed in your corn patch?"

"It would take you an hour to do that, son."

He gave her no chance to weigh a decision; he grabbed a hoe, pulled his straw hat low on his brow, and disappeared into the thick and green foliage of the corn patch.

With the threat of lye soap or a stinging branch averted, his thoughts returned to the dream of vast construction jobs.

"Someday I'm going to do it. She'll see. Everybody will see."

His words were fierce . . . certain . . . prophetic.

Chapter 22

One of the first vehicles to travel the newly graded road was a light spring wagon which the Cardigans preferred to use for the three-mile trip into the settlement of Hawk Bend. In 1915, the little town consisted of two grocery stores, a blacksmith shop, a lumber yard, and a combination restaurant and saloon. Hawk Bend had been so named to honor a minor railroad official, Lucius Hawk, who had been about to retire. The railroad buildings were the most substantial in Hawk Bend. Strung along the single track and a long siding there were section houses, a water tower for engines, a sizable depot, and stockyards. There was also a one-room school, used by about fifteen kids on school days and by an itinerant preacher on the occasional Sundays that he appeared to preach.

Exactly a week after the grading crew had put final touches on the road, Redge hitched a team of gentle black mares to the spring wagon. He checked all of the rigging with care, and then helped his wife and Carla Dunlop load an assortment of baggage and boxes. Audrey Cardigan was making her regular late-summer trip to Kate's Wagon to visit her mother. The boxes were packed with a variety of ranch and garden produce. Kate always joked that Audrey worried her mother would never eat if she didn't bring the supplies herself.

This year, Carla had decided she wanted to see Kate before returning to Denver, and the prospect of having someone with whom to talk on the somewhat tedious drive pleased Audrey, especially because for the first time she was leaving her son alone in the care of his father and Hank Kutcher at the ranch. The first term of the new Hawk Bend elementary school was opening, so Mark could not accompany his mother. Ordinarily school would not open until two weeks later, but the school board had decided to utilize a few days of August in case blizzard conditions in winter forced the closing of the school for a time.

Mark watched with trepidation as the loading was completed and his mother and Aunt Carla donned the long dusters and veils with which they hoped to combat the dirt and the harsh sunlight that would likely be with them throughout the trip. The moment for saying goodbye came, and for a moment Audrey held her son tight against her. "I'll only be gone a week, son," she murmured, experiencing a moment of regret. Carla broke the tension by wagging her finger at Mark and saying, "Watch those girls at school, Mark; they have a way of making sure you kiss them."

Mark's jaw had been quivering and his eyes getting misty. At Carla's words, he grimaced in disgust. He reached up to where Redge was arranging a blanket cushion for Audrey. Mark squeezed his mother's hand and said in a gruff tone, "If you see my friends Tim O'Connor and Sandy Beetham, tell them maybe next year I can spell them off again." His mother nodded, kissed Redge long and hard, and urged the black team into motion, as Mark turned his back to the spring wagon and sauntered a bit too casually toward the bag-swing tree.

There was an intersection of roads at Hawk Bend. The north-south one continued to roughly parallel the railroad and the course of Crow Creek, while another route diverged and for a single block was the main street of the settlement. Then it led eastward, climbing a gentle grade out of the creek valley, and leading into the undulating low hills that had been the domain of the Arapaho Indians and the herds of roaming buffalo since time immemorial. More recently, since the era of northward-moving Texas trail herds, this had been an area of huge cattle holdings, with widely separated ranches.

Now, as Audrey and Carla crested the valley's eastern rim and settled the team to a steady gait, Audrey shook her head in disbelief. Within the last year, it seemed, the homesteaders had virtually taken over the grasslands. New fences of barbed wire and close-set posts reached to the horizon, and cut the prairie into small rectangles. Plows had upturned endless acres of buffalo grass and converted it into

246

cropland. Almost every half mile was marked by a small white house, a larger barn, and the inevitable windmill.

The heavy spring and summer rains, born of the winds that swept clouds up from the Gulf of Mexico, had nurtured the crops of corn and wheat, of barley and maize, and there would be a sizable yield this harvest. There would be more buildings, more plowed-up grass, and more pigs and cows and cackling hens. And the busy land agents would range afar across the eastern states proselytizing and bringing more converts to the cause of dry-land farming.

Audrey eyed it all in silence for a while, then slapped the reins sharply across the rumps of the black mares. They jumped forward, startled, then eased back to a walk as she pulled at the reins. She turned to Carla and asked angrily, "What are they doing to this grassland? Don't they realize these are unusual years—with far more than usual moisture? The drought will come. The hot winds will tear up the soil day after day and week after week. There will be no crops—not even any grass to speak of. A wet year or so, and greedy promoters lead gullible settlers to believe this is like the rain belt. Well, if they keep plowing and harrowing and cultivating, one of these days the whole high plains is going to be a damned wrecked desert."

Carla Dunlop heard her out in silence, then remarked, "I hope you're wrong, Audrey. Too many people will suffer. They have their hearts and dreams and just about all of their future in these homesteads." She wiped off dust and sweat with a wilted handkerchief, then said, "I believe, as you do, that someday these attempts to farm the grasslands will lead to disaster. It's a good thing that Redge was far-sighted enough to file on water rights along Crow Creek."

Audrey turned on the seat and studied her companion. "And what good, Carla, would that filing have done if you and your sister had not taken a hand in the matter?"

Carla Dunlop's answering smile and chuckle carried deep satisfaction. "Jennifer and I both got a lot of enjoyment, and a few laughs, from the way that was handled, Audrey."

Audrey Cardigan drove along, her mind upon that long and hard night journey with Carla and Jennifer to Jeff Masters's headquarters so many years ago. That hasty and uncomfortable journey eastward from Denver had, in a sense, marked the end of her childhood. It was then, as she became fully aware of the danger to which Redge was returning at Cardigan Camp, that Audrey had heeded her heart—and acknowledged she was deeply in love with the stubborn, proud homesteader.

She recalled the days and weeks after Redge's showdown with Stacy Murdock when only the healing touch of her mother, the simple philosophy of Hank Kutcher, and the practical future planning of Jennifer Waverley could draw Redge Cardigan from his despondency. Jennifer had not given him any time to feel sorry for himself. On the day after his showdown, she, Carla, Kate, and Audrey had sought him out as he sat on the edge of his bed idly whittling a willow whistle. Jennifer had thrust the gleaming set of veterinary tools at him and demanded, "Isn't it about time you got acquainted with these again?"

At first, Redge seemed to recoil from the instruments, and from the past which had been thrust before him as the case was placed in his hands.

Jennifer had pointed an old, thin finger at the instruments. "Redge, these are tools of mercy and of healing. But they are only bits of steel without a skilled mind and delicately trained hands. You have such a mind. Such hands. And—I hope—the will to ease a lot of suffering."

"I'd have to go to school—for years," Redge had murmured in protest.

"Then go, dammit," Jennifer had replied. "We've talked to Hank Kutcher. He's willing to take care of things along your part of Crow Creek for a few years. Besides, you'll be free during summer months."

"It would cost—" Redge began.

Carla interrupted, "Sure it'll cost, Redge. But wouldn't your father have been excited about it?" Carla had waited a bit, then laid her thoughts and part of her heart bare. "Redge, I only knew your father for a brief time. But I know he was proud of you."

As dusk came on that same afternoon, Audrey had walked with Redge beyond sight and hearing of the buildings of Kate's Wagon. He broke their silence at last by saying in a troubled voice, "I'd be gone a long time. Most of the time for four or five years." When she did not answer, he turned and laid both hands upon her shoulders. His eyes searched her face as he asked, almost in panic, "Audrey, would you . . . would you wait for me? We're

248

both so young but I am utterly in love with everything about you—that tawny hair . . . every confounded freckle, and even with the way you thumb your nose at me."

When she answered, she snuggled into his arms and pressed her cheek to his. "Of course I'll wait, Redge. I have to finish school myself." She drew slightly back, tilted her face upward, and added, "I must be quite a gambler, making such a promise. Kiss me, Redge—just once—so I won't take a notion to back out of a wonderful deal."

Audrey's thoughts came back to the present. Noting that Carla's head was nodding sleepily, she said, "I'm just thankful you and Jennifer finagled that water decree, and also a homestead patent for Redge when he wasn't anywhere near twenty-one years old."

Carla again applied the wilted handkerchief to her cheeks and throat. "Audrey, Jennifer has been dead for seven years now. But I remember as if it were yesterday my sister's strange and contradictory feelings . . . and passions."

"I know," Audrey agreed. "She was capable of giving me holy hell for some reason, then turning about and doing something so nice it took my breath away."

Carla nodded in wistful recollection. "Jennifer could be the correct and genteel hostess of a Denver or New York or Washington reception; she could also stand in the clutter of a Telluride saloon, drink many a miner under the table, and lay a jackass driver's profanity upon the wretch who dared impinge upon her ways or her motives. She was honest, Audrey, but not averse to using every method to circumvent or defeat those who would thwart her." Carla Dunlop fell silent, drummed her gloved fingers on her knee, then added, "That claim that Redge had filed for a water decree sure set fire under a chair or so at the State House in Denver. Or at least it was the kindling to which Jennifer helped me to touch a match."

"I remember it as a legal affair," Audrey answered, recalling facts from a long-gone time.

"It started as a rather routine thing," Carla agreed. "On his way to Arizona, Redge happened to hire a Denver lawyer, Allen Van Cleve, to seek an adjudication of part of the water flowing in Crow Creek."

"Even then he was thinking of the dam," Audrey said with growing interest.

249

"I'm sure he was. Somehow he fired Lawyer Van Cleve with enthusiasm for the project. I learned later that Redge could hardly pay the lawyer and broke himself, selling all he owned."

"It was everything he'd taken on the trip," Audrey said. "He'd left his veterinary tools with my mother, as well as another horse. He was always a proud one. Still is, Carla, especially about being independent in money matters."

"The application for water came perilously near to failing," Carla continued. "Of course, the Secretary of State's office found out that Redge wasn't of legal age, and that he'd asked his lawyer, Van Cleve, to have Hank Kutcher act as a trustee."

"I know." Audrey sighed. "And Hank never had a day of schooling. Can't even sign his name—except as a witnessed 'X'."

"At that point the whole dam—or damned, if you'll pardon the pun—reservoir project seemed pretty hopeless. Especially because a shyster attorney named Fedderson got wind of the dilemma, and saw a chance to possibly file on the water rights for himself, and then try to peddle them to the Diamond-7 Ranch, or to some other landholder. So then my sister Jennifer got wind of what was going on. Van Cleve was a straight shooter and wanted to fulfill his obligation. When the matter of Redge's age muddled things, Van Cleve got in touch with Adolph Brinner. And Brinner happened to be the banker who handled most of the Waverley investments for Jennifer." Carla paused and dabbed at her brow.

"And Jennifer convinced him," Audrey affirmed. "If it weren't for her, Redge and I wouldn't own Cardigan Ranch today."

"Jennifer called in both her banker and Van Cleve for a bit of planning and strategy. She enjoyed the challenge and a chance to do battle."

Audrey peered ahead, then said with a deep sigh, "Carla, you surely know how to make time pass on a trip. See those trees peeking over the rise? They're the trees of my childhood—that's Kate's Wagon."

250

Chapter 23

The years of World War I wrought no sudden or drastic change upon the high plains of Colorado. More and more settlers arrived to carve out holdings that they hoped would provide a life of independence and security. Rainfall continued to be relatively ample, and prices for crops and livestock maintained an upward spiral. Each year brought more fenced land, more windmills to pump water, and more red barns to shelter increasing numbers of farm livestock. A few new businesses came to Hawk Bend, among them a dealer in farm supplies and implements.

It was timbers and concrete and horse-drawn scrapers that caught and held Mark Cardigan's interest. He was totally obsessed by the construction of a bridge, a house, or a segment of barbed-wire fence. The manner in which his son hung around any building project, asking endless questions of the carpenters, surveyors, and stone masons, was not lost upon Redge. Half in pride and half in exasperation, he commented often and vigorously to Audrey.

"We've a kid who's learning to know more about foundations and gable roofs and running a line for survey stakes than he does about our hay crop and heifers."

Once, the remarks brought a studied retort from her. "What's so strange about Mark liking to build . . . to create something? Like father, like son. Wasn't your dream to build a big and prosperous ranch? And didn't you make plans for the dam that makes our hay meadows possible? Mark is growing up; he is eleven years old."

Despite his fascination with construction work, young Mark found that arithmetic was his most troublesome study. By the time he had progressed to the sixth grade, in 1918, mathematics had developed into a dilemma and his despair. At his mother's urging he sought out elderly Miss Doris Kendrick, who acted as principal of the growing school.

She listened to his words of frustration, then said, "You're a very bright and energetic boy, Mark. Arithmetic should not create such a problem. Is it fractions or . . ." She fell silent, watching the way with which Mark's gaze and his interest abruptly centered on the wall off to the left of her desk. There was a small rack that supported a couple of potted plants, and a piece of board on which a few arrowheads had been mounted. Three nails had been driven into a narrow piece of board that supported the shelf; from the nails hung a rubber raincoat, a long knitted scarf, and a whip.

"Isn't that whip a quirt?" Mark asked suddenly.

"Of course it is, Mark," Miss Kendrick answered, and found herself studying the whip. At its top was a braided segment that was about half an inch in diameter and served as a handle. This was topped by a round leather knob that was ball-like and filled with heavy lead shot. The lower portion consisted of three or four pieces of well-tanned leather hanging as straps. A small loop above the heavy knob allowed the quirt to be hung on a nail or from the horn of a saddle.

"The quirt was given to me when I used to have to ride an old and obstreperous mule to school." She did not think it necessary to add that the whip had been left hanging in plain view as a caution to her older and unruly students.

Mark nodded his head brightly, then said, "Miss Doris, I know what that word 'obstreperous' means. It's just another way of saying someone—or something—is meaner than hell . . . I mean heck, ma'am."

Doris Kendrick's inward mirth was stifled except in her deep-set eyes. He knows the meaning of a little-used word like that, she thought. But finds six times eight troublesome. But he can—and he will—master mathematics. He dreams of great things he'll someday build. Miss Doris Kendrick's jaw firmed as she added to herself, Here's one builder that is going to understand algebra . . . and trigonometry. Yes . . . and someday maybe calculus too.

Very little mathematics, either practical or theoretical, was involved in Mark Cardigan's first brush with the problems of construction. He learned of the project through overhearing a somewhat salty conversation between his father and Hank Kutcher. On a spring morning of 1919, the two men and Mark were burning dry and windblown

252

weeds that might impede the flow of water in a ranch irrigation ditch.

Redge threw smoldering embers on a stack of Russian thistles and watched Kutcher shovel a bit of drifted sand from the channel. "I know where there's another shoveling job, Hank, if those rheumatic arms of yours are up to it."

Kutcher glared at him, threw a few more shovels, then asked in frosty tone, "Something you're trying to get out of doing yourself, I expect."

"Not exactly." Redge grinned. "It's just that this deal calls for an expert . . . an experienced privy digger."

"Shit!" Kutcher growled.

"Well, that enters into the general idea. "The school board—"

"School board . . . school board. That's all I hear, Redge, since you got yourself elected."

"But it's going to be a paying job. A contract," Redge explained.

Kutcher greeted the information by flinging a shovel of sand high into the air, where it showered down upon the three of them. "You mean," he demanded, "they're gonna write up papers, take bids, and all that just to have someone dig out a hole they can set a two-holer over."

"A six-holer." Redge laughed. "Three on each end of a coal house."

Kutcher stalked off a few steps, then bellowed over his shoulder, "It's no job for a self-respecting range rider. The only dug hole that interests me is the one they'll shovel out for me when I'm dead and shet of your half-assed ideas."

Mark had been listening, while forking an occasional weed. Now he piped up, "Why couldn't I make a try at the digging?"

Redge thrust his long-tined fork into the ground and wiped grime from his neck. "You'd have to shovel dirt one hell of a lot faster than you've moved weeds this morning." Then he added in a more reasonable way, "Besides, the privy digging is tied in with some other work. The contract will include building a new four-wire fence around the school yard, about sixty rods, with a couple of gates."

"I can dig those outhouse holes," Mark declared with confidence. "I know a couple of Norwegian kids who'd be good help. And I can set posts and string wire. I've watched the section hands do it on the railroad." He was silent for a moment, then added anxiously, "But it would take some tools we don't have. And I'd have to pay them Norwegians every day or so."

Redge studied his son, and the vigor with which Mark was now stacking thistles to be burned. Then he observed, "You'd be working on your own, Mark. No one to prod or to correct any mistakes. If you didn't finish—make good on the contract—it would be a disaster for you, for the school district, and for your mother and me."

"I'll make good, Dad. If it's necessary I'll keep those kids and myself working damned near around the clock. We'll build you one hell—"

"Hey! Slow up and shut up, Mark. I've got a copy of the *Notice to Bid* up at the house. If you want, I'll go over it with you. And . . . watch your words, will you? Despite what you think, you're not a mule skinner."

There was no bank at Hawk Bend, but a train of mixed freight and cattle and passenger cars made the round trip to Greeley each day. Leaving Hank Kutcher to watch over the ranch, Redge and Audrey accompanied Mark on his all-important journey to the county seat. They arranged for rooms at the Camfield Hotel, the largest structure Mark had ever seen, towering four stories above a street lined with various stores and business offices.

Shortly after opening hour, they entered the Plains National Bank. Mark clutched the page of figures by which he had arrived at a total amount he would need for labor and materials for the school's privy hole and fencing job. It was a week before the contract would be let, but Redge had pointed out the necessity for early completion of loan arrangements. Redge was inclined to believe that Mark's bid would be the accepted one, for as Hank Kutcher had pointed out, "Quite a few of the residents of the Hawk Bend district know how to build fences, but damned few would be caught dead digging privy holes."

At the bank, Silas Latham, the president, recognized Redge and waved a greeting. "Good to see you in town, Cardigan. Let me finish with a bit of paperwork, then I'll be right with you."

The Cardigans sat in straight-backed oak chairs and watched three tellers at work beyond the formidable bars that fronted their cages. "I'd hate to be cooped up like that," Mark whispered.

Redge shrugged. "Probably those fellows would hate wading mud to irrigate a meadow, or shoveling horse dung out of a stable."

"Are you sure you can borrow money here, so far from home?" Mark queried.

"I'm not the one who is going to ask for a loan. You are, my boy."

"Why couldn't you and Mom do it? Let me borrow from you?" Mark's palms were sweating, and the seldom-worn stiff collar was scratching at his neck.

"Because if you're given the contract it will be your job and your responsibility. Right now is a good time to learn—"

They were interrupted by the bank president, who had come up to them, thrust out a hand to Redge, nodded at Audrey, and was studying young Mark. "This young fellow has grown a lot since I was out to your place and we went antelope hunting."

Redge nodded and said, "That was nearly five years ago, Mr. Latham. You're welcome back . . . anytime."

"I'd sure like to make it again next fall." Latham sighed. "How are things out around Hawk Bend?"

"If you're farming, it's real good as long as there is plenty of rain. If you're a rancher, there's getting to be precious little open grazing land left. It's nearly all fenced and plowed now."

"And due for big trouble when a drought comes along." The banker nodded. "That's why we are trying to restrict our loans to the irrigated areas of Weld County."

Mark felt a tinge of disappointment at Latham's words, then the banker continued, "What can the Plains National do for you this spring, Redge?"

"But we don't live down here in the irrigated," Mark blurted in tones tinged with frustration.

Latham grinned. "So you don't. But young man, your dad has one of the best acreages of meadow in eastern Colorado, and a reservoir full of creek water to keep it green and growing."

Mark knew the time had come for him to speak up. "Mr. Latham, I may get a job contract for some fencing and . . . and toilet holes at the Hawk Bend school. I'll have to have money for tools and post and wire." He thrust the sweat-smudged estimate of costs toward the banker. "The lumber yard at home gave me these prices. And there's a couple of kids I can hire to help set posts and string wire."

Latham glanced down the listed items on the estimate and asked, "Aren't there apt to be some older people trying for the job?"

Redge responded quickly, "Likely there will be, but the boy has shaved his figures pretty close."

"Son, how much will you need?" Latham studied Mark's face closely.

"I figure eighty-five dollars should do it, sir."

"Perhaps," the banker answered. "But these things always seem to overrun. Suppose we agree to a loan of a hundred and twenty-five dollars for sixty days in case you're awarded the contract?" The banker turned to Redge, asking, "You would be willing to cosign your son's note on that basis?"

"No, I wouldn't," Redge answered.

"But he isn't of legal age," the banker said, puzzled.

"I'm aware of that," Redge said. "But this is to be Mark's loan and his responsibility. I'll tell you what I will do. If Mark makes a profit—or breaks even—I'll make sure he pays the loan immediately. If he loses his shirt, I guarantee that he will work this summer at any job he can get to pay off the part of his loan that the school board's check doesn't cover."

Mark listened, then spoke up firmly. "Maybe I'd better not bid. If I have to pay off by hoeing weeds at maybe a dollar a day, I couldn't pay off within sixty days."

The banker chuckled, then explained, "We could renew your note and give you more time, say, another thirty or sixty days, Mark. But you'd have more interest to pay."

"That interest thing could eat me up," Mark said skeptically.

"Another reason for being sure you don't bid the job too low." Latham glanced toward an impatient man who was waiting to see him. Then he said, "If you get the award, Mark, we can loan you one hundred and twenty-five dollars at four percent interest." He turned to Redge and grinned. "Keep one buck antelope earmarked for me

256

this fall. And Mrs. Cardigan, my wife would still like to have your recipe for blackberry pie." He waved aside Mark's words of thanks, then strode toward the waiting stranger.

Redge looked down at his son's elated face as they left the bank. "It looks as though you'll be in business if you get the contract. But I'll warn you, that's one piece of school-board business on which I'm going to disqualify myself to vote." He placed his hand on his son's shoulder and added, "Knowing your trouble with arithmetic, I've an idea you'd better go over those bid figures mighty carefully."

"Don't worry," Mark answered confidentially. "I've already asked my teacher to check every figure for me."

When the bids for the toilet holes and fence building were opened at an early May meeting of the Hawk Bend school district, Mark Cardigan's bid was the lowest of three submitted, twenty-one dollars below the nearest competitive figure. Audrey shared her son's elation, but Redge's only comment was, "You've got your work cut out for you, Mark. Too bad you left a twenty-dollar bill on the table."

Mark scratched his head. How could he have left a twenty-dollar bill on the table when as yet he hadn't even handled a single dollar? He had no knowledge that the amount he had underbid his nearest competitor was known as money left on the table.

His first move was to seek out his schoolmates, the Nordraak brothers, whose father was a skilled dairy-cow breeder. Earlier in the school year, an incident on the school grounds had given Mark occasion to learn the strength and quickness of these Norwegian brothers, named Halfdan and Fartein. Inevitably, they were dubbed Halfraw and Farting in the schoolyard. For a day or so the Nordraak boys took the nicknames in fun. But the fun wore thin, and when a hulking son of the town grain dealer used the names as a slur, Halfdan and Fartein issued an ultimatum to one and all to shut up or lose a few teeth.

The deftness and speed with which the Nordraaks dispatched a few challengers lingered in Mark Cardigan's mind. And now he could use such brawn and aggressiveness in fulfilling his contract.

He offered the Nordraaks a dollar per day. Boys often

worked for less in 1918, but Halfdan, the older brother, evidenced little interest in the daily wage. Instead, he made Mark a counteroffer.

"I will test the ground where the holes are to be dug for the privies. If there are no rocks, Fartein and I will take the digging job for ten dollars."

Mark screwed up his face in concentrated thought. This was a possibility he had not considered—it was subcontracting. Finally he agreed to the price, but added two provisions. "You'll have to finish the holes within a week, and they'll have to be smooth and even."

"We didn't plan to tunnel off to the side," Hafdan answered testily. Then he asked, "You'll need help with the fencing, won't you?"

"We'll talk about that after you give me a good job on the privy holes," Mark said cautiously.

He need not have worried, for the holes were completed in a fast and competent manner, done so true and even that the carpenters nodded satisfaction when they arrived to start their foundation for the building.

Largely because of his luck in hiring the Nordraak boys, the entire contract was finished well within the agreed dates, and Mark achieved a profit of just over thirty dollars, in addition to some shovels, picks, and fencing tools. He mailed full payment of his construction loan, plus interest, to Silas Latham at the Plains National Bank.

At home that evening, he studied the small tablet on which he had kept a record of the job's progress, its problems, and its costs. His mother busied herself in the living room, sorting garden and flower seeds for planting, while Redge scanned a Denver livestock magazine. Presently Mark said aloud, "I'd sure like to know how much a logging wagon and a span of mules would set me back."

Redge laid aside the journal and answered firmly, "They would cost a heap more than you've got, Mr. Construction Mogul. Besides, what use would you have for them?"

Mark riffled the pages of his tablet and selected his words with care. "There's a fellow thinking of opening a dance hall and roller-skating rink at Hawk Bend. He talked with me at the school grounds and inspected my fence. He'll buy all the house logs I can haul from the mountains. I'm to see him again—"

"Hold on a bit, Mark." His father was moving his arm in a restraining gesture. "Have you taken into consideration the work we have planned here on the ranch for the summer when your school is out?"

Mark shifted uneasily, started to speak, but was silent as Redge Cardigan continued, "Son, a lot of years ago I hauled logs from up north of the Poudre River. I was a bit older than you are, but I couldn't have done it except for the help Hank Kutcher gave me."

"I could get Hank to go along, maybe."

"No, you can't. Hank isn't all that spry anymore. Besides, he has plenty of work here, just the same as you have."

"Then I can't . . ." Mark said sullenly, feeling thwarted.

Suddenly Redge was reliving the moments when, from a high grassland crest, he had first glimpsed the virgin beauty of Crow Creek Valley, the gently folding hills beyond, and the distant and snow-crested Rocky Mountains to the west. He recalled his own exaltation as the possibility of a homeplace, a fertile and productive and secure sweep of acres, became both a vision and a goal. And his own father had understood: *It's your future we're after, son . . . Let's get down to the creek and unhitch.*

But Redge also remembered the disaster and the anguish that Cardigan Camp had brought about. So now he spoke softly to Mark, who stood before him with quiet frustration on his face.

"Son, it's your future I'm thinking of. It is pretty clear that ranching or farming doesn't excite you. But the fact remains that these fields and pastures provide our living. Someday they will belong to you, so your mom and I intend to hand them over in pretty good shape . . . God willing."

"But you helped me on my first job, at the school." Mark's tone was bewildered and hurt.

"That took just a short while, and you had darned good conditions. This pole-hauling thing is likely to run into many weeks, or even months. Mark, wait until next summer. You'll be thirteen then, and I'll have time to look for someone to help here on the ranch. Maybe old Hank might like to get up into those tall, lonesome forests again. Maybe your mother and me too . . . once in a while."

A grin, touched with reluctance, slowly spread over the boy's face. "I just hope someone wants logs or poles next summer. Besides, by then maybe Miss Kendrick, at school, will have pounded what she calls 'beauty of arithmetic' into my skull."

Chapter 24

On a dark February evening during the following winter, Audrey Cardigan peered anxiously from a kitchen window, her eyes scanning the road up which Mark should be riding home from school. A wind, nearing gale force, was blowing in from the northwest; it carried the promise of snow.

Experience warned Audrey that likely a heavy storm, perhaps a blizzard, was in the offing, and so she heaved a sigh of relief at the approaching horse and rider. Tonight would be a bad one even for an experienced rider facing into stormswept cold and snow.

Minutes later Mark had stabled and fed his horse. He stomped through the kitchen door. A single glance at him brought a cry of alarm to Audrey's lips. Mark's face was caked with blood. His lower lip was badly cut, and his right eye swollen shut.

"Mark! Oh, my God, son. What happened? Who did this to you?"

He ignored the question, but faced her with determination. "Mom, tell me the truth. I gotta know the truth. Did my dad kill a man?" As Audrey gazed at him in mute concern, he continued, "Two new kids started at our school last Monday. One's name is Collister. The other one's a kid named Dooby O'Brian. They're telling everyone that my dad is a murderer—that he killed a man right here on this ranch."

Mark's fists were tightly clenched at his sides. "I tried to beat hell out of them, but the big one grabbed and held me. Then the other one . . ." Mark paused for a couple of panting breaths. "Nobody is gonna call my father a dirty man-killer. They say when Dad was young he was no damned good. They called him a bastardly, dry-gulchin' gunslinger."

The boy poured out words in rage, pain, disbelief. Suddenly he realized his mother had not answered. Instead, she was gazing toward the outer door, which had swung open behind Mark. Through it, in a rush of wind-driven snow, came Redge Cardigan.

He pushed the door shut, then spoke thoughtfully to his wife. "Yes, I heard, Audrey. Enough to get the gist of it."

She started to answer, but he silenced her with a gesture. "Let me handle this, Audrey. It's my job. My duty." In the yellow lampglow, Redge's face seemed shadowed and older. He laid a firm hand on his son's shoulder, swinging Mark about to face him. "Don't take your coat off now. Come with me, son. Right now."

Outside, the storm was gathering intensity; already a thin blanket of snow lay across the ranch yard. Redge Cardigan seemed heedless of the oncoming night and the thickening snow as they walked swiftly past the barnyard and then upstream along the creek. Overhead, the cottonwood boughs swung to the tempo of the wind, and gave forth a loud and dirgelike sound.

They came presently to a fenced area only a few yards square. Redge held the barbed wires apart and motioned for his son to enter the enclosure. Then he followed.

"Mark, do you know where you are?"

"Of course I know," the boy answered in a perplexed way. "We're in the old graveyard."

"Right. Your grandfather is buried here." Redge's voice was quiet but purposeful. "Will Cardigan—my father— was murdered. Pretty soon I'll tell you when and why and how it happened."

"It is true, Dad? Did you kill someone?" Mark asked.

Redge slowly sifted snow through his fingers. "Yes, Mark, I killed a man. A man named Stacy Murdock. But it was in an honest gunfighting showdown. He was the one who murdered my father—and the man who laid four slashes across my naked back while I was tied to a wagon wheel. You've seen the scars, often. I just could never bring myself to tell you the truth about them."

Mark stepped backward, his eyes searching his father's face. There was great pride in his voice as he said through clenched teeth, "I hope you gut-shot him . . . so it took him seven days to die."

His father smiled in enormous relief. "When we have more time, I'll tell you about it. Right now, let's figure how you can best handle those kids at school. They worked you over pretty thoroughly."

Mark straightened as his eyes darkened in anger. Then Redge noticed a calm and calculating sureness come over him. His tone was surprisingly matter-of-fact as he replied, "You just leave that Collister kid and the other son of a bitch to me."

"But they can double up on you," Redge reminded him.

"When I get back to school," Mark said flatly, "they're gonna wish they had six other kids to help 'em." He glanced about the quiet snow-mantled cemetery and added, "Maybe I'll make them wish they were here—inside this fence—for keeps."

"Ease down, boy," Redge said seriously, preparing to crawl back through the fence. Almost to himself, he murmured, "Seems like I've raised a vengeful tiger."

They walked arm in arm toward the house, toward an anxiously waiting woman, and toward the hot meal they knew she would have waiting for them.

The storm that began that February evening became a swirling and dangerous blizzard before morning. A foot of snow fell during the night, and a steady blast of northwest wind raked across the plains, drifting the whiteness high along fence rows and the frozen roads. There was no school held at Hawk Bend for the remainder of the week. On the farms and ranches, the younger children were kept inside, while the older ones were expected to go out and care for livestock that had strayed before the fury of the storm.

Most of the chores and livestock feeding at the Cardigan Ranch fell to Mark, for his father, always available for veterinary work in the area, was kept on a constant round of neighboring farms. Many animals had sickened due to exposure and lack of ample forage. The arrangement suited Mark, for it gave his battered face a chance to heal before school could resume. It also gave him time to plan how to handle the inevitable meeting with the burly youths who had given him the beating.

First, he considered the possibility of arming himself with a pistol or a knife. The thought was repellent to him

263

and he hurriedly discarded it. Briefly, he contemplated the possibility of asking some of his school friends, such as the Nordraak boys, to take his side and to act in his behalf. But this was another obnoxious idea. His troubles were his own, and to plead for help would mean an utter loss of self-respect, and probably of his friends' esteem.

Then, a calmness stole over Mark. I am Redge Cardigan's son, Mark thought to himself. He avenged his father's death—with honor. It would be a sight better to take another beating than to act with fear and dishonor. The most destructive thing would be to cringe or whimper.

By the following Monday, the storm had swept its way eastward, and warming sunshine lay across the prairies. There were still drifts across the road into Hawk Bend, but they could be easily traveled on horseback. School would soon resume, and most of the students would attend.

Mark was quiet as he saddled his horse and rode across the ranch yard. He was aware that both his father and his mother were standing on the front porch watching as he turned onto the road. He sensed their concern, and waved a reassuring hand in their direction. When he turned in the saddle, adjusting the strap that held a couple of books, he knew suddenly what he must do. The thought brought an expectant bristling of the hair along his neck; he touched spurs to his mount eagerly and moved swiftly toward Hawk Bend and the school grounds.

Neither the Collister kid, who had held him for the beating, nor the other one, who had used his fists, were about. There was nothing unusual about this, for both of his assailants regularly skipped hours or days of school, and were apt to show up on the grounds at times of their own choosing.

That morning he had both an arithmetic and a geography class with Miss Kendrick. Twice he noticed that she was appraising him in a worried manner, but she spoke only of studies and school matters. Some of the students were more direct, staring at the damage his face had undergone. Fartein peered at him from eyes dimmed by tears. But his brother checked his words when he started to speak to Mark.

The school was large enough to accommodate two teachers and twice as many pupils as it had a year ago. There was a small house that stood separately on the yard and was known as the teacherage; here Miss Kendrick and her companion, Miss Nichols, spent a portion of each noon hour and ate their lunch.

About twenty students were scattered across the school yard when Mark chased a football close to the barbed-wire fence, a couple of hundred feet from the school's main entrance. He had stooped low to retrieve the ball when a moving shadow fell across his path. Mark jerked erect. The Collister boy, clad in riding boots and a ragged denim jacket, had vaulted over the school fence and was closing in upon him. Close by, the other boy moving awkwardly in rubber overboots, was crawling under the bottom wire toward him.

Mark veered from Collister's grasp. The boy shouted, "Didn't we warn you to keep away from this school?" The Nordraak boys had been tramping out a fox-and-geese circle, but now they stopped abruptly to watch the encounter. In an instant, Mark turned and sped toward them. "Halfdan," he challenged, "I'll race you fellows to the front steps."

Collister, enraged, broke into long strides, attempting to catch Mark, who sensed that once within this larger kid's grasp, he would be given a beating far worse than that he had already experienced. The long-legged pursuer would likely have caught Mark, but his stride was broken momentarily by his having to dodge both Nordraak brothers. Mark was conscious of the voice of the second of his enemies, Doobie O'Brian, sounding across the school yard. "You yellow bastard," he shrieked. "We'll get you!"

Mark cleared the three concrete steps of the schoolhouse with a single bound. In a blur, he saw the faces of other kids—some startled, some frightened or horrified, some with smirks of anticipation. The door to Miss Kendrick's room was closed, but Mark managed to jerk it open and dash in, eluding the long grasp of young Collister. The room was empty, save for two young girls writing a game of tic-tac-toe on the blackboard. They whirled about, dropped their chalk, and screamed.

Their eyes widened in fascination. Mark Cardigan had come to a spot where there was no possibility of further flight. He stood white-faced, crouched beside the wall close behind Miss Kendrick's desk. His eyes were watchful—

and there was a smile, almost of glee, growing over his face.

A moment later the powerful Collister boy again reached to clutch at Mark. And only a couple of steps behind him was his eager-fisted cohort. Still Mark stood motionless, but his body was as tense as a steel spring.

Then the Collister kid's arm brushed at his shirt and Mark spun about. The suddenness and strength of his movement made the other boy jump back. In that split second, Mark's arm swept across the wall against which he had been standing. When it came down in a powerful flashing movement, his clenched fingers clutched the lash end of Miss Kendrick's quirt—and the butt, filled with heavy shot, caught powerful Collister squarely between the eyes.

With a startled grunt, the attacker fell backward. He shook his head wildly, making a grab for the whip. The effort went far wide, for as it began, the shot-butted quirt circled again, this time with all of the savagery and power Mark could muster. It caught Collister an inch above his Adam's apple. He dropped writhing to the floor.

Suddenly Mark realized that Doobie O'Brian had thrown himself forward, ducking to escape the sweep of the quirt. He now was sprawled on the floor, encircling Mark's legs with his arms and attempting to wrestle Mark to the floor.

For a moment Mark stared at him, then with a jeering and obscene phrase, he tossed the whip onto Miss Kendrick's desk. Its sliding course upset an uncorked ink bottle and sent black fluid flowing wildly across books and papers. Mark's left hand reached quickly down and clutched the sprawled boy's heavy sweater. With the strength that comes only of fear or fury, he pulled O'Brian to his feet. Then with methodical precision, he swung his fist against his assailant's mouth. And again.

He would have continued had not both teachers raced into the room, and to his side. Miss Kendrick grasped his arm and restrained him.

"Mark," she ordered. "That's enough. Stop it."

He was panting, but there was a vast coldness in his narrowed eyes as he drew back. "I hope they've learned." His voice pierced the now crowded room. "They'd better know a sight more than to call my dad a murderer." His fists doubled, and he struggled in effort to strike again.

"Let me go," he begged. "They're nothing but scum any-how . . . stupid scum. I'll—" His words were cut short as his teacher clamped a firm hand across his mouth.

Hafdan and Fartein Nordraak made their way to Mark's side. There was admiration in young Fartein's face, but he kept silent and let his older brother speak.

"When you have another building or fencing contract, Mark, we'd be proud to work with you."

It took a little while for Mark to realize the friendship and admiration and trust implicit in the boy's words. Then, he managed a friendly wink and said, "I'm gonna need help right now. God . . . am I ever needing help." He was pointing toward the disaster area atop Miss Kendrick's desk.

"It's a big enough job for a joint venture," he added in dismay.

Chapter 25

Things did not progress well for Mark Cardigan during the summer of 1920. He was approaching fourteen, had finished the eighth grade at the Hawk Bend School, and was on his way to becoming a tall, well-built man.

All during the school year, he had kept in mind the proposal that he haul poles and house logs from the mountains to build the proposed dance hall and roller-skating rink. A lot of his spare time during the evenings of winter and spring were spent figuring out what horses, wagons, and other equipment he would need. He went over the cost and possible income figures time after time. Money would be needed for such items as food and horse fodder while away from home, as well as the care and feeding of himself and his assistants. The list of incidentals seemed to grow constantly. Also, cash would be needed once a month with which to pay help, for the Nordraak boys had wrung consent from their parents for one of them to accompany Mark on each trip to the mountains.

A visit to Silas Latham, at the Plains National Bank in Greeley, resulted in a limited but seemingly adequate line of credit for the hauling business. When Mark finally picked up the mail at the village post office on an early June day, he felt everything was in readiness. A letter from the forest supervisor, in Fort Collins, enclosed a cutting permit for enough logs to keep him busy for most of the summer.

Armed with the necessary papers and unbounded enthusiasm, Mark looked up the prospective customer for logs and poles. On their previous meeting the man hadn't volunteered his name, but Mark had memory of his face and form. He found his potential customer squatted on an overturned barrel in the Hawk Bend blacksmith shop, waiting to have worn horseshoes replaced on his buggy team.

"I've got everything squared around," Mark began. "If you have time today, we can work out some sort of written contract, and by next week I can have your first load of logs on the job site."

The dance-hall promoter had a jackknife in his hand; now he reached for a coal-smudged bit of two-by-four timber and whittled off a small slice, ignoring Mark's presence and his words.

Mark stared at him, puzzled, stepped closer, and spoke again. "Howdy. I've got things ready to—"

The man wheeled about on the barrel, then flung up an impatient hand. "I heard damn well what you said, kid, and you can forget the deal." His eyes dismissed Mark as he began prodding between two teeth with the whittled sliver.

Mark was angry. He had the sickening premonition that his months of work and planning had been for nothing. "I don't understand," he insisted. "Last summer you looked me up. Offered me the job of hauling timbers from the mountains for your hall and rink. Remember?"

The promoter was glowering when he mouthed an answer. "You're damn right I remember, Cardigan. That was before you put the kibosh to my whole deal. I might have known that—"

"Are you crazy?" Mark cut in, shouting. "I haven't even seen you or your building spot for months."

"You didn't see me, eh?" the promoter mocked. "But you sure as shit saw my kid. Knocked the hell out of him in a school ruckus."

"Is . . . is your name Collister?" Mark managed.

"No, it ain't. My name is O'Brian . . . Phil O'Brian. My kid used to run around with Collister's."

Perhaps a minute passed as he gazed at Phil O'Brian's face and sorted out his thoughts. Then he said, "Mr. O'Brian, I reckon I did hit your boy. Pretty hard, too. What you likely don't know is that he and that Collister kid ganged up to give me a beating just a week before that. I've an idea your son and me are just about even."

O'Brian shrugged indifferently. "Makes no difference . . .

even if that hellion of mine was wrong. Know what happened? Just about that time, someone complained to the justice of the peace about the Collisters. Some of their other shenanigans—thievery, public drunkenness, other stuff—were looked into and the whole damn family was invited to leave this part of the county." The promoter paused and stabbed his knife into one of the barrel staves. "Trouble is, Cardigan, that some old dames in the Ladies' Aid Society got all het up and said if I and my family hobnobbed with the Collisters, I wasn't likely upright and righteous enough to operate a dance hall and skating rink. And my banker told me 'no dice.'"

Mark's mouth gaped open in disbelief. After a while, he said, "I'm sorry, Mr. O'Brian. Maybe we can get things changed."

The promoter responded with a glum grin. "It's too late now. I sold the site. In a day or so I'm leaving Hawk Bend." He heaved a sigh, swung down from the barrel, then spoke again, with conviction and finality. "Cardigan, I guess you're just a kid, but you carry destruction in those fists."

Mark left the blacksmith shop, untied his horse from a hitch rail, and started the homeward ride. He let the animal choose a plodding gait that would consume a lot of time. The strengthening sun of early summer lay a comforting warmth across his hunched shoulders, but his mind was in turmoil.

Mark Cardigan, the big construction wizard, he thought bitterly to himself. So far I've had two jobs. Tore up my Mom's garden with a team of dogs, and dug some holes for the school outhouses. Maybe next I can wheedle someone into letting me bury a dead cow.

His mood of frustrated bitterness still hung over him when he reached a crossroad about halfway between Hawk Bend and the Cardigan Ranch. He jerked his horse to a halt with an unaccustomed savagery that made the surprised animal dance about. Redge and Audrey Cardigan would have to be told of his fiasco, but he wasn't ready to do it, nor did he know how.

Abruptly he glanced up the road that led off eastward, then reined the horse onto it and touched the animal's flanks with his boot heels. He had a friend—someone who was always there to listen to him, someone who understood his needs and his problems.

He approached Sam Hook's two-room tarpaper shack, fronted by a yard where two small transplanted cottonwoods clung despairingly to life. The wooden frame of a well-drilling rig thrust a foot or so higher than the shack's metal stovepipe chimney.

Mark dropped from his horse a few feet from the shack and was greeted by a collie pup whose tail was whipping in delighted excitement. He had picked the dog up and was cuddling it when the shack door opened. A tall individual stood there. His head was bald, except for a sparse black fringe just behind his large, reddened ears. The mold of his nose was akin to the beak of an eagle. He was wearing greasy bib overalls and a faded undershirt that had once been red.

"Cardigan," he said in cordial greeting. "Welcome to my abode."

"How come," Mark demanded, "you're home loafing, letting that well rig rust, when half the dry-landers need well and windmill repairs?"

"The engine conked out. Needs new piston rings. Besides, I've a batch of brew inside that's just prime for sampling."

"Sam Hook, you're a lifesaving genius," Mark said with a grin that carried both expectation and lingering frustration. "Bring out a few jars while I tether this horse."

"Come on in. Don't bother to wait for the butler."

Inside, Sam Hook cleared a table by dragging his arm across it to send newspapers and assorted debris to the floor. He uncapped a Mason jar of the home brew and thrust it into Mark's hand. Then he brushed a fly from his sweaty naked head and growled, "All right, Mark. Out with it. What's wrong?"

The boy lowered a half-empty jar, belched, and said in a guarded tone, "Nothing much."

"You're a nickel-plated liar, boy. Something bad is eating on you. You've been here to see me maybe a dozen times in the past couple of years. Before, you always just toyed with a jar of suds. Now you're drinking to a sorrow. Spill all that aching to old Sam. What's the gal's name?"

271

Mark finished draining his jar and reached for another. "It ain't a girl, Sam. It's a job—a contracting job—that went to hell and gone, after I put months of planning into it." Mark clutched his brew as though there were magic and forgetfulness within it. Then he poured out the entire story: his ideas for the timber haul, his trouble with young Collister and O'Brian, the months of careful planning. And the disastrous finale today at the blacksmith shop.

"Now ain't that a beaut of a situation?" Hook said when the boy's words trailed off. "You pop a kid in the mouth and lose a big contract." He stared at Mark, then added, "But, boy, you're not going to find the solution in a jar of brew. Just like I don't find a future in those long trips I take to New Orleans and Cisco and Bisbee. It's an escape hatch. Nothing else."

Mark's rate of alcohol consumption was slowing, but he fondled a third jar. "For damn sure, Sam," he said unevenly, "I'm cured of the construction business. To build is to butt your brains out."

"You're giving up pretty young and real early in the game, aren't you?" Hook flared. He waited for his words to take effect, then added, more softly, "Mark, I've never thought of you as a quitter. Give yourself time. One of these days there'll be a genuine chance to build, and you'll be rarin' to have at it."

"Yeah. But how about now—and in the meantime?"

Hook rose to his feet and stared out of a dust-streaked window. "Right now, take a good look at me, son . . . a half-assed mechanic with a broken-down well-drilling rig and a home-brew recipe. Know why? Because I didn't have sense enough to get a college education."

"I've been going to school steady," Mark defended.

"Who said you ain't been? But I never saw a road or bridge designed with just an eighth-grade diploma." Sam Hook slammed a fist on his table and added, "What I'm trying to say, Cardigan, is—go to college. Get ready. Then, someday, you'll hire men like me and that Phil O'Brian . . . and a scad of others worth a dime a dozen."

Mark listened with a subdued manner and thoughtful face. Now, he said, with slightly slurred words, "Those Norwegian boys said they would like to work for me."

"Sure. They've got good sense and can spot a born leader.

They're . . ." Hook's words trailed off, for suddenly Mark Cardigan's head had dropped onto his arms, upsetting a jar, which dropped to the floor, spilling its contents into the newspapers and dust. Sam smiled and let him sleep.

Chapter 26

Mark was graduated from the preparatory school of Colorado's College of Agriculture and Mechanical Arts, in Fort Collins, four years later in 1924. He now held a high school diploma, and the intricacies of arithmetic seemed less formidable. He had also achieved passing grades in algebra, geometry, and elementary calculus.

With the coming of autumn, he would return to the campus as a college freshman. But now, in early June of 1924, seventeen years old, he was eager to get home and enjoy the freedom and the everyday routine of what he referred to as "my dad's spread upstream on Crow Creek."

He had returned during each summer vacation to help his parents. The passing years had taken their inevitable toll, and now Kate Andrus lay at rest within the small ranch cemetery. Her final illness was brief. Audrey had brought her mother from Kate's Wagon and cared for her during the final days; she had followed Kate's request and buried her on Cardigan Ranch.

On the second day after his homecoming, Mark left the house and walked the short distance to the graveyard. There was a loose picket in the fence, so he found a hammer and tightened a few boards. Later, he found a dozen wild roses in bloom, placed them in a glass jar, and set them beside the headboard marking Kate Andrus's grave. Memories of his grandmother flooded him.

Especially clear was his recollection of a weekend on which he had been home from school shortly before her death. Toward bedtime, he passed the door of her room as it stood ajar. He paused, blew her a kiss, and said, "Get a heap of get-well rest, Grams."

Her face was thin and swept with pain, but she smiled and propped her head up on a doubled pillow. "Come in

274

and talk with me a bit, Mark," she urged. "I'm not the least bit sleepy."

When he had lowered himself into a chintz-padded rocking chair, she reached out to grasp his hand. "I don't get to see you much, Mark. You're growing up; in a lot of ways you're a younger edition of your father." An amused glint touched her eyes, and she added, "But you're branded with the impertinence and deviltry of Audrey too. How she used to tease and torment Redge."

"Sometimes she still does," Mark answered.

Kate Andrus continued holding tight to his hand. Her voice sounded again across the quiet of the lamplit room. "Redge has always meant so much to me. More than my own son."

Mark's voice cut in with surprise. "Grams . . . you had a son? My folks have never spoken about him."

Her grasp tightened on his fingers, and her voice faltered. "You are almost a grown man now, Mark. Yes . . . I think you should be told." She closed her eyes and for a moment was very quiet, as though marshaling the facts and memories of a lifetime. Then she began, "I had three children, a boy and two girls. Karen was the oldest; she died before she was twenty." Kate Andrus paused, as though assessing the need and the worth of divulging the painful details of her older daughter's infatuation with Stacy Murdock, and its doomed ending.

Presently she said, "My only boy was named Albert. Everyone called him Bert. Even as a little boy, Bert craved excitement . . . wanted to be doing the unusual and daring things. And there never was much excitement at Kate's Wagon. Perhaps things would have been different if I'd had time to take him to Denver, or Cheyenne. But I was a widow with a family to raise and a business to take care of. Mark, I think I failed Bert. Before I realized my mistake, my son had left home and was mixed up with some outlaw characters in Cheyenne—and also with Stacy Murdock and his band of toughs at the Diamond-7 Ranch."

Kate Andrus paused, caught her breath, then seemed to force words against her will. "It was Bert, my son, who was very much responsible for your grandfather's murder, and your father's branding."

"What became of your boy?" Mark leaned forward spellbound, trying to catch her every word.

In a slow, deliberate way, Kate Andrus stated, "Bert is still alive. Both he and I can thank your father for that—your father and a pinto gelding from Arizona."

She was tiring rapidly, and her head leaned back on the pillow. Mark started to rise, but she motioned him back to the rocker. "Mark, you'll always remember your father because of his courage and his decency. But what I have learned to respect and to love in Redge Cardigan is his compassion. The compassion he showed my Bert."

It was clear that she had more to say, although weariness was stamped on her face. She whispered, "The pinto gelding belonged to that Navajo friend of your father—Hosteen Begay. Only days after Stacy Murdock's death—and knowing that Bert would become an outcast in this area—Redge gave my son a letter addressed to a wealthy cattleman named Dade Sutherland in Arizona. The letter asked Sutherland to give Bert a job and a chance. But Redge imposed a condition to Bert's holding his job. He knew of Bert's consuming interest in the pinto horse, which the Navajo boy had trained. I believe that Redge somehow sensed that the pinto might help my boy to regain his lost values and decency. Bert was to keep the trick horse, but only if he earned money in Arizona to pay for it and took it, in person, to Hosteen Begay's mother."

"Did Bert ever come back here . . . to Colorado . . . to Kate's Wagon?"

Kate Andrus closed her tired eyes. "I have seen him twice in all these years," she murmured. "Once in Denver, at the stock show, and once when he asked me to visit him in Bisbee, Arizona." Then she was silent; in a short while she fell into a fitful sleep and Mark left the room.

It was the last time he saw his grandmother alive.

And now, walking from the graveyard, and thinking of the cluster of flowers he had placed there in Kate's memory, he realized how much she had only hinted at. For him, Bert Andrus remained but a phantom of the past. His somber thoughts led him down the creek from the cemetery to what he had always claimed as his very own tree, the bag-swing cottonwood. Although unused and weather-beaten, the rope and the sack of hay forming a seat still hung from a high branch and stirred in the breeze.

Mark clinched his legs about the sack, lifted his feet

from the ground, and let the swing move idly back and forth. It was here that his father found him a half hour later.

"I was wondering what became of you," Redge said. "I've been down to the lumber yard at Hawk Bend. Could be I've got some news that would interest you."

"You mean like there's going to be a square dance or a box social at the school?" Mark dropped from the swing, grinning, and faced his father.

"Is that all they taught you at Fort Collins . . . to dance and to eat?" Redge growled, and then added, "How'd you like a couple of weeks' work?"

"You don't have to nag." Mark laughed. "I was planning on cleaning the ditches for you."

"Are you or ain't you going to let me spill what I found out?" Redge asked. Then, before his son could reply, he squatted in the grass and began moving a small dead branch about to fashion criss-crossed lines. "There's a fellow from Kansas has bought six hundred and forty acres—a full section of land—about five miles down the creek from Hawk Bend. He plans on making it into a breeding farm for racehorses. Right now he needs fences built—miles of them."

Mark sensed what might be in the offing, and the old urging rose within him. But he remained quiet and listened.

"This horse breeder asked at the Hawk Bend lumber yard about someone to take on the fencing job. Said he'd be more than a mite particular—the job has to be a top-notch one." Redge Cardigan studied his son. "The lumberyard manager told him that if he wanted to see a good fence job he'd best take a look at the school fence that you and the Nordraak boys built. It hasn't toppled over yet."

Mark answered after a bit of thought, "Thanks for telling me, Dad. But what about my helping you with the ranch? I recall, not so long ago, you were adamant about that."

Redge rose to his feet and pushed the bag swing out over the creek. "This year, son, I think we can do both—ranch and build fences. Hank Kutcher wants to get away and see some other corners of the west. So I'm hiring another hand." Redge paused, struggled for words, and then concluded, "Dammit, Mark. Maybe there's a lot more to look forward to these days in construction than there is in ramrodding a dry-land ranch! If you want a fling at fencing hell's half acre for that horse breeder, have at it. And good luck."

On happy impulse, Mark flung his arm about his father's shoulders. "Thanks. Hey, thanks. What would I do without you?"

They were walking slowly back to the ranch house when Mark asked, "Those sections where the horse ranch is to be . . . won't they be right smack where the grazing range of the Diamond-7 used to be?"

"Right you are, son. Used to be. Nowadays most of the range down toward the Diamond-7 is homesteaded, plowed up, and fenced. Just the same as it is here around Hawk Bend."

"Dad, I've always wondered . . . who first had the guts to settle down the creek and establish the Diamond-7?"

"Mark, it was a fine old gentleman by the name of Andrew Purcell. He happened to become acquainted with your Grandfather Cardigan during the Civil War. It was my good fortune to know Andy Purcell for a short time. Before his death."

They had reached the porch, and Redge stopped and gave his son a thoughtful nod. "I guess each generation leaves things a bit safer and easier for the next. And he was one of the breed of men who left their homes, and sometimes their families, back east, then came onto the frontier to carve out a new life. A few got rich. He did—he was fortunate. A lot of others reaped only weed-grown and soon-forgotten graves."

It was plain that the conversation was leading Redge Cardigan toward painful and seldom-mentioned memories. There was a tone of finality in his words as he said, "Hank Kutcher can tell you a lot more about Andy Purcell and the Diamond-7. He worked there a good many years."

Mark knew of a certainty that if given the opportunity he would ply Hank Kutcher with questions about Purcell, about the Diamond-7. And he would ask too about a man named Stacy Murdock—a person his dad refused to discuss at length.

But now, he merely said, "Being as you think it's okay,

278

I'd like to talk to that horse breeder who needs fences. Find out if the job is worth tackling."

During the summer weeks, Mark found the building of mile after mile of fence to be both a challenge and a constant burden. The horse rancher demanded perfection and made a personal inspection of each completed segment of the work. This proved time-consuming, for there were times when Mark had to cease building, lay off his workers, and await the return of the fence owner from trips to various racetracks.

The stop-and-go nature of the work led Mark to wonder if his contract could be finished before the date upon which he would have to return to school in Fort Collins. Then Hafdan and Fartein Nordraak were told by their annoyed father that they'd be better off at home helping on his dairy. There was one bright side to the constant slowing of work. A clause in Mark's contract called for immediate payment for each finished portion of fence. Such payments enabled him to finance his labor and material costs through small and short-term loans. At no time did he have an interest-accruing loan of more than two hundred dollars at the Plains National Bank. Even banker Silas Latham scoffed a bit over Mark's frugal way of avoiding interest payments by borrowing money in minimum amounts.

By early August, the perimeter fencing had been finished, and a survey line had been run for a mile-long cross fence, with half a dozen gates that would open into small pastures. These special gates were not in stock at the Hawk Bend lumber yard, but would be supplied by a materials dealer in Greeley, and shipped by rail to a small siding near the work site.

The dealer promised that the gates, and various other items, would be shipped from Greeley on a certain Thursday. Near midafternoon on Tuesday, Mark rode his horse along the course of the cross fence. He studied the terrain where posts and barbed wire must be strung and came to a point where the land dipped for a time into a heavily grassed swale.

He considered all aspects of the situation, and realized that at either side of this lowland there would be need for sturdily braced posts to prevent slackening of the wire. He recalled seeing such braced sections on the railroad right-of-way fence. Additional strength was derived by use of guy wires running in an X design between two posts. The bottoms of both posts were utilized as anchors.

He decided to study the placement of posts and wire bracing in the area close to a railroad section house south of Hawk Bend just to check himself. He headed his roan gelding toward it, holding the horse to a leisurely gait. Presently he was a quarter mile from the railroad buildings and riding through a thick overgrowth of prairie cactus. It was also dotted by clumps of the plains yucca—soapweed, as it was called.

Evening approached, and the spiked plants cast long shadows beside him. Suddenly a coyote jumped from behind a soapweed; seeing a horseman it began to leap away.

The startled roan gelding shied violently and took a jerking, sideways jump for which Mark was utterly unprepared. Instantly, he knew he would be thrown. He managed to kick his boots free of the stirrups. Redge Cardigan had long ago taught his son the necessity of falling free, to avoid being dragged by a running horse.

He struck the ground with a hard jolt, aware that he had landed on his back and left shoulder. Momentarily, there was a stabbing of a thousand needles into his body. Then a burst of red light seemed to explode before his eyes. He plunged into unconsciousness. His horse, in another frightened leap, had grazed Mark's temple with a rear hoof.

The first realization that he was still alive came with the savage pain of a needle being jerked from his left buttock. It happened again . . . and again. At last he was conscious and yelled aloud in pain. Soft, firm fingers were exploring the flesh of his behind. He moved his head in an effort to peer about, but a shock of pain swept him into dizziness.

Later, he sensed that his head was bandaged, and that a layer of white cloth covered his forehead. Again the stabbing pain hit. His words were half curses and half pleas of protest. Then he moved his hand in effort to brush away whatever was causing the waspish stings in his bottom.

His hand encountered—and was firmly snared by—a smaller and smoother and steadier hand. And as consciousness fully flooded back, *he knew*. Knew that his pants and underdrawers had been pulled down. That his rear end was exposed to cool air, to the light of dusk—and to the gaze and busy hands of a woman.

He tried to turn to get full view of her face. He heard her quick and excited breathing. Then he roared again as another cactus thorn was plucked from his bruised flesh.

Mark struggled to get onto his side, and pull his clothing into place, but she quickly knocked his hands down. Then she spoke, quiet but stern commands. He could not understand a single word, since her language was Spanish, the broken Spanish of one who can speak English, but reverts to a mother-tongue under stress or excitement.

He lay in a pained and half-shocked inertness until he realized that she was pulling his trousers even lower.

"Let me alone," he said in agitation. "Don't you dast pull—"

She laughed then, a softly mocking laugh that sounded in clear tones across the desert. *"Madre de Dios,"* she said. "It's alive . . . it talks."

Moving too fast for her this time, Mark managed to lift the bandage from his face and gaze upward toward her. His eyes widened as he saw his benefactress, but she again covered them, and scolded with rapid, accented words, "Lie still, young gringo. Sure I pull up the shirt. Pull down the pants. The cactus—*muy grande*—you have rolled in them. Yes, I see skin . . . your butt . . . your white and bloody ass. So what? You think maybe you have too nice an ass for me to see?"

Then in an instantaneous movement he managed to push the bandage from his eyes. And then the clots of blood on it and even the painful removal of the thorns, seemed unimportant. Inches away, hovered above him, was a girl perhaps nineteen years old. She had tousled black hair, flashing eyes, and full red lips. She was the prettiest girl Mark Cardigan had ever encountered.

"Who are you? How did you get here?" he demanded in wonder.

Her hand moved across his posterior in search of more imbedded cactus. "I think the big ones are out," she said in a pleased way. Then she added, "I am Dolores Montez. My papa is what you call a . . . a straw boss on the railroad section."

Mark sat gingerly up, then cautiously moved his arms

281

and legs. "I must have been unconscious for quite a spell," he said, half guessing.

She nodded, then watched unabashed as he maneuvered his pants and shirt in an effort to be fully clad. He looked about for his horse, but in gathering darkness could not spot the animal. Turning to again face the girl, he explained, "A coyote scared my horse . . . so he dumped me."

"I know," she answered. "I saw it. You're a lucky fellow that the hoof didn't take your head off."

Mark responded with a frustrated scowl. "I don't feel so lucky. There's no one at our fencing camp today—I'll have to walk all the way into Hawk Bend."

"You're crazy. It's almost five miles. Likely your head would start bleeding again."

"And you wouldn't be there to wrap my head." Mark grimaced wryly, then added, "But I sure am glad you were around to do it once . . . and to rid me of cactus thorns."

Dolores Montez tossed her head, a gesture that caused long dark tresses to swing about her shoulders. "Haven't you wits enough to know what must be done?" she challenged. "Young gringos are slow figuring anything out. At school. At work. Or when a horse bucks 'em off."

"I suppose you could have done better?" Mark flared.

"Maybe yes. Maybe no. But I'd have ridden around this cactus patch." She was pensive, considering something for a few moments. Then she spoke again and her mood seemed different.

"I'll take you home with me," she said firmly. "That cut on your head should be washed clean. We have some salve. It will burn . . . and you will cry like a baby. After that, my papa can take you to Hawk Bend. He has a railroad motor car, a speedster. It has an engine and rides the rails."

As she thrust out a firm, darkly tanned hand and pulled him to his feet, he winced with pain. "It feels like there's a hundred more cactus . . . all the way from my neck to my . . ."

As he sought for a delicate word, she giggled and cut in, "Down to your tailbone. Likely there are small thorns I couldn't see. When we get to the section house, and better light—"

"You'll doctor my head. And that is all." When she seemed to accept the ultimatum, he said, "My name is Mark. Mark Cardigan."

"I know," she said. "You live at the Cardigan Ranch, and you've been building fence for the horse-breeding people."

"How did you know all that?" he asked, puzzled.

"My papa told me. He gets interested when any kind of building is started. Besides, I've had much time to watch. You should have finished the job days ago."

"I know . . . I know," Mark fretted. "But the owners accept the work only a little at a time."

"Don't you have a written contract?"

"Of course," he answered, irritated.

They had been walking slowly through the darkness, but now she stopped and turned, and her steady, calculating eyes probed his face. "Doesn't your contract have a time limit? Doesn't it provide extra money for delays, and for overruns of labor and posts and wire and—?"

Already she had surmised his negative answer. "Mark Cardigan," she said, "you need either a business manager —or brain repair."

They continued walking through the darkness, and now silence was about them. Soon a lamplight glow appeared before them, and then they came to the right-of-way fence, to the rails and cross ties, and to the shadowy forms of the section buildings.

Dolores's mother, a pleasant-faced, heavy-set, excitable woman, who could neither speak nor understand English, greeted them at the door of the section house. She speedily assessed his injury and with swiftly moving hands soon had his temple washed clean, medicated, and rebandaged. As Dolores had warned, the salve caused him to grunt in pain, but his mind held to a matter of greater concern. Would this motherly Mexican woman insist, as her daughter had, on examining the cactus stabs across his hind end? Mercifully she did not, but Mark suspected that only Dolores's rapid-fire explanation in Spanish, punctuated by a few giggles, saved him the dropping of his pants and unendurable embarrassment.

He was invited to have supper with the Montez family, and sensed that a refusal would be considered rude. Some of the foods were unknown to him, but he found them appetizing, and ate with real zest. Throughout the meal, Mark found himself in rapt attention at the words of Montez, Dolores's father, who spoke English with only a touch of Spanish accent.

Here was a man clearly out of place in his job. This quiet and thoughtful straw boss carried a dignity and depth that spoke of excellent family and university training. "You are wise, señor Cardigan," he said, "to be embarking on a construction career. The next fifty years will bring great opportunities for skilled builders here in the United States. Railroads, mines, great dams for irrigation. You must prepare yourself, señor. Study engineering and surveying and calculus."

"You are skilled in all those areas?" Mark asked in astonishment.

Gilberto Montez smiled, a smile tinged with both regret and pride. "I once had great plans for projects to help my countrymen in Mexico. I have university training and had a position as what you call an engineering estimator."

"And then?" Mark asked.

Gilberto Montez's shoulders moved in a defeated shrug. "And then," he repeated, "a change in Mexico's political affairs brought ruthless men into power. I had opposed them. Naturally, I became an outcast. Later I had to flee in the night. I came to your country, and last year my family joined me. Here, I am but a railroad subforeman—but my family is safe."

When the meal was finished, Gilberto Montez excused himself and went to the section toolhouse. The rail-running speedster had to be fueled and prepared for the trip to Hawk Bend. As he stepped outside, Montez smiled at Mark, and said a bit hesitantly, "While you wait, señor, perhaps you can tell Dolores something of your fence-building project. For a girl, she has an extraordinary interest in such things. Perhaps because I talk too much of them."

Mark, eager to oblige, reached into his shirt pocket and drew out half a dozen rumpled sheets of white tablet paper. He handed them to Dolores and said, "Here are all the figures I have on the fence deal—plans, costs, estimated income and profits. It's not really a big or earth-shaking deal."

She reached out for them, and for a moment was silhouetted by the soft glow of the room's kerosene lamp. He gazed at the cascade of her shining black hair, the pride and the youth of her finely chiseled features, and the swell of her breasts beneath a simple green-hued blouse. An unfamiliar stirring swept Mark Cardigan, and he avoided the directness of her eyes. She moved—and the momentary spell was broken.

She took the papers to a table with a pencil and began to scan the figures thoroughly. In a minute or so, she had scanned long columns of figures. As she came to the final page of Mark's calculations, she circled part of them with a pencil, then jotted some figures of her own. She tapped the pencil against her white, even teeth, and then looked at Mark appraisingly. "You'll make some money. But not as much as you should. Make the changes I've marked before you settle with the horse-ranch people. It may save you about a hundred and forty dollars."

He stared at her in disbelief. "Did you really add all those figures? It took me nearly an hour . . . and then I likely made mistakes."

"You did, but luckily they were not important errors. I just happen to be fast and accurate with figures. It seems to come naturally—or maybe as a gift from my papa."

Mark slowly replaced the pages of calculations in his pocket. There was tiredness about him, and his thorn-punctured back felt as if it were aflame. But now he placed his hand over hers. "Dolores . . . thanks for all you've done. You and your family." He waited, again noting the pensive loveliness of her face. Then he blurted out, "When I'm working out another batch of job costs, can I bring them here? Would you check them? I'd like . . . dammitall, Dolores, I'm just saying that I want to see you again."

"And what is wrong with that?" she said, her voice low and compelling. "But first you must ask my father; it is the Mexican custom."

Work on the cross fencing seemed to drag on, with the owner having little regard for Mark's need to finish the job. When final settlement was made, Mark found himself with only a week of free time before he would have to report at Colorado A&M College to begin classes.

On his last Sunday afternoon at home, he saddled a horse, and then sought out his father, who was in the

285

kitchen cleaning and sterilizing the steel instruments of his most valued veterinary surgery set. For a time, Mark watched Redge's steady, skilled hands, then he commented, "There's not a nerve or a tremor about you, Dad. You could have become a fine operating surgeon."

"Animals need doctoring too, Mark. Besides, you don't have to listen to their complaints."

Mark pointed to one of the highly burnished instruments. "You've had that set as long as I can remember. They're special to you, aren't they?"

Redge nodded, and his gaze grew pensive. "I guess they're a little old-fashioned now, son. But they somehow give me confidence when I am faced with a delicate job. Besides, do you know that your Aunt Carla and her sister Jennifer gave them to me when I was younger than you are now?"

Mark stood in quiet thought. He was burning to ask about Carla Dunlop, about Jennifer Waverley. And about the Diamond-7. But he was nearly certain his father would not be forthcoming with information.

So he said, "Dad, I have a free afternoon. I'd sort of like to ride down Crow Creek, below Hawk Bend, and see how my horse-farm fencing is holding up."

Redge looked squarely into his son's face and replied, "And no doubt, Mark, it will give you an opportunity to visit the Mexican girl."

Mark's face took on a defensive expression. "I've never tried to keep it secret that I see Dolores Montez . . . and that I like her. I like her father too."

Redge motioned his son to a chair. "No, Mark, you have been perfectly open and aboveboard about it. With me, with your mother, and with everybody. Perhaps that has compounded the problem."

"What are you saying, Dad?" Mark seemed mystified.

"Mark, people are talking. I guess I have to admit that we who live in this ranching and farming area are provincial and biased. Perhaps in time we will mature and outgrow it. But right now, son, it boils down to the nasty fact that people, at least a few busybodies, are trying to make something ugly of the fact that Mark Cardigan is running after a Mexican girl."

"I don't give a goddam what they say," Mark flared.

"I know some Hawk Bend girls who are practically sluts, regardless of their blue eyes and white skin."

"Simmer down, son," Redge cautioned. "We have nothing against Dolores Montez, your mother and I. Fact is, we'd like to meet her." He paused, then continued with carefully chosen words. "Mark, what you really have to consider is the damage that an affair—even an entirely innocent friendship—can have on the girl. There are those who are jealous and ridden by race hatred. They will watch every move you and the Montez girl make, hoping to somehow degrade and demean her. You are going away to college, Mark, and for you things will doubtless blow over. With this girl, things could be much nastier. She has to live here—among the rumors and gossip and downright lies."

"Then you don't think I should see her again?" Mark asked in a hostile tone.

Redge stared at his son, drew a long breath, then grinned. "No, by God. Mark, I think you should get on your horse and ride right through Hawk Bend down to the Montez house. But take another horse—a saddled one —with you, so you can bring Dolores Montez back into Hawk Bend. Then people can see the contempt in which you hold gossips and lie spreaders."

Redge's words surprised and warmed Mark. Presently he murmured, "But you mentioned the need to protect Dolores."

"That's what I'm still saying. Ride down the main street of Hawk Bend. Spike any of the talk that your meetings are secret and clandestine. Ride in such a way that everyone can see having the Mexican girl by your side is an honor. If you can, introduce her—face to face—to a couple of the town busybodies."

"What will Mom think of all this?" Mark queried in awe.

Redge got to his feet abruptly, with an ironic grin on his lips. "Mark, who in hell do you suppose put me up to this talk?"

Chapter 27

Mark's first year at Colorado College of Agriculture and Mechanical Arts seemed to pass quickly and uneventfully. It was a period of adjustment. He learned to cope with regimented hours and the compact living and studying quarters of the dormitory. After a time, he found himself with many acquaintances, but few close friends. He reveled in the nearness of the mountains and spent many free hours hiking through the foothills and up the canyons by which the Cache la Poudre River and a smaller stream, the Buckhorn, found their way onto the plains.

When approaching summer brought an end to the school term, he returned immediately to the Cardigan Ranch. He had achieved well above passing grades, and already had mastered a mathematics course that he felt would help in estimating future construction jobs. The restlessness of spring was upon him, and more and more he looked forward to visiting Dolores Montez. Throughout the school year, his mind had retained the precise memory of how she had looked when, silhouetted against yellow lampglow, she had tossed her dark hair onto her shoulders, and the beams of light had been caught and held by her dark and lively eyes.

But when he returned to Crow Creek Valley, his mother broke the news to him that Dolores Montez was no longer at her father's home, but instead had for several months been with an aunt in Albuquerque, New Mexico. "It is far better for her there," Audrey explained. "She is attending a Catholic academy." Noting her son's stunned silence, she added, "Mark, there would be nothing for her in Hawk Bend. At least, in Albuquerque, where there is a larger Mexican community, a girl with her intelligence will be accepted . . . and perhaps be assured of a decent future."

In the days that followed, Mark Cardigan began to wonder if the fates had prepared a conspiracy against his achieving even limited goals in construction. There was virtually no building work to be had that year. And when he at last learned of a couple of small proposed jobs, it turned out that the Nordraak brothers would not be available during the summer. Their father had broken a leg, and both Hafdan and Fartein were needed in the dairy.

The course of Mark's summer was fully determined in mid-June. At dusk on a sweltering day, Redge and Audrey placed some chairs on the outside porch, where they hoped a few wisps of breeze might come their way. Presently Redge called for Mark to join them, "Your mother and I have something to talk over with you, son."

Mark threw a leg over the porch railing and listened as his mother spoke.

"Mark, you are returning to A&M in the fall?"

"Of course, Mom."

A relieved sigh escaped Audrey. "I'm so glad. You've said so little about school lately."

"I'll have to give it plenty of thought come September." Mark laughed a bit ruefully. "I've got a heavy class schedule: math, science, Spanish."

"All right, son," Redge said. "Until you do go back, how about you taking hold and running this shebang of ours for the rest of your vacation? Hank Kutcher can help you. He's getting crippled up with rheumatism, and he's got a caustic tongue. But he still thinks mighty clear, and knows the ranch inside out."

"What's going on with you two?" Mark asked in surprise.

"Well," Redge answered, "our graying hair, and a few wrinkles, say it's time for your mom and me to sort of ease off. We'd like to take a trip this summer to Missouri, to the New England states. And to Virginia."

"It is about time, all right," Mark agreed. "Except for trips to Denver and Cheyenne and Greeley, you two haven't been off Cardigan Ranch, or at least out of this valley, since I was born."

In a flurry of expectant excitement, Mark's parents left ten days later. The course of their travels was marked by a flow of postcards. When they finally returned to the ranch eight weeks later, Mark had only a week to prepare to return to the busy routine of his second year at school.

Mark found his interests widening as his sophomore year

got well under way. He was chosen to participate in an engineering study designed to measure the stream flow and irrigation potential of the Cache la Poudre and Big Thompson Rivers. The work took him often to weirs and gauges built in the streams, so that he could devise means by which these could be rebuilt for greater efficiency. Before long, he was working with advanced graduate students and professionals in the field.

On a crisp November day, he found himself in Laramie, Wyoming, for the first time. Selected students from A&M had been invited to an irrigation engineering seminar at Wyoming University, at Laramie. The annual football game between the two rival schools would take place on the Saturday following the seminar. With five fellow students he checked into the Connor Hotel, where rooms had been reserved.

The seminar had drawn authorities on irrigation and irrigation law from several states, and offered a variety of challenging subjects. With the widening of irrigation projects across the west, there would be enormous opportunities in the field of irrigation construction. Vast dams were being proposed both for irrigation and for the generation of electric power. It would be up to qualified engineers to plan these structures and the networks of canals and smaller storage reservoirs to utilize the impounded water.

The seminar ended on Friday afternoon, and Mark looked forward eagerly to the fun and excitement sure to accompany the football game. By the time Mark's group reached the Wyoming University Stadium, on Laramie's eastern outskirts, a couple of bottles had passed repeatedly among them.

The game proved to be a tough cliff-hanger, with A&M finally eking out a narrow victory. It was a high-spirited group that made its way back to the Connor Hotel, proclaiming victory and good cheer.

A celebration was in order, despite Prohibition's restricting hand. The only lively, liquor-stocked night spots of the city, however, were speakeasies which would be hard to crash. They would also likely harbor rabid Wyoming University fans in the mood for a free-for-all. Then a young Swedish sophomore in the A&M group came up with an extraordinary idea.

"If you knotheads will shut up and listen," he shouted,

"I know just the place. Women. Booze. A midnight supper. Some of the best damn music you'll ever hear."

"It sounds like either a pipe dream or the governor's private party," an older student said skeptically.

"Or maybe something catered by a top cafe that runs a house of prostitution upstairs," another observed.

"Crap," the young Swede muttered in disgust. "You guys haven't the politeness or the intelligence to listen."

Mark grinned, then held up a hand to silence the doubters. "Let's listen to Kellgren. Nobody else has come up with a decent idea."

The sophomore came to the point. "All you're apt to get in Laramie is some rotgut whiskey, and maybe a bruising. But there's a place I can take you called Woods Landing— a little town at the base of the Snowy Range mountains, about twenty-two miles west."

The words brought a couple of groans from his listeners, but Kellgren ignored them and continued. "Dammit, I know what I'm talking about. There's a big dance hall at Woods Landing. That's forest country, and the tie-hacks and loggers built this dance hall themselves. It's a beauty. All handwork by some of my Swedish kin."

"We're not interested in architecture," a listener growled. "How about the gals and the grub?"

Kellgren went on, unperturbed. "Saturday night is dance night, a real Scandinavian celebration. People show up from all over the woods and from Laramie. Most of them have some good liquor stashed away. Tonight it's likely to be a fifty-bottle dance. And music—boy, you haven't heard music until you hoof it to the polkas and waltzes and schottisches at Woods Landing."

"But how'd we go about crashing the festivities?" Mark demanded.

Kellgren drew himself to his full height and laid a withering gaze on the assembly before answering scornfully, "Ye of little faith. Didn't I tell you some of my relatives will be at Woods Landing? I grew up among the Snowy Range tie-hacks."

The car in which they had driven to Laramie was parked outside the hotel. An argument ensued as to who should drive, each declaring himself less drunk than his companions. Finally, Kellgren was chosen to handle the wheel, not because of being more sober, but because he knew the way.

By the time the hamlet of Woods Landing came into view, they had drained the last swig of the last bottle and had serenaded a few lonely miles of ranchland with songs ranging from "The Bawdy Bitch" to the Colorado A&M fight song. Largely on the insistence of Kellgren, they were admitted to a spacious and well-built dance hall. But before they could walk through the front door, each of them underwent the close scrutiny of a blond giant who wore a perpetual scowl. Kellgren introduced the man as Schuck, a distant cousin. Schuck acknowledged the introduction by scowling at Kellgren and growling, "Behave yourselves and you're welcome. Tickets are six bits each . . . which includes a midnight lunch. But just remember, I'm the bouncer for this shindig. If any of you get out of hand, you'll go out of the door."

Kellgren stared back at his relative and declared in hurt tones, "All six of us are college gentlemen. Innocent. Harmless."

"Bullshit," was the bouncer's terse response.

The hall filled rapidly, and Mark was surprised at the number of women and girls who came and sat in groups, unaccompanied by escorts. The band consisted of a piano, and accordion, two violins, drums, and a trumpet. The musicians played from memory, swinging from slow waltzes into pulse-stirring polkas that wove a magic over the hall and drew practically everyone to the dance floor. The music was different, and infinitely better, than Mark had been accustomed to hearing at Hawk Bend, and sent a tingle to both his mind and his feet. Presently he was treading the floor on just about every tune. Kellgren had introduced him to two girls, and others had asked him to dance at ladies' choice.

No liquor bottles were in evidence within the hall, but there was quite a parade of men, and sometimes of couples, in and out the front door. His suspicions were confirmed when Kellgren approached and whispered, "If you've worked up a thirst, Mark, you'll find a surprise under the front seat of our car."

It was when he came in from his third trip to the car that Mark first noticed the woman in blue. The liquor had now coated his brain with a golden haze, and his one wish was

292

that this dance, with its music and lights and laughter, might continue throughout the night. He also felt a longing, a restless urge that though nebulous was becoming increasingly persistent.

There were hand-hewn wooden benches along three sides of the polished dance floor, and a few chairs clustered at each of the room's corners. Mark skirted along one wall, then started to round the corner to rejoin his companions. One of the corner chairs was now occupied by someone Mark had not previously seen; she must have entered during his refreshment break in the car.

He surmised that her age might be between twenty-five and thirty; the mode of her dress and makeup spoke of city life and sophistication. She was markedly different from the girls with whom he had been dancing. He took a few steps that brought him close to her. The hall lights had been dimmed, but Mark caught a quick breath as he took in her auburn-hued hair and hazel eyes. The intenseness of his scrutiny seemed to draw her attention, and she looked up with a subtle and mystifying smile.

She had shrugged off her waist-length silver-fox jacket and had laid it across the chair's back. Her dress, of a shimmering blue material, had lace inserts on the sleeves and was cut daringly low in front.

Fortified by a tinge of alcoholic bravado, Mark made his way to Kellgren's side. "Who is that?" he whispered, totally enraptured.

Kellgren shook his head. "She's a stranger to me. And those duds says she sure doesn't live in any lumber camp." He studied Mark with a widening grin. "Take it easy, Cardigan," he added. "You're breathing harder than a four-year-old Arabian stud has any right to."

"I wish there was some way of getting a dance with her," Mark murmured.

"Have you considered the possibility of just walking over there and asking her?"

"With one more drink I would," Mark decided.

Kellgren snorted, then said, "One more and you'd likely fall on your hot butt. Now . . . get going and leave me alone."

The lady in blue watched Mark set his course toward her and was stifling a low ripple of laughter when he approached.

His words spilled out, indicating both his boldness and his terrible fear that she would refuse. "I'm Mark Cardigan," he uttered. "I'm probably crazy . . . a trifle boozed up . . . and awfully afraid you'll turn me down if I ask you to dance with me."

She could no longer repress her mirth. It sounded in a peal of laughter, and in the sparkle that lighted her eyes. "You're going to have to ask me in order to find out," she challenged.

"Lady," he whispered in a tone of abandoned hope, "how about you and I and the next waltz?"

"Don't you realize they're playing a waltz now?" she answered, and rose to slip into his arms.

When they had taken about a dozen steps, she said, "You're not a tie-hack . . . and I don't believe you live around Woods Landing."

"And I'm not a very good dancer either," Mark answered ruefully. Then he asked, "What's your name?"

He was acutely conscious of her arm tight across his shoulders and of her cool fingers touching the nape of his neck. She pressed her bosom and thighs close to him as she said, "Mark, I'm . . . why not just call me June? June of the evening." There was amusement and irony in her words.

It seemed to Mark that during the next hour they were on the floor together for almost every dance. During the second one they sat out, Mark gathered the courage to let his fingers entwine with hers. She did not withdraw her hand, and he was positive that the firm pressure of her delicate fingers carried unspoken encouragement.

After the breathtaking whirl of a polka, she wiped her forehead with an embroidered handkerchief, and Mark became aware that the room was stifling with the press of bodies. "I'll try and find us a cool drink," he offered. "Or would you prefer coffee?"

She sat down, then placed an arm about him and drew him close. "You haven't told me yet where you're from . . . or what you do, Mark."

"I'm from Colorado," he revealed. "Just a sophomore engineering student at the A&M college at Fort Collins. Up in Laramie for the big game. We're here to celebrate."

"Isn't it fun to celebrate? To forget every responsibility and let 'er rip?"

294

"The best, the wonderful part . . . was meeting you, June," he replied.

"That speech deserves a toast," she giggled.

"I could get you a soda pop," Mark said, grinning, and her nearness caused a strange flame of something he could not identify within him.

"Couldn't we have something a bit stronger, Mark? Toasts usually are performed with champagne."

"There's a bottle of first-rate whiskey in our car," Mark replied. "We could . . ." He trailed off, not daring to suggest what he hoped for.

She rose to her feet, in a way that maneuvered her lips to brush his ear. "Help me with this jacket, Mark. I really am thirsty . . . and nights are nippy this time of year at Woods Landing." As they moved toward the door, her arm had again encircled him.

An hour passed before they reentered the dance hall. They tried to appear extraordinarily casual and circumspect as they returned to the corner chairs. Mark was seating himself when he noticed both Kellgren and the bouncer, Schuck, eyeing him in a stern way. A minute later, Schuck motioned Mark to join them.

"It's pretty late . . . almost midnight," Kellgren said nervously. "Mark, we'd better be heading back to Laramie."

Mark glanced quickly toward the corner. His partner's chair was empty, and the silver-fox wrap was gone. His gaze roved the hall, but she was nowhere to be seen. And then the stern words of Schuck began to register.

"I've got some advice for you, boy. If you've been up to what I suspect you have, you'd better flag your ass out of Wyoming on the double. Kid, you've screwed the woman who is the private property of the Union Pacific Railroad's vice-president!"

During the months between his second and third years at A&M, Mark had no opportunity to try for even a small construction contract. In late May of 1926 he was offered summer employment by the federal Bureau of Reclamation. A crew was being selected to do extensive survey work on Colorado's Western Slope, and determine the feasibility of dams in the Colorado River Basin.

The crew left A&M College and drove from Fort Collins over Cameron and Rabbit Ears passes before descending to the green, well-watered valley marking the headwaters of the Yampa River. Here a temporary camp was set up and the crew began preliminary work.

There was a great deal of surveying to be done, and Mark was glad for the physical endurance he had developed at Cardigan Ranch. The weeks passed rapidly; a variety of activities kept him busy. He progressed from the duties of rodman to those of instrument man, and always he had to take accurate notes. He was asked to draw up proposed designs of irrigation canals and laterals, as well as the structures to control water flow and diversion.

The crew moved on to the White River area, and then to the canyons of the Dolores and San Miguel rivers. These mountains intrigued Mark. He had been reared on the level expanses of prairie, and had never realized the extent of the stream-traveled mountains of western Colorado.

The surveys were completed in early August, and Mark prepared to return to the college to help with the summaries he would have to write to complete the project. He had packed his duffle bag when a note reached him asking that he stop at the headquarters of the Forest Service's district ranger at Montrose. He was met by a tall, middle-aged man with red hair and blue eyes, who thrust out a work-roughened hand. "I'm Lane Torgny," he said. "Glad you got my note and came by. How would you like to finish up the work season with us as surveyor for a forest road, for fire access into the high country?"

"There are some better-qualified men on the crew I've been with."

"Maybe so, Cardigan, but you've been recommended for the job. We're likely to run into some tricky drainage problems on the road. It will be six miles long and cross several creeks. We were told that water-control structures, and the placement of culverts, is right up your alley." When Mark remained quiet and thoughtful, the ranger added, "We're prepared to pay you about a third more than you got with the rec service crew . . . and our camp cook is the best you're apt to find hereabouts."

Mark grinned, then said, "You're pretty persuasive, Mr. Torgny. I'd like a chance to really get into the forests for a change. I'll take the job under one condition."

"Name it," Torgny shot back at him.

"That I finish in time to have a week or ten days with my parents before the school grind gets underway again."

"You've got yourself a deal and a job, Cardigan. My pickup truck is outside. Throw your gear into it, and we'll be pulling out of town in about an hour."

A sudden, excited expectation swept Mark Cardigan. For the first time since that long-ago day on the county crew's grader, he would be working on a road-construction project. And, oddly, some of his childhood words seemed to reverberate down the corridors of time. *Someday I'm going to do it . . . They'll see.* And the dreams of a builder were resurgent within him.

The camp to which they came at midafternoon was larger than Mark had anticipated. The six miles of right-of-way had been cleared of timber and brush, and the felled timber had been moved aside to be burned at a later date.

Most of the grading work would be done by horse-drawn fresnos and grading blades, but because of the rocky nature of the terrain, extensive blasting would be needed. A crawler-type tractor with a dozing blade attached in front moved dirt and rocks in quantities that no horse-drawn tool could equal. Mark was fascinated with it.

The road was not designed as a public thoroughfare; rather, it was to provide a quick route by which men and equipment might be moved into a densely timbered area in case of fire. Much of Mark's time was spent in surveying grades for the setting of stakes—routine work, but interesting and enjoyable because it brought him in close contact with the various members of the crew. Most of them had worked on previous road and trail construction, and could provide reliable data about useful techniques for building on mountain roads. When Mark told of the long, level reaches of the eastern plains, and the deep and rock-free loam, these boulder fighters often shook their heads in wonder.

The days led into September, and the aspen of the high country took on autumn's golden glow. Mark finished the design data of the final drainage culvert and turned it over to Torgny. "Unless there's something extra special you need, I'll be packing up and leaving tomorrow," he said.

The ranger studied him speculatively. "You have things pretty well wrapped up, and besides, we won't be able to get much more done before we have to call it quits for the winter." He paused, and then asked abruptly, "What are your plans for next summer?"

"Right now they're vague," Mark said. "Maybe I can find some surveying or a small building job close to home, over in Weld County."

"That's your real goal—building and contracting—isn't it?" Torgny asked.

Mark grinned. "Does it show that much? Sure . . . building of any kind has always fascinated me. Especially earth-moving projects."

Ranger Torgny shoved an envelope toward him and then spoke seriously. "Mark, I would like to have you back next summer, but I don't think you should take the job I can offer. There is not much more you can learn here. I'd suggest that you move on to other challenges and responsibilities. I have a hunch that one of these days you are going to use every damned bit of building know-how you can muster. You should get yourself to where new ideas and new projects and new machines are coming into use. So . . . I wrote this letter of introduction for you this morning. Good luck, Cardigan," he said, handing Mark the envelope.

As darkness fell, Mark boarded a passenger train at the Montrose station of the Denver & Rio Grande Western Railroad. About two hours later his car was switched onto a Denver-bound passenger train in Grand Junction. Pullman berths were available, and he was shown to a lower by a cheerful-faced Negro porter. It was the first time he had ever gone to bed on a train, and for a long while he listened to the clicking of wheels across the rail joints beneath him.

Lying awake, the events of the summer rushed through his mind. He sensed that his work and his travels had wrought a change in him; no longer would his interests and his horizons be limited to A&M College and the Cardigan Ranch. As the train moved steadily eastward, following the valley of the Colorado River, he thought of the things he meant to accomplish in the few days of vacation left to him. His mother had recently written that Hank Kutcher was now in a wheelchair and failing rapidly. Mark pondered what life would be like without this fine old range rider. He would miss him sorely.

Suddenly he remembered what his father had said to him

a couple of years previous. *Hank Kutcher can tell you a lot about Andy Purcell and the Diamond-7.*

"I sure want to talk with him," Mark murmured half aloud. "Why haven't I done it before now?"

The train's motion, and his tiredness, lulled Mark toward sleep. Drowsily, his thoughts mingled—and then focused on the night at Woods Landing and a seductive lady clad in blue. But when he thought of taking her into his arms, he somehow felt she had faded from him. And in her place was another female form bending anxiously above him. *Lie still, you gringo. The cactus—muy grande—you have rolled in them.*

When Mark awakened, they were at Denver's Union Station, and the smiling porter was handing him his boots, polished to a luster fit to dazzle a young construction man's eyes.

He had only a few minutes to change for the early-morning train to Cheyenne. About two hours later he descended to the station platform at Greeley. The mixed train to Hawk Bend would not leave until noon, so he checked his duffle bag. He had had no chance for breakfast in Denver; he left the Greeley depot and walked toward the business section in search of a restaurant.

Later, after a leisurely meal, he sought out a bench in the town's rectangular park. Two men, whose clothes announced them as farmers, settled on a nearby shady spot and were soon deep in discussion of crop prospects and prices. Minutes later, the words of the older stranger caused Mark to move a little closer and listen.

"Farming an irrigated place on credit is plumb crazy," the stranger argued. "You're just working your butt off to make the bankers rich. Most of the farmers are getting into the hands of the banks. Like the Plains National down the street. Silas Latham has a finger in just about every farm supply . . ."

Mark heard no more, for the other man had broken in with low-spoken, heavily accented words. But why not, thought Mark. It might be a good idea to walk over to the Plains National Bank and pass the time of day with Silas Latham, and even say a few words of appreciation for the banker's help on the horse-pasture fencing project. Likely he would again need to borrow money sometime.

By the time he reached the bank, a plan had bloomed.

He would ask Silas Latham for a loan of two hundred dollars. He had no contract, and no need for the money. But he would borrow it, keep it intact, then pay it back in three months, together with the small bit of interest. Then he would borrow two-fifty or three hundred. The Plains National would have a customer whom they trusted, a man who borrowed and paid regularly. And he would be able to borrow money when the time came. With a cheery whistle and the air of an entrepreneur, he strode toward the bank. He accomplished his business in record time.

The train that shuttled twice daily between Hawk Bend and Greeley consisted of a somewhat rickety passenger coach; a car devoted to express, milk cans, and mail bags; and the necessary number of freight and livestock cars. As it wound through the irrigated section and began the run up Crow Creek Valley, Mark became expectant and alert. He was not prepared for the extra stop the train made before reaching Hawk Bend. The engine cautiously backed a single freight car onto a short siding, and Mark suddenly realized where they were . . . alongside the track at the Montez section house. He turned to stare at the house —and caught his breath. A woman was standing in the door watching the train, and it was not Gilberto's portly wife. The figure, clad in a red skirt and white blouse, stood gracefully tall and erect, with her dark hair bound back by a narrow band.

It was Dolores; and he knew immediately what he intended to do. The train had already started up when he grabbed his duffle bag, hurried to the car's vestibule steps, and dropped to the ground. He strode along the ties of the main track as a dozen freight and cattle cars passed him and moved northward toward Hawk Bend.

He came onto the porch of the section house, but the girl was no longer in the doorway. His second rap summoned her—and then they stood face to face.

Mark stood in silent scrutiny, examining the girl who had once been both his stranger of mercy and his curse of intolerable embarrassment. Dolores's eyes widened in surprise, and her breath quickened. "Ah ha. He is back . . . the fence-building gringo who beds down in cactus." She looked around. "Where is your horse this time?"

His response caught her unaware. He dropped the duffle bag at their feet and his arms went out quickly to encircle

300

her, and before she could turn her head he had placed an urgent kiss upon the firm fullness of her lips. For a moment she drew close to him, and seemed to revel in their nearness, but then she pushed him away and stared angrily into his face. "I should slap hell out of you, fence-builder Cardigan. You think you are big stuff? And me maybe a Mexican bordello girl?"

Her rebuke caused Mark's face to flush, and his answer sprang from desperation. "Dolores, you know I don't think any such thing. It's . . . it's that we have both been gone, and I have missed you. That—and also I realize now that you are beautiful."

The words seemed to take her aback, and she looked about in momentary effort to avoid his uneasy gaze. "How did you get here, Mark?" she murmured. "There is no horse."

"Maybe I got bucked off the iron horse—the train—this time. Fact is, I am traveling home to the ranch. But when I happened to see you—"

"You are crazy." She laughed, then shook her head in a relenting way. "You must come into our house. My mama and papa speak often of you, wondering where you have been." She picked up the duffle bag and propped it alongside the door. Then, as she led him inside, she said, "Gilberto, my father, will have many questions."

"I'll have to leave in time to walk to Cardigan Ranch," he said. It sounded as though he was reminding himself.

"No," she replied, "it can be arranged. My father is the section foreman now, and has two motor cars that travel the tracks. Sometimes, when the railroad officers are not about, he allows me to use the small speedster. Perhaps . . ."

Her voice trailed off, but the words had conveyed her understanding of the kiss, and a gladness that he had come.

He lingered with the Montez family until shadows of dusk lay darkly across the prairies. Mark found that much of the time he was answering questions, for when Gilberto returned from work both he and Dolores inquired endlessly about Mark's work with the Reclamation Service and as a forest road surveyor. No detail seemed too small to escape their attention. Mark was soon astounded by their grasp of facts and figures it had taken him days of work to assimilate. And again he watched in awe as Dolores seemed to arrive at mathematical totals and results with an inborn skill.

Finally, he watched her pencil move across a page of computations and then asked, "Have you been studying this sort of thing at the school . . . in Albuquerque?"

"Only a little," she replied. "It is a church school, with few advanced classes in mathematics and sciences. Mostly, it prepares young ladies for marriage . . . for overseeing a household."

The answer caused Mark to ask, with not too well masked anxiety, "You're going to marry someone down there—in New Mexico?"

She sensed the state of his mind, and added to its turmoil with words that were scarcely revealing. "Of course I'll get married. Raise a family. Maybe have many *niños y niñas*. Boys. Girls. You think I should enter a convent? Become a *monja*? A nun?"

Abruptly Mark knew that her words were teasing, and he almost shouted, "I think you oughta forget marrying some Spanish dude. Then become an estimator for some big construction company."

"And where is there such a wonderful and generous company?" she demanded, with anger and irony in her voice. "A construction company that would give such a job to a Mexican girl who lives in a railroad section house?"

Mark rose to full height, his gaze encompassing both Gilberto Montez and his daughter.

"Just stick around a year or so, Dolores, and you'll see who will tackle the big jobs. Everybody will see."

They fell silent under the spell of his intensity and his certainty.

After a while, Gilberto placed the speedster on the tracks and took Mark into Hawk Bend. The trip was a quiet one, for all conversation seemed to have culminated in Mark's ringing words of determination. As they parted, Gilberto laid a work-callused hand on Mark's shoulder. "You must come and see us again. Dolores must return to school in New Mexico next week. She is here only for a brief visit." He paused and his words were a whimsical tone but vastly sincere. "Besides, Mark, she must prepare for that big, responsible job."

* * *

302

That was the summer when a telephone line had been strung to Cardigan Ranch and wired into a switchboard at the home of the town's justice of the peace. His wife, a thin-faced woman of indefinite age, acted as operator to take and switch calls. The setup had drawn caustic assessment from Hank Kutcher, whose temper had not sweetened under the necessity of spending long hours in a wheelchair.

"The damned line is nothing but a newfangled nuisance," Hank grumbled. "It'll be out of order every time some old cow gets in heat and a bull breaches the fence." About the female operator, he was even less optimistic. "That old biddy is sure gonna raise hell. Listenin' in on the secret talk of everybody from Kate's Wagon to Greeley. She'll find something sinister in the sound of a hawk on one of them line posts."

Despite Kutcher's dire prophecies, the phone worked perfectly so that Mark could let his parents know he had arrived at Hawk Bend. They hastened to town to pick him up in their shining new Model T Ford runabout.

The few remaining days of vacation passed quickly at the ranch. Like the Montez family, Redge and Audrey asked leading questions, and then listened as Mark told of his school year and the summer. Redge hungered for descriptions of the Western Slope and of the high forested ranges that stand as a great barrier from north to south across Colorado.

"I'm going to get up into that mountain country again. Your mom and me—maybe for a whole summer. I've been up above Fort Collins, in the Poudre River area, several times. And once, a long time ago, I rode horseback over Wolf Creek Pass, down toward Durango."

"It's about time you two ease down and enjoy life," Mark agreed. The new hand was now living on the ranch and helping with chores and irrigation. Also, a middle-aged woman came daily from Hawk Bend, and her largest task was taking care of Hank.

At breakfast the following morning, Mark asked, "Is my old bag swing still hanging from that big cottonwood tree downcreek a ways?"

"It is," Redge affirmed, "but likely the rope has pretty well rotted out." Redge's words carried a hope of teasing Kutcher.

Hank Kutcher, sitting nearby in his wheelchair, snorted

303

his disgust. "A hell of a lot you know about rawhide ropes, Redge. I braided that one myself. It'll be strong and limber enough for an outlaw hanging when you're too stove up to lift two fingers of drinkin' whiskey."

Mark could see how Hank felt cooped up in the house—how he longed to get free of the wheelchair and do something crazy—like swing over the creek. "Hank," he said quickly, "suppose you and I go down to the cottonwood after a bit and inspect that miracle rope?" He was more eager than ever to have a long talk with Hank about the past.

"You think you're man enough to push this goddam go-cart that far?" Kutcher challenged.

"If I can't," Mark said, "I can always dump you in the creek and let you float down."

"And I can still lay a willow switch across your ass end," Kutcher vowed.

An hour later they were sitting on a fallen log close to the creek's bank and the aging swing that moved in a tight, listless pattern. Mark helped Kutcher hobble to the log, so for a time he was free of his imprisoning wheelchair. They talked about the swing, about Cardigan Ranch and Mark's imminent return to A&M College.

Then Mark knew the time was right. If ever this loyal old cowhand was to tell him of Andy Purcell, Stacy Murdock, and the Diamond-7 Ranch, it would be right now. He chose his words with studied caution.

"What brought you to this part of the country, Hank? You must have been pretty young when you came."

Kutcher stared grimly at the horizon. "Here on the grasslands, the whole world seemed young in those days." About the old cowman was an aura of another time and a long-gone way of life.

"I was just twenty-four when I followed a herd from Texas, eating dust all the way," he continued.

"I never took you for a Texan," Mark said. "You sound more like a Missourian to me."

"There's one hell of a lot you've got to learn about accents." Kutcher snorted. "I'm from Ohio . . . nigh onto Kentucky."

"How come you strayed out here, Hank?"

"After an enlistment in the infantry, I wanted a look-see at that Texas country. Then in '82 I helped push a trail herd up from San Antonio to the Yellowstone River area in Montana. On the way back to San Antonio, my horse stumbled in a prairie-dog hole. I got a broken leg. Andy Purcell found me, splinted the leg, and took me home to his Diamond-7. Purcell was one of God's gentlemen. He was drowned in a flood on this here Crow Creek."

"Purcell had made a deal for his land? How did *he* get all this?" Mark asked.

"Who's telling this?" Kutcher growled. "There wasn't any dealing for land here on the prairies in them days. Who would you have dealt with? The buffalo? Indians? Some of the damned fools heading for gold diggin's west of Denver? No, lad, it was country that was new and open and untrampled. If you wanted a slice of it, you gathered a cow herd, built some kind of sod or log buildings to headquarter in, and settled in to stay."

"Without any legal rights? Any title?"

"There was title all right. You carried it in a holster, and hoped to hell you could draw faster than any buzzard who had ideas of jumping your herd or your graze."

Mark took a deep breath and plunged to the heart of what had long been on his mind. "Hank, weren't you riding for the Diamond-7 when there was a foreman there named Stacy Murdock?"

"Haven't your folks told you about that?" Kutcher demanded.

"No. It's something both Dad and Mom have kept silent about—except once."

Kutcher cocked his head in expectant silence as Mark continued.

"Maybe you remember the time—way back when I was in the Hawk Bend school—when a couple of kids beat the devil out of me."

"I recollect that your face was uglier than usual." Kutcher nodded. "And I sort of remember you tried to take one kid's head off with a whip."

"That's it. Those kids were telling everyone that my dad murdered a man named Stacy Murdock right here on Cardigan Ranch. My dad admitted it to me, then showed me Grandfather Cardigan's grave. Also, there's those hellish scars Dad is branded with. Later on, Hank, I wanted to know more. But all that Dad would say was, 'Ask Hank Kutcher.' "

305

The old cowboy picked up a cottonwood stick and poked thoughtfully at a black stinkbug. When he spoke, it was reluctantly.

"Maybe the first thing you should know is—Stacy Murdock was my nephew."

"You . . . you had a family, Hank?" Mark's question carried dismay.

"Doesn't everyone have kinfolks?" Kutcher muttered.

"It's just that you've always been alone."

"Not always, Mark. Back in Ohio, I had a sister . . . two years older than me. She married a fiddle-footed chap named Bailey Murdock, and they moved to a mining camp up in Montana. After I'd been with Andy Purcell a couple of years, this Bailey Murdock got himself killed in some sort of claim-jumping fracas. They had this one boy, Stacy. My sister sent me a letter saying she was pretty nigh destitute, and had no way to take care of young Stacy."

The revelation stirred fascination within Mark, but he sat very quiet, waiting for Kutcher to continue.

"Andy Purcell got hold of that letter," Kutcher said. "Nothing would do but I send for my sister and the boy. Purcell was that sort . . . couldn't bear even to read of a woman in trouble. He provided a home for my sister until she died, three years later."

"And so Stacy Murdock grew up on the Diamond-7," Mark surmised.

"Not exactly. When he was still pretty young he took off for Montana. Worked on ranches there and in Wyoming."

"But wasn't he foreman at the Diamond-7?"

Kutcher nodded. "Later he was. Mr. Purcell asked him to ramrod the outfit. And Stacy was a damned capable foreman—but I've always wished to Christ he'd stayed in Montana or Wyoming."

"Why?" Mark urged softly.

"Because of Karen—Karen Andrus." Hank Kutcher let his gaze roam out to the horizon as though seeing the far-off valley that sheltered Kate's Wagon. "God, but she was lively and pretty," he murmured.

"Karen Andrus? Was she my mother's sister?"

"Yes." Kutcher nodded. "Just a few years older than Audrey. She didn't live to see her twentieth birthday—and I hope Stacy roasts in hell a million years." The old cowman saw the anxiety in Mark's face and added, "Stacy raped Karen one night after a box social at the school. Then he panicked and murdered her, leaving her body in a dry wash half a mile south of the Kate's Wagon store." The stress of what he had revealed to Mark, after so long carrying it as a secret, caused Hank Kutcher to attempt to rise on his feeble legs. For a few seconds he stood swaying, and he looked as though he might weep. Then he fell back and sat with his bowed head on the log.

"Hank . . . Hank," Mark said softly. "Don't torture yourself. It was so long ago."

"But I recall it like it was yesterday," Kutcher whispered. "Both Stacy and I were at the box social that evening. I followed Stacy and Karen down toward that gulch, just because my horse had gone lame and I needed Stacy's mount in order to get back to the Diamond-7. When I caught up, Stacy wasn't about. But I saw Karen . . . battered and dead. He had broken her skull with his gun butt. I carried her back to Kate. Then I rode after Stacy."

"Did you catch him?" Mark murmured in dazed comprehension.

Kutcher nodded. "He had gone straight to the Diamond-7. At first, Mark, I thought only of killing him—of wanting to see Stacy as lifeless as I had found Karen. But then I thought of my ailing sister there at the ranch. Somehow her entire life seemed wrapped up in Stacy, her only child. Pretty soon I was reasoning to myself that nothing good could come of my telling who had killed Karen Andrus. Likely it would bring about the death of my sister. Maybe it would make Andy Purcell kick me and my sister and Stacy off the Diamond-7. What about our family's good name? And who would hire any of us after the story got about? So . . . I kept my mouth shut . . . and the days and months and years went by. The law was better'n fifty miles away, and didn't even investigate."

"But why didn't Kate Andrus shout out Stacy Murdock's guilt, if she was aware of it?"

Kutcher raised eyes that were dark with pain and memory. "Maybe for the same reason I didn't. It wouldn't bring Karen back to her . . . and it might rest as some sort of stigma on her other children. And I also think that Kate, with that big heart of hers, was protecting me and my sister."

"Then you let the murder pass without speaking up?"

"Oh, I spoke up plenty—to Stacy. I let him know that I was aware of what he had done. And that he better keep shaped up and go straight."

"But he didn't . . . did he?" Mark half growled. "It doesn't seem he learned a damned thing from your protecting him. It just led to his killing my grandfather, and to putting lashes on my dad that marked him for life."

"It just seemed right, at the time, to spare my sister," Kutcher said slowly, and dropped his head into his hands.

"Perhaps it was right under the circumstances," Mark murmured. "With that stress, maybe I'd have thought first of my family." And after a while, he added, "Besides, Hank, what right have I to act as a judge?" As these words closed the matter, Mark Cardigan sensed that this old cowboy, whom he had known throughout his life, would likely not be around to welcome him when another school year had passed.

Hank tossed a small stone into the placid flow of Crow Creek and said, almost to himself, "The Diamond-7 was a proud and well-managed and profitable cow outfit when Andy Purcell was alive. After he drowned, it sort of went to pot."

"Who owns it now?" Mark demanded with renewed curiosity. "I know that homesteaders have settled on a lot of the ranch's range. And it has always been somewhat of a mystery—those boarded-up and deserted headquarters buildings."

Kutcher glanced at him in surprise. "You mean to tell me you've never heard of the hand that Carla Dunlop and her sister, Jennifer Waverley, took in Diamond-7 affairs, after your dad had his gun showdown with Stacy?"

"No, I never heard of Aunt Carla, and her sister, being involved."

"Well, after Stacy was dead, most of his ranch hands took off for parts unknown. I was working for Jeff Masters, a rancher with holdings along the South Platte River, at the time. So happened I was the only one who knew that the only legal heir to the Diamond-7 was a niece of Andy Purcell's, who lived back east in Roanoke, in Virginia."

"So she came out to boss a Colorado cattle ranch," Mark guessed.

"The hell she did," Kutcher growled, with a touch of his

usual caustic response. "When me and Jeff Masters advised her of Andy's death, she wrote back offering to sell the whole shebang to Jeff Masters or me—without so much as coming west to see it. Meanwhile, she arranged for Stacy Murdock to act as manager."

"And then?" Mark urged.

"Jeff Masters had enough land and cattle troubles of his own. Me . . . maybe my pocketbook would have allowed me to buy one tenth of the Diamond-7."

"How did Aunt Carla and her sister get into the act?" Mark asked.

"They were friends of Jeff Masters," Kutcher explained. "But it went a lot deeper than that. I've always suspected that Carla Dunlop—Aunt Carla to you—was in love with your grandfather. After his death, she had a feeling for young Redge. Also for Audrey, your mother, and you too, Mark."

"But I never thought of Carla as being a rich woman, or a Denver socialite."

"Little you know about it," Kutcher scoffed. "Carla worked for a while at some sort of job at Fort Laramie, Wyoming. Had some influential friends there. And she was also the only living relative of Jennifer Waverley. Does that mean anything to you, boy?"

Mark wrinkled his forehead in perplexed effort to remember something from the past. "I remember Mom taking me to a house in Denver once when I was a small kid. A big house called the Waverley mansion."

Kutcher nodded. "It was pretty well named. The widow who owned it had been left half of the gold and silver dug out of them San Juan Mountains that circle the town of Telluride. She was as sharp as she was rich, too, that Jennifer Waverley. She bought the Diamond-7 home layout, about seven sections of land."

"She wanted a prairie-country cattle ranch?" Mark asked doubtingly.

"I didn't say that. She bought the land and said it was a long-term investment. I sort of think she was aiming to fix things so that the Diamond-7 would never again be a threat to you Cardigans. Maybe Carla had a hand in it. And mebbe not. Jennifer had quite a mind of her own."

"And does Aunt Carla own the ranch now?"

"Nope."

"Then who in hell does?" Mark demanded in exasperation.

Kutcher grinned a somewhat tantalizing and wicked grin. Then he said simply, "I do. I own it. The whole blasted shebang."

"You . . . you own the Diamond-7?" Mark stuttered.

"Sure as Satan. At least until I shuffle off this old earth and get shet of its woes."

"Then how come you aren't living on it? Keeping it in proper repair? Making it a money-maker like it once was?"

"Because there would be no future in it, Mark," the old range rider said seriously. "Lad, I've got only a few months left at best. Besides, I'm just a sort of temporary owner—a caretaker. Jennifer Waverley and your Aunt Carla had mighty ambitious plans for that old Diamond-7. Upon my death, it comes into ownership by the people of this here State of Colorado . . . as a perpetual Colorado State Park of the Grasslands. It'll have new buildings and a museum and fenced buffalo and antelope parks and God knows what-all."

Mark Cardigan breathed deeply and let his gaze move along the creek's southward course. "That's wonderful, Hank—it really is." He waited a moment, then blurted out, "And it's got to be called the Hank Kutcher Memorial Wildlife Refuge."

The old Diamond-7 rider looked toward Mark, his face a wash of emotion. "You come up with some of the most damn-fool ideas. I just got through telling you it was all Carla's and Jennifer's idea. I didn't have anything invested in that Diamond-7 spread."

Mark offered his strong arms to help old Hank Kutcher back to the imprisoning security of the wheelchair. "Nothing at all, Hank," he said firmly. "Nothing except two thirds of a lifetime, and an undying love of these prairies and the ranch way of life."

"A memorial dry-land park. It sure would beat a tombstone all to hell, wouldn't it, Mark?" Kutcher stared at the old cottonwood and its swaying bag swing, anxious that in this moment young Mark Cardigan should not see his face.

Chapter 28

The third year of Mark's studies at A&M passed with bewildering speed. Toward spring of that junior year, he was offered several summer jobs that would have taken him into either the mountains or the irrigated farming areas. A couple of them offered good pay, but in his mind was the advice that Forest Ranger Lane Torgny had offered—to go where new ideas and new machines and new projects were coming about.

It was largely because of the ranger's words and his letter of referral that Mark found himself, on a morning of early summer, sightseeing the town of Fullerton, California. He had spent a rain-drenched week in San Francisco, where the natives had assured him that the moisture-laden spring storm was "most unusual." Then an overnight train brought him to the sun-drenched orchard lands of Southern California, and into Los Angeles. After touring the city and spending a day along the coast at Long Beach, Mark ruefully noted the thinning of his wallet. The time had come to look for a job. He recalled Ranger Torgny telling him of the vast project that had turned the flooded Imperial Valley into a productive sweep of farmland. Likely an engineering student could find work in the Imperial Valley, and he could study every aspect of the sprawling reclamation project.

Mark studied a map of Southern California. He could journey to the Imperial Valley by way of San Diego, and thus see a lot more of the area. He had quickly learned that the most economical way to travel the environs of Los Angeles was by the interurban trolley cars of Pacific Electric. So it was that he came, at midmorning, into Orange County, by way of Whittier and La Habra. The cost of his ride was about a cent per mile, a leisurely start toward San Diego.

As the trolley clattered along between far-reaching groves of orange, lemon, and walnut trees, heavy air clung about him; there was no effort to breathing as there was back home. On distant hills were rectangular fields of avocado trees, and the clustered towers of oil wells. Far west, beyond a level coastal plain and a wide expanse of the Pacific Ocean, he glimpsed an island that the map indicated to be Catalina.

As the trolley car entered the outskirts of Fullerton, Mark suddenly sat up and stared through the window, fascinated. Between orchards of green trees and young oranges, there was an open field of perhaps five acres. Midway into it was a plant such as Mark had never seen. There was a steel tower with giant bins to which gravel was carried by a conveyor belt. Nearby stood sizable tanks, into which crude oil was being unloaded from a truck. There was also a massive boiler, heated by a coal-burning firebox. From this, pipes about two inches in diameter ascended the tower. There was a heavy pall of dust and of black and low-hanging coal smoke about the whole plant.

Mark's gaze followed a truck that had left the plant and was moving to a wide and carefully graded gravel road leading from the town, paralleling the trolley tracks. A moment later, the trolley brought Mark Cardigan abreast of the point where black and still-steaming paving material was being spread from the plant's trucks and was being rolled to smooth firmness.

His first thought, admiring this oil-process roadway paving and the plant where the mixture was prepared, was, God! How we could use that stuff over the miles of mud and dust back home in Colorado.

And as the Pacific Electric car brought him into the town, Mark acted on impulse. He took his two suitcases and dropped to the Pacific Electric depot platform. There would be later buses and trains to San Diego or to the Imperial Valley—after he had a chance to take a good look at that miracle plant on Fullerton's outskirts. He checked his suitcases at the depot baggage room, then strode outside and began walking. Presently, he came to North Spadra Road, leading north. This would undoubtedly bring him to the street being paved. As he moved farther from the town's business district and approached the outskirts, the buildings thinned out; soon there were stretches of citrus-fruit groves bordering the sidewalk. Then he reached a flowing canal and a steep embankment, which he climbed. He was now standing at the edge of the field, and the paving plant was scarcely a block ahead, still enshrouded in its black cloud of dust and coal smoke.

He vaulted over a low fence that wore a no-trespassing sign, then strode eagerly toward the dust and the noise of the plant. He paused within a dozen steps of the boiler that produced tank- and pipe-heating steam. There was a hand-painted sign on the boiler: "Southern California Paving Corporation."

He had edged closer to the boiler's firebox when a voice sounded in irritation behind him. "Young fellow, what in Christ's name are you doing around here in them pretty dude clothes?"

Mark wheeled guiltily about. The middle-aged man who was scowling at him was clad in dusty and grease-saturated overalls. His hands were filthy, and smudges of grime half masked his face. But Mark let out a joyous yell and thrust out his hand. "Sam Hook, how come you ain't drilling wells back at Hawk Bend?"

Taken aback, the soot-stained workman's eyes widened into a grin of recognition. His large ears seemed to tilt forward as he thrust his eagle beak nearer. "Damn my sinful soul if it ain't Fencebuilder Cardigan. Glad to see you. . . and *welcome to Californy!* I ain't no letter writer."

Mark looked about at the plant and the synchronized disorder and confusion. "Sam, this is the damnedest . . . most interesting . . . setup I ever laid eyes on. Who's in charge?"

Sam Hook swept grime and sweat from his forehead with the back of his wrist. "Depends on what part you're talking about, Mark. There's some young-sprout engineers surveying the laydown on the road. Then there's an aggregate foreman; he's in charge of the gravel crushing and hauling. Me . . . I'm charged with the duty of keeping this balky boiler from blowing sky-high, and seeing that plenty of hot, stinking asphalt reaches the tipple for mixing with the rock at just-right temperature."

Mark stared into the inferno of flame beneath the steam boiler, then asked, "You like this better than fixing windmills and fishing pipe from those homesteaders' wells back along Crow Creek?"

"It pays better." Hook grimaced. "Besides, there's more

313

of a future in this hot-mix paving stuff. Out here they're saying that in a few years every main road will be overlaid with this tar and rock—even the three hundred and fifty miles up to San Francisco."

As Hook walked over to adjust the pipeline valve, Mark Cardigan made his decision. There might be a chance to work on some great irrigation project in the Imperial Valley, but for all he knew that was a finished job. Right here was something new and different and challenging. And wasn't that what Torgny had suggested?

When Sam Hook came back, Mark asked bluntly, "How about putting me to work, Sam . . . if there's anything you think I could handle?"

Hook stared at him, then grinned. "You mean right now —in them pretty clean sissy clothes?"

"You know damned well what I mean," Mark flared. "I've got a suitcase full of work clothes up at the depot."

"Then show up in them at seven o'clock tomorrow morning," Hook growled. Then he added, "If you need a place to stay, Mark, the beds and grub at the Stafford Hotel are pretty good. I stay there; it's a workman's place. How about having supper with me tonight? I haven't had anyone to swap lies with since landing in this Mecca of sunburn and prunes last Christmastime."

"It sure suits me. And thanks, Sam," Mark agreed. "By the way . . . what are you going to let me do here at the plant?"

"You oughtn't to have asked that," Hook murmured, and pointed high atop the steel tower. "See them bins up there? There's control levers for rock and oil and so forth up there. Them levers need yanking every minute or so. That's where you'll be, my boy. Starting right at the top. Now . . . get the hell out of here, before the superintendent starts gnawing on my old butt."

As Hook had indicated, the rooms at the Stafford Hotel were clean, comfortable, and moderately priced. Mark paid a week's rent and moved in. He spent the afternoon getting acquainted with the town of Fullerton. His walking tour brought him after a while to a broad sweep of lawn beyond which were white stucco buildings in Spanish style connected by broad walkways sheltered by arcades. When a sign told him that this was the home of Fullerton Union High School and Junior College, he sought out the library.

The wide range of books on the stacks caused him to comment to the librarian, "Isn't this a tremendous library for a junior college?"

She glanced over steel-rimmed spectacles with tolerant humor. "Young man, this is Fullerton—the third-richest district in America."

"You mean there's that sort of money in growing oranges?" Mark grinned.

She pointed out a window, toward the distant hills. "See those oil fields . . . up near Brea? And those . . . and those? Most of them are on land owned by this school district."

He whistled aloud. Then he said, "And there's oil enough to lay a mat of asphalt over every street and road, every lane and driveway, too."

"That's bound to come," she said. "But I hope not too soon. For a little while, at least, let us keep our tranquil, if dusty, trails."

"Would you happen to have an atlas with maps showing the highways and roads of Colorado?"

As she handed him the large book, she remarked, "At least, with few oil wells in Colarado, folks back there will be spared this paving plague."

And Mark said, under his breath, "Not if I can help it."

An hour after sunset, Mark sat looking over the lights that gleamed off toward the sea. After a while, there was a knock on his door. He opened it and looked into the scrubbed and grinning face of Sam Hook, who said, "I hope you're hungry. I sure am."

The words brought realization to Mark Cardigan that he had forgotten to eat lunch. "I hope they're not stingy with the food, Sam. I'm starved."

"They set a table here that will satisfy you, son. I sure can recommend the seafood. It's fresh. You're within about thirty-five miles of the ocean, you know."

As they entered the small dining room, with its cane-backed chairs and white linens, Sam Hook's mood seemed to change, and to become both hesitant and serious. He dropped to a chair and fumbled to withdraw a letter from his shirt pocket. Then he asked, "Mark, how long has it been since you left home . . . left Hawk Bend?"

"About three weeks. Why?"

"Have you heard from home?"

"Not yet. I've been moving about too much. Salt Lake City. San Francisco."

"Then I'll have to tell you, lad. It's right here in a note I got from Fartein Nordraak."

"What does it say?" Mark had sensed that Sam Hook was reluctant to tell him the contents.

"Read it for yourself, Mark. Damn the poor light in here."

And it was thus that Mark Cardigan learned of the closing of an era. Of how death had come quietly in the night to Hank Kutcher. And of how people had gathered at the small burying ground at Cardigan Camp to pay tribute to their friend, a man who had once ridden for the powerful Diamond-7 Ranch.

"And now," Mark breathed, "the Hank Kutcher Memorial Grasslands."

"The what?" Sam Hook asked quietly.

"A marker for Hank. I'll tell you about it after we order, Sam."

Within one hour after he had climbed the hot-mix plant the next morning, Mark was ready to quit. He had dealt before with heat and dirt and noise. But nothing like this. Even goggles and a breathing device over his nose and mouth seemed ineffective against the dirt and the fumes and the din. I'll hold out until noon—then to hell with it, he consoled himself. But after lunch he again climbed the tower toward the bins, the gauges, and the levers. Might as well make it a full day before kissing this mess goodbye. Then he made it through two days. Three. And to the magic reprieve offered by Sunday.

He had been at the plant two weeks when, near mid-morning of a blazing hot day, Sam Hook appeared at his side and said, "The super has an idea you ain't dumping in enough aggregate on some batches."

Mark straightened, then gave Hook an annoyed glance. "Then the super better climb up here and handle the levers himself; I've put in exactly what the gauges call for every time."

"Mebbe so. But you'd better get over to the office shack quick-like. The super is waiting to nail your hide." Hook pointed to another workman climbing the tower's steps. "That fellow will relieve you for a spell."

Mark approached the small office with rising anger. The tower job was hard and dirty enough without being accused of not handling it properly. He stepped inside, ready to demand an inspection of faulty gauges. Perhaps it would have been better to look into the Imperial Valley job.

The superintendent, a graying man of perhaps fifty, clad in khaki shirt and trousers, waved Mark to a seat opposite his paper-strewn desk. Without preliminaries, he asked, "Cardigan, is what Sam Hook says true? Have you had some engineering schooling?"

"That's correct, sir. I've finished three years at Colorado A&M . . . at Fort Collins."

The superintendent nodded, evidently pleased, and he asked, "You've studied surveying?"

"For two years."

"How about practical experience? Field work?"

Mark took several seconds to answer. He was wondering why this man cared what his education had been, if all he was going to do was chew him out. "Last summer I spent several weeks on survey work for the Forest Service. Rodman, then instrument man, on drainage problems, culvert placements . . . that sort of stuff."

The super let out a sigh of relief. "Cardigan, for God's sake, get out there on the road where we're dumping hot mix, and get the grade stakes straightened up."

There was a long silence. Finally the superintendent asked, "Well, what is holding you? If it's the pay, it'll be good."

"The pay," Mark repeated, with dawning realization. "I'm sure we can agree. But, sir, right now I'm stowing up prime cuss words for that goddam Sam Hook. He said you wanted me in here to chew my ass out or fire me."

"Sounds like Hook." The super laughed. "He's the best all-round mechanic we ever had. A tinkering genius—and a man I wouldn't believe—at times—swearing on a Persian prayer rug."

The job called for ingenuity and every bit of Mark's surveying skill. The weeks of summer sped by so quickly that he was appalled when he realized that within two weeks he must report at Colorado A&M for his senior year. He was proud that he had mastered the science of hot-

317

mix paving—there was hardly a facet of the process with which he was not familiar.

He gave notice of his leaving the firm, and was immediately summoned to the company's home office in Los Angeles. Both the general manager and the personnel chief tried to persuade Mark to remain with the Southern California Paving Corporation. They each painted a brilliant picture of the firm's future in the California contracting business, and offered assurances that Mark would likely move upward to a secure and well-paying job as their engineering department expanded. Why not transfer from Colorado A&M and take a few courses in his spare time at one of the local universities, specializing in construction engineering? The firm might underwrite a sizable part of his tuition.

The offer was tempting, and Mark asked for time to mull it over. It was really Sam Hook, however, who firmed the young surveyor's decision.

"So they want you to become a little cog in the big asphalt-spreading concern? Limit yourself and your horizons . . . your future. Is that what you want, Cardigan? Is that what that forest ranger fellow Torgny had in mind for you? And how about your real dream, boy? That of having a fine big building outfit of your own?" The old mechanic paused, then added, with a shrug, "I guess Hawk Bend and Cardigan Ranch has seen the last of you. You'll settle for the beaches and some bronzed, pretty-assed young prune-picker." He slapped his knee. "Shit! I was counting on you to help me get that tank truck down from Casper, Wyoming, to Hawk Bend."

"Tank truck? What the devil are you talking about, Sam?" Mark asked.

They were sitting in Mark's small room at the hotel, and Hook lifted his tar-stained boots onto the bed. "Didn't I tell you about it? On the way out here to Californy last spring I sashayed up to Casper for a look-see at that Teapot Dome oil field. I was heading west into town from Douglas when I come across this tank truck stalled in the middle of the road. Someone ahead had been hauling chunks of concrete, and the jasper drivin' the tank truck had high-centered on a piece of that concrete that was about the size of a respectable tombstone. Wiped out the whole plumb undercarriage of the truck, including the oil pan and the transmission."

Hook swallowed, scratched in the vicinity of his belly button, and went on. "The driver of that tanker wasn't bad hurt. But he sure was disgusted. Wanted out of the trucking business there on the spot. We dickered a little. Argued like hell, then dickered a mite more. I bought the rig as was—and *was* wasn't much. The trucker took off for Cheyenne, and left me with my newly purchased wreck smack in the road and obstructing both the going and coming lanes." Hook shook his head dolefully.

"What then?" Mark urged.

"It's bitter to recollect, Cardigan. Cost me fifty dollars to get that tanker wreck into a storage lot in Casper. Worse yet, I'm having to pay three bucks storage on it every month."

Mark squinted at Sam Hook and replied, "You're making it all up. I don't think you've been within a hundred miles of Casper."

"Would I lie to you . . . my best friend?"

"You sure as hell would. How about the time you told me the plant super thought I was fouling up on pulling the levers?"

"It's a bitter humiliation," Hook said piously, "to be accused of a falsehood." He dug into a vest pocket, pulled out a couple of folded papers, and thrust them at Mark. "You'd better believe I own me a tanker—and the right to use it, anywhere in Wyoming, and south in Colorado down to Denver."

Mark silently unfolded the papers and began reading. His eyes widened and his breath quickened. "Holy Moses, Sam, do you realize what you got here?"

Hook scowled. "Sure I do. When I bought that tank truck, the fellow signed all this over. Permits to haul crude oil."

Mark came to his feet and paced the room in excitement. "Hauling permits! Hank, these are trucking permits issued by the Public Utilities Commissions of Wyoming and Colorado. You can haul any and all petroleum products practically statewide. At any time . . . with any number of vehicles. And they're nonrevocable as long as they are properly used and the annual fee paid. My God, Sam—someday these are going to be worth a fortune."

319

"Someday isn't now," Hook demurred. "It's gonna cost me a pretty penny to get that tanker rolling toward Hawk Bend."

Mark stared at the permits and remarked, "You'll have to do some hauling in order to keep these PUC permits valid."

"I don't know—I can make more money staying on here in Fullerton."

Mark Cardigan's face grew thoughtful. "Sam, I'll make you a deal. I pay for getting the tank truck fixed and on the road. And above that I'll agree to give you one thousand dollars for these permits—if I can give you a note to be paid in three years."

A light came into Sam Hook's eyes, a gleam that carried both shrewdness and triumph. "One of us is crazy. Mebbe it's me, lad. I'll take you up on the deal—repair costs plus a thousand after three years. I'll see to keeping the permits valid. But there's one condition."

"Now what?" Mark asked warily.

"A minor detail. I turn the PUC permits over to you when and if you show me an engineering diploma from Colorado A&M."

Chapter 29

Toward midmorning on a hot July day, Mark Cardigan left the office of Greeley's largest lumber yard with a materials cost estimate in his pocket. Then he walked to the main business area and approached the doors of the Plains National Bank. Three hundred dollars will handle it, he thought. And that should leave a small reserve for contingencies.

For a moment his face was reflected in a plate-glass window. Mark paused, and stared thoughtfully at himself. Just what am I doing here? It's 1928; I'm twenty-one years old. For over a month, I've had that sheepskin from Colorado A&M College that say's I'm a civil engineer. Right now I could be working for the Forest Service, some engineering firm, or even the Southern California Paving Company.

Mark's lips twisted in a wry grin as he recalled an item he had spotted in the previous evening's *Denver Post*. The Colorado Department of Highways was preparing to call for bids on an assorted list of road-paving projects.

The state will need inspection engineers to supervise the jobs, he thought. Likely I could earn as much in a month as I'm going into this bank to borrow . . . three hundred dollars. So that I can build some hog-tight woven-wire fence for a dry-land farmer.

He shrugged, then pulled open the door of the Plains National Bank, knowing within himself that his reverie had not touched the core reason for his being here. Even with the Southern California Paving Company, he would be a salaried employee, carrying out the instructions of others. But while building half a mile of hog-tight fence, he would be Mark Cardigan, independent builder.

Inside the bank, he was quickly aware that remodeling and enlargement had taken place since his last visit. The rear of the spacious lobby held several cages, fronted by small barred windows, where tellers were at work tending to the needs of perhaps a dozen customers.

Off to one side, in a spot that offered a strategic view of the entire room, was a waist-high counter. Beyond the counter was a huge, flat-topped desk, a swiveled office chair, and two not-too-comfortable upright chairs. The occupants of these would not find encouragement to linger after their business had been finished.

Mark's eyes adjusted to the lesser light. He saw Silas Latham, president of the Plains National Bank, rise from the swivel chair to stand with his hands firmly grasping the polished edge. Mark realized then that Latham was a tall man, slim of build and muscular. It was well known that he had gotten his start in business by collecting and selling the bones of cattle that had perished by the hundreds in a winter blizzard that swept the prairies.

Latham made it a point to greet everyone who entered the bank personally. "Ben," he now addressed a middle-aged customer in ranch garb, "I hear you're set on feeding lambs this winter. How many?"

A half-amused and half-calculating grin broke across the customer's weathered face. "You heard correct, Silas. I figure I can lose more of the bank's money in sheep than I can in steers."

Latham's hands toyed with a pad of green-tinted notes payable. "Stop by before you leave, Ben. I'll be unwise enough to listen to your plans."

Mark was next in line. He strode over to the banker's desk.

"Good morning, Mark Cardigan," the banker said, shrewdly appraising the boy. "What brings you in from Crow Creek Valley?" Latham's resonant voice reverberated, and filled the bank.

"Howdy, Mr. Latham," Mark responded in low tones. "I'm here because I need three hundred dollars."

"You need what?" Latham shot back in a loud and seemingly dismayed voice which canceled any possibility of confidentiality.

"I . . . I need three hundred dollars," Mark repeated, and knew that his face was becoming crimson with humiliation.

"So, my young friend," the banker continued, "you expect me to loan you three hundred dollars of this bank's resources?"

Mark nodded in misery, then added, "I need it for sixty days. I'll pay it promptly—just as I always have." There was a moment of silence, and then anger and embarrassment surged within Mark as he added, "Do I or don't I get the money, Mr. President?"

Evident enjoyment swept Silas Latham's face. He was well aware that every employee and customer in the bank was listening to this drama in which he held center stage.

"And just what do you have for security, Mr. Cardigan?"

For a moment Mark eyed him in an oddly impersonal way. Then he lifted his hands and laid them, palms upward, on the counter, only inches from Latham's face. "Here's your precious security, Mr. Latham," he grated. "My two hands. They can pitch hay, pull a calf from a weakened cow, dig post holes, or skin coyotes. They can also handle a surveying instrument or set drainage stakes. They've done most of that before to pay you. Now, do I get the money?"

With a gesture of defeat, but of showmanship, Latham flung the pad of notes payable to the floor, then ground his heel upon them. "Three hundred dollars," he shouted. "You come begging for three hundred dollars!"

"Listen, Mr. President," Mark said in a voice so calm that it seemed deadly. "Who the hell do you think you—"

"Mark . . . Mark," the banker said calmly. "Cool down. It's just that you come in time and again for two or three hundred dollars. You did it when you were a kid in grade school. Why, you almost two-and-three-hundred me to death. Of course you can have the money." Latham stooped to retrieve the notepad, then as he wrote rapidly he added, "Take this to a teller and get your money." Latham savored the quietness of the room. Presently, in a voice that was just a trifle lower, he said, "Cardigan, it's just that anyone should grow above the two-or-three-hundred-dollar mark. You're out of college now, aren't you? I want to see the day when you can walk in here and persuade me to lend you twenty-five thousand dollars."

Mark reached for the outthrust note. His first impulse was to rip it into pieces and throw it in the banker's face for the embarrassment he had caused him. But reason warned that he was already committed to the hog-fence job and that he had no other way to procure the money. Then he assessed what Latham had said about bigger sums. After a minute, he straightened, forcing a bleak but determined smile. "Twenty-five thousand dollars, you say, Mr. Latham," he said slowly and decisively. "Twenty-five thousand in hard, cold cash." He paused, to again lay his steady hands on the counter. "Silas," he said, emphasizing the banker's name, "if this bank has that kind of money to loan . . . just hang onto it. Keep it nice and safe for sixty days. I'll be back with the need for it—and a solid proposition to back it up. I'm going to build something big. Maybe an empire. Twenty-five thousand will be a good beginning."

Mark Cardigan turned on his heel, adjusted his work-stained hat, and walked quickly toward a teller's cage to pick up three hundred dollars. Because he did not glance back, he failed to see the unfathomable smile on Silas Latham's face.

The building of the hog fence proved a simple and somewhat tedious job for Mark. The ranch where it was needed was less than five miles from Cardigan Ranch. At his father's suggestion, Mark used a team of the ranch work horses for hauling materials and stretching wire. He drove to and from the job each day, and found extra time to do odd jobs at home for Redge and Audrey. Nowadays, they spoke occasionally of retiring and moving either to Hawk Bend or Fort Collins. But Mark sensed that only some serious disability would ever force his parents away from the fields and the livestock, the prairie vistas and lifelong friends.

The small burial ground a little way upstream was now surrounded by a white picket fence, and lawn sprinklers had been installed. Mark visited the graveyard in respect to those he had known who now rested on this quiet tree-lined knoll. He had vivid memories of Kate Andrus, his grandmother, and of crotchety but tender-hearted Hank Kutcher. About the other graves, he could only ponder . . . those of Will Cardigan, of a gunfighter named Willoughby, and of the Indian boy, Hosteen Begay.

Mark had been able to hire two boys in Hawk Bend to aid in the fence building. Each rode his own saddle horse to the job site and provided his lunch. When not busy with his own ranch work, Redge Cardigan would sometimes join his son for a few hours of setting posts and stretching hog fencing. Once, after squinting down a long line of perfectly aligned and tightened wire, Redge scratched his graying temple and remarked thoughtfully, "I wonder how long such a barrier as this would have stayed put when Andy Purcell was running his cattle over half of this county?"

"He must have foreseen plowed fields and stock-tight fences," Mark answered. "Else why did he let Grandfather Cardigan and you squat on his range?"

"It was a business deal," Redge answered, and he was recalling how, over the furious protests of Stacy Murdock, he had gotten the job of caring for the crippled stock of the Diamond-7 Ranch.

Mark glanced toward the west, where the mountains shone in brilliant blues and mauve against a morning sky. "I've never been able to understand why you and your father didn't settle up in the high country where there was timber and streams and mountain meadows. Half of the country was open for grabs in those days."

Redge laid down his fencing pliers and let his eyes roam the softly folded hills and the undulating grasslands that lay eastward. "Others can have all that country that stands on end up there. I . . . and your Mom . . . prefer the prairies, where the winters are warmer, where wind seeks its way through the buffalo grass, and where a morning sun peeks early-like over the eastern rim." Redge paused, aware that his words were becoming perilously near a poem. Then he added, "We've lived here, and save for a few years we've had peace and security. And, son, when the time comes, we want to be laid away with the others . . . there along Crow Creek."

They worked for a while in silent and mutual understanding, using a team and wagon to tighten a length of woven wire. After stapling it tight to a cedar post, Redge asked, "How come you haven't been riding down to that section house below Hawk Bend to call on the pretty Mexican girl?"

"She's teaching at a parochial school in Albuquerque just now. She'll be home for a visit in August."

"I hope we've got all of this confounded hog mesh up by then," Redge said, "or likely I'll have to take over your contract."

325

Mark eyed him seriously. "I'll never default on a contract, Dad."

"No," Redge Cardigan murmured, with sureness in his voice. "No, by God, I don't think you ever will." He studied his son's face, then went on, "But Mark, don't settle for a whole series of piddling little jobs."

"You mean like this hog fence?" Mark's question was blunt.

"Now that you mention it—yes."

"I don't intend to. Right now I'm waiting for some papers from Denver . . . the state highway folks. What would you think if I bid on a sizable asphalt road-paving job?"

"I'd ask," Redge said in startled voice, "if you intend to mix the stuff in a washtub, or maybe a wheelbarrow."

"Come to a meeting I'm setting up for the second Monday in August and find out. I've asked several people to get together with me. Sam Hook—he's been back from California a couple of weeks—the Nordraak boys, Gilberto Montez."

Redge looked up. "Montez," he said finally. "You mean Dolores's father, the section foreman?"

"I sure do," Mark replied, a bit defensively. "Do you happen to know that Gilberto Montez is a graduate engineer, and that he worked on big jobs in Mexico until a political change drove him out?"

"I wasn't aware of it, son. But I've talked with Montez a few times. He strikes me as a quiet, decent person. In a fracas, I'd like him on my side. All in all, you're calling in some pretty dependable people. But you haven't said yet how you expect to get set up to smear oil and grind up rock."

Mark wiped sweat from his neck and lowered himself thoughtfully onto the wagon's open end. "Dad," he asked, "where can I get hold of lots of gravel?"

"You mean for a building foundation?"

Mark shook his head. "No, I may need it for hot-mix paving material. Thousands of tons of clean, crushed, and screened aggregate."

Redge shook his head. "There's some gravel along the creeks, but not in any such quantities. The only place I know you'll find it is down on the South Platte River.

326

There's land there that is practically waste because of the deep veins of gravel."

Mark silently computed his finances. The fencing job would be finished within a week, and should show a satisfactory profit. Also, he had spent only half of the three hundred dollars he had borrowed at the Plains National Bank. "I don't suppose a person could get hold of much of that gravel land for five hundred dollars."

His father looked up with sudden interest, asking, "What use would you have for a river sand bar with a lot of gravel in it, son?"

Mark sighed, knowing that the time had come to reveal the plan that had been growing in his mind. "I have sent for the plans and specifications for a couple of highway-paving jobs the Colorado Highway Department has advertised."

Redge nodded. "I've heard that paved roads are the coming thing. The way automobiles are taking over, we're gonna need to get shet of all the sand drifts and mud holes."

Mark squatted beside a newly set post and stared thoughtfully at his father. "The process isn't too complex, Dad. You use a plant with a boiler and tanks, to heat a type of crude oil; then you mix it with screened rock or gravel, dump it on a firm roadbed, and roll it smooth while it's hot. There's even a way of making it pretty much waterproof if the road has been graded to shed moisture." He shrugged, then got to his feet. "But I don't own any gravel pits, and likely if I had one it wouldn't prove out to be within hauling distance of any job I could bid in."

"Hold on a minute, son," Redge said briskly. "Maybe there is a way. Did you ever hear of options? Options to lease?"

"Sure, but—" Mark began.

"Yep," Redge interrupted. "It's sure worth a try. Find three or four good gravel deposits between Greeley and Sterling, maybe along the South Platte River, north of Denver, then option them until you find which ones you are apt to need for a paving job."

"That would take a heap of money," Mark said uneasily. "I'm not going to be able to scare up more than maybe five or six hundred dollars."

"It's not going to set you back a fortune just to take

327

options. Ranchers sometimes do it. Fellows who own land usually consider gravel or sand streaks pretty useless. You can't raise much hay or sugar beets on gravel. Besides, son, you can talk *royalties*. Tell the landowners you're willing to pay a reasonable royalty on every cubic yard of gravel you dig and haul away."

"That could get daggoned expensive on a big job," Mark demurred.

"Not so bad," Redge continued patiently. "Besides, it will get you more and cheaper options. Also, those landowners won't feel you were out to cheat them." Redge paused, then said, "There is going to be a big demand for gravel in a few years; I wouldn't mind having some money invested that way. Let me talk it over with your mother."

Mark grinned his appreciation of the offer. Then he asked, "How can we tell if there is a good gravel deposit? Usually there is several feet of soil overburden, and a mat of cactus and grass and sagebrush."

"There are ways. I've had to scout along Crow Creek for gravel for foundations. One way is to watch for what gophers and prairie dogs have dug up. Then study the streambanks where they are cut by flood waters. For larger deposits, try to determine if the land was once the course of the river, even thousands of years ago. Besides, you can probe pretty well with a post-hole digger, using a long piece of pipe for a handle."

Mark sensed the enthusiastic interest building within his father. "How about you taking a trip and looking for a few prime gravel deposits? And in areas out away from gravel beds, but where highways are apt to be paved some day, keep a lookout for formations that have good rock we can put through a crusher for aggregate."

Redge responded with a penetrating stare, then he demanded, "How much would one of those road-paving jobs bring in—say a medium-long one, maybe three or four miles?"

"You're sort of asking how high is up," Mark said, laughing. "But I saw one contract of the Southern California Paving Company, for a job close to Fullerton, that ran close to a hundred and fifty thousand dollars."

Despite his effort to seem unimpressed, Redge Cardigan's eyes widened and the muscles of his jaw tightened. "Maybe," he muttered, "I should take a ride along the Platte—after a lawyer draws us up some option-to-lease forms!"

His journey in search of gravel lands caused Redge to miss a meeting that was hurriedly called at the Hawk Bend school. It concerned a matter that had long been perplexing and somewhat irritating to the landowners of Crow Creek Valley. Several years previous, improvement bonds had been issued to finance an ambitious and far-flung irrigation project. The project had been initiated when Joe Edmundson, an irrigation developer who lived in Denver, had carried out comprehensive surveys.

There is a portion of Colorado, beyond the first great barrier of peaks, where the rivers drain toward the north. Both the North Platte River and its tributary river, the Laramie, have their origin among the vast peaks of northern Colorado. The North Platte flows far northward into Wyoming, makes a giant bend in the vicinity of Casper, and then moves eastward into Nebraska on its way toward the Missouri River. The tributary Laramie River also flows from Colorado into Wyoming, and merges with the North Platte in the vicinity of historic old Fort Laramie. The situation created an opportunity for some farsighted irrigation projects. And Joe Edmundson was farsighted.

The plans Edmundson prepared called for a trans-mountain diversion of the Laramie River's heavy flow. By utilizing natural grades, and a tunnel beneath the barrier range of mountains, a portion of the Laramie's flow could be channeled to supply reservoirs along the foothills north of Fort Collins. From the storage reservoirs, canals would carry this mountain water into the broad valley of Crow Creek, and onto the level plains that lay adjacent to the creek. Thousands of acres of fertile plains-country land could be farmed, and have the security of ample water for irrigation.

Edmundson's project had gone ahead speedily at first. Much of the mountain tunnel was completed, as well as the necessary ditches for drawing the water from the Laramie River. Recently, however, the project had encountered both legal and financial setbacks.

Aware of the project's potential for both Cardigan Ranch and the Hawk Bend community, Audrey Cardigan insisted on attending the meeting, particularly since Redge was not around. She persuaded Mark to accompany her. "You're a trained engineer. Maybe you can explain all those blueprints and specifications that Joe Edmundson is apt to spring on us." Audrey shook her head and then commented, "I hope Edmundson has found a way to go ahead with his project; it has been lying half-completed and idle for several years. And meanwhile everyone around here has to pay on those Improvement District Bonds."

Mark recalled the remarks his favorite professor at A&M had made in assessing the project's prospects. "Don't get your hopes up too high, Mom."

"Why?" Audrey asked. "Isn't it a feasible plan?"

Mark nodded thoughtfully. "Entirely feasible. The water is up there, in the Laramie River. Plenty of it. And the law of gravity says it will flow down through the tunnel into Jimmy Creek, and on down to the reservoirs."

"Then what's the hindrance?" Audrey demanded.

"Mom," Mark answered, "before this is over there's going to be one hell of a legal battle—a lawyer's heyday—all the way to the U.S. Supreme Court. That Laramie River water flows into Wyoming, and then into Nebraska. Both of them are arid states and need irrigation projects. They'll fight to the last inch to keep Joe Edmundson from diverting even one teacup of water."

"I see," his mother responded. "But I've learned a lot about Edmundson over the years. He'll fight, and he has some powerful friends in Denver and in Washington, D.C., too."

If there were any doubts in Edmundson's mind, they certainly were not evident at the evening meeting, which drew an overflow crowd to the Hawk Bend school. This dynamic man seemed to have absolute faith in himself and the water-diversion project. "We of Colorado will be able to keep our water," he assured his listeners. "It is on our high snowfields that the streams are born. The water of the Laramie River, although it follows nature's way northward, is the birthright of Coloradoans."

Edmundson went on to say that he was now prepared to back his faith and his fortune—plus the bond holders' equity—with new work. With his own resources, he would immediately begin construction of a new canal, one reaching twelve miles from the easternmost of his storage reservoirs to the western rim of Crow Creek Valley. A survey had already been made and the necessary right-of-way acquisition completed.

Mention of the new canal construction brought Mark upright in his seat. He heard little of Edmundson's closing remarks, which dealt with water allocation to prospective users. Instead, Mark was striving to recall the contour and the physical makeup of the soil through which the canal would probably be built. He was also remembering the challenge that banker Silas Latham had bellowed out. "Nobody can be hanged for merely thinking," Mark muttered to himself, then pondered how he could best approach this energetic project developer.

As it happened, within ten minutes after the formal meeting had ended, while refreshments were being served, Edmundson sought Mark out. "Son," he said, after a few words of introduction, "your mother tells me you are a graduate engineer, and that you understand surveying. Tell me more about it."

Mark Cardigan grinned, trying to contain his excitement. "There's not much to tell, sir. I graduated from Colorado A&M last spring. I have had field experience with the U.S. Forest Service and with the Southern California Paving Company."

Edmundson eyed him shrewdly, then said, "I'll be needing a reliable surveyor on those twelve miles of canal. Why don't we set a time to talk it over?"

"I would be interested," Mark agreed, and then he decided to lay his whole plan on the line. "Mr. Edmundson," he asked, "who is your contractor for the canal?"

"I haven't quite settled on that, Mark. Why?"

"Because I would like to make you a proposition, sir," Mark said with cautious assertiveness, choosing his words slowly. "I'd like a chance at all aspects of the job. Engineering. Right-of-way clearance. Excavation. Flood safeguards. The whole ball of wax."

Joe Edmundson seemed taken aback. "How would you manage all that, Cardigan? You'd need a complete organization—men, equipment, horses and graders, someone with office skills."

"I know that, sir. But I've sort of been preparing for something like this. I believe I can give you a top job at a favorable price. And don't worry about my capital, or a

331

surety bond . . . I'll have those, to your satisfaction, before we sign any papers or turn the first shovel of dirt."

The older man sipped his coffee and stared into space for what seemed an endless time before answering. Finally, he said, "Son, maybe I should be telling you hell no, or giving you a polite brush-off. But you're Redge and Audrey's son. Besides, I have heard how you build fences that last. I'll be back here next week, on Tuesday. Have at it, Mark, and prepare your proposition. I warn you, you'll find me pretty rough to convince."

"I'll need preliminary papers," Mark said quickly. "Profiles of the canal. Contour maps, canal dimensions, and your estimate of quantities."

Edmundson gestured toward a table on which several bulky folders were lying. "You're welcome to what's there. I wouldn't think you'd need much more. I keep the original copies in my office, but take care of these. Paperwork and overhead cost a fortune."

The meeting ended on an optimistic note. If anyone had the political and financial clout to bring the trans-mountain project to a successful culmination, it would be Joe Edmundson. And with the imminent building of the big ditch to Crow Creek Valley, the prospect for ample irrigation water appeared very real.

As Mark and his mother started home, Audrey wondered about the possible impact of the irrigation system on their own property. "We've been the lucky ones for many years, Mark, because your father saw the possibility of putting the dam across Crow Creek when he was a boy."

"What was shrewder," Mark agreed, "was his filing legal claim to a good share of the creek's flow."

"Of course, we've never had as much water as we could readily use. The creek flow varies a lot from year to year. Snow and rainfall is never the same for two consecutive years. And nowadays the dams upstream, around Grover and Cheyenne, make a lot of difference. Even Redge agrees that we could sure make use of our share of the diversion-project water."

Mark drew their car to a halt in front of the Hawk Bend post office. Although they were now on an RFD route, they had elected to keep a lock box at the Hawk Bend post office, so that they would pick up mail during evening hours and on weekends.

He got out of the car and said, "I'll check our box; I'm expecting those bid papers from the State Highway Department." A glance at his mother showed Mark that she was still preoccupied with Edmundson's talk. "Mom," he said tenderly, "I hope the canal brings you and Dad water enough for every acre of Cardigan Ranch." But he knew there would be a big fight in the Supreme Court before Audrey saw a drop of water. He turned in the cool darkness and entered the post office.

When he reappeared and climbed to the driver's seat, there was a bulky brown envelope in his hand and an excited grin on his face. "This is it, Mom. The bid-form envelope. Think of it! Me, Mark Cardigan. All I've ever built by myself is a privy hole and a few fences. And now I've got a chance at two big jobs. Road building. Canal building." He thought a minute and then added, "I'll have to form a company. The Cardigan Construction Company— how does that sound, Mom?"

Audrey threw her arm about his shoulders. But innate common sense mingled with the pride of her reply. "Why not just call it the Cardigan Corporation, Mark? I've a feeling you will need a lot of help from a lot of people before too long." As Mark mulled over the name, Audrey added, "I wish your dad were here right now, instead of being somewhere along the Platte River punching holes to find gravel. He would be proud—Redge would be very proud."

During the following few days, as Mark studied the plans and specifications for both the highway and canal jobs, he often glanced at the wall calendar on which he had carefully marked the second Monday in August, the date of the meeting at the Montez house. There had been a twinkle in the section foreman's eyes as he had agreed to the time and the place. Of course it was entirely coincidental that this Monday evening was exactly twenty-four hours after Dolores would be arriving from Albuquerque on a visit.

Redge Cardigan arrived home on the third day after the meeting at the Hawk Bend school. After Audrey had brought him up to date, he appeared at the door of Mark's room and surveyed the disorder of blueprints and documents strewn over a table and the bed. "Why, Mark," he demanded with doleful groan, "can't you tackle one impending disaster at a time? There is paper enough here to

333

stock an outhouse for six months, even with a diarrhea epidemic."

Mark looked up with a tired and wry grin of welcome. He pushed a chair toward Redge and said, "Someone has to tend to the details—we can't all take off for a pleasure trip to the banks of the South Platte." He let the barb fly, then before his father could growl a reply, he asked, "How about the gravel and the rock for crushing? Did you find any sizable deposits?"

"Sure I did," Redge answered after a stretch and a yawn. "Why else would I have ridden more than a hundred miles, and shoveled dirt at half a dozen sites?" His tone became serious. "Son, I took the bull by the horns. Managed to get options signed for a couple of gravel deposits and a ledge of flint-hard rock about halfway between Greeley and Denver."

"I hope you held costs down," Mark fretted. "Right now my bank account is pretty slim."

"Don't worry about it. I used my own money for the options. But I had to offer some pretty hefty royalties. Those landowners don't give anything away."

There was silence in the room for a time as Mark jotted figures onto a bid form, studied them, and finally drew an X through the work.

"I just hope you're not getting beyond your depth, son," Redge remarked.

"Maybe I am. My math was never too great. Gilberto Montez spent years as an estimator. He'll help me."

"I wasn't talking about those figures," his father persisted. "How come you're sweating to get bids ready on two big jobs when you haven't a thousand dollars of capital?"

Mark threw down his pencil and rose to pace the floor. Presently he stopped and peered into his father's questioning face.

"Why am I charging into this, you ask. Because I'm a stubborn, determined, daydreaming Cardigan. I have an education to put to use—and some experience. I have friends with even better qualifications, and I intend to call upon them for help. Yes, dammit, Dad, to use their abilities and their skills. Most of all, I am going to call the bluff of that bastardly old banker friend of yours in Greeley. Yes . . . I'm talking about Silas Latham, the head honcho of the Plains National. He gave me hideous hell for asking to borrow three hundred. Said he wanted to see me in shape to ask for twenty-five thousand." Mark paused to point at the spread of papers. "I'm getting ready, Dad, to go after that big loan—if either of these contracts comes my way. At least I'll give Latham a chance to turn tail and renege."

"Fine, Mark," his father responded. "Count on me—and your mom—if we can help. And let me tell you one thing: Silas Latham didn't become president of the Plains National Bank by reneging on his word!"

Mark again studied the calendar. "Day after tomorrow we're having a meeting at the Montez section house. I've asked Sam Hook to be there. Also Halfdan and Fartein Nordraak. And a fellow from the Forest Service, a ranger friend of mine named Lane Torgny, may be able to attend. How about you and Mom sitting in on the session too?"

From the corner of his eye, Redge saw that Audrey had appeared in the doorway, so, with a cunning grin, he asked, "Will the lovely señorita from Albuquerque be there?"

A flush mounted to Mark's face, but he kept his voice even. "It's her home, isn't it? Sure—she's expected there tomorrow."

Redge rose from his chair whistling, and moved a few steps to a Latin rhythm. "I should brush up on my fandango, and the Mexican hat dance. Once I was acclaimed for—"

Audrey immediately cut him short. Very slowly and very seriously she raised her hand—then thumbed her nose. "Tell it right, Redge. Tell your son that you ran off like a scared jackelope—and hid—to avoid your first dance at Kate's Wagon."

The day wore on, with Mark engrossed in study of the papers by which the two jobs would have to be bid. Then he concentrated on the specifications for the irrigation canal. It was clear the highway project was very complicated—only the expertise of Gilberto Montez would enable him to reach figures to use in bidding. The list of items and quantities seemed endless. If I just had some idea what other contractors are bidding for such items, he fretted to himself.

It was near midnight, and both Redge and Audrey had

335

gone to bed, when the frenzied barking of the ranch dogs caused Mark to turn from his work table and go to the window. There was a gleam of headlights, and he heard the throbbing of a motor. A car swung from the county road into the Cardigan Ranch driveway. Mark hurried to the porch and was waiting when the auto pulled up. A man stared nervously from behind the steering wheel at the two dogs that undoubtedly had him cornered. Finally, his gaze zeroed in on Mark, and he yelled, "Cardigan, I'm not budging an inch until you call off these mankillers."

At sound of the stranger's voice, Mark laughed aloud, then silenced the dogs and called them onto the porch. "Lane . . . Lane Torgny . . . crawl out and be recognized. Lord almighty, but I'm glad to see you."

Torgny mounted the steps, and the car's headlights revealed the smart cut of his green uniform. They shook hands, and Mark caught sight of the pine-tree badge at Torgny's coat pocket. "Wait a minute, stranger," he yelled. "Don't tell me I'm hobnobbing with a full-fledged forest supervisor?"

Torgny nodded. "That's why I was so late getting in, Mark. I was called into Denver by the Regional Forester's office. They pinned this on me and gave me a week off. After that I have to report as supervisor of the Harney Forest, in Nebraska."

They turned off the headlights after unloading Torgny's luggage. As they entered the house, the dogs again set up their barking, this time in answer to the call of a distant coyote. The commotion had awakened Redge and Audrey, and presently they too came into the living room. There were introductions, and then, after demanding when their visitor had last eaten, Audrey scurried into the kitchen.

"She shouldn't bother, at this hour," Torgny protested.

"It would be a lot worse for her to be tossing and turning and fretting because a visitor might be hungry under our roof," Redge said. "Now you two can visit while I help the cook stir something up."

Lane Torgny tapped his fingers thoughtfully on the arm of his chair. Abruptly, he asked, "What's up, Mark? Your letter said you need help. I sure don't know much about preparing bids, other than Forest Service figures."

"Lane, I'm about to start out on my own. Set up a construction business. There are a lot of questions that need answering. I'm real scared, Lane. I could make a big flop of it."

"Then we can commiserate together. I'm scared of tackling the responsibility of administering the Harney Forest. Now—what sort of job are you planning to tackle?"

"Either a state highway oiling job—road mix—or a contract to excavate twelve miles of irrigation canal."

"Why not both?" Torgny asked in a matter-of-fact tone.

Mark shrugged. "Actually, I don't have a contract yet on either job; maybe I'll be underbid on both jobs."

"But you feel capable of handling the work?"

"Sure I do. Besides, I think I can gather experienced people for the projects." Mark described the knowledge and skills of Sam Hook, of the Nordraak brothers, and of Gilberto Montez. Thoughts of Dolores came also to his mind, but he did not speak of her.

Lane Torgny nodded attentively, then said, "You've been planning this for a long time, Mark."

"Ever since I was a little kid, and the county road crew came by our place with a mule-drawn grader."

Forest Supervisor Lane Torgny's gaze became suddenly penetrating, and he leaned forward. "Mark, I'm about to ask a mighty personal question—but a vital one. How do you stand financially and credit-wise?"

Mark's answering gaze was a bit rueful, but steady and determined. "I don't have but a few hundred dollars. But right now I don't owe one damned cent. I have never had a lot of credit—or any credit difficulties." He took a deep breath, then plunged ahead, telling of his relationship with Silas Latham and the Plains National Bank. "Latham sort of laid it on me the last time I was in his bank. I asked for three hundred dollars to buy material for a fence job. The old boy threw a fit. Said he wanted to see the time I'd come to the bank asking for twenty-five thousand dollars."

Torgny laughed, then demanded, "What did you tell him?"

"Just that if he had that sort of money to loan, he'd best keep it handy. That I'd be back with sound proposition to slap down before him."

A grin of anticipation swept Lane Torgny's face, and there seemed about him the confidence and authority which

337

Mark had first noted when his friend was a district forest ranger organizing the diverse duties of his assignment. "Mark, do you have the plans and specs of both jobs handy?"

"Do I ever, Lane! I've been struggling over them all day."

"Do you mind if I scan them?"

The question was firmly answered by Audrey Cardigan, who had entered the room with a tray of sandwiches, milk, and pie. "There'll be no more blueprint rustling or column adding in this house tonight." She smiled. "What both you and Mark need most right now is a snack and then a long night's sleep. But tomorrow I will see that the house is quiet, and that Dad and I keep out of the way so you empire builders can *figger like fury*."

Much to Mark's surprise, Torgny spent only about an hour the following morning studying the canal drawings and specifications. Then he asked abruptly, "Would it be possible for us to drive a car along the indicated route of this ditch?"

Mark shook his head, then brightened. "But the lower end of the canal site is close enough that we can ride out and look it over for two or three miles . . . and be back shortly after noon." He paused, then asked, "But how about the highway job, Lane? You haven't even glanced at that data."

"First things first, Mark. We can't possibly visit the highway route today; besides, I have an idea that your friend Señor Montez will interpret that job better than I can."

They were walking toward the horse corral when Mark said, "I'd like to show you a dam that my dad planned when he was just a kid. It has provided enough water from Crow Creek to enable our ranch to survive for about thirty years."

"Let's insist that your father go along," Torgny suggested. "I'm sure he's familiar with every rise and fall of the terrain, and has a bunch of sound ideas as to how water will move in the type of soils we'll find. You know, Mark, I've taken a liking to Redge and Audrey."

When they asked Mark's father to accompany them, he grinned and said, "Hell, just let me get my old sorrel stud horse from the barn. I've had him saddled for an hour hoping you two would give me an invite."

Audrey stood on the porch to see them off. "Mark," she

338

reminded her son, "don't forget that tomorrow night is the meeting at the section house."

"Are you coming, Mom?"

"Just try and keep me away! Perhaps I can persuade Señora Montez to give me a recipe or two. Besides, I'd enjoy a chat with that lovely daughter you're aching to see."

"A lovely daughter, eh?" Lane Torgny repeated, and raised his eyebrows in interest.

"Just wait until you see her," Redge offered in gleeful voice. "Wow! If I was back in my lamented twenties, I'd be learning some Mexican honey-do words—pronto."

Audrey smiled sarcastically and then gibed, "Mr. Cardigan, if you were really in those long-gone, cherished twenties, you would be wearing out the trail to Kate's Wagon."

"And you are so right," Redge murmured as he blew her a kiss, and then touched heels to his mount.

They found that the final four miles of the projected canal would flow along a gently descending contour line, with only two small washes where some fill would be necessary. Likely in these spots either flumes or galvanized pipe should be used in order to avoid washouts.

"It will be reasonable digging," Redge said. "Mostly loam, with some deep sand and soft shale. I doubt you'll have to do much blasting. If the season gives us good weather, we could do a lot this fall." Then he added, "It'll take a lot of horses and men and scraping fresnos for the job."

Lane Torgny turned thoughtfully to Mark. "How many miles of the project are you thinking of tackling?"

"All of it. The whole twelve miles." Then he doubled back a bit. "I want to undertake just two miles for this year. But only if I can be assured of a per-cubic-yard figure that will assure a profit. Only if I am given a written option to perform the other ten miles over a period of three years. And only if Joe Edmundson agrees to a weekly settlement for completed work. I want payment every Monday for the previous week's completed work."

"You've done some hardheaded thinking," Torgny said approvingly. "Be sure to keep some money on hand for your teamsters and fresno dumpers. And you're going to have to set up some sort of tent or wagon camp for your men."

"I've thought of that," Mark answered, "but there aren't going to be many horse-drawn outfits. We're going to dig our stretch of this ditch with a dragline. I know where there is a coal-burning Marion Model 36, with a one-half-cubic yard bucket."

"That sort of smoke belcher would cost a fortune," Redge objected. "I saw one working when I was down near Denver last week."

"Sure it will cost," Mark agreed. "With freight to Hawk Bend, it will set us back about twenty-four thousand, five hundred dollars. But Dad, it will move a lot of dirt fast. That half-yard bucket will pick up and dump approximately a yard of this type of soil every minute. That means about six hundred cubic yards in a six-hour day. It'd take a bunch of horse-drawn scrapers to match that."

Lane Torgny had listened quietly. Now he dug a pad and pencil from his vest pocket and jotted figures, before saying, "With the dimensions of the canal being close to ten by four feet, you'll be moving right at a hundred and forty cubic yards of excavation for every hundred linear feet of canal. Counting down-time, Mark, such an outfit should drag and dump at least two hundred and fifty feet of completed work a day. Let's see . . . that should figure out to about twenty days per mile. But remember to allow plenty of leeway time for breakdowns, difficult terrain, and those inevitable rocks and hard places."

"Do you realize," Redge persisted, "that after you get your miracle machine set up—and paid for—you'll have just about five hundred bucks of operating capital left out of Silas Latham's twenty-five thousand? *If* he lets you have it."

Mark grinned. "You're right, Dad. I'd be just about as broke as I am right now. But of course it doesn't quite work out that way. I've already found out I can get the Model 36 —a brand-spanking-new one—for forking over a seventy-five-hundred-dollar down payment. The company can arrange financing for me through a Denver bank at four and a half percent interest on the balance. I'll have a payment to make once a year, based on the quantities I've moved, provided I pay about six thousand a year principal and interest."

340

Redge heard his son out in astonishment. "How in holy Herefords did you get all this information? You've hardly been off the ranch, what with you and me stringing barbed wire."

"By mail. Those stamped pieces of mail. I don't know why you've always born a grudge against the postal service, Dad."

"Most of what they send around is either an endorsement for some patent medicine, or confidential advice about where some old prairie hermit can get a dewy-eyed third-hand bride." He pondered the dragline proposition a minute, then he rendered his verdict. "Son, if that hulk of iron can outdig a dozen teams of mules—like you and Mr. Torgny seem to think it can—damn it, Mark, make your deal for it."

A glance of deep understanding passed between father and son. Then Mark said simply, "Thanks, Dad. But right now buying the rig is just a possibility. Something to be gone into only if and when Joe Edmundson signs on the dotted line for me to build the canal. And when I'm satisfied my weekly net is earmarked for me and on hand.

"How much do you expect to charge a cubic yard?" Redge asked.

Mark shook his head. "Right now that has me stymied. But Sam Hook and Gilberto Montez can help me out with various cost figures. They'll have to include a lot of things besides dirt throwing. Like structures, some concrete reinforcing, and a lot more. The fencing I can pretty well estimate on my own."

"Right now," Lane Torgny spoke up, "I can tell you that soil excavation is being bid at around twenty-four cents a cubic yard. More for hard dry stuff, or any wet gumbo sort of thing. At least, those are figures I've seen lately for forest-road bids."

Redge glanced at the sun, now an hour past noon. "That old sun, and my empty belly, say we'd best be heading back to the ranch. You two can shuffle papers and drink lemonade on the porch. Me, I'm going to demolish some roast beef and spuds. Then get caught up on my irrigating."

They turned and rode toward Cardigan Ranch, each quietly lost in his own thoughts. But at last Mark said, "I sure wish I had Gilberto's help with those state highway bid papers today."

"Then wait for him," Lane Torgny answered firmly. "The man can undoubtedly make quick and accurate work of them."

"Yep," Redge put in dourly. "Let the Mexican gentleman do the work while you hold hands with his daughter."

"Sure," Mark agreed.

Chapter 30

In later years, Mark Cardigan would always remember the meeting at Gilberto Montez's railroad section house as the moment when years of hope and planning became a reality. The men carefully scrutinized plans and documents by the yellow glow of kerosene lamps. This night's activities would soon culminate in the legal enterprise which would be known as the Cardigan Corporation.

Those who mean the most to me, and upon whom I must depend, are all here, Mark thought to himself. Mark and his parents, together with Lane Torgny, had been the first to arrive at the section house. They were greeted at the door by Gilberto, in a courteous and dignified manner. He ushered them into the living room, and they could see that hours of careful preparation had gone into this reception. After all, it was unusual for a sizable group of *americanos* to spend an evening in a Mexican dwelling, and the hosts were eager to display their pride in their race and heritage.

A short time later, Sam Hook's vehicle appeared, stirring the dust on the road leading from Hawk Bend. Hook had taken a Buick roadster, sliced off the rear-seat section, and fashioned a small boxlike sleeping quarters on the chassis. When Mark exclaimed over the expertly fashioned structure, Hook ignored him, looked about, then shook hands with Gilberto Montez. After being greeted by Redge and Audrey Cardigan and being introduced to Lane Torgny, Hook gazed quizzically about. "It's nice to get an invite to whatever is gonna take place here tonight. But what is gonna be nicer is sight of your daughter. I saw her a time or so up at Hawk Bend; she's prettier than a rain-fresh sand violet."

Gilberto Montez gave a slight bow, acknowledging the compliment. "Shall we return to the house? My daughter should be free of helping her mother in the kitchen. We shall see."

A significant glance passed between Redge and Audrey Cardigan, then Redge said, "Sam, why don't we wait outside here a bit for the Nordraak boys to show up?"

Lane Torgny instantly realized the implication of Redge's words, and nodded agreement. "Sure, Sam, it'll give me a chance to ask you about your interior cabinets." He turned to Mark and added, "You go inside with Señor Montez; perhaps he'd be interested in your canal cost figures." Torgny waved him inside, and his gesture implied, *Now's your chance. Get the hell to wherever she is.*

Mark and his host had hardly seated themselves in the living room when Gilberto rose, saying, "Mark, as always, our home is your home. Now I must be excused to go outside to check the pump of the railroad water tower. It will take only a few minutes." Then he went to the kitchen door and called in low voice, "Dolores, bring your mama and attend to your guest; I shall return shortly with the others."

The older man's words brought Mark to his feet, and he felt breathless with urgent expectation. He was not even aware that Gilberto had left the room.

Within seconds, Dolores came across the room with quick steps and stood before him. With wide eyes and quickening pulse he saw the beauty of her shining black hair as it tumbled to her shoulders. At one side, it was highlighted by a single wild rose. Her eyes told him how glad she was he was there. She seemed a trifle taller and perhaps somewhat thinner than he remembered her. The cut of her pale-blue blouse subtly showed the graceful lines of her throat and the curved fullness of breasts that were touched with her own excited breath.

Mark felt a stab of almost physical pain as he repressed desire to sweep her into his arms and crush his lips against the fullness and the promise of hers. But he knew that tonight he and his friends were guests in this home. The social rules and graces of Dolores's heritage must be honored. And then he recalled that time when he had dropped unexpectedly from a train and kissed her. *Fence-builder Cardigan,* she had stormed, *I should slap hell out of you. You think you're big stuff? And me maybe a Mexican bordello girl?*

So now, in this moment, Mark gathered her smooth hands into his and lifted them only part way toward his lips.

"God, but you are lovely tonight, Dolores . . . and I have missed you so much, for so long."

"Mark," she answered in a tone scarcely above a whisper, "I too have counted each long day." She broke her hands free of his. Then for a moment her arms were about his neck as her lips brushed his. She pulled quickly back, and the old vixen tease came back to her voice. "Señor Cardigan, why you did not write to me? So many days I looked for a letter. Days almost as many in number as the cactus I plucked from your skinned-up butt."

"Dolores," he answered after long hesitation. "I've always intended to write. Really I have, so many times. But I just put it off. It seemed every time that school or other work got in my way." As his words ended there was an air of guilt about him.

They would have said more, but footsteps approached from the kitchen, and Dolores turned to stand beside Mark, their fingers still entwined as a beaming Señora Montez came into the room.

"Mister Cardigan, I . . . I am . . . how you say it, Dolores? No . . . no . . . now I remember. I am delighted you honor our house by your presence."

"You see, Mark," Dolores broke in, "my mama is becoming an *americana*—learning to talk English."

Mark bowed before the middle-aged, beaming señora. "Tell her, please, Dolores, that of all the homes in Colorado —or in the world—this is the one where I shall be the happiest tonight."

When the Spanish translation had been spoken Señora Montez smiled. Then she moved toward the door to greet the others visitors, who could now be heard on the wooden porch.

For dinner, Señora Montez and an elderly woman who had come to assist had prepared a variety of Mexican dishes that were both colorful and delicious; tostados, tamales, tortillas. There were also mouth-watering sopapillas, done to a golden brown. And from some unknown source, Gilberto had procured a red wine of tantalizing robustness. The meal lasted for an hour. This was a time of getting acquainted, of breaking language barriers, and of recalling events that had led to their being together.

Mark insisted, after the long table had been cleared and his construction documents brought out, that the women rejoin the group. Then he began speaking, quietly and confidentially.

"I am grateful that everyone I asked Señor and Señora Montez to invite here tonight found it possible to attend. And with such food and companionship as we've enjoyed, I'm darned sure each of you is glad you came.

"I wanted to get this group together because I need your help—the help of every one of you—in undertaking something pretty big—maybe in chasing a rainbow. Ever since I was a kid I have dreamed of someday building a big construction company." Mark paused and let his gaze move from face to face.

"Right here we have the skills, the integrity, and, I believe, the determination to plan and to build. To build big. To construct things by which our country grows. We will have to take risks and chances. There are bound to be times of anxiety, of worry—perhaps of failure. But, by God, with your help, there are going to be a lot more successes than failures." A flush of confidence and zeal covered his face as he concluded, "In honor of my father and mother, Redge and Audrey Cardigan—and of my grandfather, Will Cardigan—I would like to name our enterprise the Cardigan Corporation. And now, thanks for your patience in listening. I have asked our host, Señor Gilberto Montez, to tell you a little more of what I have in mind."

The Mexican section foreman rose to his feet and smiled. "Thank you, my young friend. Before coming to your Estados Unidos I had considerable experience as construction estimator in my native land. I am not unfamiliar with the industry, its goals, and its sometimes difficult but challenging achievements.

"Now . . . what Mark is offering, and asking for, is a pooling of our respective experience and capabilities. Yes, *amigos,* we are asked to come together in a joint venture in the widest and most challenging sense of the term. As individuals, we are restricted by our own skills and our resources. Yet, joined together, our powers are multiplied many times over. Mark has offered, and wishes to make it legally binding upon himself, that each of those here tonight who see fit to join with him will become a stockholder of the Cardigan Corporation and share in its profits."

Gilberto paused and looked about, then added, *"Amigos,* I sense the beginning of not only a new and vigorous com-

346

pany, but of enduring friendships to be born of common work . . . sweat . . . worry . . . and achievement."

Lane Torgny, at whom curious glances had been cast, spoke when Gilberto was seated.

"I am just a visitor to this vicinity, but two things impress me. The patience and thoroughness with which Mark has prepared for this venture, and also the diverse skills that you people represent. A trained civil engineer, an expert construction estimator, a mechanic with training and skill in operating heavy equipment." He turned to the two Nordraak brothers. "And two strong and loyal young friends whom I predict will go far as job foremen and then project managers of this new firm." Torgny grinned, and concluded by saying, "My situation as a newly appointed forest supervisor precludes my being a part of the Cardigan Corporation. But damned if I don't wish every one of you good luck—and sort of envy you."

They all sat quietly for a few moments, and then Mark broke in, "All I can say is—*thanks for your confidence.*" He unrolled blueprints from a cardboard tube. "We've a couple of hour's work ahead studying the plans and specs of the two jobs I'm interested in. I'd like each one of you to become as familiar as possible with the details, and I want you to know I'm sure open to suggestions." Suddenly he stood up, looked around the room, and said, "There is one position we must fill that neither Gilberto nor Lane has mentioned. It is a task of endless work with figures, and other vital office functions. I have chosen the one person that I know to be fantastically fast and accurate with detailed and wearisome computations. One who can get the right totals of columns of figures while I am sharpening a pencil." Mark turned abruptly and gazed into Dolores's dark, lively, and intelligent eyes. "How about it? Will you risk becoming office manager to help each of us? What . . . what I'm trying to say is, I need you as financial officer of the Cardigan Corporation."

She thought for a long moment and studied her parents' faces. Then her clear laugh lilted across the crowded room. "Fence-builder Cardigan, knowing how you add nine and eight to get sixteen, then smudge the hell out of every paper, what other choice do I have? Yes, Mark, I will join the others in trusting you and working with you—but *madre de*

Dios, how you'll regret this if you smear smudges—like hen shit—across my records."

Mark joined in the laughter, but again, deep within him, came the stirring of desire, of wondrous yearning.

At Gilberto's recommendation, it was decided to forgo bidding on the state highway job for the present. "We have too little to go on in arriving at competitive bid figures. It would be best for us at the beginning to work out bid prices and then wait and compare them with the figures other contractors submit, especially those of the contractor to whom the job is awarded. Let us do that on perhaps half a dozen different projects. Then, on the right contract offering, we can make some of our competitors really use a sharp pencil —and yet lose the work to us."

The pencils of the Cardigan Corporation were both sharp and proficient in preparing bid figures for Joe Edmundson's irrigation canal. The initial award to Mark's firm was for three miles of excavation, structures, and fencing. The agreement further stated that the remaining nine miles would be awarded to Cardigan Corporation upon successful completion and approval of the first unit.

Edmundson agreed also to prompt payment of weekly estimates, and that funds would be placed in escrow to assure such payments. "You've come up with one hell of a binding clause to tie me up," he admitted before signing.

"It's about all we can do, and arrange our own financing," Mark explained. "I wish as much as you do that Wyoming and Nebraska hadn't filed lawsuits in the Supreme Court."

The promoter shrugged. "Son, you just worry about the digging, and leave the lawyering to me . . . and to some of the smartest attorneys in Washington. We'll have Laramie River water flowing mighty quick after you dredge out those twelve miles." Then he added briskly, "You've hogtied a slice of my available funds. Now I assume you are prepared to show me a performance bond."

With evident pride, Mark drew a folded document from his shirt pocket. "Here it is, sir. Signed, sealed—and now delivered." He did not tell Joe Edmundson that it had required personal pledges from every member of the Cardigan Corporation, plus a stiff qualifying penalty, to secure the bond. Nor did he reveal that he had not yet approached the Plains National Bank for the sum of twenty-five thousand dollars. If I don't get that money, he grimly told himself, goodbye to the dragline. But somehow I'll contract for every mule and horse and scraper handler within twenty-five miles. This ditch is going to be built. Built by the Cardigan Corporation.

Two days later he made the trip to Greeley. He told Redge and Audrey, "Now I'm gonna call old Silas Latham's bluff. Make him put up or shut up. And he's not going to throw my contract on the floor and grind a heel on it."

Redge grinned spiritedly at his wife. "I'd give my saddle-warped old hind end to see this Cardigan-Latham fracas today. Two knot-headed, stubborn financial geniuses throwing insults at each other."

"He's a good banker—but I hate his guts. The way he ranted and raved," Mark commented. "If you and Mom want, just tag along. I'll need moral support."

They entered the Plains National Bank during a mid-morning lull in business. Silas Latham, who Mark thought looked a bit older and heavier, waved a greeting, then rose and shook hands with all three Cardigans. To Audrey, the banker said, "I wish you folks could get into town oftener; I miss seeing acquaintances and customers from up Crow Creek Valley."

"If you ever get shet of mortgages and thousand-dollar bills," Redge offered, "drive out to the ranch. You'll size up how Hawk Bend is growing. There'll be a steak with your name on it in Audrey's skillet."

With the pleasantries finished, Redge and Audrey moved quietly from the counter, and seemed intent on scanning a Charles Russell painting in the lobby. Mark remained at the counter and said to the banker, "If you've a bit of time, Mr. Latham, I am here to do business."

The old glare leapt to the banker's face. "I suppose, boy, you need three hundred for another farm fence. Let's see . . . you're all paid up with us, aren't you?"

Mark's face was expressionless as he stated, "I don't owe the Plains National one dime. I don't want three hundred. Mr. Latham, I'm here to take you up on that offer of twenty-five thousand dollars—or were you just bluffing?"

"Twenty-five thousand, Mark." Latham's voice was low and had a calculating quality.

"Yes, sir. Remember I asked you to keep those thousands on hand? Well, here I am, and I have a practical business proposition—if you want to hear it."

"You're a brash young man, Mark Cardigan," Latham said. "But bankers are known to favor practical business ventures." He unlatched a counter gate and motioned Mark toward his cluttered desk. "Bring your folks in too; I imagine they're tired of staring at Russell's bear painting."

Within half an hour Latham had studied every paper pertaining to the canal construction project. He had also examined several other documents: the options held on certain gravel and rock deposits, the executed fidelity bond for the project, and the permits issued for trucking of petroleum products in both Colorado and Wyoming. Latham's face registered utter disbelief when he looked at the last. "Son, do you realize the potential value of such interstate trucking permits?"

"I imagine they will get hard to come by," Mark answered.

"They already are, with few being issued. But about the twenty-five thousand dollars. You won't need that much to hire mules and fresnos and laborers."

"But I will to dig a canal the new and fast way, Mr. Latham. I've checked it out. The canal is a natural for a dragline. I'm going to buy one. Seventy-five hundred dollars down, and the balance to be paid from earnings."

"And you want me to loan you twenty-five thousand dollars—on the basis of this contract?"

"No," Mark replied in steady voice. "I want to borrow it in the name of the Cardigan Corporation. A legal Colorado corporation. Here is a list of our officers and stockholders."

Latham studied the papers before him, and he was evidently very impressed. He asked Redge and Audrey, "How long has this son of yours been preparing to build? To have a business of his own?"

"Ever since a county mule-pulled road grader cut a swath along our ranch. Mark must have been eight years old then," Audrey answered.

"As long as that," Latham murmured. "I'm gratified, Mark, that a college degree in civil engineering hasn't taken away that dream and that determination."

"Someday," Mark responded, "we'll do it. The whole

country is going to want the Cardigan Corporation for the big jobs."

"Yes . . . yes, it may very well come about." Latham picked up the Public Utilities Commission trucking permits again and asked, "Have you kept these paid up? Current? In good standing?"

"He sure has," Redge cut in. "About twice a year Mark and old Sam Hook make a run into Wyoming, either to Casper or to that new refinery at Parco, up by Rawlins, and haul out gasoline, kerosene, or whatever they've been able to get orders for."

There was satisfaction written on the banker's face. He reached for the loan documents. "Mark, this bank is going to loan you the twenty-five-thousand dollars, to be used in whatever you and I decide is the most practical manner. I will have to bring it before our board of directors, of course, but that won't create any problem." He paused, looked searchingly into Mark's face, and said, "There is one condition, however. I am going to ask that you not dispose of those trucking permits, or pledge them in any manner, during the course of your borrowing relationship with this bank."

An excited flush glowed on Mark's face. "Mr. Latham, I fully agree to that condition. And . . . and, you know, I'm about to forget the way you tore into me when I wanted three hundred dollars . . . said I was three hundred-ing you to death!"

They had all risen to their feet, and the Cardigans were already at the front door, when Silas Latham's bellow sounded loudly across the lobby. "Another thing, Mark Cardigan—don't you twenty-five-thousand me to death!"

Chapter 31

Despite concerned forecasts by the more astute business and financial experts that national chaos might be impending, Americans were busy and prosperous as the summer of 1929 came on. It was a busy time for Mark and his associates. Sam Hook had taken on the operation of the Marion dragline like one born to the task. He insisted that there be no delay on the excavating work because of other problems. To assure progress, Mark gave a lot of his time to the surveying and structures. Both of the Nordraak boys had joined the work force, despite dire predictions from their dairyman father that they would soon come dragging home for money to buy a square meal. Mark had found that Hafdan took quickly to surveying and made a helpful rodman and assistant, while Fartein, with his cheery ways and quick quips, got along well with the laborers and kept the necessary team-and-scraper or team-and-wagon work underway.

Only two of the company's associates were seldom seen at the job site. Gilberto Montez had shaken his head when offered a place on the payroll. "I will stay with my railroad job for the present, Mark. Bring your estimating or other problems to me; I can handle them in my spare time, and that will save our company money."

Because of the remoteness of the Montez section house from the canal job site, it was agreed that Dolores should have an office in Hawk Bend. Although quite a few eyebrows were lifted, and a few dirty-minded jokes whispered about town, the pretty Mexican girl found a suitable place to board. Within weeks she was accepted as part of the tiny business community of Hawk Bend, and people motivated by curiosity or with time to kill dropped by frequently to visit with her.

The awarding of all additional miles of the canal project to the Cardigan Corporation came almost as a matter of course, and by early June Sam Hook was neatly stacking excavated dirt at a spot well into the fifth mile. And Joe Edmundson had promptly paid every weekly estimate.

On June 20, 1929, Mark picked up the firm's mail and strode toward the Hawk Bend office. This was a pretty standard routine for him these days, for now the corporation was receiving regular notices of Colorado State Highway and other jobs open for competitive bidding. There were also notices of bid openings and of the unit prices of both successful and unsuccessful bidders. One return address quickened Mark's pulse, and as he entered the small, neatly kept office he tore open the letter and dropped the envelope to the floor. Dolores was seated at her desk, writing figures in a ledger, but she quickly rose to pick up the discarded envelope.

"Mr. Big Boss Cardigan," she snapped in irritation, "why do you think this room is a pigpen? Drop things everywhere. Track in mud. I think I won't sweep anymore. Let the crap get deep. Up to your ass maybe."

Her words went unheeded, for suddenly Mark let out a whoop, flung an arm about her, and danced her toward the door. "We got it, Dolores. That seven-mile stretch of highway grading and surfacing just east of Denver. Look at this, beautiful! Contract 0198-A, awarded to the Cardigan Corporation for two hundred and thirty-eight thousand, five hundred and eighty dollars. The lowest of six bidders."

In stunned comprehension, Dolores reached for the envelope and read the return address: Colorado State Department of Highways. "Mark," she breathed. "Can it be? So many thousands of dollars."

Mark was sharply aware of her tight grasp on his arm, and of the clean scent of her hair as it touched his shoulder. "You bet it's real, sweetheart. Gilberto sure sharpened his estimating pencil on this one. We beat out the second-lowest outfit by less than two thousand dollars."

Dolores' eyes danced. "Papa will be excited; he worked many nights. When can we tell him, Mark?"

Mark glanced at a clock. It was near noon. Work was progressing smoothly on the canal, there would be no great harm done if he missed a few hours, and Halfdan or Sam Hook could always keep things going on an even keel. He tucked the contract letter into his shirt pocket and pointed her toward the desk. "Close that confounded book, cork your ink bottle, and get a jacket. Hear me? Now—pronto. You and I are going to celebrate by driving down the Union Pacific tracks until we find Gilberto and his section hands. Then we're going to inspect every draglined mile of the canal."

"But to get to the canal, we would need horses."

"Well, we'll get horses—later. What in hell do you suppose we have at Cardigan Ranch besides cattle? Horses to ride. Horses to feed. Horses to build a sweetly aromatic pile of manure."

"I think you're crazy." She laughed. "But I'll go, if you can wait while I hurry to my boardinghouse and put on something suitable for horseback."

They quickly located Gilberto, for his crew was cutting trackside weeds less than a mile south of Hawk Bend. As they handed the section foreman the award letter, Mark was tempted to shout aloud the exciting news. He repressed the urge so that Dolores could enjoy the triumph of telling her father what his long hours of work had accomplished. She spoke rapidly in Spanish, faster than Mark could follow. Gilberto beamed satisfaction as his eyes swept down the open pages. "Mark," he said presently, "at last we have the job that may be your perfect beginning with the Highway Department. We must plan quickly and very carefully for the move-in phase; the deadline for starting work is July 10, less than three weeks away." He turned to his daughter. "You are going to be very busy, now, with two jobs." Montez studied his daughter's skirt and commented, "Is that not meant for horseback riding?"

As Dolores nodded, in silence, Mark explained, "We're going to celebrate, Gilberto, and I wish you could join us. We're going to drive to my folks' ranch—they're expecting us—then take an inspection ride along the canal."

"I would like nothing better, Mark. But should I leave my crew and tasks, the railroad roadmaster would have what you call a . . . a conniption fit." He handed the letter back to Mark, turned to rejoin his workmen, then glanced back. "Señor Cardigan, you have your new contract, your day to rejoice, but please do not give in to my daughter's demands for too spirited a horse."

At the canal job site, they were delighted to find that Sam Hook had made excellent headway with his dragline

354

and was excavating at a rate that would assure a sizable weekly estimate. They tarried for several hours, riding most of the segment of canal yet to be built. By the time they were nearing Cardigan Ranch, the sun was retreating beyond the rim of far-westward peaks. Both were hungry and a bit sore as they unsaddled their horses and turned them into a creekside pasture.

They fully expected an exuberant welcome from Redge and Audrey. Instead, on the kitchen table they found a hastily written note:

Hi, Dolores and Mark,

Sorry, but we've been called to Kate's Wagon. The Lattimers have two sick horses and want your dad to treat them. We should be back by nine or ten.

There's a pot of beef stew simmering, and a pie in the icebox.

Dolores, do come soon and gather strawberries for your family.

In haste, with affection,
Mom. And Redge says so too.

They turned up heat under the stew and cut the pie into enormous sections. Outside was the sound of crickets and of a swiftly diving nighthawk. Presently Dolores rose and walked to an open window. "Mark," she asked after moments of scrutiny, "that small grove, up the creek . . . and the white picket fence. Is . . . is it a graveyard?"

"Yes, Dolores, it is the Cardigan burying place."

"So quiet . . . so peaceful it seems, Mark. Can we walk up near it."

"Of course," he agreed, and gathered her hand into his as they stepped into the warm night.

They paused just outside the enclosure, and Mark pointed out the various stones. He felt a tremor in the hand he was clutching. "There is history here, Mark. Unwritten and untold," Dolores said quietly.

Her mood caused him to draw her gently from the picket fence, to retrace their steps down the heavily grassed banks of Crow Creek. "There's something else you must see," Mark said eagerly. "It's my old bag swing."

"Your what?" she asked blankly.

355

"My boyhood super-duper swing. Old Hank Kutcher braided a rawhide rope for it, then tied on a sack of straw as a seat. It's anchored high in a big cottonwood tree just down the creek a piece. It's still there. Kutcher swore that rope would last a lifetime. Come on!"

They sought out the venerable old cottonwood and the spot where once Mark's dragging feet had trampled the grass. And the old swing was there, swaying gently when touched by a wisp of breeze in the darkness.

Dolores seized the rope and would have dropped astride the straw sack, but Mark stopped her. "Wait. There's a better way. See that big branch, and the next one slightly behind it? If you stand on the higher one to jump onto the swing, you'll swish way out over the water. Then you can drop off the straw bag when it swings back, onto the lower branch. I've swung that way for an hour. Nobody has to push you."

She stared at the two branches with determination. "Mark, will you boost me up, onto the lower branch? It's way above my head."

"Sure. Now don't fall. I'll swing the sack up to you, then I know a way to shinny up this old cottonwood. I'll help you get started."

Before he had clambered to the lower branch, she had grasped the rawhide rope, sprung onto the bag, and was already arching toward the ground, then upward and out over the placid flow of the creek. A gasp of delight broke from her as she gazed down, then began the descent. "Oh, Mark, it is wonderful—perfect!" She dropped beside him on the lower limb, then hastily climbed to the higher one for another leaping takeoff. She was soaring upward again when an errant moonbeam lighted the zest and the beauty of her face, and the hair that now followed behind as a dark streamer on her course.

As she came soaring toward him for the fifth time, Mark yelled teasingly, "Stingy! How about me?" Then before her feet could touch the lower branch, he jumped, caught hold of the rope, and dropped with his legs astride hers on the bag of straw. They felt a jolt, but the braided rawhide rope held. They skimmed the ground and swept upward in a climbing curve, out over the pool where Mark had so often splashed on sunny, childhood days.

There was a sudden, ripping sound, and Dolores screamed

as she dropped from beneath Mark. There was burning pain in his palms as they slid down the rope, for in her descent Dolores's arms had seized his legs and pulled him downward. Both of them hit the water near midstream, creating a huge splash, and went under. The rope continued its gentle swaying, the shreds of age-rotted burlap hanging from it.

Mark was first to surface, wiping water and straw from his face and blowing cold water from his mouth and nose. A moment later, Dolores's face bobbed above the water as her feet pushed off against the creekbed. With both hands, she threw back her hair, then spat out a dark piece of burlap. Both shock and anger were written across her wet, dismayed face. "Cardigan—you dumb son of a bitch. You too-heavy, too-big jackass!" She paused, staring at his remorseful expression. And then she laughed. A gay, wondrous laughter that seemed to engulf both of them and the old and gnarled cottonwood tree.

He moved to her side and aided her, stumbling and splashing, to the grassed creekbank. For a time they stood there dripping. Then Mark tore open his shirt and pulled it off, followed by his undershirt. "You'd better get that sopping dress off. We'll have to wring these duds out and let them dry."

She was fumbling at her shoelaces, but stopped to stare at him. "Listen, you bag buster. If you think I'm going to undress—stand naked—"

He noted that her teeth were chattering. And then he was again hearing words she had once spoken: *Yes, I see your skin . . . your butt . . . your white and bloody ass. So what? You think maybe you have too nice an ass for me to see?*

And now he mocked: *"Madre de Dios.* You think maybe you have too nice an ass for me to see?"

It took her a moment to remember. Then with a contemptuous toss of her head she pulled off her blouse and dropped the riding skirt from her. And then she continued. With swift hands she removed her stockings and her underwear, and stood proudly before him without a single garment. "You think you bluff me, Mark. See . . . I am here. All of me. And you sit shivering in wet pants."

The taunting, teasing ring of her words was still in his ears as he finished undressing, and wrung streams of creek

357

water from his socks, his underdrawers, and his pants. But he avoided her eyes, and remained silent. After his belly was reasonably dry, he rolled over and lay full length in the grass to let the whisper of breeze warm his back. And he was painfully aware of one thing: Hers was the most perfect form, and the most tantalizing, he had ever hoped to see.

He lay with his face away from her, not wishing to see her or worry about her. And then he felt her soft fingers touch the nape of his neck. He lay, scarcely breathing, as she forced his face toward her. "Mark . . . Mark . . . it is all right. Don't you know it is?"

The wonder of her words and her warm tone caused him to roll over and face her. For a moment, in the moonlight, he saw tenderness and something more in her face.

Suddenly his arms crushed her close, and his lips sought the fullness of her mouth. With demanding kisses, her thighs and breasts welded to him. The sudden, undeniable demands of their passions rose to the fury of their total ecstasy.

Later, they rose to squeeze a few more drops of water from their clothing, which was drying rapidly in the warm breeze. When the task was finished, they sat side by side, with fingers tightly interwoven. Moments later, they again came together, this time with slower and more gentle words and movements as they explored and gloried in each other's body. They each experienced a vast contentment and a conviction that this night was meant to be.

At last she said, "Our clothes are dry enough, Mark. You must take me home to Hawk Bend."

Chapter 32

Mark was able to lease three acres of brushy and cactus-matted ground as a base site for their first state highway project. The headquarters offered immediate access to the work area and was large enough for the equipment they would likely need. The first structure pulled onto the site was a one-room trailer. Sam Hook had drawn up detailed sketches. "Have it built like this, on a farm wagon's running gear. It'll be large enough for a desk or two, some cabinets, and a draftsman's table. The wagon tongue has been shortened and modified. You can hook it behind any truck—or even a tractor. This way, Mark, we won't have to come up with a new shack for every job."

On his first weekend off, Gilberto Montez and Dolores visited the new field office. As they toured the lot, Gilberto's attention was attracted to another small structure that had been skidded from a Highway Department truck. "Ah, yes," he said gloomily, "the inevitable supervision."

"Supervision?" Mark repeated, puzzled.

"Yes, Mark. There are government and state funds involved here. And bureaucratic underlings will make the most of it. We will be constantly watched, and our work scrutinized, measured, tested, and analyzed by scales and thermometers and test tubes."

Mark shrugged. "I guess it's all right. Just so they don't hold up work progress."

"Try to cooperate with them, Mark; they too have assigned duties. And often the state inspectors can be invaluable to the contractor."

A telephone was connected in the field shack within a week. As soon as Mark saw the instrument, he thought again of his need for a field clerk, and an office such as that at Hawk Bend. But it had been decided that for the present at least, the Cardigan Corporation's headquarters would remain at Hawk Bend, and daily work, quantities, and man-hour figures would be mailed to Dolores. Mark scowled at the telephone. "Likely if any calls come, it will be from some job hunter."

There were a few job seekers, but the deluge of phone calls, and of personal visitors, came from salesmen declaring their indispensable products.

Mark stayed late into the evening studying the specifications for gravel-screening and rock-crushing setups with one of these salesmen, who represented a heavy-equipment distributor. The processing and stockpiling of such aggregate would have to be among the first contract functions.

They were interrupted by the telephone. Mark ignored it for a couple of rings. "I'm not up to the patter of another lubricants or bolt-and-nut salesman." When the jangling persisted, he lifted the receiver, then said brusquely, "Cardigan Corporation."

"One moment, sir," a distant feminine voice replied. "Is this Mr. Mark Cardigan? Washington, D.C., is calling, sir."

There was a short delay, and then a man's deep, anxious voice came through the receiver.

"Mark? Well howdy, old son."

"Lane . . . Lane Torgny," Mark said louder than was necessary. "Where are you?"

"Right now in a private office in the National Forest Service headquarters. Mark, are you alone? Can we talk private?"

Mark turned to the salesman. "It's a long-distance call—sort of private." The man smiled understandingly and passed through the outer door, closing it behind him. "Now, Lane," he said into the telephone transmitter. "We're alone."

"Mark," the forest supervisor's voice sounded urgent, "how well has Joe Edmundson been keeping up on those weekly production estimates on his canal?"

"We never let him get more than a week behind. There's been no problem yet."

"How much would you estimate Edmundson owes you right now?"

Mark made fast mental calculations. "Not over twenty-one . . . twenty-two . . . hundred dollars."

"Fine," Torgny replied quickly. "Is there any way you can get every cent tomorrow?"

"Maybe. But for God's sake, Lane, why?"

"Because it's being whispered here in Washington tonight that Joe Edmundson's trans-mountain diversion project is in big trouble. The Supreme Court will render a decision tomorrow. I have it on damn good authority that the decision will adjudicate enough of the flow of the Laramie River to Wyoming and to Nebraska to leave the diversion canal high and dry. A hell of a big project with no source of water."

"Oh Christ," Mark Cardigan murmured, and his thoughts at the moment were not of his outstanding money, but of the horror of defeat facing Joe Edmundson, and all he had promised owners of Crow Creek Valley, to whom the canal project had become a symbol of a better life—a tomorrow free of almost yearly drought. "Lane, thanks for calling," he said. "Are you stationed there in Washington now?"

"No, and thank God for that. There's been one of those periodic Forest Service reorganizations. It may land me in Idaho, possibly to supervise the Sawtooth National Forest."

"Call me tomorrow night, Lane; I'll be at the ranch up on Crow Creek."

"I don't think I should, Mark," Torgny said reluctantly. "I'm not supposed to know any of this, and you'd be surprised how telephones back here sprout ears. But let's keep in touch, old son . . . and good luck."

The next issue of the *Denver Post* was delivered to the Hawk Bend office by a sober Sam Hook. Earlier in the day, Mark had pulled every man off the canal job and had prepared the equipment for an indefinite shutdown. And now his employees had clustered into the office. Dolores was white-faced and quiet.

Mark unfolded the newspaper, and the banner headline, printed in bold red type, jumped out at him.

HIGH COURT DECISION
STEALS COLORADO WATER
Joe Edmundson, canal promoter, dies a suicide

There were columns and pictures, describing the trans-mountain diversion project and its various phases. This was followed by several paragraphs detailing the long court fight that had culminated in the agricultural areas of eastern Wyoming, and western Nebraska receiving title to the major portion of the Laramie River's flow. The paper also ran a photograph of Joe Edmundson, and described him as a farsighted thinker of vast drive and vision and purpose. The news dispatch related that within hours after hearing the Supreme Court decision, Edmundson had shot himself in the Willard Hotel.

Mark knew that now he must quickly put a final stop to all work on the canal. Men and equipment must be moved immediately to the highway project east of Denver. And now a decision would have to be speedily made as to the best spot for a new Cardigan Corporation office; this he would talk over with both Gilberto and Dolores.

He drove to the job site and called Sam Hook, Halfdan and Fartein Nordraak, and half a dozen teamsters and laborers about him, to discuss the crushing news. Then he said, "I wish Gilberto Montez were here; sometimes, when I seem at wits' end, his calm assessment of things seems to indicate the correct way."

"You've got others who want to help," Fartein Nordraak said reassuringly.

"You bet I have." Mark smiled his appreciation. "Much as we all hate to leave a job unfinished, it has to be done. But this isn't going to kill off the Cardigan Corporation. Not by a long shot. We've got a good, solid highway contract to get going on. I've got a job for every one of you that wants to help me tie into that roadbuilding."

"Son, I hope you can use this here Marion dragline down there," Sam Hook observed. "I've got real fond of it."

"Just don't give your heart to that lump of iron and cable," Mark said, grinning. Then he said confidently, "We're going to build that stretch of highway with some new tools, at least new for us—a rock crusher and a roadmix spreader plant for maxing macadamized paving." Even as he uttered his brave, determined words, Mark was wondering just where he would find the money to pay for all that.

Then Sam Hook asked, "You mean a rig like we worked on at Fullerton? Splashing hot road oil onto the rock and tumbling it in a mixer?"

"Not quite, Sam. That was an experimental hot-mix plant, somewhat ahead of its time. Just now, according to the bid invitations, we'll be dealing with a process where the aggregate is spread on compacted road surface, and then a machine, called a spreader, sprays road oil to be mixed in."

"Depend on those road engineers down in Denver to do things the hard way," Hook growled.

"Okay, Sam, I have an idea we can show the highway engineers the benefits and lower cost of a hot mix operation."

By the time he left the job site, in late afternoon, preparations were already underway for a transfer of activities to the Denver area. He drove back toward Hawk Bend immersed in thought, and his mood bordered on melancholy. To what a great extent, Mark mused, was the fate of most people governed by the desires, the whims, and the greed of others. All but two of the canal employees had expressed their desire to continue with the Cardigan Corporation. Upon his ability and his judgments would rest the financial stability of those who were choosing to follow and to place their trust in him.

So too had the people of a large area of northern Colorado placed their trust in Joe Edmundson. Bonds had been issued, money borrowed, and rights-of-way granted for the trans-mountain diversion project. And now the decision of nine elderly men in the nation's capital, none of whom had ever seen a single mile of Joe Edmundson's hope and dream, had sent it crashing into oblivion. Edmundson had been neither a fool nor a crook, Mark thought; rather, he had been an energetic, forward-looking innovator, who had wished to bring water and verdancy and hope to a semi-arid section of the High Plains.

Mark gritted his teeth, remembering that two days hence Joe Edmundson would be buried from a small Episcopal chapel in Denver. "I'm going to attend his services," Mark said aloud. "I guess I am his sort. My wanting to build the biggest project on earth. But God help the man who ever brings one dollar to the coffers of the Cardigan Corporation if he gets it by laying a bad yard of asphalt, length of bridge timber, or bucket of concrete. When we do it, it'll be done right."

Work got underway on the state highway project just ten days later, beginning with a clearing of brush and an old barbed-wire fence line from the right-of-way. Toward midmorning, Mark left the work in charge of the Nordraak brothers and sought out Sam Hook, who was applying thick grease to the rollers by which his dragline crawled along. Mark opened the door of the small secondhand pickup truck he was using. "Climb in here, Sam," he invited. "I'm heading for the office shack."

Sam Hook sniffed disdainfully. "You just ain't gonna put me to pushing no pencil, kid."

"Of course not. But you're going to look over some equipment catalogs and price lists with me. Maybe later today we can visit a dealer or two and wheedle for bedrock prices."

"You got that kind of money all ready?" Hook demanded.

"Who needs money nowadays?" Mark grinned. "Hasn't President Hoover said we're just a bit slow on the glory road? Seriously, Sam, I need some solid figures to back me up when I face a certain Silas Latham." Even as he spoke, his inner sense told him that he was facing a gamble . . . one goddam big, beautiful, risky gamble.

They arrived at the shack and noted with interest that a shiny new Buick coupe was parked close to the door with a man seated in the driver's seat. He was middle-aged, heavily built, and looked a bit impatient.

Mark drew the pickup to a stop and gazed at the stranger. "Hello, sir. I hope you haven't had a long wait."

"I tried earlier to contact you by telephone. Don't you have an office clerk?"

Something hostile in the stranger's clipped words rankled Mark, but he remained pleasant. "We've a phone, but don't receive too many calls yet." The man had climbed from his car, so Mark extended his hand. "I'm Mark Cardigan, and this is Sam Hook. Now, what can we do for you?"

The newcomer flipped ashes from a cigar and stared intently at both Mark and Sam. His eyes were unsmiling and protruded slightly. The lids drooped to mask cold pupils. Inexplicably, at that moment, Mark remembered an incident of his boyhood . . . a moment when he had gazed into the dead stare of a prairie badger he had shot near his mother's chicken coop.

They had entered the field office and were seated before the stranger offered his hand or his name. "I'm Charley Lenholtz. Maybe you've heard of me. Came by to get acquainted, seeing as how we'll be doing business together."

Mark's reply was guarded, and he was aware of Sam

Hook's shoe touching his leg in warning beneath the desk. "We're always agreeable to meeting construction people," he said sociably.

"Then we can get down to business, Cardigan. I own the Lenholtz Sand and Gravel Company. We'll be furnishing your aggregate for this job. To save time, I've brought a subcontract form with me. It's filled in with our going prices. A deal you can't beat."

Mark accepted the forms and laid them face down on his desk. "We'll go over the figures and possibly be in touch with you, Mr. Lenholtz. I appreciate your stopping by."

Lenholtz nodded and attempted to sound genial. "I understand this is your first sizable highway job. It sort of took the boys by surprise . . . the way you sneaked in and got the award. We figured this job was set to go to—"

Mark's eyes flashed, and his voice hardened. "Mr. Lenholtz, I don't think 'sneak in' is exactly the right phrase. The bidding was competitive, and we happened to make the most reasonable bid."

Lenholtz waved his cigar, seeming unaware of the ashes it was strewing on Mark's desk. "Everyone has some way of breaking in, of getting their feet wet. We'll help you learn the ropes, Cardigan. You'll need to get wised up." He rose from the chair. "Just call on Lenholtz Sand and Gravel, day or night. I'll expect the subcontract in a day or so, after you've signed it."

Mark would have put the man in his place, but he caught the admonition in Sam Hook's eyes. "I'm sure we will meet new challenges and need some expert advice," he said a bit flatly. "But thanks for dropping by, Mr. Lenholtz."

The owner of Lenholtz Sand and Gravel Company strode toward his car. And he muttered to himself, "You're damn right you'll hear from me—and from the boys—you young whippersnapper!"

When the Buick had left, sending up dust plumes in its wake, Sam Hook flipped the subcontract face up and for several moments studied the unit prices. "Jesus Christ, Mark," he breathed. "Get ready to buy your own crusher—or risk losing a bundle on this here job."

Within an hour, Mark had summoned both Halfdan and Fartein Nordraak to the office, and he and Hook filled them in on the details of their visitor from the gravel company. Halfdan nodded and said, "I've sort of been expecting something like this. A couple of our new-hires, men who have worked on jobs around Denver for a long time, have been talking of how unusual it is for a firm from up north of Greeley, and an unknown one at that, to underbid a group of Denver road and street builders."

Fartein added pointedly, "Mark, you told me a few weeks ago that you and your dad had optioned some gravel pits and a likely rock deposit. Where are they? Close enough that we can afford to stockpile and haul our own aggregate?"

Mark dug out a worn, penciled map of Colorado, then one of Adams County, where the job would be located. All four men studied it, and finally Sam Hook said, "It looks as though the rock ledge is our best bet. It will mean a haul of about ten miles, but the gravel pits are too far down the Platte River, too far north."

Mark took a deep breath. "I wish we had Gilberto here with us. Yes, and Dolores too."

Sam Hook grinned agreement. "That Mexican section foreman must have been one hotshot road-building expert before they chased him across the border." He paused and went on, "And that pretty gal of Gilberto's could get cost estimates for the crushing operation, while Mark and I are taking wild guesses."

"Sam is right," Mark agreed. "Right now what I need—" His words broke abruptly as he heard a light but insistent rap on the outer door of the office shack. He moved to open it, and then all four men rose to their feet.

A young woman, perhaps four inches above five feet tall, was standing there, slimly erect in a somber black dress and a tan jacket. She was wearing a small, chic felt hat, tipped slightly to the side. It revealed her carefully combed, burnished hair, hair that just now caught the glint of the setting sun. But it was this woman's eyes, set in her pale, determined face, that caused Mark to remain speechless for a moment. They were deep-blue eyes, serene eyes, yet masking some overpowering grief.

"Do you happen to be Mark Cardigan?" she asked, in a pleasant, subdued voice.

"Yes, I am. Won't you come in, please?"

Her eyes moved about the group of four men, seeming to gather assurance from their faces. Then she thrust out a slim but firm hand. "Mr. Cardigan, you don't know me . . . but I often heard my father speak highly of you. My

366

father, Joe Edmundson, died several days ago. You were working on a canal for him, were you not?"

In utter amazement, Mark nodded, then moved his own chair toward her. "Won't you sit down, Miss Edmundson?"

The Nordraak brothers and Sam Hook moved toward the door, but this intense young woman motioned for them to stay. "I don't want to interrupt your meeting; what I have to say will take only a few moments." The men stood paralyzed, as though she had cast some sort of spell. Then she continued. "I have a certified check for you, Mr. Cardigan—or rather for the Cardigan Corporation. It is for twenty-two hundred dollars. I believe that is close to your estimate for the work done during the week before . . . before . . ." Her voice broke in a sob and she passed the check to Mark with a trembling hand.

He looked at it in stunned amazement. The first thought that came to him was that this unexpected sum would enable him to finish repaying the Plains National Bank. The Marion dragline would be free of encumbrance. But within seconds the thought vanished, as he looked into their visitor's troubled face. She must have made some personal sacrifice to do this. It couldn't be funds from bond-issue money. The courts had doubtless taken action that would preclude such distribution of bond funds. "Miss Edmundson," he said slowly, "you are paying this out of your own money, perhaps from insurance or a savings account, aren't you?"

Her eyes, now seeming more gray than blue, lifted determinedly to Mark's face. "Does it matter, Mr. Cardigan? I am Joe Edmundson's daughter. I am here to pay off a family obligation."

Mark turned, seeking guidance from the faces of Sam Hook and the Nordraak brothers. Something in them sustained him and impelled his thoughts and his hand. He placed the check back in her hand. "Keep this. Please do. You owe us nothing."

For moments her face crumpled, and she attempted to hide it behind a shaking hand. "Thank God," she murmured, "there are those who still care . . . men who are not utterly possessed by greed." Her eyes swept the table, noting the papers and catalogs which the men had been riffling through before her coming.

"I used to help my father with the business. It was such fun then—selecting supplies and equipment. And how we used to try to squeeze dollars. Deal. Dicker. Demand discounts."

Halfdan spoke up. "Then I wish you had more time. This purchasing is all new to us, and we're likely not to be blessed with beginner's luck."

"Could you stay? Could you take time to help us get some rough figures together for a crusher and a road-mix plant?" Mark asked.

For the first time, despair seemed to leave her face. Presently she smiled, and said firmly, "I will do it, gentlemen—on one condition."

"And that?" Mark asked.

"That you accept this cashier's check."

"And we'll do that—but also on one condition."

"And that is?" she repeated him.

"Upon condition that this twenty-two hundred dollars is in payment for a hundred shares of Cardigan Corporation stock, and that you accept a temporary receipt right now. And my name is Mark, not Mr. Cardigan."

She nodded agreement. "I've a feeling my father would have been excited about you—about all this. God bless each of you." She reached for a catalog. "Let's drive some dealers crazy." She smiled. "And by the way, my name is Lois."

Two days later, Mark was again seated in the railed-off section of the Plains National Bank. After the usual pleasantries had been exchanged, the banker quickly scanned a file labeled "Cardigan Corporation." Then he studied Mark in a shrewd and contemplative way. "Let's see, Mark. You've been right on time, and frequently ahead of time, on the dragline payments. A little over two thousand dollars will clear you with us." He pondered a moment, then added, "You were wise in making sure of weekly estimate payments on the canal job. Joe Edmundson's suicide is going to put a lot of plains-area people in a bind—and add to the hopelessness of those who expected water."

"Sir," Mark answered, "I agree that Joe Edmundson's taking his own life was no way to solve the bond holders' problems. I can't say he was justified. But as I see it, the damnable folly was that of the Supreme Court. Nine blind

368

old men giving Colorado's rightful share of the Laramie River's flow to downriver states."

The banker had listened with rapt attention. Now he asked, "Mark, did you know Joe Edmundson?"

"Not well, Mr. Latham. I met him only two times, briefly. But I have reasons for my convictions. I'm here to finish paying our corporation's loan for the dragline. And do you know where the money came from? It was given to me by Lois Edmundson, Joe Edmundson's daughter. She insisted on doing it. Said it was a family obligation, to make the final week's payment in full. Perhaps you should know that her payment was unexpected, coming, I believe, from her own savings."

Silas Latham nodded in admiration of the act, then said, "It's that money that is enabling you to pay off this bank completely, I presume."

Mark handed the cashier's check to Latham. "Here it is, and I'll endorse it to your bank."

Latham reached over to grasp Mark's hand. "I've come to believe, son, that somehow you're going to make it, do well in a tough, competitive business."

Mark grinned broadly, then chuckled. "I'm glad you said that, Mr. Latham. For right now the Cardigan Corporation wants to borrow sixty thousand dollars."

"For what, Mark?" Again there was the note of executive caution in his voice.

"You probably know by now that we have landed a nine-mile stretch of state highway to grade and surface. It's just east of Denver. Our bid price was slightly above two hundred and thirty-eight thousand dollars. We're getting moved in and set up right now—and we need money to get hold of a rock crusher and a plant for mixing oil-surfacing materials. Also, a couple of graders, and enough to rent some dump trucks."

Latham tapped a pencil on the desk. "Mark, I am disturbed by the economic news coming out of Washington and New York these days. For several years, we've been riding a surge of seemingly great prosperity. But right now, the rest of 1929 looks uncertain. I've a feeling that our financial condition, as a nation, isn't really healthy. Overpriced stocks. Runaway consumer spending."

"But we have a State Highway Department contract, sir. Backed by the resources and the integrity of the state of

Colorado. Do you foresee we might have difficulty in getting paid?"

"No. Of course not. Such funds must be on hand and earmarked before a state contract can be awarded," Latham admitted. "And I believe your corporation might be wise to confine its work largely to such public projects, where the counties, states, and the federal government will be legally and morally bound to pay in full." Latham heaved a sigh, shrugged and added, "Perhaps I'm just getting old, Mark. Too cautious. Too suspicious."

"And maybe I'm just getting too big for my britches. Trying to become a renowned worldwide builder when I ought to be branding calves out at Dad's ranch."

"God forbid," Latham laughed. "Right away you'd be back three-hundred-dollaring the life out of me."

After a pensive half-minute, Silas Latham spoke firmly and decisively. "The bank can loan you sixty thousand dollars, Mark. We'll need some security, of course. You can pledge your dragline, now that it is clear. And we may ask for a second mortgage on the new equipment. Does that sound agreeable?"

Mark nodded, then offered another thought. "We can arrange to have the Highway Department make its estimate payments to us payable to this bank, Mr. Latham."

"That won't be necessary. Son, banking is a matter of mutual trust—and you've always been pretty trustworthy."

Mark could not resist having the last word, for once. "How do you know I'm not going to sixty-thousand you to death?"

Latham rose to his feet. "Because, Cardigan, if you keep your brains level, and your nose clean, one of these days the Cardigan Corporation's operating needs are going to exceed the lending capacity of Plains National Bank. Glory to God, I'll be shet of you."

"I don't think so," Mark challenged.

"Why?"

"Because right now I'm going to sell you ten qualifying shares of Cardigan Corporation. You can do your fretting as one of our corporate directors."

The banker's response was a controlled gasp. And then his voice sounded loud and strident, but triumphant too, throughout the bank. "Christ almighty," he howled. "Cardigan, how you do milk a situation!"

Feeling totally elated, Mark left Greeley and drove the dusty road to Hawk Bend. He would have stopped to discuss the Denver road project with Gilberto Montez, but could not find him anywhere along the railroad. Undoubtedly he had taken his crew to help on some section down the line.

He entered the canal construction office, to find Dolores packing ledgers and office supplies into cardboard boxes. She was wearing a gray skirt and a rumpled red blouse. She turned when he came in, and he noticed the dust smudges on her forearms and across her lip.

"I like you in a mustache," he quipped.

"Ha! for once Cardigan takes notice of his poor peon."

His arm went around her, but there was a preoccupied remoteness that forestalled his intended kiss.

His momentary awareness of her gave way as he exclaimed, "Dolores, you see that this is the big break for the Cardigan Corporation. We're going to have our hot-mix plant." There was no reply, as she turned to gather more office supplies, but her eyes were baffled.

"Just where are you planning to take all this stuff?" he inquired.

"Home to my *casa*. Mark, we mustn't spend money anymore for office rent." She leaned with both hands on a table, stared at him, and demanded, "Why aren't you at work in Denver, boss man?"

He told her of his visit to the bank, and its successful outcome. "Now, Dolores, I need to get a lot of advice from your father."

"Not today. He is in Denver. Some time ago, there was a section-boss job came open at a place called Henderson. Papa bid the job in; we'll be moving there."

"Great!" Mark beamed. "Henderson isn't twenty miles from our job."

She was quiet for a long time, then looked into his face with somber intensity. "Perhaps it is not so good. You and me. Close together."

"Dolores," he began haltingly, "about what happened that night at the cottonwood . . ."

Quickly she placed a silencing finger on his lips. "It is something that is past, Mark, with no need for guilt."

371

"But dammit," he almost shouted, "Dolores, are you too blind to know I'm in love with you?"

"Mark," she answered, "we have much to learn about love. About ourselves. About living. Now . . . will you help me load these boxes into my truck?"

"Sure we'll load them, Dolores—in my car. For me to haul to our Denver office. I'll expect you there ready for work, the day after Gilberto gets you moved to Henderson. There's so much . . ." He paused, noting the possible refusal building within her. "Forget I need you, if you want it that way, Dolores. But remember this: the Cardigan Corporation needs you, and a lot of our employees are asking when that adding-machine señorita is going to show up for work."

She remained quiet, but Mark's deepest instincts told him that his persuasion had worked.

372

Chapter 33

Immediate delivery could not often be secured on pieces of heavy equipment such as draglines, rock crushers, and asphalt plants in those busy days of 1929. Sometimes delays of six months occurred before the factories could fill an order. It was therefore surprising to Mark that a Denver dealer happened to have a new rock crusher in its lot that could be delivered to the job site immediately.

When he questioned the salesman, he was told the crusher had been ordered for a firm that had decided to get out of the aggregate business at the last minute. When asked bluntly how this had come about, the salesman became evasive. "I'm just here to demonstrate and sell them," the salesman answered tersely. "Our manager handles the ordering."

"Then I think I'd like to talk to your manager," Mark bristled.

The manager, sensing Mark's irritation and the possible loss of a cash sale, was more vocal, but still reticent, shaking his head anxiously. "These cancellations for heavy equipment have been causing us trouble for two years now. Some firms are dropping out of the heavy-construction business, and others, who used to do lots of work around the Denver area, are inclined to go after work over on the Western Slope, or even out of state."

"But there have been quite a few substantial contracts awarded by the Colorado Highway Department. Why would the contractors shy away from the jobs?"

The manager pursed his lips, studied Mark's face, then said, "You're new to the business hereabouts, aren't you, Cardigan?"

"Yes, we are. In fact, we're getting this crusher for our first job."

373

"I see. And have you had a call from Amos Shinn, the business agent for the local contractors' group?"

"Not yet. Just one fellow dropped by, named Lenholtz. Pretty determined to sell us aggregate."

"I take it you didn't sign with him," the manager answered.

"We didn't—and we won't. His prices would have put us in a bind before we got started. So, we're buying a crusher."

"Cardigan, I can guarantee you two things. This crusher carries a full warranty. But you are going to have a visit from Amos Shinn of the contractors' group. Surer 'n hell you are."

Facts were fitting into place in Mark's mind, and he asked, "Those companies that are dropping out . . . quitting the business. Did they have visits from Mr. Lenholtz and then from Mr. Shinn just before calling it quits?"

The manager's face paled slightly, and he spoke in a much lower tone. "Mr. Cardigan, we're in business to sell machinery. Good machinery at competitive prices. And . . . and as a favor, please forget what has been said about the contractors' group."

"You mean forget the boys, don't you?" Mark shot back.

The remark provoked utter silence. Mark wrote out his check for the crusher and left the dealer's lot.

When Mark reached the job site the following morning, he bypassed the office and drove the entire nine-mile length of the project. He noted with satisfaction the progress of land clearing, and the demolition of old fences and a couple of abandoned farm buildings. Both Halfdan and Fartein Nordraak came to talk over details of the work ahead. Mark listened, made a couple of suggestions, and then told them, "Seems to me you're getting along ahead of schedule. Get grade stakes surveyed and set, so we can get graders to roughing out the roadbed course. Likely you'll need a bulldozer—one of those tractor-mounted ones—for some cut and fill. Just rent one, with an operator if necessary."

He stooped, picked up a handful of sandy loam, and let it sift through his fingers. "This stuff will handle well, and I don't think you'll encounter much rock problem here on the grading segment. Now. I am going to get hold of

Sam Hook. We've a rock crusher to be delivered to that outcropping that my dad got hold of a few miles north. We will try to have it crushing and screening our aggregate late this week."

"What are your plans for getting the aggregate down here and distributing it?" Fartein queried.

"We'll rent trucks for the haul. Four or five ought to handle it. If you hear of anyone looking for such a haul, have them see me. Otherwise, I know a chap up by Greeley who would likely be interested. Any questions?"

They shook their heads, and Mark peered along the right-of-way, thinking, as always, of the next problem once he had taken care of the previous one. "I wonder where in thunder Sam Hook is?"

Halfdan laughed. "He hasn't been here for fifteen minutes. Come by and said he had to hurry to your office. To unlock it for one pretty bookkeeper señorita."

"Dolores is here?"

"Who else," Halfdan chided gently, "would meet old Hook's glowing description?"

Dolores was already working on the project cost estimates when he arrived at the office.

"Howdy, honey," he greeted her. "Am I ever glad you decided to show up. This concern needs a pencil wizard."

She smiled slightly, perilously close to tears, then swept scornful eyes about the clutter of the office. "And like always you need a cleaning woman. What a mess you big, important road builders can make of an office."

"It's the dirt moving outside that concerns me," he said. "And where in tarnation is Sam Hook?"

"Señor Hook," she answered, "is down at your little machine-parts shed, making a proper blueprint rack for me."

"For now, my dear, toss the prints in a corner. I'm taking Hook to set up a rock crusher and get it grinding along."

"Oh! Sure . . . sure. More machinery, more piles of rock. And for Dolores, paperwork up to her . . ." She turned with disdain to the dust-coated box holding more ledgers. But as Mark strode toward the door, the corner of his eye caught the secretive toss of a kiss toward him.

He had not taken half a dozen steps from the office when the jangle of the telephone stopped him. Dolores picked it up. ."Mark . . . wait. It is for you. A man. Wouldn't say who he was."

He reentered the office and picked up the instrument. "Hello. Yes, this is Mark Cardigan."

"Cardigan," a voice boomed back, "how goes the job?"

"I'll know better in a week," Mark answered. "Who is this?"

"This is Charley Lenholtz, Mark. Remember? Lenholtz Sand and Gravel. We haven't received our subcontract back from you."

"I haven't mailed it."

Lenholtz made no attempt to mask his irritation. "No sweat, boy; I'll drop by today and pick it up."

"If you want the unsigned copy, come ahead."

The voice coming back through the receiver shed the facade of friendliness. "What's the matter, Cardigan? We're set up to start your deliveries."

"Then hold them," Mark barked. "Cardigan Corporation has no intention of paying your prices—or of doing business with you."

"You're going to be in a bind, Cardigan. Who in hell has underbid us?"

Mark's voice was steely. "Mr. Lenholtz, I said *no go* on our buying at your figures. And what other arrangements we make is strictly our business. We will mail the unsigned contract back to you today."

Lenholtz yelled savagely, "Kid, you've got a lot to learn. This ain't the end of it—not by a damn sight!" His slam of the receiver cracked loudly in Mark's ear.

The next three weeks were among the busiest of Mark's life. The rock thrusting from a low gully wall proved suitable to crushing, and daily production soon soared. Upon Sam Hook's recommendation, more men were hired for the crusher operation, and it was put on a two-shift basis. There were no local trucks available to undertake the haul of aggregate, but Halfdan made suitable arrangements with a small Colorado Springs firm that had experienced drivers and good serviceable trucks.

The roadway grading was under way, on an alignment preset by the Highway Department specifications. For a time Mark found himself shuttling back and forth between the crusher and the grading and compaction work, with intermittent visits to the office to telephone various vendors for needed supplies. He would also frequent the new section-house residence of Gilberto Montez, at the hamlet of Henderson. Together they would study the Highway Department's plans and specifications for additional jobs.

"Mark, I think that for the present time, at least, we should keep away from contracts that call for work in the mountains. It calls for much blasting, and special rock-handling machines, and we would be on unfamiliar ground in estimating costs."

Mark nodded agreement, saying, "I worked on a Forest Service road in the mountains a couple of years ago—I'm not totally unfamiliar with the procedures. But we should at least begin to look toward mountain-road work. There's bound to be a lot of it throughout the state." He paused, then added, "When we're through here, Gilberto, and land a half-million-dollar job, I want you with us full time."

"Perhaps the time will come, Mark. Do not be impatient. It is wise that I protect my railroad pension yet."

Even before placing the bid which won the nine miles of roadwork for the Cardigan Corporation, Mark had satisfied himself that the newer method of mixing asphaltic paving oil with rock or gravel would be acceptable to the Highway Department. The experimental plant near Fullerton, California, where Mark and Sam Hook had worked had improved methods considerably. By use of oil-fueled heating units, the asphaltic paving oil could be heated, and then piped to a tumbling mixing unit mounted on a tower. The aggregate, sifting down through predetermined screens, would then blend with the oil. The hot mix could be trucked and spread to provide a more satisfactory layer of paving. For heavier-traffic areas, double layers could be applied and then rolled firm.

The lowest price quoted for such a ready-mix plant was that of a firm near Stockton, California. Immediate shipment could be made, and a mechanic sent to aid in proper installation. A deal was made, and suitable concrete footings prepared. Bulk tanks, each with a capacity of several thousand gallons, were set to hold and supply fuel oil and asphaltic road oil. Meanwhile, a nearby pile of crushed rock aggregate was trucked in from Sam Hook's quarry operation.

The first day of experimental plant operation proved a

fiasco, and heralded disaster. When the crushed rock was carried up a conveyor and dropped onto a screen where it was to be reduced, the system broke down. The rock built into a dangerously heavy pile atop the screen and would not filter down. Sam Hook was the first to notice what was happening. "Stop that blasted conveyor!" he yelled. "That rock's gonna start spilling onto some heads down below—or topple the whole contraption."

Mark heard, and shut off the power to the conveyor. "What do you suppose we've done wrong?" he demanded.

Hook scratched his head. "Maybe the gears aren't meshing right to operate the screen shaker. I'll get down close and have a look." He descended to the screen and waved a hand. "Start her up easy-like." Then in a moment he called out, "Shut 'er off, Mark. It ain't the shakers. Them screens are shuttling back and forth just like they're supposed to."

Men with shovels climbed up and removed the aggregate from the overburdened screens. The conveyor was disconnected, and the screen rockers again put into motion. Yet only dust and a shower of pebbles sifted through.

"Are you sure we've put in the right screen for the rock of specified diameter?" Mark asked.

Hook studied a grease-smudged operations manual and said testily, "That square screen mesh is just what's called for. Specified diameter. Damned if I understand the balky bitch, Mark."

They worked until the sun had set, but found no solution. The rock crushed and initially sized at the crusher would not pass through the control screen. And it would have to do so to meet Highway Department specifications.

At last, feeling totally defeated, Mark strode to the rock stockpile. "I just don't know, Sam." He picked up a handful of the rock fragments, stared harshly at them, and dropped them in his pocket. "Maybe it's something in the crusher's pressure. The shattering." He clenched his fist, then chided himself. "Wise boy Cardigan, always thinking he knows all answers. Here we are set with maybe ten thousand tons or so of rock that may be useless. Waste stuff. Won't that guy Lenholtz laugh his guts out?"

Sam Hook stared soberly at him. "Maybe an assayer or a geologist can explain it, son. I'll have another go at trying to coax the stuff through the screen tomorrow. Why don't you drive up to the School of Mines at Golden and ask some professors to run tests on some pieces of obstinate rock?"

When they stopped at the office, Dolores was still working.

"You should have gone home an hour ago," Mark scolded.

"Why? Does it matter? There are letters for you, and some checks you must sign."

When they had finished the day's batch of paperwork, darkness lay across the city. Mark stared at distant corridors of street lights and abruptly asked, "Know what we're going to do . . . you and Sam and me? We're going to a restaurant that has good steaks and a booze cellar. We're going to forget the crusher. Forget that miserable screen. Sam, I'll buy you three fingers of the best bootleg bourbon; then I'll have the same myself—as a starter."

He slammed Dolores' ledger shut and caught her arm, lifting her from her chair. "I've an idea, Mexicali Baby, we may even find a sip or two of tequila for you. Get your coat, and we'll lock up."

She stared at him excitedly. "You mean we go like this?" she demanded. "To a fancy restaurant? In work clothes?"

"What's wrong with my duds?" he snapped. "They're just right for the young corporation president—who may be flat broke tomorrow."

"Caramba." She laughed. "How come one setback has brought you to such craziness? Made of you a *loco* fool?"

An hour later they arrived at a lovely house with a wide veranda discreetly screened by elms and pines. They were given careful scrutiny by two husky, no-monkey-business individuals at the door, but inside they were courteously ushered across deep carpets into a room where flames from a stone fireplace reflected in the mirror of an old and highly polished bar. There were tables aglow with white linens and spotless crystal; theirs was somewhat secluded, but close enough to the fireplace for light and shadow to play across their faces. The glow of many candles enhanced the atmosphere. The service proved flawless, the food excellent, and the liquor assuredly from bonded bottles.

There was music and a small dance floor, and down a hallway was a room from which came the low chant of a croupier calling out the fall and fortunes of dice.

Despite the wonderful surroundings, they ate in almost total silence, nor did the liquor lift the pall of anxiety and disappointment from either man.

After the meal, they moved to a fireside couch and watched sparks swirl upward from a new log. Dolores could offer little encouragement about their problem and sat with her chin cupped disconsolately in her palm.

Presently Mark stirred, reaching into his pocket. His fingers grasped the stone fragments he had taken from the stockpile. He peered angrily at one piece, then tossed it toward the hearth of the fireplace. It fell short of the hearth by a few inches, but landed on a cleverly designed cold-air vent topped by a grating and level with the floor. He did not bother to take aim as he flung a couple more of the rock chips.

Sam Hook sat up abruptly on the couch. "Do that again," he said excitedly.

"Do what?" Mark demanded.

"Toss a couple more of them rock fragments onto that air vent—onto the metal grill."

"You think you can pitch 'em better?"

"Shut up . . . and just fling 'em," Hook exclaimed.

Irritated by Hook's tone, Mark dug into his pocket and came up with some more bits of rock. Then with a careless air he tossed them. They spun upward, fell to the mesh-work of the grille—and disappeared.

"They went through," Mark pointed out with growing interest.

"Of course they went through. Damned if they didn't—every one. Mark, have you got a pocket ruler?"

Mark shook his head, but Dolores, her eyes again excited, dug into her purse and handed Hook a six-inch steel ruler.

The old mechanic bent over the grate and measured both the width and the length of an individual opening in the mesh grating. "It figures, Mark. By God, it figures. These dimensions are almost exactly the same as the mesh of our balky, no-shake-through screen. But you know what? These holes are six-sided—hexagonal."

In his excitement, Hook took Mark's remaining chips from him and one by one dropped them onto the cold-air grating. A few clanged sharply, then bounced, but all fell through.

380

They stood entranced and smiling, unaware that others had gathered about them. Presently a middle-aged man in a tuxedo pushed forward angrily. "Just what do you think you're doing, dropping rocks into the cooling system? If it's some fool game or if you're making bets, just remember our repairs may cost you fifty bucks."

For once, Sam Hook spoke up quicker than his young boss. "For damn sure," he told the irate manager, "we'll pay the fifty dollars—and, by Gadfrey, make maybe fifty thousand!" He turned to Mark. "Let's go take Dolores home. Then you and me are gonna be up maybe all night laying out a drawing for a new plant screen—with hexagonal openings. My Lord o' Hosts, how them extra corners can handle your aggregate!"

The next day Mark and Sam were waiting at a Denver iron-fabricating plant when it opened. They found the foreman, showed him a scale drawing of the screen they needed with hexagonal mesh. They had brought with them a burlap sack of the stockpiled aggregate. It was early afternoon before the screen could be fashioned and welded to match precisely the drawing made of the restaurant's cold air grating.

As soon as it was done, they dumped the sack of rock onto the screen; then they lifted it above the floor and, each standing at one end, vigorously shook the new screen. The rock sifted easily through the six-sided openings and clattered dustily to the room's cement floor.

"We've got it, Sam! It works like a charm!" Mark gloated.

Sam Hook turned to the shop foreman. "Make us up half a dozen of these screens just as fast as you can. We sure want to avoid downtime if one breaks or is damaged."

Mark muttered to himself, "Maybe the Cardigan Corporation isn't 'on the rocks' after all."

The time had come now to hire more men and work the project steadily toward completion. Save for two afternoon rain showers, the weather held; within ten weeks, Project 0198-A was nearly finished. All nine miles of sub-base had been graded, leveled, and compacted. The right-of-way fence was practically complete, and the two small culvert structures had been installed.

Finally, they met the greatest challenge of all: the application of the ready-mix asphaltic material which would then be rolled to a slightly convex, water-shedding hardness.

Mark had ordered only small quantities of boiler-heating and fuel oil for the trial plant run. He had procured the few barrels of fuel oil at a small bulk plant in north Denver. For the asphaltic road oil, the Highway Department specifications called for use of a somewhat different grade than that used in the conventional in-place spraying of aggregate already applied. Heating, penetrating, binding, and wearing qualities had been laboratory-tested in several states, and formulas provided to refineries. Such asphaltic tar was available at two Denver refineries. Mark chose to buy his initial supply at the plant of Roundtop Petroleum near Cheyenne, Wyoming. Using this supplier would mean a round trip of two hundred miles, but he was obliged to keep utilizing the permits issued by the Colorado Public Utilities Commission and the Wyoming Public Service Commission, granting the trucking rights he had bought from Sam Hook so long ago.

For this present job, the company lacked enough tankers to provide all asphaltic oil from Wyoming, but a dependable source was located locally.

The first two days of plant operation went smoothly. Minor problems were adjusted without delay, and the quality of paving materials being hauled in steaming loads from the mixing tower to be spread met the approval of the Highway Department's engineers and material checkers. Soon the first half mile of completed blacktop was in place. Only a seal coat, plus the passing of ever-increasing traffic, was needed to make of this stretch a wide avenue for cars and trucks. It would be quite a while before the second half mile of plant-mix paving would be placed.

On the third night of operation, Mark was awakened by a phone call from the night caretaker at the mix plant. The man was scarcely coherent, but he managed to stammer out that the plant was on fire. By morning it had burned to the ground. When the smoldering embers cooled enough to allow inspection, it was determined that no part of the plant equipment could be salvaged. At the hour when the blaze started, only the caretaker had been on duty, keeping the boilers fired so that pipelines would not cool and congeal. He was also there to sign for loads of fuel oil and asphaltic tar now coming by night from the refinery.

Firefighting units had been slow to reach the isolated plant, and the intense heat of the oil-consuming flames created the possibility of explosion. And, oddly, it was the tank holding less volatile asphaltic mixture that flashed, becoming a rapidly spreading inferno of flames.

It was near noon that day when Sam Hook bounded into the small office, from which a county fire investigator had just departed. "That's it," Hook roared. "That dumb son of a bitch of a night watchman. If he shows up, just let me know, Mark. I'll kick—"

"Whoa up, Sam," Mark said, and stared at his mechanic's agitated face. "Now . . . start over. Just what are you talking about?"

"I'm talking about a night man that doesn't know his butt from an alfalfa bale, not even a jackass turd from Pike's Peak."

Dolores had listened in a stricken way, staring out of the office window at the charred ruins. But now Hook's fury caused her to whirl about. *"Que trata usted de decir?"* she demanded.

Hook stared at her in utter incomprehension, then asked Mark, "Damned if I savvy that lingo. What's she saying, Mark?"

"She wants to know what you're driving at with all these wild accusations."

"What do you mean . . . wild? I tell you I know how it happened. That watchman got the hoses mixed; them that run from the tank truck to our storage tanks. That asphaltic road oil was pumped into the heating-oil tank. And that explosive heating oil was connected to the asphalt tanks. When heat was applied, the boiler fired up; under the heating oil it flashed—blew everything to hell and smithereens!" Hook paused, panting, then asked, "Where can I find that watchman?"

"Hold it. Just hold everything, Sam. I happen to know that our watchman didn't go near the unloading last night. He told me, this morning before he went home, that he was working in the shop shed all night sharpening tools. He said the trucker brought delivery tickets there for him to sign, then took off."

"But the watchman started firing up the boilers early this morning?"

"Sure, Sam, but that was hours after the truck had delivered oil and left."

"Then we'd better get ready to sue one refinery and their damned delivery driver," Hook snapped.

Mark was about to nod his agreement, when something struck him. The oblique and veiled threat Lenholtz had made. This, and the reluctance of the equipment dealer to discuss the falling off of the number of job bidders. The prediction that the Cardigan operation would be visited by someone named Amos Shinn. Yet Shinn had never put in an appearance on the job site.

His nebulous thoughts were interrupted by Dolores's hand on his shoulder. "Mark," she said in a worried tone, "does it mean we are finished? What . . . what you call *busted?*"

He grinned with more confidence than he felt. "Not by a long shot, honey. We've insurance, and . . ."

"But can we meet the contract's date for completion?" Hook muttered. "There's a daily penalty if we can't."

The urge for action, for continuing against all odds, swept Mark. "Have the men spend the day bulldozing the rubble from the plant site. Sam, see if you can find replacement fuel and asphalt tanks for immediate delivery. I'll get on the phone to California and find out when and how quick we can get a replacement mixing plant. And Dolores, you . . ." He paused, his eyes narrowing thoughtfully. "Sam, don't mention to a soul what you've told us about the switched hoses. Keep it mum even from our own men." His eyes again sought out Dolores. "And you, honey, the big job is yours. Go home. Dress up pretty. Then meet me in two hours at the Denver Dry Goods Store downtown."

"You are sick . . . crazy, Cardigan. I should call a doctor," she gasped.

"Just do as I ask!" he shouted. "The Denver. In two hours."

When she had cleared the door, with a bewildered shake of her head, Mark strode across the room, stared at the wreckage, then said, "Sam, I want a general meeting tonight at Gilberto Montez's section house if you can arrange it. If you can, then call my dad up at Hawk Bend and ask him to get down here for it if he can. And call Silas

Latham at the Plains National Bank, in Greeley. Tell him exactly what happened, but that we have insurance. Tell him I'd like him to attend the meeting. If he doesn't want to come, remind him he's a stockholder and director—and had better flag his chair-polished butt down this way."

He left Sam Hook open-mouthed and drove speedily into Denver. His first stop was at the State Highway Department headquarters, where he sought out the district engineer and came quickly to the point. "I'm Mark Cardigan, I head up the outfit that has the contract on Project 0198-A, east of town. You've probably heard by now that our plant-mix setup was totally destroyed last night."

"Yes, Cardigan, we've heard. It's a nasty blow, especially for a new firm. What do you have in mind now?"

"Several things, sir. But the most important is to have a duplicate plant in operation as soon as possible. I am not asking for any favors. Just wanted to tell you that the Cardigan Corporation will move hell and high water. We're going to have that new plant on the ground, set up, and ready to roll within two weeks."

"But if you can't?" The engineer's query was both sympathetic and doubtful.

"If we can't, you have my personal assurance that I will come here immediately and aid in every way in having our contract completed by another firm—with the Cardigan Corporation to assure liability for any additional cost to the state of Colorado."

The district engineer stood up and extended his hand. "Thanks for coming to talk to me, Cardigan. See what you can do, and keep us advised."

Dolores was waiting for him just inside the Sixteenth Street entrance of the Denver Dry Goods Company store.

"Mark, I never understand you," she greeted him. "How come we take time this morning to look at clothes?"

He appraised the neatness of her attire, the graceful curves accentuated by the blue street dress she had on. Then he went to the rack, glanced through it rapidly, and chose a low-cut cream-colored model with a tight straight skirt. "It should do . . . do very well . . . for a visit to a refinery. Now to find the right pocket watch."

She stepped back, eying him from about a yard's distance. "Contractor Cardigan, what in the name of Holy

Jesus are you talking about? A pocket watch—that I do not need."

His hand cautioned her to speak softly, and then he explained, "It isn't for you, Dolores. You're going to make an award to one of the refinery's truck drivers. For driving so extremely carefully through the streets where Mexicans live and their children play."

A gleam of understanding leapt into her eyes. "You want to know who he is, that one who misconnected the oil lines?" She hesitated, then asked, "How will I know him? There are so very many men working at a refinery."

"You won't know, Dolores. That is what we must find out. He is a tank-truck driver who makes local deliveries. And . . . and get this, Dolores. He is the one driver who would have had to load and carry extra lengths of fuel-discharge hose on his truck last night." His arm went tightly about her as he murmured, "It's best I send you out to the refinery by taxi cab, but be careful, very, very careful, darling."

Within half an hour they had found a suitable but not too expensive watch, had arranged for gift wrapping, and had enclosed a short commendation of an unknown truck driver for his concern for Mexican pedestrians written in both English and Spanish. Dolores went into the back and changed into her new dress. Before the cab bore her away, Mark leaned inside and touched his lips to hers. "I'm going out to the project office. Call me there, just as soon as you get back downtown. My God, how the hours are going to drag."

"But probably not for me," she chided, and then blew him a kiss that was half lost as she called, *"Hasta la vista."*

She phoned him three hours later, and the excited triumph of her voice lent instant assurance of her safety. "It has gone well, Mark. I am at a pharmacy near the Tabor Theatre."

"Wait right there," he yelled. He dropped the receiver onto its cradle and strode to his car.

They found a clean-looking restaurant within a block of the drugstore and sought out a secluded booth.

"Mark, here is the name of the man—and the place where he lives." She pushed a slip of folded paper toward him.

He did not immediately open it, but searched her face. "How did you manage it?" he breathed.

Her response was an excited peal of low laughter. Then she said, "It was almost too easy. There was a fence around the oil refinery. What a big and noisy and stinking place it is!" She wrinkled her nose. "The taxi let me off at a gate where there was a little shack. A man, maybe a guard, stared at me—mostly at my chest—then waved me ahead to go inside. The first building was offices, and I asked to see the general manager. Instead, a sour-faced old lady, with her hair made into . . . into a doorknob, came and asked what I wanted. I told her I was there to make an award to one of their workers." Dolores paused, savoring the recounting of her experience.

"What then?" Mark urged.

"They called someone they said was a public-relations man. He suggested that I just leave the award. I told him I was ordered to give it only in person. When he hesitated, Mark, I lifted my skirt about to here." She indicated a point slightly below her two shapely knees. "And you know, Mark, he smiled."

"I'll bet he did," Mark growled. "What other crazy thing did you do?"

"He wanted to know for whom the award had been made. I told him that it was for someone the Mexicans wanted to honor, but whose name was unknown, since he was but a truck driver. But one who drove frequently and, ah, so carefully through our crowded streets. He told me they had several delivery drivers and without a name he couldn't identify the man. But it was then I remembered what you said, Mark—about the extra hoses. I told him that several of the children had seen the careful driver only last night—with many hoses on his truck."

"Lord almighty," Mark chuckled in admiration.

"So then, Mark," she continued, "that personnel man made a phone call. I guess to the loading docks, or racks. He asked which driver had taken extra hoses last night." She pointed to the paper that lay between them on the table. "He scribbled the name there."

"That's incredible, Dolores. It really was simple."

"Not quite," she flashed back. "The refinery wants two or three citizens of the Mexican community to come to the refinery next Wednesday evening to make a formal presentation of the watch. They're keeping it in their safe until then. And, Mark, they promise to have your driver there to receive his reward."

"The hell they do!" Mark snapped, then read the name and address. "Ed Lukens. North Clay Street. Even the house number. That's our man." Mark glanced at the restaurant clock. "You're a jewel, sweetheart. I wish I could stay and buy you a sandwich and a jug of wine. But we've got to get back to the project, so I can gather up a couple of men. We'll be waiting for our Ed Lukens, right smack in front of his house, when he gets home this evening. Come on!"

"No," she replied, and shook her head firmly. "Go back to your dusty, noisy road job. Me? I am going shopping for another dress. A lovely red evening dress." She smiled impishly and added, "Maybe a dress that costs a hundred dollars. And know what? I may charge it to the Cardigan Corporation."

"You do just that." Mark grinned. "One of these nights we'll go dancing."

"Maybe I go dancing *esta noche*. Tonight. That public-relations man from the refinery, the one who liked my legs. He asked me."

For silent moments Mark felt anger, and the new emotion of jealousy, within him. Then her eyes and upturned lips assured him that he was being baited . . . teased. "Sure. Go dancing, my sly señorita. The man from the refinery, is he tall and handsome?"

Dolores nodded. "Of course, what other men would I pick?"

Mark turned to leave, but took a parting shot. "I'll bet he doesn't have a bag swing—and a cozy, grassy creek-bank."

Before he could get clear, her foot flashed upward and butted his rear end. "Dumb, *loco* gringo!" Then in an almost inaudible whisper she added, "I love you, Mark."

A surprise awaited Mark when he arrived, near sunset, at the construction shack. He opened the door and let out a yelp of delight. "Dad . . . Mom . . . and, can it be? Sure enough, Aunt Carla!"

He went to the older woman first, and took Carla Dunlop into his arms. As he drew her from her chair, he was aware that her form against him was still that of a vibrant and supple woman.

"You haven't changed a bit," Mark marveled.

"Rubbish. Pure rubbish and flattery, Mark. I am seventy-six years old. I have to use eye shadow and mascara and hair dye to keep from falling apart." She pointed toward the side of her chair. "And nowadays I have to carry a cane."

"Mostly to keep younger fellows at a respectful distance," Mark observed.

She held him at arm's length. "God, only a Cardigan could say that with sincerity. They breed true to form. Will. Then Redge. And now you, Mark."

When Carla was again seated, Mark turned to his parents. "You folks got down here in a hurry. I'm glad you did."

Audrey Cardigan studied her son's face, aware of the strain and tiredness upon it. "Your Aunt Carla and I were going to stay at the ranch; she just got in from Santa Barbara, California, yesterday. Then we decided you could use some moral support, son."

Redge had been staring out of the window, was shaking his head. "Something sure made a nasty mess of your plant."

"Not something, Dad. Someone! And we know who touched it off." He paused thoughtfully. "Trouble is we're not sure who's behind this sabotage."

They all listened intently as Mark told of Hook's discovery of the switched tank hoses, and of the information and name Dolores had uncovered at the refinery. Then he asked, "Have you found a decent place to stay yet, a hotel? It's too bad my apartment is so small."

"Yes," Audrey answered. "But your dad spotted a pretty good place over on the Greeley Highway."

"I'll have to see you over there later," Mark said reluctantly. "Take care and get some rest. Right now I want to look up Sam Hook and the Nordraak brothers. We're going out to Clay Street and pay a call on the bastard who switched those fuel hoses."

Redge turned and laid a firm hand on his son's shoulder. "How about me going with you instead? Before you were born, Mark, I had to handle a few troublemakers. I don't think I've entirely lost my touch."

Audrey Cardigan's face tightened, but she evidently

agreed with the suggestion. "Carla and I will be waiting for you at the hotel. We'll need to rest and spruce up before we go to the get-together at the Montez house."

Carla Dunlop came spryly to her feet and stabbed her silver-handled cane at a knot in a floorboard. "Mark," she interjected, "this señorita, this Dolores, your mother tells me she's quite beautiful."

He reddened as he nodded.

And Carla's voice rang out in a firm question. "What is she to you? Is she your mistress?"

Mark gasped, then with an embarrassed face and halting tongue he murmured, "Well . . . well, not exactly."

Carla Dunlop's smile was understanding and compassionate. It was also loaded with conviction. "Well, if she is as nice and as pretty as she's supposed to be, and isn't your mistress—you're the slowest and dumbest Cardigan of three generations!"

The address on North Clay Street was a one-story frame house, set well back from the street and in need of repainting. There was no car in the driveway, and although dusk was beginning to settle across the city, no lights had been turned on inside the dwelling. They had taken Redge's auto for this trip as it would not be readily identified, and now Redge brought it to a halt at the curb on the opposite side from the address they were scrutinizing.

"I don't think there's anyone home," Redge said presently. "Maybe our Mr. Lukens has already come home from work, and gone out again. If we stay, Mark, we may be in for a long wait."

Mark frowned his disappointment. "We haven't got that much time. We've that meeting at Gilberto Montez's place."

They waited about fifteen minutes, and scanned the streets carefully. "What are you going to do about a replacement mix plant?" Redge asked.

"I've called the manufacturers in California, and they're figuring how soon they can ship another unit. But first, I have to settle with the insurance people. Find out how soon the claim for the burned one can be paid. If we can . . ." Mark's words trailed off. He was watching a heavy touring car that had rounded the corner and was now executing a turn into the driveway across the street. Both Mark and

Redge sat very quiet, seeing the lights of the car go off as it got into the driveway. And then a man stepped down from it. They could not clearly see his features in the lessening light.

"Come on," Redge said in low voice. "Let's get going."

They came up quickly and noiselessly behind the stranger just as he was digging into a pants pocket for a door key. Then Mark asked aloud, "Mr. Lukens?"

The stranger wheeled, in evident surprise, apparently unconcerned. "Yeah, I'm Ed Lukens. Why?"

Redge and Mark came to a stop on each side of the man. He was probably in his mid-forties, with a thin face, which was badly in need of a shave.

Redge spoke again, his voice almost sociable. "Are you the truck driver, Mr. Lukens, that the Mexican community is going to honor for safe driving?"

Lukens grinned, then said, "I guess I am. Ain't it something? The Mexicans saying I watch out for their kids on the street?"

Redge nodded vaguely, his eyes ascertaining Mark's readiness, and also determining the possibility that Lukens might try for a weapon or chance a getaway. Then he asked, his voice suddenly flat and cold, "And are you the Ed Lukens that hauled a tankload of fuel oil and asphaltic oil to the Cardigan Corporation's road job out east—and then deliberately switched the hoses to the tanks?"

Lukens stiffened, the grin dropping from his face. "Who the hell are you?" he demanded. "That's bullshit. You're not gonna pin any rap like that on me."

"We already have, Lukens," Mark put in. "We own that plant you sent up in smoke by filling the asphalt tanks with fuel oil."

Lukens's face clouded in fear—it was a weak face. "Must have been a mistake," he said. "Maybe I got the hoses mixed up—it was pretty dark."

Mark grabbed the scared man's arm and wheeled him about until their faces were only a foot apart. Then he said, with growing fury, "It wasn't dark when you loaded extra lengths of hose at the refinery. You knew what you were up to when you did that!"

"So what are you gonna do about it?" Lukens challenged.

Redge noticed slight hesitation on his son's face, and said, "Maybe that depends on you, Lukens."

"How?" The man was grasping at a straw.

"We've got you nailed," Redge continued flatly. "We know you burned the plant, and how you did it. But there's something we don't know: why you did it. Who paid you for the job. And you'd better start talking, pronto."

"Nobody paid me. Hey, you're nuts." He made a move as though to wrench free.

"You're a goddamn liar." Redge's voice was low, but carried a menacing quality that startled Mark. This was a side of his father that he had never before seen, or even guessed at.

"I'm not passing out any names. Not till hell freezes over," Lukens growled.

Redge sensed that some fear, greater than that of their threats, was behind Lukens's stubborn defiance. They were all silent for a moment. Then Redge said, "Mark, see if you can turn on the lights of this man's car. Go ahead. If he tries to move, I'll break his neck."

An entirely puzzled Mark Cardigan answered, "I'll need his keys."

"So that's what you're up to—stealing my car," Lukens snarled.

"Just hand them over," Redge said. His tone made the man thrust the keys into Mark's hand.

The lights came on, sending forth a soft beam that was reflected from a shabby garage at the back of the lot. Mark peered about, wondering if their voices had been loud enough to attract the curiosity of neighbors, but there was nobody to be seen.

"Let's move out there a few feet in front of the headlights," Redge said slowly. "All three of us."

"Why? For Chrissake, why?" Lukens asked.

Redge did not respond, but when they were in the headlight's beam, he said to Mark. "Watch the miserable firebug; if he takes more than one step, shoot him."

Even as he watched in puzzled amazement, Mark knew that his father was bluffing. Surely Redge was aware that Mark had brought no firearms.

In the revealing glow of the headlights, and with unhurried movements, Redge Cardigan removed his coat, his shirt, and finally his light summer undershirt. He turned to reveal his whip-scarred and welted back.

Ed Lukens stared at the wounds with fascination and un-

392

easiness. Then, as Redge leisurely replaced his undershirt, he said, "Lukens, I carry those scars as the result of whip lashes. I was cut to ribbons, branded, by a bullwhip." He paused dramatically, then added, "You've got a choice to make. You can tell us who put you up to that burning rampage at our plant—and just how he paid you for it— or you and my boy and I are going to take a ride out to a nice quiet gully. One where your screams won't do one bit of good. And I've got a whip in the car. Take your choice. Talk or feel that lash!"

Mark noticed the quivering of Lukens's knees. The man would have collapsed from fear had not Mark grabbed his shoulder and steadied him.

"I'll give you the money. I've still got just about all of the two hundred dollars," Lukens panted.

"No," Mark cut in. "We don't want money. We want a name. Who hired you? Name the son of a bitch."

"He'll kill me," Lukens panted. "But either way I'm a goner. It was . . . was Charley Lenholtz."

"You mean Lenholtz of the sand and gravel company?"

"Yes. That's him." Lukens's teeth were chattering. "Oh, God, now let me alone!"

"Pretty soon," Redge answered, and there was mixed contempt and pity in his words. "First, I'm going to write down everything you've told us—and you're going to sign it."

And Ed Lukens nodded in hopeless acceptance.

Both Mark and his father were quiet and emotionally drained as they drove north toward the Montez home. Mark suddenly realized that the hectic happenings of the day had caused him to skip both lunch and dinner. They wheeled into a cafe in the suburb of Adams City and settled for a sandwich, soup, and black coffee. As they were finishing their light meal, Mark shook his head, exhausted. "I've got Ed Lukens's signed confession in my pocket. It explains a lot, Dad. But, you know, in a way I wish we hadn't had to wring it from him as we did. When you see a man go to pieces as he did, it somehow takes the edge off your own pride."

"I know, Mark. How well I know." And as Redge spoke there was within him a vivid memory of the day when, a smoking gun in hand, he had stridden across the yard of

Cardigan Camp and gazed upon the dead face of Stacy Murdock. A moment later, Redge said, almost tenderly, "I'm glad you feel that way, son. It shows you have that intangible quality people call compassion. Never lose it, Mark. Fight for what is right when you must. But let the moments of reason and compassion be the ones on which you build."

They were the last to arrive at the Montez home, and as they came into the already crowded living room, Mark gazed about. There were his mother and Aunt Carla. Sam Hook. The Nordraak brothers. Dolores. Silas Latham. The sweep of his gaze fell on another face—a thoughtful and hauntingly lovely face—that of Lois Edmundson. He stepped to her side and took the hand she extended. "Lois, I'm glad you got my letter and could come. How are things with you these days?" He noted that she was no longer wearing mourning, and there was an acceptance, a certain tranquillity in her face.

"I keep busy, Mark. There are still trans-mountain diversion affairs to which I must attend. And I'm taking some classes at the University of Denver."

Mark knew that he must not ignore the others, but as he moved toward Señora Montez, he glanced back. "Later, Lois, please tell me about the classes."

Within minutes, the room quieted in the expectancy of the business meeting. Gilberto was the first to speak. "Welcome to our small home, and please be as comfortable as you can. We have a saying in Mexico that roughly translates, 'My house is yours.' You are welcome guests." He paused, then went on, "Mark, I know we have troubles to discuss. Big troubles. But perhaps I can lighten them somewhat. Have any of you seen this evening's *Denver Post*?" Nobody had, and Gilberto's voice took on an unexpected tone of triumph. "Then I am happy to announce it. Our Cardigan Corporation was today awarded a quarter-million-dollar grading and surfacing contract by the state of Wyoming. The work is to be done next summer, between Cheyenne and Douglas."

There was excited murmuring and then a burst of applause. When it died, Gilberto bowed toward Mark. "My own congratulations, and those of my family, each of us. Mark, will you please take over now?"

Mark rose to his feet, conscious of his grimy work clothing. He moved his chair in front of him and grasped the back. "It has been quite a day, and I haven't even had time to clean up or wash up decently. Gilberto's news of the Wyoming award sort of cuts through the worry and tiredness. There is probably a letter of award in my mail at the post office. It should be a good job. But first we have to solve our problems here. I mean get this Denver work done right and done on time.

"Now. I don't have to tell you what you already know. Our hot-mix asphalt plant was destroyed last night. We do have insurance, but just how much and how soon we can collect I don't know yet. I'm going to telephone the plant manufacturers in California again in the morning. They don't have a unit on hand, but may be able to locate a used one we can buy or rent."

Mark paused, bit his lip and then looked directly at the Greeley banker. "Mr. Latham, is our credit good enough to see us through—until the insurance money is in hand?"

The banker studied his folded hands, then spoke in a troubled way. "Everyone here is a friend of mine; I've known most of you for years." He paused, shaking his head regretfully. "I wish to high heaven that I could say to you, 'Go right ahead; the bank will provide the necessary funding.' But the truth is I can't. New regulations, and the uneasy money market, make it impossible—until we are sure of a sizable insurance settlement." Latham looked about the circle of concerned faces, then spoke again. "I'm willing to use my personal funds, to back you in every way. But it will take time. I will have to liquidate—" The banker's words broke off, as Carla Dunlop raised her hand to break in. But Audrey Cardigan touched Carla's arm and motioned her not to interrupt.

Then Redge got up, moved to Silas Latham's side, and laid his hand on the banker's shoulder. "Silas, what you are offering to do will be remembered and appreciated for a long time. But let me have a minute. Do you remember, several years back, when you asked if I would guarantee my son's very first loan. I told you I damned sure wouldn't. I wanted my son to have his own responsibility—to handle things on his own." Redge paused, scratched his earlobe, then said suddenly, "Dammit, folks, there comes a time when even two firmly planted feet need support. Silas, Audrey and I will be in your bank as quick as it opens tomorrow. The Cardigan Ranch—a good slice of Crow Creek Valley—will be pledged so that Mark can keep going. Have some sort of mortgage ready as soon as you can." Redge grinned, dropped back to his chair, then added, "Besides, I'm a stockholder in this shebang. I've got a right to protect my dividends, don't I?"

When the murmur of approval had calmed, Mark spoke in a low, subdued voice. "Dad . . . Mom . . . thanks." He waited, then went on, "We do have some good news. Maybe now is the time to tell you. We have found out who set the fire at the hot-mix plant. And we have his signed confession."

"What did the lawmen say to that?" Sam Hook growled.

"Nothing at all; they don't know yet."

"How come?"

"Because, Sam, there's someone bigger than our firebug behind this. It was Lenholtz, of that sand and gravel outfit, who made the payoff. But there's a higher level to this vandalism."

Redge's face registered surprise. Then he asked, "If this Lenholtz wasn't the coyote stirring up trouble—as I figured he was—who? Why?"

Mark's reply was guarded. "What I'm about to say may be pure speculation. Maybe hogwash. So I am going to ask that nobody mention this after we leave this room. Now. I'm getting surer by the day that we are up against some sort of organization. Maybe we threw a monkey wrench into things when we bid and won this Denver job." He paused, aware of the group's attention and shock. "I've been told I am bound to have a caller, and it seems he represents some sort of contractors' association. He hasn't showed up yet. I've a hunch that when he does it is going to shed light on some serious things. Some queer goings-on."

Fartein Nordraak spoke up. "Mark, if there's trouble ahead . . . well, I just want you to know you can count on Halfdan and me. Yes, and I believe that everyone here tonight will back us up."

The meeting was breaking up when Carla Dunlop, moving briskly with the aid of her cane, maneuvered Mark into a quieter corner of the room. "Mark," she asked pointedly, "just how widespread do you think this troublesome element may be?"

396

"Right now, I don't know, Aunt Carla. I wish I did. It may be just a molehill. Again, it could be damned far-reaching. Maybe into the Highway Department or even the State House."

"You mean there may be fraud, or a conspiracy?"

"I don't know . . . yet. Maybe I never will."

Carla Dunlop grasped his hand and clung tightly to it. "Mark, you'll find out. You're a stubborn Cardigan." She smiled tenderly, and her face registered determination. "Mark, promise me just one thing. If this mess reaches into Denver or Colorado politics, let me be the one to handle it. Give me that satisfaction."

He nodded his consent reluctantly. "There may be hell to pay, Aunt Carla. Even danger."

She rapped the cane sharply on a chair and answered, "Mark, my sister Jennifer taught me to laugh at danger. Son, just remember what I have asked of you."

Later, as Mark was leaving, Dolores was waiting for him near the door, with a light shawl about her shoulders. "I will walk with you to your car, Mark."

In the darkness, he put an arm about her. "Dolores, being alone with you after such a day is like coming home from a wearisome journey."

She smiled, but there was a touch of reserve, almost of sadness, about her. Presently she said, "She is a very lovely lady, Mark . . . your friend Lois Edmundson."

"She is nice," he agreed. "But I hardly know her."

"You will, Mark. You may not even know it yourself, but she is very much interested in you."

"Dolores . . ." He laughed. "You are just imagining things. And maybe just a little jealous."

"Jealous? Me?" she scoffed to hide bitterness. "How could I be jealous of any other woman, Mark, when you are married to your work—to your Cardigan Corporation? Sure, boss man. One minute you make love to me. Then in the next breath you ask what bills have come in, or whether we received a bid invitation. Think about it, Mark. And be very honest with yourself. Your love is construction. Women will always be secondary to that. Just conveniences for your office or your bed."

She lifted her lips, touched them casually to his, and then turned and walked quickly toward the house. At the door, she paused and waved. Then she was gone from his astonished sight—but still very much in the turmoil of his mind.

Mark's second call to the plant manufacturer at Stockton, California, brought some encouragement. "Mr. Cardigan," the sales manager reported, "we've been checking other contractors to see if they have an idle plant that might be for sale, or that possibly you can rent. We may have a lead for you. Morrison-Knudsen Company, out of Boise, Idaho, has several of our units. It seems they have one on a job near Billings, Montana, that isn't presently in use. I would suggest you give them a call."

With a relieved sigh, Mark jotted down the telephone number of the Boise firm and then voiced his thanks.

"Let us know how you make out, and meanwhile we'll try elsewhere to find a suitable unit."

From a trade directory, Dolores soon ascertained that the Boise firm was headed by a Harry Morrison, and Mark surmised that to expedite his request, he should try to speak to the top man. A person-to-person call to the company headquarters brought the information that Mr. Morrison was en route to Provo, Utah. A later call ascertained that he had left Provo for Kemmerer, Wyoming, where he might be reached after dinner at the Hotel War Bonnet. It wasn't until almost nine o'clock that Mark's persistence paid off.

A briskly firm but friendly voice came over the long-distance line. "Harry Morrison here."

Mark took a deep breath, then wasted no words. "Mr. Morrison, my name is Mark Cardigan, of Denver. We have a serious problem, so I hope you will excuse this late call."

"They're a way of life with me." There was a slight pause, then Morrison asked, "What can we do for you, Cardigan?"

In precise sentences Mark told of the burning of the hot-mix plant, of the immediate need for a replacement unit, and of the suggestion made by the plant sales manager at Stockton.

"What sort of job do you have?" Morrison queried.

"A Colorado Highway Department contract. Nine miles of grade and surface. And, sir, it's our first big job."

"Trouble at the outset, eh? That sounds familiar. Our Morrison-Knudsen Company lost better than a thousand dollars on our first job, back in 1912. It almost scuttled us. How long would you need the plant?"

"Not to exceed ninety days, sir. We would like either to buy it outright, or to lease it, with the Cardigan Corporation to pay the cost of transportation both ways, of course. If you need a summary of our financial status, I can offer Mr. Silas Latham, of the Plains National Bank, in Greeley, Colorado, as a reference."

Morrison was silent, considering. "I'd like to help you out. We do have such a plant that is idle just now near Billings. The trouble is, we're having trouble getting crushed aggregate to pass through the screens of this new-type plant. I wouldn't want to saddle you with a lemon."

Mark's voice took on an excited tone. "Mr. Morrison, we had exactly the same trouble with our unit—the one that burned. We found, quite by accident, that redesign of the screens, using a hexagonal mesh, eliminated the trouble. It works perfectly. I'm . . . I'm not sure that our modification would meet your conditions. We have an idea the shattering—the type of crushing—as well as the composition of the rock may call for variations. Perhaps an elongated type of mesh opening would help."

Harry Morrison listened eagerly. "You know, Cardigan, I think you have stumbled onto the solution. And I tell you what. Why don't we ship the outfit to you on a standard-rate equipment-rental basis? We ought to get it on its way to Denver in three or four days."

"Mr. Morrison, you're a lifesaver. Thank you, sir. Would you like us to send men to help in disassembly and shipping?"

"It won't be necessary," Harry Morrison replied, and then asked, "You sound like a young fellow."

"Yes, sir. I just finished at Colorado A&M College in engineering, several months ago."

Morrison's voice took on surprise. "And already you have a company, and you've landed a state highway job?"

"Yes." Mark laughed. "But I've been tinkering in heavy construction since I was eight years old."

"Cardigan, someday I want to meet you. Goodnight. We'll confirm this by mail."

Activity at the road project quickened in preparation for the arrival of the new plant from Billings. To Mark's surprise, his father decided to learn how to operate a leaning-wheel grader, and stated his intention of remaining on the job until its completion. He explained to Audrey that he was having fun, and thought it about time for her to have a few weeks of city life. But when alone with Mark, he spoke differently. "As soon as that new plant is railroaded into town, this project is going to have night-and-day guards—call 'em watchmen if you'd rather—but they'll be armed and ready. There's a few of our neighbors from up on Crow Creek who can shoot the left ear off a jackrabbit high-tailing it at a hundred yards. I've talked them into coming down here for a spell."

Mark thought about Redge's words two days later, when he was alone in the office one morning. Dolores was off for the day, working at home on a bid proposal about which Gilberto had become enthusiastic. She had left a stack of invoices, each with a check to be signed.

Because the morning was hot, Mark had left both the office door and a window open, although each wisp of breeze carried dust from the outer work area. The clock had nearly reached ten, and he was almost finished, when a shadow against the doorway light caused him to glance up. A man had entered, and the contrast of his elegant clothing to the rough garb of the workers caught Mark's attention.

The newcomer advanced briskly toward the desk, extended a well-manicured hand, and said in a clipped voice, "I presume you are Mr. Cardigan, Mark Cardigan, sir?"

Mark nodded and waited, as without invitation the stranger dropped into a chair directly opposite. As he did so, his gray, expressionless eyes swept the office. Mark sensed that the man was assessing the possibility of there being others within the reach of his voice. He was small of stature, with neatly parted gray hair, and wore steel-framed glasses that accentuated the thinness of his face and the tight lines of his mouth.

"Mr. Cardigan," he said presently, "I am Amos Shinn. Perhaps you have heard of me." He paused, waiting for Mark's reaction or answer. When none came, he continued, "I represent the local contractors' group. You might say I am their business agent."

"What can I do for you, Mr. Shinn? If there are association dues, I'll have my secretary—"

Shinn suddenly dropped any pretext of friendliness.

"Let's just can that crap, Cardigan, and get down to business. You got this road job by sneaking in the back door. For damned sure you won't get another—and maybe you won't finish this one—unless you want to cooperate and play ball with the group."

Mark's impulse was to seize the little man bodily and throw him out the door. Instead, he kept his control and asked calmly, "The group? Am I to understand they have something to do with the awarding of state contracts?"

Shinn's answer was a sneer. "God, young fellow, but you're naive. Don't you realize no contractor can survive under the asinine system of competitive bidding? We have a right to protect our investment, to assure profits."

"I always thought," Mark replied, "that a contractor had his freedom of decision either to bid a job at his own figure, one that gave reasonable assurance of profit, or let it alone —stay out."

"There's a surer way, Cardigan, and you'd better learn it fast. The group has a way of disseminating bid information, and of allotting jobs. Sure, a realistic, down-to-earth member may be asked to lay off bidding on certain jobs. But it's a trade-off. When his time comes, others of the group either ignore the bid invitation, or bid so damned high you're in free. Besides, you'll know, on important items, what the others of the group are using for base prices."

"And if a contractor refuses to go along with this shit— with your damned deals—then what?" Mark's words were spat out with venom.

"In that case," Shinn replied, and grinned in a vicious way, "there are means. Even the idealistic fools, if they manage to pick up a contract, will need suppliers. Of equipment, supplies, aggregate. Oil and asphalt."

"Such as the hot-mix aggregate Lenholtz Sand and Gravel offered to supply," Mark observed, as he carefully watched his visitor's face. There was no indication that Shinn was aware of Ed Lukens's confession. Mark rose to his feet and briefly stared out of the open window. Then he turned back to Shinn. "Tell your group, sir, that the Cardigan Corporation has no intention of cooperating in such—shall I be polite and call it activity? Or tell it as it is, and call it dirty and downright fraud? We are going to stay in business, and bid on every job within this western region—including the

401

Denver area—in which we become interested and which we believe lies the possibility of reasonable profit."

"You obnoxious young fool!" Shinn answered. "You're signing the death warrant of your ridiculous corporation."

"Be that as it may, Shinn, perhaps you had better get this straight. We have our own gravel and rock deposits. A lot of them. We have highly qualified men—and others waiting in case they're needed. You know we had a fire; I think you also have a good idea of why and how it started. If something like that is planned again, be on the lookout for our watchmen. They will shoot—to kill."

Shinn seemed just a bit less sure of himself as he answered, "None of our refineries are going to supply oil products. I'll pass the word."

"You just do that, Mr. Shinn. I don't believe you'll find the Denver refiners as amenable to your racket as you think. You see, the Cardigan Corporation holds old, priority-type oil and oil products trucking permits with the public-utilities people of both Colorado and Wyoming. Not only can we haul petroleum products as we damn well please—but we can also put a crimp in the hauling of those having more recent permits. And some refineries now depend on hauls under the permits with less seniority."

Amos Shinn was white-faced and furious as he came to his feet. "You think you've got it all sewed up and cozy, don't you? Maybe you're just supid. But you better know I'll stop you. Just try to get bonding—" Shinn cut off his words, almost as though sensing that in his anger and frustration he had for once let his calculated control slip, that he had uttered one word too many.

Without another word, Amos Shinn walked out of the office and left the job site.

For almost a half hour after Shinn's departure, Mark sat at the desk striving to remember every word the man had uttered and to compare them with those of a reluctant equipment dealer, and of Charley Lenholtz. He recalled the domineering fashion in which Lenholtz had first presented his outrageous subcontract to furnish sand and gravel. Then, with a few penciled notes on a notepad, he reached for the telephone and gave the operator a Denver number. When the receiver was picked up he smiled, then said, "Hello, Aunt Carla. Know who this is?"

"Of course, Mark. Why haven't you called a lonesome old lady before?"

"Because I've been plugging along at the problems of a greenhorn construction stiff." He chuckled.

They chatted for a few moments, and then Mark's voice became serious. "Aunt Carla, remember what you asked— that I let you handle certain matters if they led anywhere?"

"Are you ready?" she demanded briskly.

"Not yet. But we may be making progress. Want to help me?"

"It would sure beat knitting on an afghan," she came back testily.

"All right. Here is what I need. It is reasonably certain that some Denver businessmen, mostly contractors, have dropped out of the local picture because of conditions that make them uneasy, or disgusted, or wary. Would you possibly have any way, or any contacts, through which we can check this out? Very quietly, of course. Maybe someone can drop a hint as to what has been keeping them out of the Denver construction business. What do you think, Aunt Carla?"

"I am thinking about how my sister, Jennifer, would have handled this, Mark. She knew a lot of people. Men and their wives. Sometimes wives are more apt to talk. Leave it to me, Mark. The name Waverley still opens quite a few doors, and possibly a few mouths." She heaved a determined sigh, then asked, "I'll call you back—when and if."

"I may not be in town, Aunt Carla. I've good men here, including my dad. There are some jobs coming up for bid in other parts of the state, so I may take three or four days and look them over on the actual location."

"What if I think it calls for handling at a certain State House office?" she persisted.

"Then go to it. My dad can fill you in, especially on that firebug's part, if you need it. And good luck, Aunt Carla."

He replaced the receiver on its hook. For a long time he stared, unheeding, at papers on his desk. "My God," he muttered. "We can do it."

Chapter 34

A week passed before Mark was free to leave on his planned trip to inspect work on which the Highway Department was calling for competitive bidding. For several of the jobs, plans and specifications were already available. Mark passed them on to Gilberto Montez and gave all of his time and attention to unloading the hot-mix plant, which had arrived from Billings, just as Harry Morrison had promised.

After a day of faultless operation, and satisfactory yardage of pavement in place, Mark was free to visit with Gilberto and discuss the pending jobs. He found the Mexican estimator hard at work on data concerning a stretch of seven miles of road bordering the Colorado River, on the state's Western Slope.

"Gilberto," he remarked, "that is mountain country. Steep grades. Lots of borrow and fill. And rock that'll call for blasting. I thought you said we should keep free of that sort of thing."

"But this one excites me," Gilberto said eagerly. "It is so much like the terrain and the problems which I faced at home in Mexico." He paused, laid down his pencil, and added wistfully, "I only wish I were free to examine the project in person. We have profiles and engineering data. Yet only an on-site inspection, a thorough one, can answer my questions."

"Isn't there a chance the railroad would grant you leave?"

"I doubt that."

"Wait, Gilberto. I've wanted to take a trip and look over some projects. Why couldn't you write out instructions for me? And I could keep in touch by telephone."

"But what of the work here? Your new plant?"

"Why do you suppose we have experts like Sam Hook and the Nordraak boys? Besides, my dad is pretty handy at keeping things going."

"But what if there is an emergency?"

Mark's face was serious. "If the Cardigan Corporation can't deal with an emergency without me, its greenhorn president, we shouldn't be in business."

Gilberto listened in thoughtful silence. Then he said, "Mark, I will prepare a list of questions. And as you say, we have the telephone." He straightened, and eagerness came into his voice. "You have asked me to quit the railroad, but always I have been cautious and said wait until the time is right. Now, my young friend, the answer is different. If we are successful bidders for this mountain job, I will turn in my resignation. I will devote full time to the project, to others yet to come, and to our Cardigan Corporation."

Mark smiled warmly. "Thank you, Gilberto. I am both grateful and eager. I will leave for the Western Slope tomorrow. If only I understood estimating—had your knowledge of it."

"You will get along," Gilberto said reassuringly. "Now, with your permission, I shall get busy on your instructions. While I am writing them, you may wish to visit with Dolores. I believe you will find her out front on the porch."

Dolores was pensively easing the new porch swing back and forth by the pressure of one bare foot against the railing when Mark found her. The darkness had deepened, but her face and form were silhouetted in the faint yellow glow of a street lamp close by. Again there was the stirring of primal emotions within Mark as he gazed at her.

He was almost at her side before she seemed aware of his coming. His hand moved out to stroke the dark softness of her cascading hair. "By daylight, you are pretty, Dolores; in the darkness, somehow you cast an aura of . . . of . . . I think the word is enchantment."

Her response was a pleased but teasing laugh, before she said, "Wherever did you learn to talk like that, Señor Gringo? At engineering school?"

He slid into the swing, placing his hand firmly over hers. "Guess what? Tomorrow I am going over on the Western Slope, across the mountains, to size up a state road project.

And if we nail this one down, your father is going to join the company to supervise it."

"That's fine," she replied. "Papa has talked much about it to me, hoping that somehow you could include this river-valley project in your trip."

His arm cncircled her in excitement, and he felt a thrill as her cheek pressed his. "Oh, dammit, Dolores," he murmured. "I wish we were married, and that you were going with me."

Her hand freed itself and moved to firm strong, steady fingers about his chin, to turn his face until he was conscious of the calm and clear depth of her dark eyes. "Mark, I am going with you—if you desire it so. But I will not marry you."

He wanted then to shout aloud, and to protest her refusal. "But what do you mean, Dolores? What will your father say if you go with me and you won't marry me? And your mother? They are my friends, almost my second family. I couldn't—"

"Mark," she pleaded, "listen to me. It is because I love my papa and my mama so much that I have been honest with them. For a long time they have known of my love for Mark Cardigan. And they know now that I am yours —your woman to love, your woman for passions. But never your wife. I am Mexican, and I am demanding. I need a husband who will give me more of himself than you ever can."

He felt the clean softness of her hair on his shoulder, and was conscious of her silence and her quick breathing. There seemed to be an elemental sadness about this child of Mexico. But quickly she drew his lips to hers. "Mark," and the word seemed both serene and excited, "won't it be fun, working together along that big river valley? And I can help. Already my papa has taught me to make accurate estimates of quantities and costs."

They left Denver at midmorning of the following day and headed forward on the largely unpaved and narrow roads climbing swiftly into cool forests and along tumbling creeks. They passed through the towns of Golden, Idaho Springs, Georgetown, and Silver Plume. They thrilled to the valley's grandeur, then to the steep climb that brought them, near nightfall, to the historic two-mile-high settlement of Leadville, where they spent the night. They slept in separate rooms.

Their route out of Leadville, through Tennessee Pass and the hamlet of Redcliff, heightened the excitement and wonder of the previous day. To the west loomed the Mount of the Holy Cross, rising 14,000 feet, with lifted arms of eternal snow. After a time, they descended to the Eagle River Valley and followed it to its merging with the Colorado River, and the rocky battlements guarding the beginning of Glenwood Canyon.

Despite stopping frequently to admire the canyon's beauty, they came into the quiet, tree-shaded town of Glenwood Springs at midafternoon. They registered at the Colorado Hotel, asking for separate rooms that would face onto the large hot-springs swimming pool. The disinterested manner in which the room clerk noted the arrival of a young American traveler accompanied by a beautiful Mexican girl was noticed by Mark and Dolores. They let it pass without comment, and did not even discuss how long they might remain quartered in their own rooms.

After a leisurely drive along the route for the proposed road improvement, Dolores spoke firmly. "Now I will spend my time at the hotel. *Madre de Dios,* but there is much figuring to be done."

"The paperwork can wait, can't it?" Mark protested. "I sort of wanted you with me on the job." He grinned and added, "I need a good assistant, a rodman."

"Such a helper you can hire." She shrugged. "Now I must get ready for the hundred smeared pages of figures Boss Cardigan will dump on top of the plans and specifications I already have." She pecked lightly at his lips, then pushed him toward the door. "*Vamos.*" But, Mark, come back when the sun is throwing long shadows."

It was on the evening of their third day that Mark's field work and her accurately moving pencil brought their understanding of the project into sharp focus. She had prepared a full estimate of costs, and he read it through thoughtfully. "Dolores," he said, looking up from the paper, "I don't think it can be done; it seems to me that this job is out of our reach, beyond our financial strength. Look here . . ." He pointed at salient figures. "We would have to borrow heavily, for many months. The interest, plus the straining of our resources, would likely drain the corporation completely."

Seemingly unaware of his arm about her shoulder, she picked up another sheet of neatly written figures. "It may be that you are right, Mark, but again there may be a way . . . an alternate handling of the bid items."

Mark studied the second sheet with growing excitement. "You've figured the first items to be completed at high-bid figures, then compensated by lowering the bid figures of work that comes along later. That would bring a lot of cash during the first phases."

She agreed, her eyes bright and excited. "Exactly, Mark. I read of this method in one of my papa's books. It is called an unbalanced bid, to provide the greater amount of revenue upon finishing the earlier portions of the project. There is nothing crooked or reprehensible about it. Contracts are awarded on the basis of total bids, regardless of individual items."

His arm about her tightened as his mood soared. "We *can* do it this way, sweetheart—swing the financing through short-term loans for a time, then on our own money."

"But don't forget," she cautioned, "others will be bidding."

"But we'll get this job," he affirmed stoutly. "With your genius, and Gilberto's know-how—we'll crack this big one."

She leaned back, her hands clutching his elbows. "Right now, Mark, I would like to crack even a tough steak. I am famished."

He stared out of the window, then pointed. "That valley leading up south is the Roaring Fork River way to the old mining town of Aspen. It's pretty well deserted these days, but I've heard of a good restaurant up there that caters to hunters and fishermen. And they say it's magnificent country. Want to drive up there before we eat?"

"Perhaps tomorrow, Mark. Tonight let's eat here in the hotel."

"And then?" he asked in a voice mingling tenderness and amusement.

She looked at him with love and honesty and excitement. "Perhaps then, Hard Rock Cardigan, we may even find another bag-swing tree."

Later, when he came with eager steps and pounding pulse to her room, she was seated near the window, peering out across the village. She wore a soft, sheer dressing gown, and a scent of exotic intrigue.

Mark knelt beside her, his arms reaching out to draw her close. "Oh, God, Dolores. I love you so. Want you so much. Not just for now. Not for just tonight. But for all of our lives. Dolores, why can't we get married?"

Her fingers caressed his tumbled hair. "Mark, take me as I am. As it must be. There can never be marriage between us."

"But why?" he whispered.

"For so many reasons. I am a Mexican. I am of a different faith."

"What little I care, Dolores, about those things. They are nothing."

She shook her head sadly. "You would come to care about such things. Mark, someday you are going to be very rich and very famous. If we were married, I would always be your Mexican wife. The spic . . . the greaser . . . on whom Cardigan threw himself away. They would say it, Mark, the jealous men and their fork-tongued wives."

"I'd be proud of you. Gloriously proud."

"Yes, Mark, I know you would. But there is another reason our marriage cannot be."

"What?" he murmured.

"I can never bear children." At his questioning gesture, she hastened on. "Oh, I know it to be true. I had a childhood sickness. I am what I am destined to be—forever childless."

"But it is only you for me, Dolores. It is only you I have ever loved or wanted."

She crushed him against her, and her words were low and intense in their outpouring of truth and emotion. "You will have me. Mark, someday you will marry one of your race, your creed, and your kind. But when you want me, I will be yours as much as I can be."

With mingled anguish and desire, his hands slipped beneath the gown and cradled her breasts. She gasped, laid a searing kiss on his mouth and rose to shrug free of the garment. "Mark," she murmured, "your hands. Run them over me—every inch of me. They set me afire."

When again they had consummated raging desires, they lay snuggled together. About Mark was a sense of foreboding, of resignation. He was struck by the fact that

Dolores knew more about him than he knew about himself.

They lingered over a late breakfast the next morning in the hotel's dining room. Mark was in no hurry to leave for another day's routing of inspection and estimation of rock quantities. Nor was Dolores in haste to resume penciled calculations and unit costs. They were content to bask in the remembered wonder of the night, and to sit with knees that touched with the wordless message of love.

It was a hotel bellhop who brought them abruptly back to reality. "Mr. Cardigan, you have a long distance call, from Denver. Do you care to take it on our hallway phone?"

Mark rose, shaking his head. "I'll take it in my room, thank you." He flipped a coin to the bellhop, then turned to Dolores. "You'd best come upstairs too; it may be Gilberto calling for figures and data."

It was Redge Cardigan, and he sounded shaken. "Mark, we have trouble over here, perhaps one hell of a lot of it."

"What's up, Dad?"

"Last night one of our oil tankers, coming down from Cheyenne, was rammed by an old, beat-up dump truck. Whoever did it was an expert, and knew exactly what he was about. Our tanker was split open, and the oil spilled to hell 'n' gone across the highway. Worse, though, son, we lost a driver. He went through the windshield."

"Who was it?" Mark asked in concern.

"I don't think you knew him; he was a new employee, a fellow about forty years old. Fartein Nordraak had hired him."

"Did they get the bastard who hit him?"

"Not yet. When the wreck was discovered, there wasn't anybody around. And listen to this. That old relic of a dump truck had been plucked free of its license, its papers, and everything else by which it might be traced."

Mark sighed, then replied, "Dad, get word to our driver's wife, or family, that I will be in touch with them soon. Now, what in hell else has gone wrong?"

Redge's voice seemed puzzled. "This one I don't understand. Silas Latham has been working with the fidelity bonding people for us, making financial statements, filing forms."

"Sure, what about it?"

"Mark, Silas called me from Greeley about an hour ago. Something queer as hell is going on. He has received word from both the Colorado and Wyoming highway departments saying that our bonding is under serious review. That possibly it may be either rerated or canceled."

For a minute Mark sat stunned, then his thoughts recaptured his fiery exchange with the little man who described himself as representate of the contractors' group. What was it Amos Shinn had said in parting? *You better know I'll stop you. Just try to get bonding.*

Redge's voice sounded anxiously again, after the long silence. "Mark, are you still there? Son, can you hear me?"

"Sure, Dad. Now . . . will you do some things for me? First, have Silas Latham call the bonding companies if he hasn't already done so and find out if they are themselves back of this reinvestigation thing. I've an idea they aren't. But when you know, get word to Aunt Carla. Also, give her that confession we wrung out of Ed Lukens, the firebug. Then tell Aunt Carla I said the time is now—today."

"What can she do? I mean, she's a wonderful woman, but . . ." Redge's voice was doubtful.

"Dad, this may lead to the Colorado State House or the Division of Highways. If it does, believe me, Aunt Carla is our ace in the hole." Then he added, "Give my love to Mom; I'll be home in two or three days."

Dolores had heard his side of the conversation and stood beside him, unsmiling and worried. "Shouldn't we hurry back to Denver, Mark?"

"No," he answered firmly. "If the Cardigan Corporation is to grow, we must have men who can act on any emergency on their own. No, Dolores, we will finish making sure we have every bit of information, every rock and soil sample, and every local subcontract possibility to cinch this job."

"Then get out," she said, "and let me get my pencil moving."

On that morning in mid-August of 1929, Governor Joe Whitlock arrived at his Capitol Building office in good spirits. There was a reassuring article by a Washington financial analyst in that morning's *Rocky Mountain News*, saying that the nation's strong economy would continue in the months ahead. As he walked the last two blocks his spirits were raised by the spectacular view of the mountains, clear and bold, from Pikes Peak far north toward Wyoming.

Scarcely five minutes after he eased himself into the chair behind his desk, he heard the voice of his secretary from the next office. "Governor, there is a lady calling you. A Miss Carla Dunlop, who says she is Jennifer Waverley's sister. She says it is vitally important."

Whitlock picked up the phone, then heard his secretary say, "Miss Dunlop, Governor Whitlock is on the line."

"Hello, ma'am," Whitlock said in a deep, resonant tone.

"Governor," a firm feminine voice came back, "it is extremely important that I see you at once, today if possible." When he remained quietly listening, she added, "Probably you don't remember me. You will recall my sister, Mrs. Jennifer Waverley, who used to live on Pennsylvania Street."

"Of course. I would be delighted to visit with you, Miss Dunlop, but unfortunately today my schedule—"

"Governor Whitlock. It is most urgent that I see you immediately. It may affect the very financial and governmental integrity of this state." Carla was quiet for a moment, and then added, "I would also advise—yes, dammit, *request*—that you have certain people in attendance at our meeting."

"Who, Miss Dunlop? You know this is irregular—most extraordinary."

"The circumstances are deserving of your attention, sir," she answered. "You should arrange to have present your highest officer of the Colorado Department of Highways. Also a man named Amos Shinn—I believe he represents, or claims to represent, some sort of contractors' association. Most important, have Charles Lenholtz, of Lenholtz Sand and Gravel, on hand—if he has to be dragged in. Governor —what time this afternoon should I be at your office?"

Whitlock looked about in confused amazement, then answered, "May I call you back, Miss Dunlop? Say in thirty minutes."

"Of course, governor, but, sir, I must ask you to prepare yourself for some revelations that may rock the unwary complacency of even your closest advisors, and yes, yourself."

412

The governor had scarcely hung up when again his secretary called out, "Sir, there is another call, this one from Silas Latham, president of the Plains National Bank, in Greeley."

Whitlock grinned relief and reached for the phone. "Good morning, Silas. How are things with our northern Colorado constituency?"

"Governor," the banker's brisk and serious voice sounded on the other end of the line, "excuse me for being abrupt. Have you had a telephone call this morning from Carla Dunlop?"

Surprise wreathed the governor's face. "Why, yes, Silas, I have. Just a few minutes ago."

Latham's answer was brusque. "Joe, I am leaving right away for Denver. By all means do as Miss Dunlop has asked. Set up an emergency meeting, and request, or demand, or order, that the people she mentioned be in attendance."

Governor Whitlock whistled sharply into the mouthpiece. "For God's sake, Silas. What has happened? What's wrong?"

"Just let Carla Dunlop spread it out before you. Yes, and document it. Joe, listen. It could save your administration lots of embarrassment—and possibly a recall election."

The connection broke; Latham had hung up before Colorado's governor could think of additional questions. For a couple of minutes he stared at the ceiling. Then he pressed a buzzer and his secretary came to his side. "Get Miss Carla Dunlop back on the phone. Tell her the meeting is scheduled for three-thirty this afternoon. Also, get hold of these three men." He handed her the handwritten notes of those Carla had mentioned. "Tell every one of them that the governor wishes to see them here at three-thirty— without excuses or delays." Then again he repeated in a soft murmur, "What in heaven's name is going on?"

Both Carla Dunlop and Silas Latham walked into the governor's reception room at three-twenty-five that afternoon. Presently, Whitlock appeared in the door to greet them. Pleasantries were passed, but each of them was noticeably tense. They stepped into the spacious executive office, where already two other men were seated. Carla surmised that the younger man, seated behind a small desk, was a stenographer, prepared to take down a record of what would be said.

The governor's entrance brought the other stranger to his feet. He was past middle age, was dressed in a gray business suit, and wore an air of puzzled incomprehension.

"Miss Dunlop . . . Mr. Latham . . . I would like you to meet Carl Seawell, our state highway engineer. I have invited him to sit in on our conversation." Whitlock waved them to comfortable seats, indicating that Carla Dunlop should occupy a chair close to him. He glanced about, making sure that the room's doors were closed, and then asked Carla, "Would you like to have the other two men you mentioned, Mr. Shinn and Mr. Lenholtz, in here? They are now in my outer office."

"Not for a few moments, Governor Whitlock," she replied. Then, seeing all eyes curiously upon her, she began, "Mr. Seawell, as state highway engineer, in charge of highway construction work statewide, have you noticed, within the past year or two, a change in the pattern of those bidding for project work, specifically in the Denver area? Have there been fewer potential bidders? Or ones different from those who have been your regulars over the years?"

Seawell glanced momentarily at the governor, in evident surprise.

"Go ahead, Carl, answer her."

"Denver and its environs are but a small—although highly important—part of our state system. But since you mention it, yes, there are fewer bidders in this area."

Carla leaned forward, her face a little pale, but intense. "Have you given any thought as to why this change has come about?"

"Not really, Miss Dunlop. In construction work there is always a percentage of attrition among contractors. Old ones fade out. New concerns spring up."

Carla produced a neatly typed sheet from her purse and laid it before Joe Whitlock. "Governor, what I am getting at goes far beyond natural changes and attrition. Here are the names—and the facts. Six reputable firms that have chosen not to undertake bidding of Denver-area jobs because of corruption and bribery."

The state highway engineer jumped to his feet. "Governor, if this is an assault upon my personal integrity, and that of my department . . ."

414

Carla held up her hand for silence. "It is not, Mr. Seawell. But I believe you will be most interested in other statements I am prepared to make." As Seawell sank agitatedly back into his chair, Carla, smiling somewhat apologetically, turned again to the governor. "May I suggest that you ask Shinn and Lenholtz to join us?" There was a note of contempt in her voice as she spoke their names.

The two men, both wary and sullen, were ushered in and quickly introduced to those already seated. Then the governor said, "Miss Dunlop, I believe you have something more to say."

She picked up her heavy cane, rested her folded hands upon it, and asked abruptly, "Governor, Mr. Seawell, are you aware that just last night an oil-tanker truck belonging to the Cardigan Corporation was intentionally rammed while en route from Cheyenne to a project on the eastern outskirts of Denver? The driver was killed." Before they could answer, she added, "And are you aware that only a few days ago a mixing plant belonging to this same Cardigan Corporation was set ablaze and burned by a paid firebug? Also, it is interesting to note that very recently Mr. Amos Shinn, now seated here, called on Mark Cardigan, the president of the Cardigan Corporation, and threatened to drive him from the Denver construction scene."

Her words dropped off, leaving an almost unbearable silence in the room. Both Governor Joe Whitlock and his chief highway official stared at her with unbelieving shock.

Within seconds a white-faced Amos Shinn spoke up. "Governor Whitlock, sir, is this all I have been asked here for—to listen to the ranting accusations of a crazy old woman? This impingement of my honor . . ." Shinn was rising to his feet as though he intended to leave.

"Sit down! Sit down and listen, you mealy-mouthed old son of a bitch!" As she spoke the words, Carla Dunlop raised her cane and poked Shinn sharply in the belly. But it was the shock of her words, more than the cane's pressure, that caused an outraged and plainly fearful Amos Shinn to drop again into his chair.

Carla unfolded another document, which she dropped before the stunned governor. "As for Mr. Shinn's cohort, Mr. Lenholtz, I have this to offer—a confession signed by an Ed Lukens, and witnessed by two men, that Lukens was hired by Lenholtz to burn down the Cardigan hot-mix

415

plant. This was after Mark Cardigan refused to contract for road aggregate material to be furnished by the Lenholtz firm at ruinous prices."

"Miss Dunlop," the governor asked in awe and restrained fury, "is that all?"

"Not quite, sir. The truck that last night wrecked the Cardigan tanker had been stripped of license plates and all identification. Even the engine serial number had been removed. Within the last few hours, we discovered, it has had a rebuilt transmission installed. We believe a check of all Denver transmission suppliers will likely reveal . . ." Carla left the thought unfinished, but cast a stony glance again upon Amos Shinn and said, "You know what it will reveal, don't you? It is one of the things you know as head of the reprehensible contractors' group."

Governor Whitlock swiftly read the Ed Lukens confession. "Why was this not immediately turned over to the police for action?"

"Because," Silas Latham explained, "it was needed to build our proof of fraud and conspiracy."

"Mr. Latham," the state highway engineer asked, "are you insinuating that my office—my department—is a party to fraud?"

The banker looked at Carl Seawell in a troubled manner. "Carl, I hope not, but I hardly know what to think or believe. There is an even more serious aspect to this." He paused, turned to the governor, and asked, "Should I expand on this?"

"Hell, yes," Joe Whitlock snapped. "Let's get to the bottom of this—right now."

"As a banker, and also as a stockholder of the Cardigan Corporation, I handle all details of their bonding, of the surety papers that must be properly executed and submitted before a job can be awarded. Now, I was flabbergasted to learn yesterday that our bonding integrity—the very heart of our financial stability—is suddenly being questioned. I, of course, got in touch at once with the firms that supply our bonding. They were amazed. None of the investigation had originated with them. *It had somehow originated at the offices of the Colorado State Highway Department.*

"And listen to this, gentlemen. Someone using a fictitious name phoned a warning to the Wyoming Highway Department, saying the Cardigan Corporation was a bad risk, likely to default. That call originated within your Highway Department offices, Mr. Seawell."

The governor stared thoughtfuly about those assembled. Then his gaze focused on Amos Shinn, and he asked, "Mr. Shinn, have you anything to offer in explanation?"

"Not until I can confer with my attorneys," Shinn rasped.

"As for you, Mr. Lenholtz," Whitlock continued, "I have no choice but to turn this confession, signed by an Ed Lukens, over to civil authorities for further action."

With weary resignation, the governor turned back to Carla Dunlop. "Have you anything to add, Miss Dunlop?"

"Only this, sir. I am not an official of the Cardigan Corporation. But I know that the enterprise is conducted by highly reputable and conscientious persons. And, sir, I am confident there has been serious misuse of public trust and confidence by two men within this room." She was pensive for a moment, and then added, "Collusion is a nasty word, gentlemen. One that can strike at the very heart of our form of government. Collusion is a secret understanding between two or more persons prejudicial to another—in this case a threat to the dignity and integrity of Colorado, my beloved home state."

Governor Joe Whitlock replied, "Thank you, Miss Dunlop." Then he added, "I appreciate the presence of each of you. Now, after we adjourn, I would like Engineer Seawell to remain."

When the others had left the room, the governor demanded, "Carl, what do you know of all this?"

"Not one damned thing, governor," Seawell replied, and there was honesty in his face.

"Good. Now, Carl, we're going to follow this through! I want this mess cleaned up within seventy-two hours—especially if it touches someone within your bonding documents division. Keep in touch. Straighten it out—fast. I would sure as hell hate to ask for your resignation."

Later that evening, in a small warehouse in northeast Denver, a group of ten men were listening to a distraught Amos Shinn.

"You mean you and Lenholtz blew it?" an angry voice demanded from the group.

"Lenholtz threw the shit into the fan," Shinn defended weakly. "But we've got to face it. That young bastard

417

Mark Cardigan has got us by the balls. They'll trace that transmission, all right."

"And then you'll be facing murder charges, won't you, Shinn?" someone jeered.

"I'm getting out of your chickenshit contractors' group. It ain't worth the risk, and surer 'n hell the heat is going to be on." The heavy-set speaker was putting on his coat.

"I know about that Dunlop dame," another volunteered. "So count me out too. She inherited millions from that rough old sister of hers. Believe me, she won't hesitate to use a wad of it to stir up more trouble—maybe a grand-jury investigation."

As they rose to leave, one contractor asked in disgust, "Shinn, ain't you got some deal, say in Hong Kong, needing your quick attention?"

Within one week the Cardigan Corporation had received full clearance and approval of the bonding necessary for the jobs on which they had been successful bidders.

Chapter 35

The growth of the Cardigan Corporation during the twenty-five years that followed was a phenomenon born of both the Depression years and those of World War II. In October of 1929, the stock market faltered and then crashed, bringing on an era of business stagnation and inertia. But long ago Silas Latham had pointed out the wisdom of the company's bidding only such contracts as were state obligations, and those of federal agencies such as the Forest Service and the Department of the Interior.

Thus it was that after their successful completion of the Denver road project, the corporation was able to get on with the Wyoming job between Cheyenne and Douglas. Much to the delight of both Dolores and Gilberto Montez, they also were successful bidders for the construction along the Colorado River, on the scenic western slope. True to his word, Gilberto at last left the security of his railroad job to give full time to the Cardigan Corporation.

Within seven years, Mark felt that his dream had been realized, for his builders had completed a variety of projects throughout a seven-state area. With the growth, they had acquired new and highly skilled personnel, and the ability to take on varied jobs: bridges, canals, railroad relocations, water-storage reservoirs.

In late autumn of 1939, Mark was summoned to Washington. The impending war was sure to involve America. Vice Admiral Ben Moreell at the Navy Department had urgently requested that Mark come as soon as possible. The message came at an inconvenient time, for earlier in the month of October, Gilberto Montez had been dispatched on an important mission to Mexico. Political changes had taken place south of the border, which made it expedient for Gilberto to return to his homeland. Once there and settled in Mexico City, he would open the first of the Cardigan Corporation's foreign subsidiaries, the Cardigan Construcción de México. Halfdan was now at an earth-fill dam site in Montana. Fartein had recently undergone surgery and was recuperating at the old homestead near Hawk Bend. Yet Mark went to Washington anyway, following his firm belief that his trained men should be able to take over all phases of the company's activities.

He made the trip to Washington, D.C., alone; for several weeks Dolores had been in Mexico City helping her parents get located. He was acutely lonely without this beautiful and unpredictable Mexican girl, although he was glad of her frequent letters pouring out her excitement, and the assurance that she would soon return.

He was brought with some delay through the maze of Washington naval command to the office of Admiral Moreell. With a few sharp, incisive questions, Moreell probed the experience, the stability, and the present status of the Cardigan Corporation. And with hardly a chance to protest, Mark accepted the vice-admiral's proposal. The Cardigan Corporation became one of the companies designated for the secret, top-priority building of far-flung Pacific naval air bases. This commitment would require many months and tax the manpower and the expertise of the corporation to the full.

After the catastrophe of Pearl Harbor, a crushing burden of work was imposed upon the Cardigan Corporation. Mark found that more and more frequently, he would be flown by military airlift from the islands of the South Pacific to the searing desert reaches of North Africa. High-level conferences with both construction and military leaders had become a way of life.

It became increasingly impossible for him to request that Dolores be allowed to accompany him. But she was almost always there upon his return to the United States— to be, as she had once said herself, his woman. His refuge from loneliness and pent-up passions, and often sheer exhaustion. She had always sensed his pride and his need, and she herself, still slim and graceful, gained a certain limited joy from their relationship.

Dolores was on a brief trip to Mexico when Mark was summoned to Hawk Bend by his mother's death, in 1943. Audrey Cardigan had always appeared vital and active.

She succumbed to a sudden heart attack during the pre-dawn hours of a mild spring day.

The flowers and the long line of quiet-faced friends and neighbors told of the love and respect which Audrey Cardigan had inspired. After the services, when his mother had been laid next to Kate Andrus in the white-picketed cemetery, Mark turned to accept the hand offered by a woman whose face was tear-stained and grave. "Lois . . . Lois Edmundson," he breathed, and then held her tightly as she cried out her grief.

He stayed at Cardigan Ranch all of the three days which his emergency leave would permit. He was greatly concerned for Redge, but his father surprised him by asking, "Mark, isn't there one of your jobs, somewhere in the west, where I can be of use? Keep busy? Audrey wouldn't want me to mope and brood. Someday you'll lay me by her side, but just now I gotta keep busy."

"As soon as you're ready, Dad, phone me. There are half a dozen places where we need your abilities and common sense."

Mark rode back to Denver with Lois Edmundson. They were nearing the city, and the rows of street lights were reflecting from low-hanging clouds, when he said without warning, "Lois, perhaps it is crazy to ask you at such a time—but will you marry me?"

Her face whitened, and she clutched the steering wheel with a tight-knuckled grasp. "Mark, you have never given even a hint that you care for me, that you love—"

"Because," he interrupted fiercely, "I really haven't the right." His hand lifted and tightened on her shoulder.

"You are thinking," she said brokenly, "of Dolores. Of your years together. Your love. Your passions."

"I won't deny it, Lois. But now, with Mom gone, I realize how desperately I want a family. Boys of my own. Girls."

"But you have Dolores, Mark. She loves you greatly."

"But of all our love there can never come a child. Years ago a sickness took that possibility away from her."

Lois drew the car to a halt and parked. "Is that all I mean to you, Mark—the possibility of children?"

He bowed his head, and his suffering was clear to her. "Lois, in my damnable way, I am fickle. I cannot, and will

421

not, deny that I adore Dolores, and that sexually I would be lost without her. But by her own choice, she will never be more than a companion to me—she fears the cruelty of race hatred and prejudice. I can't promise, in fairness either to you or to her, that I can ever be constantly apart from her."

"Then how would you fit me into the scheme and turmoil of your life?"

"Lois . . . Lois," he murmured, and in his voice was a plea for understanding. "I need someone to walk proudly by my side. Someone to organize my life and my home. Yes, and please God, my children."

With both compassion and long-pent-up love, Lois put her arms about him. "Mark, I would be honored and thrilled and very happy to be your wife. But before I take the step, there are things that must be understood. For your sake and for mine."

There were tears in Mark's eyes as he said, "We've got time to discuss everything, to be totally honest."

"Mark, dearest, I have been close to construction people all of my life. I have watched the reaction of wives whose husbands must, by the nature of their work, be away from home much of the time. Women have different ways of facing the situation. Some of them simply acquire lovers . . . sex mates. Others try to go to every country and every job, hanging desperately on to their husbands' coattails. Some love the constant travel, the adventure of trains and ships and airplanes. Others, a very few, are caught up in the spirit of construction and want to become an integral part of it. But I suspect most women fly from one job to another, and from one continent to another, simply because they cannot bear the possibility that their husbands may seek out younger and prettier, and perhaps more passionate, women to take to bed."

"You understand a great deal, Lois. Perhaps, now that I think of it, most of the couples I know in the business do behave that way."

"Well, I will never get caught up in that sort of merry-go-round," she said forcefully. "If we marry, I'll try to walk by your side with dignity, and love and honor. But I will not pursue you to the ends of the earth. I, and I hope our children, will wait at home for your times of peace and fulfillment."

422

He drew her to him, placing a delighted kiss on her lips. Then he felt her draw slightly from him.

"Mark, one other thing. We must be entirely honest with Dolores. You must tell her how I feel before we are married. We are each destined to play a different role in your life—for I shall not be so foolish as to try to quench the desires that flame within you when you and I are hundreds or thousands of miles apart, and Dolores is by your side."

They were married within the month. Their honeymoon was a trip by train far north into Canada, where Mark had been asked by the Secretary of War to review and report upon a unique project. At the time, the creation of the atom bomb was being rushed at plants near Oak Ridge, Tennessee, and Hanford, Washington. The American production of uranium needed for the bomb was meager, but large quantities of pitchblende, a uranium-yielding ore, were available at a Canadian outpost on the eastern shore of Great Bear Lake. It could be freighted by barge to the Mackenzie River, upstream to the Athabasca River, and then transferred to a railroad at the frontier settlement of Waterways.

Mark and Lois admired the width and the magnificently broad northward flow of these Canadian rivers. And a dream was born in Mark. These rivers flowed unused into the Arctic Ocean. What if someday an international agreement could be reached whereby this unused flow, this tremendous rush of mountain-born water, could be diverted in part to the wheatlands of southern Canada and the gently undulating plains of Montana . . . Wyoming . . . Colorado . . . Kansas? He would have to study the engineering feasibility, and find if others had considered the daring possibilities. He returned home from his honeymoon with every map and document he could lay his hands on.

By 1955, the Cardigan Corporation was acknowledged as one of the greatest companies specializing in engineering, design, and heavy construction. From Cardigan Construcción de México, set up by Gilberto Montez, had sprung related enterprises throughout South America. Now there were also affiliates or wholly owned subsidiary companies across other continents.

Mark had been thirty-eight years old when the war ended in 1945. By 1952, he was the father of two small boys and a baby girl. It was also in 1952 that he sadly took his father home to Crow Creek Valley and the little graveyard at Cardigan Camp. Death had claimed Redge as he had attempted to save a fellow worker who had fallen while high-scaling rock for an abutment at an Arizona project.

Dolores traveled with Mark less frequently these days, but there were times when the surges of love and loneliness brought them together, and they slept locked in each other's arms. And looking at Mark's slightly widening girth, she would flash the old, tantalizing smile, then call him Worldwide Cardigan. In turn, he would slap her naked butt until she vowed, "I'll kill this gringo bastard. *Madre de Dios,* what I endure for love of this beautiful, horny construction stiff!"

Chapter 36

A letter from his old friend, Lane Torgny, brought Mark to Las Vegas on a blustery early-March day in 1955. The letter had caught up with him at his hotel in Chicago, and it was clearly an appeal for expert advice. It read:

> Dear Mark,
> Through our correspondence you are aware that about two years ago I was named regional forester for the Southwest Region, which includes the state of Nevada. Now the Reclamation Service has drawn up specifications for a dam and irrigation district, in which I have become more than ordinarily interested. Much of the drainage area lies within the Cathedral Peaks National Forest, which is one of several in my region. Mark, I really want to approve the construction, yet I would be more assured—more comfortable—if you, with your wide experience and a world of such evaluations, could see fit to tour the area and give me your thoughts. This is a whale of a lot to ask of a busy man, but perhaps a few days at Lake Mead, Mt. Charleston, and the casino musical reviews is just what we both need. Pleasure—and business too.
> Give my best to Lois and the children. Also to Dolores, wherever she may be.
>
> Personal regards,
> Lane Torgny

When the Cardigan Corporation's new DC-3 plane taxied up to the Las Vegas terminal, Lane Torgny was waiting eagerly at the designated parking spot. At sight of his friend, Mark recalled the first time they had met, in a raw construction camp in western Colorado. He thought also of how this man's encouragement had helped to get the Cardigan Corporation off the ground during the early years of struggle.

"I've reserved rooms for you, Mark," Torgny said, as they shook hands. "Thought it best, with one big vim-filled liquor dealers' convention about to swamp every hotel on the Strip."

"Thanks, Lane. It was thoughtful of you. I suppose we could pass ourselves off as thirsty tavern owners and belly up to their samples handout."

There was little said of the potential dam until they drove out of Las Vegas the next morning, heading northwest in Torgny's official car. They had covered perhaps forty miles, and Mark was studying the sun-drenched chilly desert, when Torgny said with enthusiasm, "You're not going to believe your eyes when we come to what I want to show you—in about an hour, after some chuckholed and dusty driving."

The twisting, ungraveled road zigzagged and then began to climb a high, steep range of brush-covered hills. After a long time, they crested the ridge. Abruptly Torgny pulled his car to the side of the road and cut the motor.

Mark's eyes widened as he gazed ahead. Before him was a canyon perhaps a mile or so in width, with guardian walls of rock that glowed pink and crimson and amber in the morning sunlight. There were also green meadows, alfalfa fields, and orchards in which fruit trees and grape vines stood in orderly rows. Mark stared in amazement, for coursing down this remote, sheer-walled valley was a swift-moving stream that caught the sun's reflection and broke it into diamonds.

As though spellbound, Mark stepped from the auto and strolled to a nearby rock that offered an even better view. Memories flooded him. How many times, in boyhood, had he climbed an eastern ridge and looked down upon the meadows of Cardigan Ranch? But this stream, here in the midst of a lonely desert—it seemed to be born of wonder, flowing toward adventure. "Lane, what's the name of this place?" he called aloud.

"Cathedral Gulch—at least that's what the old-timers named it. The stream comes down from Cathedral Peak up north, with a couple of tributaries from heavily timbered

426

country off east. There's not a lot of area with great elevation, say above eight or nine thousand feet, but a heap of snow falls up there in the winters. Quite a few summer rains too."

"These farms and ranches . . . they have the appearance of being quite old."

"Most of them are, Mark. Cathedral Gulch was settled by pioneer Mormons shortly after the Civil War, and furnished produce and beef for some rip-roaring gold mines hereabouts."

"It isn't all so ancient," Mark commented, and pointed to a long freight train laboring its way north.

"This happened to be the best, and just about the only, route for the railroad from Salt Lake City to the Los Angeles area," Lane explained. "Which creates part of our problem. You can't believe the devastation of floods that come down this gulch once about every ten or fifteen years. Ruined fields and orchards. Livestock and even houses washed away. The railroad grade and bridges torn to hell 'n' gone."

"Then why any objection to a dam?" Mark frowned.

"It's a ticklish question, Mark. Very controversial. Down here, the dam would likely be vastly beneficial. But above where the dam must be—and there's only one suitable location in the length of the gulch—quite a few fine farms, a little town, some abandoned mines, and a cemetery site will go under a hundred or so feet of water. Also, the lake is going to flood out a couple of sawmills in really magnificent timber stands."

"Look, forget my schedule, and try to revamp yours if necessary," Mark said. "You've brought me to something utterly fascinating and challenging. I want to see every foot of this gulch, visit Cathedral Peak, do some tests at the dam site. I'll give you my best, if it takes us a week. Of course, ultimately the decision to build or not to build lies with the powers that be. In Reno. In Washington, D.C." Mark paused and smiled, then added, "But when and if bids are let, you can be sure that the Cardigan Corporation is going to figure this one with sharp pencils. It intrigues me."

The bid openings for Cathedral Gulch Dam were held in Las Vegas just thirteen months later, a fact that led Mark to surmise that even at the time of his inspection of the proposed project it had already been cleared by the government for construction. There were four bidders, with the Cardigan Corporation submitting the lowest figure: the bottom-line figure was $28,750,280. The second-lowest bidder, a San Francisco firm, turned in a figure of slightly over $30,000,000.

Jubilation marked the corporation's success and Mark was showered with congratulations by employees, hopeful suppliers, Bureau of Reclamation officials, and even representatives of the competing firms. As quickly as possible he sought out Gilberto and Dolores, who had arrived at Las Vegas months before with a staff of engineers and estimators. Dolores's uncanny ability to assemble and evaluate intricate calculation had been the touch of genius that inspired the estimating staff.

The dam would be a three-zoned, or three-layer, rolled earthfill structure, nearly three thousand feet in length, creating a reservoir fifteen miles long, with branches reaching into half a dozen small creeks and dry washes. There would be extensive installation of hydroelectric generating units. The dam itself was designed with a central core of compacted clay, silt and sand, impervious to water. A zone of gravel and cobbles, also compacted, would protect the core. The upstream slope would be guarded by rock installed as rip-rap. The structure would rise 331 feet above the silty, boulder-strewn bottom of Cathedral Gulch. During construction, an upstream cofferdam would divert the creek's flow into tunnels that would bypass the earthen and rock structure.

Studying the intricate drawings and specifications with his staff, Mark Cardigan often smiled in triumph. His corporation had undertaken and successfully completed larger projects, but they had been in conjunction with other firms that would share in profits or assume proportionate percentages of loss. These had been joint ventures, the type of partnership common in the industry and limited to one project. Cathedral Dam would be different, to be built and financed entirely by the Cardigan Corporation.

"With this one," Mark told Gilberto, "I have an idea we have come of age. You and many other dedicated employees have made us an acknowledged power in worldwide construction. Not yet as big at Peter Kiewit Sons or Morrison-Knudsen, but a vital growing entity."

Halfdan Nordraak overheard the remarks, and presently spoke up. "You know what, Mark? Most of what we've been able to achieve stems from our boss—from you. Few men have one special ability you possess."

"What is that, Halfdan? My ability to trounce on some poor bastard and cuss him out for sluffing off?"

"Oh, you're a master of that, all right, Mark. But I'm talking about something a hundred times more important. Your confounded knack of making people want to follow you, work for you. Fartein and I fell under that spell when we were digging a privy hole and stringing a school fence back at Hawk Bend."

Halfdan paused, then plunged ahead with his compliment. "Nowadays you send men to the ends of the earth. They endure heat, and cold, and isolation, and foreign lingo, and sometimes monotonous or bad food. Sometimes tents or barracks with stinking latrines. Some of these men are killed in accidents or are shot by hostile natives. Yet . . . yet those who live stick to the job.

"Sometimes the loneliness and the conditions cause them to say, 'Shit on Cardigan and this job,' and they catch a plane home. Then you, you sly, understanding son of Satan, you meet them at the train station or airport when they arrive. And you've already lined up luxurious rooms, fine food, Canadian liquor, and a bevy of willing gals for those who want just that. For others, you see that they have a vacation at company expense with their wives and kids. Then what? Within a week those deserting construction engineers or bosses are on a plane bound back to finish the job. And swearing to anybody who will listen that Mark Cardigan's company is the world's top outfit—and offering to knock hell out of anyone who disagrees."

Mark listened in utter and surprised silence. Likely Halfdan had never before spoken so many words at one time. "Thank you," he murmured, and turned so those about could not see the tears welling up in his eyes. Halfdan's truths touched him.

Two miles below the dam site was the hamlet of Canyon Vista. In previous years, it had been a coaling and watering stop for the railroad trains. It had never had more than fifty people, railroad workers mostly. A grocery store. A school. The homes of some older people who had retired to this serene and shaded place upon leaving their farms and ranches in younger hands.

Construction of the dam necessitated a fifteen-mile re-routing of the railroad, and Canyon Vista was bypassed, except for the rutted road along the creek. A few construction workers moved in, mostly laborers with wives and children. And it was this secluded and quiet little village with which Dolores Montez fell instantly in love. She bought a rather spacious building that had once been the railroad depot, and soon had various tradesmen from Las Vegas at work transforming it into a distinctive home in Spanish style. Ample water had been diverted from the creek to provide for orchards and gardens. Soon Dolores's home was surrounded by a wide lawn, with borders of flowers.

Her father had chosen to remain on the dam project until its completion. He told Mark that this was a job that would better qualify him for the building of irrigation systems in Mexico, but it was evident that the aging Gilberto now felt the need of a permanent home and of his daughter's presence; his wife had recently passed away in Mexico City.

The scope and demands of worldwide contracts kept Mark from spending much time at Cathedral Dam, but he hurried to the project on several occasions when it was possible. Lois had chosen to remain in Denver, where more advantages would be available for their children, and Mark flew often to Denver.

It took just short of three years to construct Cathedral Dam. At the peak of construction, several hundred workers were employed, some finding living quarters in towns and homes as far as fifty miles from the job site. Others existed bleakly by choice in tents and shacks wherever a spot of vacant land could be found. At the dam site there were company-operated barracks and mess halls for single men.

The complex nature of the dam's construction called for the subletting of many contracts to smaller and specialized building or construction firms. Among the many such subcontracts which Mark signed was one assigning the work of grouting the dam's upstream surface; this work consisted of pouring or blowing thin, almost liquid, concrete into drilled holes. From such holes, it would spread and saturate the somewhat porous rock at the dam's base. The purpose was to create a protective concrete shield to prevent hydraulic penetration, or washing away, of the dam's heavily impacted and water-impervious central core.

The contract for grouting was awarded to Searchlight Drilling Company, headquartered in a Nevada town near Las Vegas. Upon signing of the subcontract, after its preparation and approval by his office engineers, Mark noted but took little heed of the company's name.

It would come to his attention later, in a manner he would remember for the rest of his life.

With the dam's completion in 1958, a change came over Cathedral Gulch, the little town of Canyon Vista, and the surrounding area. A new townsite, with broad, straight streets, a spacious park, and comfortable homes had been built on a tableland above the dam's crest two miles distant. Offices were built for the Reclamation Service, the Forest Service, and the units charged with maintenance of the dam and the hydroelectric generating plants. From here, the amount of water to be discharged downstream could be computed and controlled by electronic connection to the dam's great spillways.

In Canyon Vista, where upstream could be seen the high, arching outline of the dam, a quiet prevailed. Cathedral Creek ran, clear and sparkling, through the town, but only a few families remained, for the rush of construction workers to other jobs had swept away much of the population.

The reservoir behind this newest of western dams filled quickly after the coming heavy snows in the spring of 1959. The spring thaw had created seventy miles of shoreline, and the area was now a recreational area for boating, fishing, and water-skiing.

Dolores had grown to love the hamlet of Canyon Vista. It seemed that her house would never be completely finished, for she was never satisfied, always making changes: replacing a brilliantly woven Navajo rug, building a bookcase, moving a vase of jonquils or roses.

Every phase of Cathedral Dam's operation had now been taken over by the permanent operating forces. It had been dedicated by the United States Secretary of the Interior in an impressive ceremony. Mark attended with his friend Lane Torgny, who would soon be retired as regional forester. After the speeches, the band music, and the opening of the dam to let water flow briefly through a great concreted spillway, Mark sought out Dolores.

"Mark, this is really your day of achievement, of fulfillment. How proud you must be."

They were walking the great length of the dam's crest, with the blue, quiet lake stretching miles above them. The old valley bed and canyon of Cathedral Gulch lay below on the downstream side.

"Strange to think of it completed. Two days ago the final acceptance of all this was made by the Reclamation Service. From now on, it will be just a memory for our company and a picture on our office wall in Denver." His voice trailed off. He felt tired, empty, as he always did after finishing a long job.

"Dolores," he asked, and laced his fingers through hers, "how about you? Where to now? We have over fifty projects currently underway. Mexico. Brazil. A few in Europe and Africa. You are needed at all of them."

She paused, and looked up with the old, tantalizing smile. "Am I, Mark? Am I really needed—except in the loneliness of your heart?"

Heedless of workmen adjusting a crane nearby, he stooped to kiss her. "*Chiquita,* I need you, and the business does too. Yes, there are times when my loneliness is far greater and more far-reaching than the world of the Cardigan Corporation. But the important thing is you . . . your future."

She glanced down the gulch, where the village of Canyon Vista, and her own house, sat peacefully basking in warm sunshine. "Mark, just now what I value most, what I sense is home, is there. My books. My garden. Even the speckled trout in Cathedral Creek. Someday perhaps I can build a small adobe church, with a bell, for the community." She brightened and added, "Would you like to see my new patio? Come, we can disappear for a time."

Mark shook his head wistfully, "God, my lovely one, how I would like to spend today with you. But I can't now. Any minute a committee will catch up with me. Sweep me off to that ceremonial dinner tonight. Dolores, come with me—to the dinner."

With great sadness she shook her head. She pointed to Canyon Vista, and the red-tiled roof of her home. "There is my place and my security, Mark. The spot I love, and where I love to have you all to myself." She touched her lips lightly to his cheek and walked away briskly.

The rain began in the early-morning hours of August 10. A steady wind from the southwest had brought dark, heavy clouds from the Gulf of California, and stacked them about Cathedral Peak and the surrounding forested mountains. As the day wore by, the patter of raindrops picked up tempo and became a torrent beating on the red tiles of Dolores's house in Canyon Vista.

She busied herself with baking and the knitting of an afghan. When she went to bed, the rain was still beating down, accompanied now by strong gusts of wind.

In the gray of early morning, she peered out her bedroom window. Her eyes widened with concern as she noted the rapid flow of Cathedral Creek, and the manner in which small waterfalls were cascading down from the surrounding canyon walls. Minutes later the phone rang. It was her father. "Dolores," and Gilberto's tone was worried. "The reservoir is at full capacity, and soon the spillway must be opened." He was at the new, upland town where administration of the dam was handled. "There is no indication of trouble—yet. But it might be well to caution the people down there in the gulch—have them prepare to seek higher ground." Then he added, "Possibly I get uneasy too hastily. There are patches of blue sky. Of the storm breaking." After a parting word of endearment, Gilberto hung up.

Dolores slipped into a raincoat and light plastic overboots. As she left the house, her eyes caught sight of the letter lying on her hall table. It was from Mark, in Omaha, where he was discussing a large Ohio installation with representatives of Peter Kiewit Sons. "With any luck," he wrote, "I'll be able to spend a couple of days in Canyon Vista in about two weeks. I want to see the reservoir behind the dam—and I'm frightfully lonesome for you, *chiquita*."

She stepped outside, noting that the rainfall was lessening, and there was even an occasional errant beam of sunlight. Two of her neighbors were on a nearby porch; she stopped to chat for a moment, and passed on the warning Gilberto had voiced. "The storm seems about over," she told them. "But it might be wise for everybody in town to be ready to seek higher ground. Will you tell everyone you see?"

They nodded, and she left them, for she suddenly felt an urge for a walk in the rain. There was a hillside trail leading upstream the two miles to the dam; she chose to follow it.

She had come within a quarter mile of the dam when she stopped and stared. Below her, in the boulder-strewn canyon bed, close to the creek, water was surging upward as though pumped from a small artesian well. Perhaps, she reasoned, an inactive spring has come to life. Yet she was uneasy and fearful.

There were several maintenance workers on the dam, and she told them of the flow she had just discovered which seemed to spring from some subterranean depths.

"We know," one of them acknowledged. "There are a couple more of them downstream. The engineer crews are checking and watching them."

The rain had stopped, and the heaviest clouds were lazily drifting eastward. Dolores scanned the impounded waters of the reservoir, and marveled at their great width, and how near they came to the safety zone marked on the dam's embankment.

It was nearly noon when she returned home and switched on the radio for any news. Canyon Vista had received official warning of potential danger. People were asked to leave their homes temporarily and take shelter in the new administrative town on higher ground. Some of Dolores's neighbors had already prepared to leave; others took the attitude that it was probably a false alarm. Had not the storm already passed?

It was nearly sunset when Dolores went out to take another look at the mysterious "springs" and view the level of the reservoir's wind-rippled water. She chose to drive her Chevrolet coupe to the dam this time, for the oiled road had dried. She began the two-mile climb, but before she had gone a mile, she slammed on her brakes. Where there had been the one upward thrust of water forming a spot near the creek, there were now half a dozen, and their flow was swift and deadly.

She drove hastily onward. There were Caterpillar tractors and trucks on the dam, pushing rock over the downstream embankment in an effort to rip-rap a dark, wet spot where a length of the dam's fill material had slid. Then she uttered a scream. Before her very eyes, one of the tractor-dozer

434

units had slid from the dam's crest and was sliding and then tumbling down the steep embankment. In its wake was another dark and slippery trench of caving fill material.

It was but a hundred yards to the dam's crest. She threw the auto into low gear and ground her heel onto the accelerator. She was upon a concrete apron at the dam's west bank when she felt a jarring and a rush, a rushing terror that became a crescendo. Only a dozen yards away, a segment of the dam was now missing, as angry water, knowing only the force of gravity, tore and plunged into the valley below.

Dolores jumped from the car, to stare in fascination and then in horror.

"My God! My God! The water is deeper . . . faster. The dam, it's crumbling like rotten paper. Oh, Mark, why? Why?"

She threw shaking and stricken hands before her eyes, but quickly snatched them away and turned to reenter her car. Her words had become tortured sobs, but about them was determination.

"Those people down the canyon. The women and the children at Canyon Vista—they'll drown like helpless rats. I must go. Warn them."

She was nearing the spot where she had first seen the geyserlike spring when the wall of water, born of the final rupture of the dam, pounded down on her. It lifted the car, sending it like a spinning top into the churning, rushing hell of destruction.

Two days later, a stunned, sorrowful Mark Cardigan sat amidst a group hastily brought together to see the cause of the disaster. Already the bodies of forty-two people had been recovered downstream. The final total might rise to seventy or more. Dolores's body had been among the first recovered, for she had not been thrown from the battered, mud-caked car. Now her white-wrapped form lay among those which had been tagged and counted. A warehouse in the administrative settlement, far above the devastating flood, had been converted to an emergency morgue; the railroad had brought in iced refrigerator cars to store the dead.

At the inquiry board's meeting, Mark could not concentrate. Voices floated around him, speaking nothing. He was horrified, not only by Dolores's death, but also by the manner of its coming. Presently, words of an investigating engineer came through to his consciousness. "We have been fortunate in so quickly determining what I believe to be the foremost contributing factor to the dam's failure. Tests show that the base grouting, in a considerable section, was substandard, causing the protective concrete curtain to allow seepage through bad concrete into the dam's central core— into the densely packed, impervious zone. This seepage increased at a rapid pace, soon allowing hydraulic erosion and collapse of the central core."

Abruptly, another voice asked, "The grouting? Has a chemical analysis been made? What was the deficiency?"

"Our present evidence indicates rather conclusively that the percentage of $CaCl_2$, calcium chloride, was twelve point eight percent of the grouting mix, extremely in excess of the two to three percent allowed as standard by the industry."

Mark looked suddenly up, his eyes burning into the speaker's face. "Why would that be done?"

"Mr. Cardigan, you are aware, I am sure, that calcium chloride hastens the hardening and setting of concrete. There may have been a mistake, though I seriously doubt it. I believe the large percentage was intentionally introduced into the mixture so that there could be more rapid pouring and a lessening of man-hours."

Grimness marked the outthrust of Mark's chin. "How could that have gotten by our supervision, and the bureau's constant checking?"

"I don't know, sir. Possibly by keeping a supply of $CaCl_2$ hidden, and quickly injecting it into the grout between inspections."

"Who was the grouting subcontractor?" Mark asked sharply.

Another investigator ruffled through some papers. "Here it is. The subcontract was held by Searchlight Drilling, a firm headquartered near Las Vegas."

A two-page list was thrust into his hands, and he started to scan it. Seconds later, his eyes hardened and his mouth twisted to savagery. "See there. God almighty—look at that. Their vice president of operations! *Amos Shinn.*"

Mark's fists doubled in fury and he dropped his head upon them. Then he rose to his feet and stared at those about him. "I had a go-around with this slimy bastard Shinn once before. Years ago, in Denver. He spent too damn few years in the penitentiary. Now . . . I want him. Bring him here under arrest or any other way that is necessary. I'd go myself to haul him before this board—dead or alive."

A Forest Service helicopter delivered Amos Shinn, irate and shaking, onto the Cardigan Corporation's old landing spot near the dam at midafternoon of the next day. Mark stared at him, "Maybe you remember me, Shinn. Not that it makes any difference."

"I should remember you—that frame-up in Denver," Shinn muttered.

Mark ignored the words, and his next question was cold. "What do you know about the calcium content of grouting concrete?"

Shinn was silent. Mark motioned to two of his trusted employees and indicated that they bring Shinn to his waiting car. "Get in there and sit down," he ordered.

The dapper but frightened little man voiced shrill protest. "You have no right. Are you going to have those thugs of yours kill me?"

Mark laughed bitterly. "Christ no, Shinn. I have no intention of killing you, or having it done—though you deserve it. We're going for a short ride. Before this day ends, I think you will pray to God to let you die."

Within fifteen minutes the car drew up alongside the temporary mortuary. "Will you please tell whoever is in charge here that Mark Cardigan would appreciate a word with him?" Mark asked the guard.

After a little time, a white-frocked man of about fifty years appeared at the door; and they talked for about five minutes. Finally the assistant coroner gave a nod of consent.

"Come with me, Shinn," Mark said in an almost sociable tone.

A wave of comprehension, or of premonition, caused the face of Amos Shinn to slacken. "No . . . no," he yelled, "I'm not going in there." He tried to turn away, but his two bulky escorts seized his arms and half dragged him toward the first of three refrigerator cars.

The four men mounted the plank steps, Mark jerked

open the door and came face to face with another attendant clad in white and wearing a surgical mask. There was an overpowering, nauseating odor, and beyond was row upon row of canvas cots, each with a quiet form over which a sheet had been thrown.

Mark was breathing heavily as he thrust Amos Shinn into the refrigerator car and followed. "The coroner has okayed this," he said to the attendant. "We have here the man who is more than anyone else responsible for the death of those who lie here, and of others yet to be brought in. He is to see what hell his greed and hatred have brought about." He motioned to a cot on which a small form was outlined beneath the shrouding sheet. "This one will do—to start."

The attendant hesitated, then with a reluctant motion pulled back the sheet. On the cot lay the battered form of a child of perhaps three years, a girl whose hair was bright yellow, and in whose death grasp was a small toy rabbit.

In agony, Mark glanced at Amos Shinn, knowing that the man's spirit was breaking.

"Show him the next one, and the next, and the next. Until he sees all of those his act has killed."

"You're kidding," the attendant replied.

Mark shook his head and motioned for his men to follow him and leave the car. "It is up to his endurance, his guilt, and if he has one, his God."

When he reached the car, Mark Cardigan threw his arms upon its hood, bent to hide his ashen face, and cried out his own hurt and desolation.

Later, Gilberto found him, "Mark, I have a request," he said solemnly. "Long ago, after visiting Cardigan Ranch, Dolores said to her mama and me, 'Someday I would like, when death takes me, to rest in that little Cardigan graveyard, within the white picket fence.' Mark, my *amigo*, would it be possible for . . . ?"

Mark placed his arm about the man. "Gilberto, we will leave in the morning. By helicopter to Las Vegas, then by our company plane to Denver. From there, another helicopter can carry you and me—and her—quickly to Hawk Bend. I will arrange everything."

"I have a friend in Denver . . . a priest," Gilberto whispered. "May we take him also with us into Crow Creek Valley?"

Mark's last act at Cathedral Dam was to ask all Forest Service and Bureau of Reclamation officials to a meeting. "There is a long and terrible cleanup job ahead, whether or not Cathedral Dam is rebuilt. You who are here will doubtless direct the rehabilitation efforts of Cathedral Gulch. But I promise you this: Every available resource of the Cardigan Corporation will be at your command, whether to rebuild a ten-mile section of railroad, to bring a new town out of desolation, or to help a farmer set one solitary fence post. Call on us. We will be awaiting your summons."

The evening shadows of the Rocky Mountains were lengthening as the helicopter made its way over the checkered farmlands between Greeley and Denver, and then followed the thin tracery of trees and sand marking the course where once Crow Creek had flowed strong and clear. At last it hovered close to the ranch house, then touched down softly.

Dolores Montez was home. Where both Redge and Audrey Cardigan now rested. Those who had prepared the grave had left, for Mark and Gilberto had agreed that only they and the second woman in Mark's life—his wife, Lois —should be there. The black-robed priest spoke the final words in English, and then repeated them in the softly musical language that had been Dolores's native tongue.

For a long time, Mark gazed upon the spot where she had been brought to rest. "God, take her in kindness. She was proud. She was beautiful. She was mine."

The helicopter lifted from the cottonwood-sheltered cemetery. Above the seven graves. Above the Cardigan Ranch buildings and above the old, gnarled bag-swing tree. As the aircraft banked to begin its return trip, Mark glimpsed the old weeded canal. At that moment he felt utter desolation.

Soon the hand of his wife met his, and pressed an old map into it. It traced the course of his greatest dream, the MacKenzie River–Great Plains International Canal.

"Mark, don't torture yourself. How she would have scolded you for that! Time is healing, and surely, for you, great things lie ahead. You may be the one to make those waters of northern Canada flow through Joe Edmundson's trans-mountain system—perhaps even into Crow Creek Valley Canal."

His eyes lifted to her with new understanding and meaning and purpose. "It is coming closer, Lois." He caressed her hand. "I'll be in Washington next week, and will check on the progress of the international-relations aspect."

Mark was thoughtful, but his face took on a serenity. "Do you suppose that someday . . . perhaps . . . this home section of our first big project will be flowing water to nurture fields and orchards? Wouldn't it be so right, Lois, if it were named the Dolores Montez Memorial Canal?"

As she smiled agreement, he closed his eyes. The valley below them doubtless looked much as it had when his father and grandfather had chosen it as a homeplace. Here too had been the beginning of his own dream and the place of his meeting with all those who had helped him to achieve it. He sensed that whenever he might return here Dolores would seem very close to him. So would his parents and grandfather.

Someday, in this grassland valley, Lois and he would also rest—for upon them was the imprint of the land.